A PLUME BOOK

THEY DID IT WITH LOVE

KATE MORGENROTH is the author of *Kill Me First* and *Saved* and the YA novels *Echo* and the Edgar-nominated *Jude*. Visit her Web site at www.katemorgenroth.com.

Praise for Kate Morgenroth's novels

"Mesmerizing. I am as delighted by Kate Morgenroth's nerve as much as by her skill."   —Toni Morrison

"I read *Kill Me First* in one sitting. Kate Morgenroth has created an exciting and formidable character in Sarah Shepherd."
                    —Lisa See, author of *Snow Flower and the Secret Fan*

"Compulsively readable . . ."   —*Entertainment Weekly*

"Nearly impossible to put down."   —*Time Out New York*

"Riveting . . . Morgenroth writes with quick, razor strokes."
                                                    —*New York Post*

"Intensely absorbing . . ."   —*Publishers Weekly*

"One knockout story . . . Morgenroth succeeds not only in creating something different but in doing it well."   —*St. Petersburg Times*

"An appealing heroine supported by savvy plotting. Morgenroth's second outing: [*Kill Me First*, 1999] proves again that she knows how to weave a spell."   —*Kirkus Reviews* (starred review)

"A must read for those who like their women tough but vulnerable."
                                                    —*USA Today*

THEY DID IT
with *Love*

A Novel

Kate Morgenroth

A PLUME BOOK

PLUME
Published by Penguin Group
Penguin Group (USA) Inc., 375 Hudson Street, New York, New York 10014, U.S.A. •
Penguin Group (Canada), 90 Eglinton Avenue East, Suite 700, Toronto, Ontario,
Canada M4P 2Y3 (a division of Pearson Penguin Canada Inc.) • Penguin Books Ltd., 80
Strand, London WC2R 0RL, England • Penguin Ireland, 25 St. Stephen's Green, Dublin
2, Ireland (a division of Penguin Books Ltd.) • Penguin Group (Australia), 250 Camber-
well Road, Camberwell, Victoria 3124, Australia (a division of Pearson Australia Group
Pty. Ltd.) • Penguin Books India Pvt. Ltd., 11 Community Centre, Panchsheel Park,
New Delhi–110 017, India • Penguin Books (NZ), cnr Airborne and Rosedale Roads,
Albany, Auckland 1310, New Zealand (a division of Pearson New Zealand Ltd.) •
Penguin Books (South Africa) (Pty.) Ltd., 24 Sturdee Avenue, Rosebank, Johannesburg
2196, South Africa

Penguin Books Ltd., Registered Offices: 80 Strand, London WC2R 0RL, England

First published by Plume, a member of Penguin Group (USA) Inc.

First Printing, March 2008
10   9   8   7   6   5   4   3   2   1

 REGISTERED TRADEMARK—MARCA REGISTRADA

LIBRARY OF CONGRESS CATALOGING-IN-PUBLICATION DATA

[tk]

Printed in the United States of America
Set in Adobe Caslon

"To have trusted someone! To have believed . . .
and it was lies—all lies."

—Agatha Christie, *They Do It with Mirrors*

for Carrie

Acknowledgments

Cast of Characters

The Couples

Sofie and Dean

Priscilla and Gordon

Susan and Harry

Ashley and Stewart

Julia and Alex

The Detectives

Detective Peters: Detective from the Greenwich
Police Department

Detective Ackerman: Detective from the DA's office

THEY DID IT
with *Love*

It was autumn. Early morning. The air was sharp, and the sky was a deep October blue. The cars on the narrow suburban street whizzed by, churning up little whirlpools of leaves—but none of the people in the cars noticed the body hanging among the trees.

The feet were suspended in midair not far from the ground, and they looked like they had maroon stockings on—the deep purple color due to the blood pooling in the lowest parts of the body. The long, blond hair hung in a curtain around the lolled head. A light wind ruffled the hem of the nightgown and shivered the leaves in the trees, but the body hung motionless.

A dozen cars drove by without noticing anything. It might have been hours before the body was discovered—if it weren't for Sofie.

Afterward Sofie's life would never be the same, but a year earlier she hadn't even known the woman. For her it had all started with another death.

NEW YORK
December

Prologue

he phone call came early Friday December 14 at seven fifteen a.m., ensuring that Sofie would remember that particular morning forever. That's what happened with death. It took otherwise small, unmemorable moments and fossilized them. This would be the second time she had experienced the phenomenon. It had happened once before when she was three years old and had wandered into her mother's bedroom because, though she'd waited *forever*, her mother hadn't come to get her up. Even twenty-five years later Sofie still remembered those moments as clearly as if someone had taken a photograph. The open windows. The rumpled sheets. The slowly revolving ceiling fan. Then the sharp smell of urine. And the feeling . . . as if all the joy had been sucked out of her heart like water rushing down the drain when her mother pulled the plug in the bath.

Now it would be these moments—before the phone call—that would be preserved in her memory. She was sitting in the window seat, her mug of tea balanced precariously on the sill. The heat from the tea had made a small hazy patch of fog on the window pane just above the lip of the cup. The newspaper—opened to the second to last page of the Arts and Leisure section and folded to frame the crossword puzzle—lay on the cushion beside her, and her cat, Agatha, was curled in her lap, a small spot of warmth.

Outside the window a few snowflakes drifted through the air. Across Fifth Avenue the trees of Central Park were a tangle of dark gray branches against a pale gray sky. In a few minutes the sun would rise, and the first rays would hit the facades of the buildings across the park, turning all the windows into mirrors of light.

But at seven fifteen on December 14 the sun wasn't up; there was only the flat emptiness of the sky and the aimlessness of the tiny flakes of snow. And her mood matched the day. That morning she felt . . . suspended. Poised on the edge of something. (Though later she wasn't sure if this was true or if it was something she had retroactively inserted into her memory. Does the calm before the storm seem calm at the time? Or does it only seem calm in retrospect, knowing what is to follow?)

At that moment, sitting in the window seat, looking out over the dreary view, Sofie realized that the feeling of discomfort wasn't purely internal; the tip of her nose was almost completely numb. She had been waiting for the heat to come up, but her husband, Dean, must have put the heat on manual override (he slept better when it was cold) and forgotten to switch it back. Cupping her palms around the mug, she lifted it to her face and exhaled, letting her own breath send a little cloud of steam billowing up. It warmed her nose, but only for a moment. As the steam ebbed away, the cold crept right back in, so she gently dislodged Agatha from her lap and stood, making her way through the dining room, then the living room into the foyer and over to the master climate control for the apartment.

As she was adjusting the heat up from an arctic fifty degrees she saw Dean's gym bag tucked underneath the hall table. He must have forgotten it in his rush out the door earlier that morning. She sighed in exasperation. He always came home cranky when he didn't work out. Now she had to decide if it was worth the bother to take his bag over to him at the office or risk his mood later. Maybe she would take it over to him. She nudged the bag out from under the table with her foot so she would see it when she went out, then turned to go back to finish the crossword puzzle.

The call came precisely as she was passing the phone extension in the living room, as if her presence had somehow summoned it into action. The abrupt jangle also echoed from the extensions in the bedroom and kitchen, and the hand that held the mug jerked, sending a little tidal wave of hot tea spilling over the side of the cup and onto her knuckles. It left a red mark where it splashed onto her skin.

She set the tea down and reached out to pick up the receiver. But her hand hovered in the air as if to delay the moment of knowing— though the truth was, she knew already. She knew it wasn't Dean calling about his forgotten gym bag. She knew it wasn't a solicitation offering her an opportunity to get the *New York Times* delivered right to her door. She knew it wasn't the bookstore checking on her availability. She'd been expecting this call for weeks now.

She picked up the receiver.

1.

Sofie went from the hustle of Manhattan on a Friday morning through the smooth automatic doors and into the stillness of the hospital lobby. She'd gone through those doors dozens of times over the last three years, but every time she was struck by the contrast—from the careless rush of the city into the hushed calm of the hospital, from the world of the living to the world of the dying. Every time she passed through those doors, she thought about how the two worlds felt so far apart and yet only the space of a breath actually separated them. For her mother, only the time it took to swallow a handful of pills. For her father, only the time it took to get the results of a biopsy.

She crossed to the elevator and pressed the button for the third floor. They grouped patients with the same type of cancer together. The section for pancreatic cancer was small and grim. As she exited into the familiar hallway, she wondered how many times had she been there in the last few years? Ten? Fifteen? More? How many times had the doctors told her that it looked as though her father wouldn't make it out of the hospital again? But somehow (by pure willpower he claimed) he'd always fought his way back. So when he'd been admitted again yesterday she came to visit, listened to the doctors say the same thing they always said, then went home when visiting hours ended. The only difference was that this time the doctors had been right.

When she reached her father's room she found the door open. The sun was streaming in through the windows, and the vase of orange tulips that she'd brought was still perched on the sill, but all the curtains around the bed that her father usually kept closed were now drawn back, and the bed was stripped down to the plastic mattress pad. A nurse was bent over the bed removing the pad, and she must have sensed Sofie's presence at the door because she looked up.

"I'm so sorry," the nurse said. "He's not here anymore."

"Where did they take him?" Sofie asked. She was amazed that her voice came out so calm. So even.

"They took him to the lower level," the nurse told her. "Do you want to view the body?"

Sofie nodded.

"Just take the elevator down to the basement."

So Sofie retraced her steps back down the hallway and waited patiently for the elevator. When the doors slid open and she got in, she saw the button next to the one for the lobby labeled "B." If she'd ever noticed it before, she would have assumed that it was a dark, musty basement filled with buckets and mops and supplies. She pressed it and the elevator took her down. Down past lobby level. Down below ground level. Why had she never thought about the fact that a hospital needed somewhere to store their failures?

When she exited, she found not the concrete walls and the buckets and mops she'd imagined, but a carpeted reception area. And there weren't silent men in blue coveralls, but a very pretty, very young girl sitting behind a desk. The girl didn't look old enough to be out of high school, and it seemed incongruous to have someone so young manning the reception desk for the hospital morgue. But maybe, Sofie thought, only someone young would be willing to work down there. For the young, death was something that happened to other people.

Sofie gave the receptionist her father's name, and the girl checked the computer. She picked up the phone, but before dialing she said, "It will be just a few minutes," and motioned for Sofie to take a seat. Five minutes later an orderly appeared. He was dressed in green scrubs with a plastic identity card clipped to his pocket. Sofie noticed his name was James . . . the same as her father's.

"If you'll come with me," the orderly said. So she followed James down the corridor. Just past the reception area the carpet ended and the floor was a slick, hard linoleum. As Sofie walked, the sound of her footsteps seemed embarrassingly loud, and it felt like it took forever to get down the hall. They took a right, and the orderly stopped in front of a closed door.

"Do you want me to go in with you?" he asked politely.

"No, thank you."

She waited while he turned and retreated down the hallway. Only when he had disappeared back around the corner did Sofie open the door. As she slipped inside and closed the door behind her, she felt as if she had entered yet another reality. This wasn't the hospital, the world of the sick and dying. This was the world of the dead. Her father's body lay on a steel table in front of her, a thick white sheet pulled up to his shoulders. *My father's body* she repeated to herself, as if it had only been some possession that he had relinquished. Her father's town house, her father's vacation homes, her father's cars, her father's businesses, her father's body. He owned none of them anymore.

She crossed the small space to stand beside him. She had thought that he might simply look like he was sleeping, but he didn't. His face looked different. In life there was always something tense about it—the lips pressed together, the eyes creased into a squint, even the skin had seemed to stretch tight over the bones. It was the same face, but now everything was slack—not peaceful, just slack.

At that moment Sofie suddenly realized that this was the first time in her life that she had been in the same room with her father and not felt a nauseous, clutching sensation in her stomach like how you might feel right before a big test that you haven't studied for but desperately needed to pass. And with that realization she finally believed her father was dead. The body hadn't done it. The slackened face hadn't done it. Only this—this sense of calm in his presence—made it real.

Sofie had never really believed he would die. She'd always had the sense that he could do whatever he wanted, that the laws of the universe didn't apply to him. That was why when he was diagnosed three years ago and the doctors told him that he only had a few months to live and he might want to consider forgoing the painful treatment and trying to get the most out of the time he had left, she hadn't been surprised when he ignored the advice, did the treatment, and went into remission. He'd had her convinced that he would live forever. Now looking down at his body she felt a strange, unnatural lightness as if she'd been hiking for hours with a heavy pack and had finally taken it off. The only thing she knew for sure was that this wasn't how you were supposed to feel when you were standing over the body of your father.

She was distracted from this thought by voices outside in the hall. And then the door was opening, and her husband, Dean, was there. Having him arrive felt like fitting that last piece of the puzzle into place. It came with a feeling of relief. She was about to speak when she noticed that hovering behind his shoulder was the pretty receptionist. The girl must have decided that Dean warranted a personal escort to the room instead of calling the orderly. That kind of thing always seemed to happen to her husband.

"Let me know if you need anything else," the girl said to Dean.

"OK, thanks," Dean said.

Sofie could see the girl still standing there even as Dean shut the door. He was a heartbreaker even when he wasn't trying. Maybe part of the reason he'd pursued her so hard when they first met was that he couldn't believe Sofie wasn't interested in him. It was amazing for her to think back on that now—that there had been a time when she had looked at him with absolute indifference. That when she first met him, she thought he was a little too good-looking with his sandy blond hair and a dimple on one cheek, a little too slick with his ability to turn on the charm. She'd turned him down three times, but he had pursued her with a single-mindedness that eventually secured him a date. Who could resist being wanted that much? And during that first date she realized that he wasn't just handsome, he was also sarcastic and smart and a little bit insecure and trying so hard to impress her while at the same time making fun of himself for it. She wasn't sure exactly when it happened, but she fell for him—hard. So hard that she never admitted except to herself exactly how much. She knew that that kind of love tended to frighten men off, even husbands.

As Dean came up beside her, he put an arm around her shoulders. "Are you Ok, Cara Mia?" he asked. That was his pet name for her. He'd started out calling her Mia because he insisted she looked like Mia Farrow's twin (though Sofie thought that he was glamorizing what was simply the Swedish inheritance she'd gotten from her mother: blue eyes and white-blond coloring). Over the years the nickname had morphed into the Italian endearment.

She nodded. "I'm fine."

Then he looked down at her father.

By some miracle of fate Dean and her father had actually gotten along. Her father often said that Dean was the only thing she'd ever done right. And Dean had never in the three years they'd been together (the same three years her father had been sick) made a negative comment about her father. So now she expected Dean to say something about missing him or about how he was a tough old man. But after a long moment of silence Dean said, "He was such a prick."

Sofie was so surprised, she started to laugh. But then the laugh caught in her throat. And then, to her surprise, she began to cry instead.

2.

$\mathcal{I}$t was a few weeks later, after another crazy, exhausting day, that Dean brought up his idea.

They were lying in bed in the dark, looking out over Central Park and the carpet of trees and the buildings with their tiny twinkling lights on the other side of the park. Dean liked to sleep with the windows open and the heat turned down, so they were under the heavy down quilt. Dean was curled up behind her, his arm draped over her waist, his chin nestled in her shoulder.

They had been talking about the day—what she had gotten

done, what happened at his work—but in the last few minutes they had fallen into a comfortable silence. Sofie was watching the lights wink on and off in the buildings when Dean spoke.

"I was thinking," he said slowly. "These last few weeks have been rough on you, haven't they?"

"A bit," she said.

Dean snorted. This was classic Sofie, always understating things.

If pressed, she would have had to admit that the last few weeks had been more than "a bit" rough. First there had been all the details to take care of: the funeral arrangements, making phone calls, writing letters. Then there was the inheritance to deal with. Her father had a brother and a sister, both married with kids—six nieces and nephews all together. He'd also gotten married (and divorced) twice after Sofie's mother died. Both ex-wives were alive and well. But her father hadn't left the brother or sister, nieces or nephews, or the ex-wives a dime. Sofie as the only child had gotten everything—all the houses, all the cars, all the antique furniture, his art collection—everything. And she had to make decisions about what to do with it all.

It was a nightmare.

Sofie remembered reading an article about what generally happens to lottery winners after they win; they are barraged by family, friends, and strangers. The same thing happened to Sofie. Everyone seemed to have an investment scheme, or some service that she couldn't live without, or they simply thought they deserved a piece of the pie. With many of the people who called and wrote she wondered how they even knew about the inheritance. Her father had been a relatively well-known businessman, but nowhere near the level of the true titans of industry. His death appeared in the obituaries and in a few trade magazines and that was it, but there seemed to be some sort of network that passed around this type of information and then descended in a swarm.

It was all so overwhelming, and beneath the details and the daily hassle was an aching sense of loss. The feeling of lightness that she'd felt initially while standing over her father's body hadn't lasted. It had been replaced by a chasm of regret. It wasn't that she missed her father. The way he had been in life—angry, contemptuous, vindictive, critical—she knew she was better off without him. What tortured her was the loss of the possibility for change. Not that *he* would change—she'd always known that was never going to happen—but she thought that *she* might.

She always had the idea that one day she would stand up to him. Her father sometimes taunted her, daring her to do it. "How can you just stand there?" he'd sneer at her (though she thought it took more courage than her father could know—to stand there quietly, keeping her face a mask of indifference while he screamed or yelled or mocked, depending on his mood). "You're a damn victim," he would say. "Your mother would roll over in her grave if she could see you. She'd never let someone talk that way to her. She had spirit. She had *guts.*"

Sofie had a hazy memory of screaming voices, voices so piercing that they penetrated closed doors and hands pressed over ears and pillows burrowed under. She thought this might be a memory of her mother's guts and that this memory might also explain why she usually chose to avoid confrontation. The only problem was that she found the price of conciliation was her self-respect. And now her father was gone, and it was too late to change.

So the idea of change was already on her mind when in bed that night Dean said, "I was thinking we might need a change."

From the way he said it, Sofie knew that it was a suggestion he thought she wouldn't like. "What kind of change?" she asked.

He hesitated then said, "Before I tell you, I just want to make sure you're going to take some time to think about it before you give your answer."

She was definitely not going to like it, Sofie thought.

"OK," she said.

"All right, well, I was thinking maybe we should move out of the city. Not too far away," he said quickly, anticipating a protest. "I could commute to work, and you could still come in to work at the bookstore if you wanted."

Sofie had been working at the Black Orchid Mystery Bookshop since she was sixteen. As a freshman and sophomore in high school she spent so much time there—just hanging around, buying books by the armful, and trying to avoid going home—that she had gotten to know the owners, Bonnie and Joe, pretty well. She spent so much time there in fact, they finally suggested a part-time job. She'd jumped at the idea and found she loved it. She was surrounded by what she loved most in the world—books. And not just any old books—mysteries. Dean joked that she loved mysteries more than she loved him.

Dean went on, "Or if you didn't want to commute in to the bookstore there's also another possibility: Haven't all your friends been saying for *years* that you should write a mystery? Well, this could be your chance to do it—get away from the city and all the distractions, somewhere quiet where you can think. We could set up an office for you. You could use this as an excuse to finally get started. And I was also thinking—"

"Dean," she broke in.

"I thought you said you weren't going to answer right away," he said. "I thought you were going to take some time to think about it."

"I don't need to think about it."

"But—," he started, ready with more ammunition to persuade her to leave the city.

She rolled over, turning her back on the hulking buildings and their beautiful, twinkling lights. It was too late to change what happened with her father, but it wasn't too late to make a change.

"I don't need to think about it," she said again. "The answer is yes."

Sofie could see the look of shock on Dean's face even in the dim light filtering through the window.

"Really?" he said. "You're not joking?"

"Really."

He started to smile. "Just when I think I've got you figured out, you go and surprise me again," he said. "How is it you always do that?"

"You're not too bright?" Sofie suggested.

"You're in trouble," he said, making a grab for her. But when he'd wrestled her, pinning her beneath him, he suddenly turned serious again. "Listen, I know how much you love the city, but this is the right decision. You'll see."

But it was this decision that eventually brought Sofie her third dead body. The first had been her mother, lying sprawled across the bed, sunshine streaming through the windows. The second was her father, in the cold fluorescent light of the hospital morgue. The third would be swinging gently from a tree, surrounded by brilliant red autumn leaves.

PART I

GREENWICH

January

3. Priscilla & Gordon

$\mathcal{P}$riscilla Brenner woke up in a foul mood. It was January. The sky outside her bedroom window was gray. It looked like it was going to snow again. And she was forty. She'd been forty for almost a week—and at the age of forty she'd discovered that she wanted to change everything about her life. But at that moment, waking up to another dreary winter morning, Priscilla saw no hope.

What she saw was her husband, Gordon, sleeping beside her. Just looking at him she felt a surge of irritation. She'd reached the point where everything about him annoyed her—even the way he slept. She hated the way his mouth hung open. She hated the way the loosening skin of his neck (invisible when he was awake) was pushed into little rolls under his chin. She even hated the sweep of his impossibly long dark lashes against his cheek, because it reminded her of how handsome she'd thought he was when they first met.

It wasn't that he'd changed so much in the fifteen years they'd been together. He was still in good shape and, though his hair had gone gray and was thinning at the crown, he'd inherited the kind of patrician features that weathered well. But in Priscilla's mind it was as if there were two different men—the man she *thought* she'd married and then the man he had turned out to be. When they first met, Gordon had seemed aloof and somehow mysterious. There were those long dark lashes of his and the quiet secretive way he had of smiling as if he were laughing at his own private joke. He also had an aura of glamour because he came from a wealthy Boston society family—though, being Yankees, they were very discreet about it.

But after they got married Priscilla discovered that she had been all wrong about Gordon. What she'd thought of as aloof was merely awkward. The smile she'd thought of as secretive was simply self-conscious. And the idea of Gordon being glamorous—*that* turned out to be so completely ludicrous, she would have laughed if she could have managed to find the humor in it.

Gordon's alarm went off and Priscilla quickly closed her eyes and pretended to be sleeping. In the morning Gordon liked to hit the snooze button and roll over and spoon her. Even the word made her shudder and his actually doing it made her feel trapped, pinned down, smothered. She finally told him that it was bad manners to wake her when she was still sleeping, and Gordon in his perpetual reasonableness had accepted the rebuke and had never done it again—and she despised him for that as well.

She lay there, rigid in pretend sleep, while he slipped out of bed and padded over to his bathroom. She waited a few seconds until she heard the hiss of the shower, and then she got out of bed as well and escaped into her bathroom.

Half an hour later she was in her dressing room morbidly inspecting her pores in her magnifying mirror (she'd actually thought she had good skin before she'd bought it, but the mirror showed her how wrong she was) when Gordon knocked on the door. Usually he would just call through the door that he was leaving, but today he poked his head in.

"I just wanted to let you know that I have to stay late today. That OK?"

"Fine," she said still peering into the mirror. It came with rows of lightbulbs that you could adjust to evening, indoor, or sunlight. She kept it on the harshest sunlight setting.

"I don't know why you insist on looking in that thing," Gordon said.

"Why do you think? I want to see what I look like."

"You look amazing."

"I'm getting wrinkles."

"I can't see any," he said.

"I can see the wrinkles in the mirror. The mirror doesn't lie. This tells me the truth."

"The truth? You mean if someone stood you under a spotlight and magnified your face, what, five times?"

"Seven times," she said.

"Imagine yourself walking around with a head seven times the size it is now."

"That's not the point."

"I think that's exactly the point," he replied.

She finally turned away from the mirror to shoot him a look.

"Sorry," he apologized automatically. Then, to try to smooth things over, he asked, "What do you have on for today?"

She was about to snap—"Nothing except having to call all the members of the Junior League to remind them about the Leadership Development and Council Meeting next week"—when she remembered that her mystery book group was meeting that afternoon. It wasn't the only book group she belonged to, but this was *her* group. She'd formed it, she ran it, and she (usually) enjoyed it. She wasn't sure about today's meeting though. There had been a bit of a shakeup in the last few months. They'd lost two members who'd gotten divorced and moved away, so she'd invited two new members to join and Priscilla wasn't sure they were working out. But she still had Candy and Susan, she reminded herself. They had been in the group since the beginning, and Priscilla knew she could count on them.

4. Susan & Harry

*S*usan knew she was in trouble. *Big* trouble.

She hadn't finished the book.

"Harry, what am I going to do?" she asked, taking the pot of coffee from the machine and pouring out a cup. "I didn't finish the book. Priscilla is going to kill me. She's always saying that she doesn't want to turn into one of those clubs where half of the members don't even read the book."

Susan had to step over Bo and Hector—her two huge dogs who were both sprawled out on the tiles—to carry the cup of coffee over to where Harry was sitting at the kitchen table, scanning the front page of the business section. His hair was wet from the shower, and with his head bent she could see the marks from the comb. The strands were a combination of gray flecked with silvery white.

She set the coffee down next to him.

"Hmm?" he said without looking up. Then he noticed the coffee. "Oh, thanks."

Harry always said that she might not be able to cook, but she made the best pot of coffee he'd ever tasted. When she pointed out that it didn't take a lot of skill—that all she had to do was measure out the beans—he'd told her that it didn't pay to look too closely at a compliment. It was a smart move on his part because, as a result, he hadn't made a pot of coffee in years.

"Is this decaf?" he asked.

"It's half caf, half decaf. You said your doctor told you to cut back on the caffeine."

"I know, but I need the caffeine today. I've got a big meeting this morning."

"Well, you didn't tell me that. But if you have two cups, you'll get a full dose."

"And I'll be jumping up to go to the bathroom every two minutes," he said.

"Fine, I'll make you a fresh pot."

"How long is it going to take?"

She rolled her eyes. "About five minutes. Do you think you can wait for five minutes?"

She poured out coffee into the sink, threw away the old filter, and measured out the beans for a fresh pot. They had one of the machines that did everything including grinding the beans. She even could have set it up at night and put on the timer so that the coffee was ready when Harry came downstairs, but Susan preferred to get up to make it herself. She liked the feeling she got from doing little things for him. It suited them both.

It had suited them from the very beginning when they met at

her parents' summer house in Newport. She was home after her sophomore year at Barnard. Her older brother brought Harry back with him for a visit; they were classmates at Wharton. When Susan first met Harry, he had seemed to her so serious, so focused, and so much older than most of her brother's friends. It turned out that he actually *was* older. While most of the other boys had spent a year or two at most working at Goldman Sachs or Salomon Brothers before applying to Wharton, Harry had spent almost ten years working before returning to grad school. The first evening, Susan, intrigued by the intense friend her brother had brought home, had maneuvered to sit next to him at dinner and listened while he confided to her that from what he could tell, you didn't actually learn very much at business school—at least not compared to what you learned when you were out working. But he'd decided to go because that was what you needed to do if you wanted to get to the top. He didn't actually say that he was planning on getting to the top, but he didn't need to.

And he hadn't changed. At least not in that way. As she looked over at him Susan noticed that Harry had put down the business section and now he was bent over a stack of papers literally a foot high, doggedly plowing through them. She poured out a fresh cup of coffee and brought it over. He looked up briefly to receive the cup from her and take a cautious sip, but then he went right back to the stack. He flipped through, eyes darting down each page. He must have gone through at least ten pages in less than a minute, but watching him she got the feeling that he didn't miss anything. *He wouldn't have had any problems finishing the book for this afternoon, Susan thought ruefully. He'd probably do it in half an hour.* He had been like that ever since she'd first met him. She'd never encountered anyone with that much drive. He seemed to want things so much more than other people. And it turned out one of the things he wanted was her. It made her feel special, chosen, like she was necessary to his happiness. So maybe she didn't get quite as much appreciation anymore, but what could you expect after almost two decades? It was understandable: as CEO, he didn't have the time that he used to.

Harry looked up at the clock on the wall to check the time. "Is Kevin outside?" he asked.

Susan crossed to the window, and she could see the nose of the car out front.

"Yes, he's here."

"OK, gotta go." He stood and started gathering up his papers.

"You didn't drink your coffee. Do you want it for the car?"

"Sure."

Susan got a travel mug out of the cupboard and poured another cup. "Will you be back out tonight?" she asked.

"I probably won't be. I've got a couple of late meetings so I'll probably skip the commute and stay at the apartment."

She felt a flash of annoyance. If she hadn't asked, he probably wouldn't even have remembered to tell her. Instead she would have gotten a call from his secretary sometime in the evening when he remembered in the middle of a meeting.

Harry was trying to balance the huge pile of papers under one arm while he stooped for his briefcase.

"I'll get that," she said quickly, envisioning the pile of papers cascading onto the floor. She bent to retrieve the briefcase. The dogs scrambled to get up and flanked Susan and Harry as they walked through the foyer to the front door. Susan handed Harry his briefcase. He didn't even bother with an overcoat anymore since he never had to be outside for more than the amount of time it took to walk to the car that was always waiting for him, ready to whisk him to the office, to the lunch meeting, to their apartment in the city, or back to Greenwich. Susan had grown up around money, but even she was surprised by the amount of luxury that the top executives enjoyed. She thought the only thing missing were sedan chairs to transport the CEOs and presidents from the lobby to the waiting car.

Harry bent down to kiss her good-bye. As his lips brushed hers she suddenly had another surge of memory. It was something she hadn't thought of for ages—a memory of a morning more than ten years ago. At the time, they'd already been married for about six or seven years. They had settled into their routine, which was why, at the time, what happened was such a surprise. Harry always gave her a kiss good-bye in the morning. That morning ten years ago, he'd given her the usual quick kiss on the lips. Then he pulled back and looked at her. And he bent and gave her another, longer kiss. They only stopped kissing long enough to make it into the bedroom, and Harry, who was so conscientious about his job, had been late to work that morning. Very late.

Why did she think of that just now, she wondered? It was true that she'd been feeling strange lately. Melancholy. Maybe it was because she'd be turning forty soon—though Priscilla hadn't seemed to have any trouble with turning forty. Just last week she'd thrown that big bash down at the country club. But Priscilla, with her willowy height, blond silky hair, and flawless skin, barely looked thirty. She was easily the most beautiful woman in a neighborhood populated by trophy wives. Well, Susan corrected herself, at least Priscilla *had* been the most beautiful until Julia moved in.

Susan, on the other hand, had put on about a pound per year of marriage. She wasn't fat—she was what people usually referred to as curvy. She wished she were living back in the fifties when Marilyn Monroe had the perfect figure; these days Marilyn would probably be considered plump. Of course she wasn't exactly Marilyn Monroe, she acknowledged to herself. She tended more toward the cute end of the scale rather than the sexy. She was probably closer to Sally Field.

Harry had turned toward the door as if to leave, but then he turned back again and looked at her. He was frowning slightly as he said, "Are you OK, Suze?"

She was startled that he'd noticed something was wrong. She thought she was hiding it better than that.

"Me? Oh, I'm fine," she assured him.

"I bet if you went to sit down right now and read, you could finish that book easily by the time you have your book group meeting," he said.

She was confused for a second until she remembered that in the kitchen she'd asked him what she was going to do about the book club. He obviously thought that was what was bothering her. She didn't correct him.

"You know what," she said brightly, "that's exactly what I'm going to do."

He leaned in and gave her another kiss. Then he turned back and opened the door. The dogs crowded in around his legs, and Susan had to grab their collars to make sure they didn't run out. A moment later he was gone.

Just as she said she would, Susan went and retrieved the book and settled into the armchair by the window that looked out onto the rolling hills of the golf course.

And then she burst into tears.

It was the kind of noisy, un–self-conscious crying that she only ever did when she was alone. The sound was loud enough to attract the attention of Bo and Hector. They jostled around her, obviously worried by the strange noises she was making. Bo, the Newfie, even put his paws up on her knee and then tried to climb up as if he were a lapdog. This made her half laugh through her tears as she pushed him off.

"What is *wrong* with me?" she said aloud once she'd gotten a little more under control. She pulled out a tissue and blew her nose. Then she took another and dried her face. "Nothing's wrong," she said firmly. "I'm just being silly. Everything's going to be fine."

She picked up the book and started to read.

5. Ashley & Stewart

"Time to get up." Stewart leaned over the bed, feeling under the covers until he found Ashley's foot. Then he tugged on it until she came sliding toward him.

"Stewart, stop." Ashley sleepily tried to kick her foot free. "It's *early*."

"I've been up for an hour," he said. "Did five miles on the treadmill, lifted weights, and took a shower."

She opened her eyes carefully, keeping them slitted against the light. "Sounds like it's time for you to come back to bed," she said.

"Oh yeah?" He leaned over and kissed her.

"That's not back in bed."

"I know. I can't, baby. Not today." He stood up and crossed to his closet, pulling out a blue button-down shirt wrapped in the plastic from the dry cleaner's.

"You don't love me anymore," she said.

He tore off the plastic and tossed it toward the trash. The wicker basket was only a few feet away, but the plastic didn't have much heft, and it floated and fell short. He couldn't get over the fact that Ashley didn't even seem to notice. Pam would have jumped all over him to "pick that thing up off the floor and put it where it should be—in the trash—and if you don't do it who do you think is going to?" Her voice was almost like a tape in his head. It used to be that when he tossed the plastic wrapping he got it into the garbage about half the time, but toward the end of the marriage Stewart had started missing on purpose, just to prove that he could do whatever he wanted in his own damn house. He got pleasure out of leaving the ball of plastic lying on the floor. He still did even now that Pam was gone.

"No," he said, threading his arms through the sleeves of his shirt. "It's just that if I'm late to work one more time, I'm not going to be able to live it down. Ever. Not if I lived to be ninety."

"Aren't you pretty close to that now?" she said slyly. Ashley liked to tease him about their age difference. It was an invitation to tickle her or pretend to wrestle her—and it was an invitation he usually took her up on.

But today he shook his head and said, "I'm not falling for that old trick."

"You're no fun," she said, sitting up and throwing a pillow at him. "Anyway, they don't know *why* you're late."

"Are you kidding me? Two months married and showing up late every day? They never let up. Especially since the Christmas party. Forget it. It's almost nonstop."

"Why? What happened at the Christmas party?"

"What happened? They got a look at you is what happened."

"What's wrong with the way I look?"

He knew she was fishing for compliments, but he was happy enough to give them. "That's the thing. There's nothing wrong. You're absolutely perfect."

She leaned back against the pillows and smiled.

"And that dress you wore . . ."

"It was Versace," she said.

"It was practically indecent."

"I thought you liked it."

"I loved it," he said. His ex had always worn turtlenecks to the company parties. Turtlenecks, for God's sake. "But it's the reason I've got to get in on time for a while. Besides, you've got a big day today, right?"

She looked at him blankly.

"Isn't today the book club meeting?"

"Oh. That," she said.

"Yes, *that*. I told you that it's going to be a way to get a foot in the door and start making some friends here. You know, book clubs are the new social—"

"Fabric of the suburbs," Ashley finished in unison with him.

"You . . ." He jumped on the bed and mock tried to strangle her. "I'll teach you to be impertinent," he said while she shrieked and laughed and tried to push him off. But she didn't try very hard.

He leaned over and gave her another kiss. "It hasn't been so awful, has it?" he asked.

"The book was actually pretty good," Ashley said.

"Oh, and this is coming from the woman who said that she didn't mind joining a book club, she just didn't see why you had to read books to do it?"

"It's not like I *can't* read," she retorted. "I just choose not to. Don't start treating me like everyone else does."

"How does everyone else treat you?"

"Like I'm stupid. They're mean to me."

"They need to get to know you, and that's going to take some time," Stewart told her. "You need to be patient."

"They're nice to Julia, and she's been a member for even less time than me."

"That's a bit of a different situation though, honey. You can't expect them to welcome you with open arms. After all, they knew Pam for years."

"I know, I know. And *everybody* loved Pam," Ashley said, crossing her arms over her chest and looking away.

"Not everybody."

She looked back at him.

"I didn't. I love *you*. And everyone else is going to love you too."

"No they're not."

"They will."

"They think I'm some bimbo with boobs and no brain."

"So you go in there and show them, right?"

She shrugged.

"Right?" he insisted.

"Right," she said.

6. Julia & Alex

*J*ulia heard the garage door open, then a moment later close again, and that's how she knew that Alex was gone for the day. She rolled over in bed and threw her arm across her eyes. Waking up in Greenwich made her not want to get out of bed at all. She wasn't sure if she could last the year. It had only been six weeks and it seemed like an eternity.

She hated the outdoors.

She hated the dirt.

She hated the grass.

She hated the fashion—they wore country chic here.

She hated country chic.

But most of all, she hated the women. They were so tedious. All they talked about was Junior League and town gossip and *books*. Apparently out here if you weren't a member of a book club, they thought you were illiterate. So Julia had joined one, and they were having one of the silly meetings today. She'd even gone to the trouble to read the book. At least it was short—too bad the meeting wouldn't be. The woman who ran it, Priscilla, blathered on and on and on, and whenever she spoke it always sounded condescending. Julia had caught herself a few times on the verge of opening her mouth and telling Priscilla exactly what she thought of her. Julia had been famous in her social circle in the city for her withering attacks on women she didn't like. But for now she was trying to be good. She just wasn't sure how long she could last.

7. The Mystery Readers

"*C*andy," Priscilla's voice sang in the cadence of welcome as she opened the front door. "Come on in."

"Darling, how are you?" Candy said. She had the low, throaty voice of a smoker and, though she'd done her best with chemical peels and laser treatments and expensive facials, she had the skin of a smoker too. She stepped inside, bringing in a swirl of cold air and leaned in and kissed Priscilla's cheek.

"Did you walk over?" Priscilla asked.

Candy pulled back to look at Priscilla in mock amazement. "Of course not. In this weather? No, I was just having a quick ciggi."

Candy had probably spent double the amount of time standing outside smoking than she would have walking over. The truth was Candy didn't walk in *any* weather. Candy was not a walker; she only lived three houses down, but she drove whenever she came over—winter or summer.

"I mean I know *you're* out there every morning," Candy said—because Priscilla was a notorious walker, doing loops of the neighborhood religiously every day. "But I prefer my little gym in the basement and my elliptical machine. The best thing about it is, I can read at the same time."

"How many books have you gone through in the last week?" Priscilla asked.

"Oh, not many this week," Candy said, waving her hand. "And almost no good ones. The books I pick out myself are terrible. And the picks from my other book groups aren't much better. So am I late? Is everyone else here?"

"Susan's here"—then Priscilla's lip curled a little as she added—"and Ashley's here."

"No Margaret? Or Julia? And I thought I was going to be the last one to arrive."

"Julia's not here yet. And of course you must know that Margaret's not coming," Priscilla said. "And I wasn't sure if you were coming either," she added, annoyance creeping into her voice.

"But I told you on the phone the other day that I'd be here," Candy said.

"And then you practically hung up on me, you got off the phone so fast."

Priscilla wasn't sure if it was her imagination, or if Candy looked a little nervous. Candy never looked nervous.

"When's the last time I missed a meeting?" Candy asked as she pulled a pair of high-heeled sandals from her bag. She kicked off the heels she was wearing and bent to put on the new ones. Priscilla didn't allow shoes beyond the foyer unless they had never been worn outside, so all the women had a special pair they saved only for the book group.

"Are those new?" Priscilla asked.

"Spring line," Candy said.

"I haven't seen them."

"They're not available here yet. I got them from Paris. We decided to fly through Europe on our way back from Beijing."

"They're gorgeous."

Once Candy had her shoes fastened, Priscilla walked back with her to where Susan and Ashley were sitting in the living room.

When *Architectural Digest* did a spread on Priscilla's home the year before, this was the room they had featured. It had a soaring cathedral ceiling, and it was decorated all in white—white rugs, white couch, white tables, modern white-toned paintings. The entire back wall was glass: glass windows reaching up to the ceiling and, at floor level, glass doors leading out to a terrace and the view of the twelfth hole and the big pond that served as the water hazard in front of the green. Usually the window was a counterpoint of color—green in the summer and reds and yellows in the fall. But the landscape now was a monochrome. The ground was white from the dusting of snow they had gotten in that morning.

"Hello, darling," Candy said, stooping to kiss Susan's cheek.

"Oh, you're cold," Susan said.

Candy turned to Ashley and looked her up and down. Ashley was wearing a low-cut blouse with Seven jeans and stilettos. "Don't you look pretty today," Candy said, bending to kiss Ashley on the cheek as well.

"Thank you," Ashley said, though she wasn't so sure it was a compliment.

"What can I get you?" Priscilla asked Candy.

"Green tea. I'm only drinking green tea these days."

"I should have had that," Susan said, looking down at her coffee. "It's supposed to be some sort of fountain of youth."

"It's the antioxidants," Priscilla said. "They're supposed to be good for you."

"I'm counting on it," Candy said. "I'm so bad in so many other ways."

"Do you want green tea instead?" Priscilla asked Susan. "I'll just tell Danielle to make a pot," she said without waiting for an answer, and disappeared through another door.

Candy dropped into a white armchair, tossing her bag at her feet.

"I haven't seen you since Priscilla's party three weeks ago," Susan said. "We missed you at the last 'Done in a Day' project."

"I know," Candy said. "And I heard I also missed a trip to our favorite used-book store. How was the selection?"

Candy was referring to the Greenwich dump, which had a place where people dropped off their unwanted books. There was a time, years ago, when people just dropped off boxes of old books that were actually quite valuable. Then the dealers heard about it, and for a while the dump was overrun. Now people knew better and called the dealers into their houses to go over the collections.

"Selection was pretty good. There were ten or fifteen boxes. Someone must have been moving."

"Or died," Candy said.

"I don't like to think about that." Susan shuddered.

Priscilla reappeared from the kitchen. "Isn't it funny that your favorite thing to read is murder mysteries," she said, overhearing the last part of the conversation.

"And the gorier the better," Candy put in.

"I know," Susan said. "But please don't ask me to make sense of it."

"Of course not. Some things just don't make sense," Candy declared. "So did you get any good mysteries at the dump?"

"A signed, first-edition copy of *The Alienist*," Susan said. "It's not really valuable, but I loved the book."

"I wish I could have come along."

"Well, why couldn't you? Where have you been?" Priscilla asked. "I haven't seen you since you got back from Beijing."

"I've been a little busy," Candy said.

"A *little* busy?" Priscilla repeated. "When I called you the other day, you couldn't even talk for two minutes. And I called you before that, too," she said, just remembering. "I called you last Tuesday and left a message, and you didn't even call me back."

"I know, darling. I'm sorry. Truly."

"What's going on?" Priscilla demanded. "I know there's something."

At that moment Danielle pushed open the door and came in carrying a tray. She set it down on the bleached wood coffee table and proceeded to pour out four cups of green tea from the teapot. She put one down in front of Priscilla. Candy reached out to take hers, saying, "Thank you, dear."

Susan was still holding her coffee cup.

"Done with coffee?" Danielle asked in a thick, Eastern European accent.

"Yes, thank you," Susan said, exchanging her coffee for green tea.

Danielle tried to take Ashley's coffee as well, but Ashley held firmly on to her cup and said, "I'd actually like some more coffee."

Danielle put the extra cup of green tea on the tray and disappeared back into the kitchen.

"Danielle's wonderful," Candy said.

"I know," Priscilla agreed. "But you're changing the subject again."

Candy sighed. "I wish Margaret were coming so I could tell everyone together."

Margaret was the fourth member in the book club. She had moved into the neighborhood a year and a half earlier—and into the neighborhood's nicest house. It was an enormous old Tudor, built in 1907. Of course it had been hopelessly outdated inside, but the previous owner sold it to a contractor who'd gutted and totally refurbished the interior and then sold it to Margaret and her husband for an enormous sum. The selling price had been whispered around: fifteen million. The price itself wasn't unheard of for Greenwich. There was an estate that sold for more than fifty million, but that was on eighty acres with a guest house, pool house, caretaker's house, and a stable. Properties in the twenty- to thirty-million-dollar range were more common, but were usually waterfront. The houses in Priscilla's neighborhood had generous plots of land, but weren't quite in the realm of the really top-end Greenwich properties. The price Margaret and her husband had paid for their house was by far the highest for the area. They bought it without even bargaining, people said. The rumor mill soon had it that Margaret's husband ran a hedge fund that had netted him personally more than twenty million in one year alone.

"Why did she have to miss today," Candy said, half asking, half complaining.

"Don't tell me you haven't talked to her," Priscilla said.

"She called a few days ago, but I haven't had a chance to call her back," Candy said. "I figured that I could just catch up with her today. What happened?"

"Her husband's hedge fund," Susan said.

"Blew up," Priscilla supplied. "Apparently he was leveraged to the hilt. Trying to make a comeback before the end of the year. Instead he ended the year down something like thirty to forty percent. Maybe more. Margin calls all over the place."

They had all picked up more than a little of the business lingo over the years.

"But weren't his personal assets—"

"No. They lost everything. Margaret's packing now. I think they have to be out by the end of the month."

"I heard the house is already listed," Susan added.

"Poor Margaret," Candy said. "How is she taking it?"

"She's amazing," Susan told her. "You know what she said? She said, 'I didn't have anything before, and we managed.' "

"But I hear her husband isn't doing quite as well," Priscilla put in.

"Suicide watch," Susan murmured.

"That's terrible."

"You know these men and their egos," Priscilla said.

"I don't think Harry would think about killing himself," Susan said. "He'd just start figuring out how to get to the top again."

"Gordon never cared that much," Priscilla said.

"Stewart would never even think about killing himself. He loves himself too much." Ashley laughed gaily to show she was joking.

"That's probably true," Priscilla said tartly.

Candy brought them back to the topic. "I can't believe that about Margaret. That's terrible."

"I know. I'll miss her. She was a great reader. And she was better than all of us at the Sunday crossword."

"That's not saying much in my case," Susan admitted.

"This makes what I have to say a bit harder," Candy said.

There was a moment of silence as Priscilla, Susan, and Ashley all looked at her.

"What is it?" Priscilla asked, almost ominously.

"I just want you all to know that . . . that . . ." Candy faltered.

"You're moving too," Priscilla said. "I *knew* it was something."

"No. It's not that. I'm not moving." Candy said.

"Oh, thank God. I couldn't bear to lose you, too."

Candy grimaced. "Well, that's the thing."

"What's the thing?"

Never in a million years would Priscilla have expected the answer Candy gave her.

"I'm going to be a mother," Candy told them.

Priscilla started to laugh and only stopped when she saw the look on Candy's face. "You're kidding, right?" Priscilla didn't know her exact age, but she knew Candy was over forty-five.

"No," Candy said a little stiffly. "We're adopting a baby girl from China. Her name is Anna."

"So *that's* what your trip was about," Susan said.

"I didn't want to say anything until I was sure," Candy went on. "In case it didn't work out. But it did, and we're going to get her next week."

"Candy, that's wonderful." Susan glanced nervously over at Priscilla then said again, "I think that's just wonderful." She got up and gave Candy a hug. "Congratulations."

"Congratulations," Ashley echoed.

Priscilla didn't say anything.

There was an awkward pause, then Priscilla said abruptly, "You know, you don't have to leave the group. It's not like there's this rule that says you can't have a baby and stay."

Actually there *was* a rule—one that both Priscilla and Candy had fully agreed on when it was instituted, though Susan loved kids and would have happily talked babies instead of books. But as a result of their ban another book group formed, one consisting solely of women *with* children. Priscilla knew that Candy would be switching book groups, and switching book groups in the neighborhood had come to represent switching social circles.

"Oh, honey," Candy said. "Thank you. I really appreciate that . . . but I think it's best this way."

"Oh," Priscilla said.

"I still want you to call me Sunday about the crossword. Well, not this Sunday because we'll be on a plane back to China," Candy said as she rose to go.

"You're not going to stay to talk about the book?" Priscilla asked.

"We're leaving Sunday, and we don't even have a crib yet. We're thinking we might co-sleep, but Michael is worried about rolling over and crushing the baby, and so we think we'll get a crib just in case, but—" she broke off, laughing. "See? I'm baby-obsessed already. I'd better go."

"Call and let us know when you're back," Susan said. "I'd love to come over and meet Anna."

"I will. I promise I'll let you know when I'm back." Then she disappeared into the hallway. A moment later they heard the door open, and then Candy's voice: "Hello, Julia. No, I'm just going. Sorry I missed you. But they're all inside. Go on in."

A moment later, Julia appeared in the doorway. She paused there, one hand against the doorframe to balance as she slipped off her shoes and pulled on a pair of slingbacks from her bag. "I'm sorry I'm late. Don't tell me it's over already? I just saw Candy leaving."

"She had to go," Priscilla said.

Susan was the one to add the details. "Unfortunately, Candy's not going to be part of the book group anymore."

"Oh, no?" Julia raised her perfect eyebrows. "Why not?"

"She's having a baby. I mean, she's adopting," Susan corrected herself. "From China. They go to get her Sunday. Her name is Anna."

"How wonderful for her," Julia said.

Susan hesitated for a moment. Sometimes she found it hard to tell if there was something underneath Julia's innocuous comments. She decided that Julia was being sincere, so she replied, "Yes, isn't it?"

"But now we need to find someone to replace her," Priscilla said.

"Maybe someone nice will move into Margaret's house," Susan suggested.

"But that will take ages," Priscilla said.

"Actually, it won't," Julia said.

Priscilla turned to look at Julia. "Why do you say that?"

"There's already a couple scheduled to come look at the old Tudor."

"Margaret's house? How do you know that?" Priscilla demanded.

Julia shrugged with a little smile on her face. "A little bird told me."

"Who?" Priscilla persisted.

Julia tossed her hair back, slightly annoyed at being forced to reveal her source. "It's being shown by the same Realtor I used. She told me."

"Well, OK," Priscilla said. "But even if they buy it, it's not going to be anyone like Margaret."

The constant optimist, Susan said, "You never know. She might be better."

8. Sofie & Dean

"*I* found it," Dean said first thing when Sofie picked up the phone.

"Found what?" Sofie tried to think of what he might have lost. His wallet? His briefcase? His cell phone?

"I found our house."

She should have known; when Dean started thinking about doing something, there was almost no gap between thought and action. Once when he said he thought he wanted a new car, he'd driven home in a BMW the next day. It was what she had loved about him when they first met—she hadn't realized how annoying it could be to live with. It had been only a few weeks since Dean first brought up the idea of moving. A few days later he mentioned in passing that he'd gotten the name of a real estate agent from a colleague. But after that he hadn't said a word about it.

Where Dean was impulsive, Sofie was deliberate. Deliberate was her word—Dean's way of describing her behavior was a little less flattering. When Sofie tried to defend herself, saying that she liked to take her time and consider all the possibilities before she acted, he replied that she could spend hours trying to decide whether or not to get out of bed in the morning.

"I'm telling you this house is perfect. I've made an appointment to see it tomorrow."

"But it's a Tuesday. You've got work tomorrow," she protested, but Dean knew she was really saying, *I need more time*. He heard the unspoken message in the way that people who have been together for years hear the meaning beneath the words as clearly as if it had been spoken.

"I'm taking the day off. I'm telling you, this is our house. It just came on the market a few days ago, and if we don't move on it someone else could come along and snatch it up. What do I always tell you? Slow and steady doesn't win the race. They made that up to make all the slow kids feel better. You have to go for what you want. Otherwise someone else is going to get it first."

She sighed. "What time tomorrow?"

"That's my girl! Our appointment is at ten. We'll drive out bright and early."

"What do you think?" Dean whispered in Sofie's ear.

The real estate agent had stepped outside supposedly to check her messages, but the real reason was to give them a chance to talk about what they thought of the house. Sofie could see her through the sliding glass doors, her ear glued to her BlackBerry.

"It's a little big," Sofie said. "It'd be like living in Versailles."

"You shouldn't joke about that," Dean told her. "There's actually a house here in Greenwich that's modeled on the Petit Trianon. I could have suggested we buy that one instead."

"You're kidding."

Dean shook his head. "I'll drive you past it when we're on our way home. This isn't even close to big out here. And anyway, that's why we're moving out of New York. To get some space." He flung his arms out as if to demonstrate. "You've lived in the city your whole life. You just don't know what it's like to have room to breathe. Besides, who cares how big it is. We can afford it."

She supposed it was true, but she still hadn't adjusted to the fact that her father's money was now hers. Even though she had grown up in luxury in a town house manned by an entire staff, she never had any money of her own. She could have whatever she asked for, but she'd had to ask.

"We might be able to afford it, but should you buy something just because you can afford it?" she asked.

"Of course not. You should buy it because you love it. And I love it."

The house was a Tudor, set back from the road and surrounded by huge old oaks. The rooms in the front were a little dark, but the back rooms had been adapted, the windows enlarged, and sliding glass doors installed leading out to a veranda. There were more oak trees in the backyard and then beyond that, the rolling green carpet of grass that was the fairway for the fifth hole of a golf course.

The truth was that Sofie loved it too. And she had to admit that Greenwich was beautiful with its narrow, winding roads lined with stone walls and overhung by towering century-old trees. But Sofie's cautious side stopped her from saying "Let's do it." Instead she said, "It's beautiful . . . but don't you think we should look around just a little?"

"And then when we decide this is the one, it'll be gone," Dean said impatiently.

While they were talking, Sofie was staring absentmindedly out through the glass doors. She cocked her head to one side then said, almost thoughtfully, "The thing is, I don't want to buy anything through that woman. She's such a bitch."

Dean snapped around to stare at her, but what was more interesting to Sofie was that the Realtor made a sharp movement as well.

"What are you talking about? She couldn't have been nicer to us."

Of course what Dean meant was that the woman couldn't have

been nicer to *him*. Women were always nice to Dean. That's what happened when you looked like a male model, had a BA from Cornell and a law degree from Columbia, and had already made partner.

"Oh, you know I was just kidding," Sofie said.

"Sometimes your sense of humor is a little strange, you know that?" Dean was obviously trying to hold on to his patience. "But can we forget about the Realtor? I don't care about her. It's the house I really—"

"Can we go take another look at the backyard?" Sofie broke in.

Dean shot her another strange look, but then he shrugged. "Sure. If you want."

He led the way through the sliding doors out onto the patio where the real estate agent was saying, "Yes. Yes, I realize that. But we can't just . . . well, I know." She held a finger up to them, asking them to wait a moment. "Yes, OK. Listen, could you hold on a sec?" She took the phone away from her ear, covering the mouthpiece. "How is everything?" she asked them.

"We're going to take another look around the property," Dean said.

"Do you need me to—?"

"No, no, we'll be fine," Dean assured her.

"OK, I'm just going to finish up with this. Let me know if you need anything."

"Yes. Thanks."

Sofie had already started walking away, down the lawn toward the golf course. Dean had to walk quickly to catch up.

"What the hell is going on with you?" he said.

"I'll tell you in a second," Sofie replied, continuing down the sloping lawn. She kept going until she reached the edge of the property, and only then did she stop and turn around to look back up at the house. It really was impressive. For all its size, the Tudor architecture made it seem cozy—like a hamlet tucked in a glen.

"So what's bothering you?" Dean asked after a moment. "It's something, isn't it?"

"Mmm." Sofie turned back to look at her husband. "This Realtor is representing the sellers, right?"

He shrugged. "I guess so. What does that have to do with anything?"

"It means that she's not just working for us. Not to mention the higher the purchase price, the more she gets in commission."

"That's the way it works," Dean said. "That's business. And it's up to us to get the best price we can."

"The only thing is, we're at a bit of a disadvantage," Sofie said.

"You mean because I really want the house?"

"Yes, that. But even more because she knows how much you want the house."

"I don't think I was *that* transparent. I barely said anything while she was showing it so I don't see how—"

"She bugged the kitchen and was listening to our conversation," Sofie said.

Dean gave a shout of laugher. "You take the cake, Sofie. I swear, that's the most ridiculous thing I ever heard. What do you think this is, the CIA or something?"

"It would be the FBI. CIA is international," Sofie informed him.

"Honey, you've been reading way too many mysteries."

"Why is it so hard to believe? I mean it's not like it's difficult. You can buy a bugging kit for less than a hundred dollars on the Internet. Any twelve-year-old could do it. And think of the advantage it gives her. She'll know if we're waffling and she has to bring the price down. She'll also know if we really want it, she can keep the price high and pretend to be willing to walk away."

"You're such a conspiracy theorist," Dean said. But his voice was less certain.

"You know what they say: 'Just because I'm paranoid doesn't mean they're not out to get me.' And when have you known me to be wrong? Remember when I said those two antique dealers we called to give estimates on my father's furniture were fixing the price on a lot of the pieces? You laughed at me then too. But I was right, wasn't I? And in both cases, we're not talking about peanuts. We could be talking about a difference of millions. How do you figure out how much something is worth? Well, it's worth what you can get someone to pay. And she's hoping to find out just how much we want it and how high we'll go. She might even tell us that there are other people interested—and they're just about ready to put down a bid. Then she'd really have some leverage."

Dean frowned. "OK, so how did you figure this out?"

"I don't know. I was just watching her out the window. And there was something about the way she was talking—or maybe it was *when* she was talking. She only seemed to speak at the breaks in our conversation. The timing was too weird. So then I said the thing about—"

"Her being a bitch? So that's what that was about!"

Sofie grinned. "You should have seen her jump."

Dean laughed again. "When they made you, they broke the mold, you know that?"

Sofie shrugged but looked pleased nonetheless.

"So . . . what about the house?"

"Do you really want it that much?"

"I really do," Dean admitted.

That was enough for Sofie. "If you really want it that much . . ."

He whooped and picked her up and spun her around.

"Dean, put me down," she said, laughing.

He gave her a big smacking kiss, then put her down. "So shall we go up and face the gorgon? I have to admit she is a little scary."

"Did you see her nails? I feel like she might stab me in the jugular with one of them."

"Don't worry, I'll protect you," Dean said, snaking an arm around her waist as they walked back up the lawn.

"What, with these little sticks?" she teased him, squeezing his bicep.

When they reached the house, the Realtor was in the kitchen, drumming her long manicured nails along the marble countertop. She looked up and said brightly. "So? What do you think?"

Dean smiled back. Sofie always marveled at his ability to turn on the charm—like some sort of tap. "My wife wants to take some more time, and she's the boss."

The Realtor cut a sharp glance at Sofie, then turned her focus back to Dean. She seemed to sense that he was the lynchpin—that he was the one to sell to. "Well, just so you know, there has been quite a bit of interest. Personally I don't think it's going to be on the market long. I have another couple already very interested, and they could move on it any day. I think they're getting their financing in order. Maybe if you sneak in now, you can avoid getting in a bidding war."

Sofie looked at Dean and raised her eyebrows as if to say, "See?" Just as she had predicted, the woman was trying to push Dean's buttons. Sofie could see how Dean tensed at the Realtor's words, but when he answered her, he spoke nonchalantly: "We'll try to get back to you soon."

"Do you have any specific concerns about the house?" the woman asked, addressing Sofie this time. There was a note of saccharine sweetness that fell just a shade short of condescending.

"Well, I guess I was thinking I wanted to find out a little more about the neighborhood."

The Realtor bridled at this comment. "But this is one of the best neighborhoods you'll find. Do you know that this is one of the wealthiest counties in the country?"

"I don't think my wife meant exactly that," Dean said, coming to her rescue.

"Well, what did she mean then?" The woman seemed genuinely puzzled.

"I think she meant what the people are like, didn't you, hon? Oh, that reminds me," Dean said to Sofie, "I meant to tell you I heard that some of the women in the neighborhood have a book club. And guess what they read? I'll even give you a hint. You read a lot of them." He paused, waiting for a reaction. When Sofie didn't respond, he said, "They read mysteries, silly. Come on, I thought you'd be at least a little excited about that." He turned to the real estate agent and explained, "Mysteries are her favorite thing."

"That's very nice," the agent said with a little smile. "But I believe you have to be invited first."

Sofie was sure the nastiness was in retaliation from the earlier comment the agent had overheard.

"So who do I have to bribe to get my wife an invitation?" Dean asked. "If we move here, of course," he added with a glance at Sofie.

The agent said, "That would be Priscilla Brenner."

February

9. Priscilla & Susan

$\mathcal{P}$riscilla rang Susan's doorbell, and as she waited on the stoop she marched energetically in place. Priscilla was very serious about her power walking. Their neighborhood was a spider web of quiet, tree-shaded streets that branched off the main road. There was barely any traffic, because all the roads ended in a cul-de-sac or looped around in a semicircle. Priscilla had worked out a circular route: One lap was about a mile long, and she always did three laps. Her route also happened to pass the houses of all the book club members; if they looked out they could see her doing her three laps every morning. Susan didn't need to look, because Priscilla stopped at Susan's house to pick her up for the last lap.

Susan opened the door dressed in her favorite workout outfit—a Juicy tracksuit in bubblegum pink.

"Ready?" Priscilla asked.

"Could I—"

"No dogs," Priscilla told her.

"But they'd love a walk," Susan said.

"You always let them stop and sniff."

"Otherwise it wouldn't be any fun for them."

"This isn't supposed to be fun. This is exercise." Priscilla checked the band on her wrist. "Come on, my heart rate is dropping. I've got to keep it in the target zone."

"Oh, sorry," Susan pulled the door shut behind her, and Priscilla took off, Susan hustling to catch up.

"So have you talked to Candy yet? She's back, you know," Susan said.

"I know. I got a message from her. I haven't had a chance to get back to her."

"But that was almost two weeks ago," Susan pointed out.

"I've been busy."

"Oh, *right*," Susan said.

There was a pause, but Priscilla couldn't quite pull off total disinterest. "How is she?" she asked after a moment.

"She's good."

There was another pause.

Then Susan added, "Well, other than the fact that she hasn't slept through the night in three weeks, and she's trying to quit smoking."

"Candy's *quitting*? Oh my God." Priscilla started to laugh.

"It's not funny," Susan said, but she couldn't hold back a smile.

"You'd think that would be something she'd try to do *before* she got the baby in the house."

"I know," Susan said, laughing now too. "I was going to go over and visit, but I think I'll wait until things calm down a little."

"What else did Candy say?"

"Well, she was talking about how much she missed real, adult conversation. And she was saying how the women in the other book group were great and smart and everything, but they couldn't ever have a real conversation, because there were always kids running around, and they couldn't manage more than two consecutive sentences without getting interrupted."

"They don't leave the kids home with the nannies?"

"Some of them don't believe in having nannies."

"Good lord," was all Priscilla could say.

"I wouldn't want to have a nanny. At least, not full-time."

"How on earth did Harry ever convince you not to have kids?" Priscilla said. "You were born to be a mother."

"I didn't want to force him into doing something he didn't want to do."

"But what about what *you* wanted to do?"

"I'm fine with not having kids," Susan insisted.

Priscilla opened her mouth to speak again, but Susan hurried on, "Oh, I meant to ask, did you hear that someone bought the old Tudor?" She knew she'd be able to change the conversation with that piece of news.

Priscilla almost stopped in midstride. "No. How does everyone suddenly know everything before me?"

"I heard it from Julia. I ran into her the other day, and she mentioned it."

"Julia? How does Julia know everything all of a sudden? Who bought it? And did you hear when they're moving in?"

"It's a young couple. And next month maybe?"

"Anyway, I hope it's soon. And I hope she reads. We need another member to offset the boob job."

"You invited her," Susan said. "I still don't understand how you could invite Ashley, after what Stewart did to Pam. I mean, that was—"

"I don't want to talk about it," Priscilla snapped.

"OK. Fine."

They walked in silence for a minute.

"Um . . ." Susan hesitated, then said, "I wanted to ask you something."

"As long as it doesn't have anything to do with Ashley and Stewart."

"No, it doesn't have anything to do with them."

Priscilla heard something in Susan's voice that made her glance at her friend. "What is it?"

"It's actually about Harry."

"What about Harry?"

"I wanted to ask if you noticed anything different about him."

"Different? What, did he dye his hair or lose weight or something?"

"No. I mean . . . I think he's been acting strange," Susan said.

"Strange? How do you mean strange?"

"Strange like . . . well, he's been really quiet recently. And you know Harry—he's anything but quiet."

Harry had a booming voice and very strong opinions, which he didn't hesitate to share.

"Did you ask him about it?" Priscilla said.

"Yes. A bunch of times. He just says he's tired. I suppose he has been working longer hours recently—as if he didn't work enough as it is."

"Longer hours? You mean like lots of late nights?"

"I know what you're thinking," Susan said. "But he's working on the acquisition of a company."

"What company?" Priscilla asked suspiciously.

"I don't know the name of the company. Why is it you always expect the worst from people?"

"Experience," Priscilla said succinctly. "But don't go trying to make me the bad guy here. If you're so sure that Harry's just tired from this acquisition, then why did you bring it up?"

Susan didn't have an answer to that.

"I'm only saying aloud what you were thinking," Priscilla said.

"What should I do?"

"Nothing."

"Nothing?"

"Nothing," Priscilla repeated firmly. "If you kick up a fuss, you'll just drive him away. Besides this kind of thing happens all the time."

"I know . . . but not to me and Harry," Susan said plaintively.

"Apparently it does."

"You wouldn't sit around and do nothing if your husband were having an affair."

"Gordon?" Priscilla laughed. "Gordon have an affair? I wish. He doesn't have the imagination."

"I never thought Harry would do it either."

"You're probably making too big deal out of a little thing. I bet it's all in your mind."

"You think?" This was what Susan wanted to hear. She wanted Priscilla to tell her that she was being silly—to tell her that it wasn't true.

Priscilla went on, "I'll tell you what—I'll watch and see how he acts at Julia's dinner party tonight."

"If he even comes," Susan said morosely.

"But you'll come either way, won't you? You couldn't pass up the opportunity to get a look at Julia's husband, the mystery man. I mean, it's been more than three months in the neighborhood, and we haven't had a single glimpse of him."

"I've seen his car," Susan said. "But the windows are tinted."

"And do you even know what he does? How he made his money?"

"I think he's some sort of entrepreneur. But Julia was pretty vague about it."

"I think she's trying to hide something," Priscilla declared, "probably the fact that he's a toad."

"Speak of the devil," Susan said.

They could see Julia's Jaguar convertible pulling out of her driveway. A moment later she spotted them and pulled up alongside.

"I can't believe you haven't switched to Pilates," Julia said as she lowered the window.

"I like my walks," Priscilla replied.

"Well, you might want to try Pilates sometime. Anyway, I just wanted to make sure you were both still coming tonight."

"Wouldn't miss it for the world," Priscilla said. "I'm looking forward to meeting your husband. He'll be there, won't he?"

"I expect so, since he does live there," Julia said a little sharply. "Well, anyway, eight o'clock. See you then."

10. Julia & Alex

"*J* don't believe it," Priscilla said. "It's just not fair.

"No, it's really not," Susan agreed. "Not fair at all."

They were standing in Julia's living room, sipping Julia's wine, and staring at Julia's husband.

"If there was any justice in the world, he'd be old, short, and pudgy with lots of hair on the backs of his hands. Or at the very least he'd be bald with that little fringe around his head like a monk. Instead he's" Priscilla gestured toward him, wordlessly—"what is he?"

"Gregory Peck," Susan supplied. She had a knack for comparing ordinary people to movie stars.

"Exactly." Priscilla said.

"Ashley is practically throwing herself at him," Susan observed.

"And he's barely looking at her," Priscilla said with satisfaction.

"I've never known a man who could resist staring at Ashley's cleavage. Do you think he's gay?" Susan said.

Priscilla cocked her head and observed for a moment before declaring, "No, he's not gay. I would love to be able to tell you he is, but I can't. He's just a very cool customer. And Ashley's way too obvious for him."

"Cool customer is an understatement," Susan said.

Priscilla put her hand on Susan's arm. "Look at that. Ashley's getting the brush-off."

Julia's husband glanced down at Ashley briefly, said something, touched her elbow to gently move her aside, and walked off across the room to where Priscilla's husband, Gordon, was deep in discussion with Ashley's husband, Stewart.

"And here she comes."

Ashley walked up a moment later and announced, "He's gay."

"I don't think so," Priscilla said.

"Yes. Yes, he is," Ashley insisted. "I can tell about these things."

At that moment, Julia emerged from the kitchen and announced, "It looks like everything is just about ready." She turned to Alex. "Darling, will you take everyone into the dining room? I'm just going to coordinate the serving." Then she disappeared back into the kitchen.

"It's just through here," Alex said, gesturing toward another doorway.

They filed through into the dining room, and there was the inevitable pause as everyone considered where they should sit. But it turned out that Julia hadn't left it to chance. Each napkin had a name stitched into it.

Priscilla was seated next to Ashley's husband, Stewart. At one time Priscilla and Gordon and Stewart and his wife had all been quite close—that is, Stewart and his *first* wife, Pam. Their breakup had sent shockwaves through the neighborhood—mostly because for years the great mystery was what Pam saw in Stewart. And yet *he* was the one to file for divorce. And even more astonishing was the fact that Stewart kept the house, and Pam was the one who took the kids and moved—to California. A few months later Ashley showed up. No one could understand how Stewart could go from a woman like Pam to one like Ashley. Pam was the seventh wonder of the world—the kind of woman who, when people were around her, they felt better about themselves instead of worse. Even Priscilla, who talked about everybody behind their backs, never had a bad thing to say about her.

After Pam left for California, Priscilla vowed that out of loyalty to Pam, this new wife would never get an invitation to the book club. But when she made that vow, she had forgotten that Stewart's fund was a major client for Gordon's sales group. Before Priscilla could give Ashley the cold shoulder, Stewart made sure Priscilla understood that his new wife was to be accepted—or his firm might reconsider their business. Ever since, Priscilla's relationship with Stewart had been strained. At best. And now she was stuck sitting next to him.

After everyone had settled in, Priscilla turned to her other side to seek refuge in Harry, Susan's husband, who was seated on her left. But Harry had his back to her—and all his attention was fixed on Julia. And Julia wasn't even talking to him. Julia was in fact listening intently to Priscilla's own husband, Gordon. Gordon was talking in an animated fashion while Julia had a little, amused smile on her face.

Priscilla was annoyed: annoyed at being trapped next to Stewart, annoyed that Harry was fixated on Julia, annoyed that Julia was talking to her husband, and annoyed at her husband for talking. Priscilla called across the table, "Oh, Gordon, will you stop boring Julia with the details of spreadsheets and corporate accounting?"

Her voice was sharp, and it cut through all the other conversations. Everyone stopped talking, and there was an awkward silence.

Gordon looked as if he were about to say something, but then his mouth tightened and he just stared down at his plate. It was Julia who answered.

"Well, if anyone could make spreadsheets interesting, I'm sure it would be your husband. But he was actually telling me about how you first met. I wish Alex was as romantic. Gordon said the way you met was like the fairy tale of seeing someone across a crowded room—but he didn't see you. He heard you laugh. And he said when he heard it, he immediately thought that he'd like to spend the rest of his life with a woman who could laugh like that."

"Oh, that old story. I don't know why he insists on telling it." Priscilla said, unsettled by the fact that Gordon had shared that with Julia.

"He was saying he wishes you would laugh more," Julia said.

"Well, things aren't so funny anymore," Priscilla retorted.

"No?" Julia said suggestively.

Susan, with her impeccable breeding, was ready to head off any uncomfortable conversation. "Your house is beautiful, Julia," she broke in. "I love what you've done with it. Where did you get your ideas? Did you use a designer?"

The house was furnished with a combination of antiques from different periods, set against unusual Persian carpets in bold colors. The overall effect was striking and elegant but somehow also managed to be cozy at the same time. Most of the other women's houses had been designed by decorators, and the rooms looked more like set pieces than places where people could live. As usual Julia had outdone them all.

But then Julia admitted, "Oh, I had nothing to do with it."

"I have to get the name of your decorator, then," Susan said.

"Alex did the house."

"Alex . . . ?" Susan repeated as if waiting for the last name of the decorator Julia was referring to. Then the truth dawned on her. "You mean Alex, your *husband*?"

"He has quite a flair for it, don't you think?"

"It's *amazing*," Ashley jumped in, with an arch look to Susan and Priscilla to show that she thought this proved her point.

"Yes, you'd think he was gay," Julia said with a laugh.

Alex made a noise from his seat down the table.

"It's a compliment, darling," Julia informed him. "I was just telling everyone that the house was your vision."

Alex shrugged and said, "I like nice things."

Those were the first words he'd uttered since he sat down, and he hadn't actually produced a sentence longer than that all evening.

"I know what you mean," Priscilla agreed. "And the nicest things are always the most expensive. It's the curse of having sophisticated taste."

"So where does your sophisticated taste come in with you just reading mysteries for that book club of yours?" Harry said.

Priscilla treated him with one of her best drop-dead looks, but he didn't even seem to notice.

"You could be reading something useful like biographies," he went on. "I'm reading that new biography of Churchill right now. It's fascinating. You can really learn something from that man."

"Mysteries can be useful too," Susan said before Priscilla could attack.

"What, you mean for all the murders you have to solve?" Harry asked.

"You never know," Alex said drily.

At the time it was just a random remark, but later, when they remembered Alex's comment, they all wondered—what was the chance that it was simply a coincidence?

March

11. Sofie

$\mathscr{M}$oving day finally arrived, and after weeks of anxiety Sofie's practical side took over; she was too busy overseeing the packing and labeling and moving to worry about what her new life was going to be like.

When the movers finished loading up the truck and started out, Sofie went back up to the apartment for one last walk-through. She scooped up her cat, Agatha, and held her as she drifted through the rooms, her footsteps echoing on the hardwood floors. This was how it had looked when they'd first seen the place. But then it had been filled with possibilities. Then she had walked through thinking, "The couch could go there, the bed over by the window there. . . ."

Even though she knew they were moving to a new home, the empty rooms still seemed unbearably sad. With everything stripped bare it was as if they had never lived there at all. With all the memories—the horrible fights, the talks that kept them up late, the plans they'd made for the future—it seemed like they should have left some sort of imprint. But it was just an empty apartment, until someone else moved in and built their own memories here.

As she wandered through, she found some odds and ends that had been shaken loose from carpets or revealed by the removal of the furniture. There were a few loose coins, an old grocery list, a single diamond stud earring, and one of Dean's cashmere socks.

She picked each item up as she found it. Then, clutching them tightly in one hand, she bent her face into Agatha's soft fur. And Agatha, who was usually so finicky, held still in Sofie's arms.

Sofie stayed in the apartment until she regained her composure, then she went downstairs to get the car. Dean had offered to take the day off and help, but Sofie knew he was hoping that she would say no, so she did. At the time he'd smiled and kissed her and said it was probably for the best, since God knew if he tried to help, he'd probably just get in the way.

So Sofie had prepared, knowing she was going to be handling it all herself. She'd mapped out where all the furniture was to go beforehand on sheets of paper, and she gave copies to the movers so they would know exactly where to put everything. She even went through the new house with a pencil and measured and marked the walls where the paintings were supposed to be hung.

Not only were the movers arriving with the furniture from the apartment, but another van with another set of men was coming with furniture they had purchased and put in storage. When their bid on the house had been accepted, Dean had pointed out that the furniture they had in their apartment wouldn't come close to filling a house. Wasn't it a shame, he said, that they had just sold off all her father's antiques. Though she didn't say so at the time, Sofie was hugely relieved. Having the furniture she'd grown up with in their new house would be like a nightmare come true. She still remembered the fit her father had thrown when she was six and put a glass down on an antique table and it left a watermark. He screamed at her, he screamed at the nanny, he screamed at the housekeeper, and then he kicked the piece of furniture to pieces—saying that it might as well be used as firewood, because it was ruined as an antique. After that Sofie wasn't too keen on antiques, but she never shared that story with Dean, because she couldn't figure out a way to tell it without sounding self-pitying and melodramatic. So he didn't know about her antipathy for expensive antiques, and it turned out he had formed his own bias in childhood. Apparently he had grown up with Danish modern and had a horror of blond wood and clean lines. Plus, after reading some copy of *Architectural Digest* in the waiting room of the dentist, he had inexplicably fallen in love with furniture from early eighteenth-century England. He showed Sofie pictures, and she told him there was no way in hell she was going to live in a house that looked like a museum. They finally agreed on a compromise. Sofie was going to decorate their bedroom, her own study, and the kitchen any way she wanted, and she would let Dean have the rest of the house.

So, in planning the move, there was the furniture from their apartment, the new furniture that Sofie had bought, and the new that Dean had purchased. It was an organizational nightmare, but somehow Sofie managed it—with the help of a small army of men—and that night when Dean came home to their new house, there wasn't a box in sight. He stepped through the door and, setting his briefcase down, looked around in awe. Then he called for Sofie, but she didn't answer. He went through all the rooms on the first floor before he climbed the stairs and finally found her in the master bedroom, sprawled out on top of the fully made bed, fast asleep. Agatha was nestled in the crook between her neck and shoulder.

Crossing to the bed he sat down gingerly on the edge. "Hey," he said, "naptime's over."

Agatha got up, stretched, and stalked off. Then Sofie opened her eyes, pushed herself up, and looked around as if she didn't know where she was.

"The house looks incredible," Dean said, rubbing her arm. "Have I ever told you that you're amazing?"

"No," she said sleepily. "But you've told me that I'm compulsive and obsessed with details and . . . and . . ."

"And precise to the point of insanity?" Dean added, starting to smile.

"No, that's a new one," Sofie said.

"All right. Precisely amazing. How's that?"

"Better."

"There's my girl. Have you had dinner?"

She shook her head.

"I bet you haven't eaten anything all day, have you?"

She shook her head again. "Too busy."

"We'd better feed you then. Let me take you out to eat. Anyplace you want."

"I don't know anyplace out here," she said. Now that the actual move was over, she was feeling a little lost, and Dean must have heard it in her voice because he took her hand and said, "So we'll explore."

12. Sofie & Susan

The next day the doorbell rang while Sofie was putting things away in the kitchen. When she opened the door, there were two people standing on the stoop. One was a deliveryman holding an armful of flowers. The other was a plump, pretty, smiling woman holding a pie.

"You're sure popular," the woman said.

"Believe me, it's not a usual thing for me," Sofie said as she awkwardly tried to hold the flowers and sign the deliveryman's clipboard at the same time. The deliveryman went back to his truck, and Sofie was left standing with the woman holding the pie.

"I wanted to welcome you to the neighborhood. I'm Susan Altman."

"Oh . . . um . . . would you like to come in?" Sofie asked.

"As long as it's not a bad time . . ."

"Not at all." Sofie led Susan into the living room.

"Didn't you just move in yesterday?" Susan asked, looking around at the immaculate room.

"Yes, but I can't relax until everything is put away."

Susan nodded knowingly. "Control freak. Me too."

"The problem is remembering where everything is."

"I know exactly what you mean."

"So, can I get you something? Coffee, tea?" Sofie offered.

"I'd love some coffee, but only if you'll let me keep you company in the kitchen. Kitchens are so much cozier."

Sofie led Susan into the kitchen and, laying the flowers down on the counter, said, "I have caf and decaf, skim and whole milk. I'm sorry I don't have half and half."

"You moved in yesterday," Susan said laughing. "And you have more in your kitchen for entertaining than I do. Not to mention it's a whole lot cleaner than mine as well. I'll take caffeinated coffee with whole milk. I know it's bad, but being good isn't much fun. But before you do anything, you'd better get those flowers in water. They're beautiful. Is it a special occasion?"

"Not really." Sofie took out the card and read it. "My husband just wanted to say I did a good job with the move."

"I can't remember the last time my husband sent me flowers. You must have gotten yourself a good one."

Sofie grinned. "Oh, you mean cause he picked up the phone and called a flower shop after I spent weeks planning everything?"

"Yeah, that counts as a good one, at least as husbands go," Susan said. "I hope you like key lime." She hefted the pie.

"I love it," Sofie assured her. "You shouldn't have."

"Actually, I didn't. There's this wonderful little bakery downtown. The cherry pie and the pecan pie are excellent, but I've never had the key lime."

"Would you like a piece with the coffee?" Sofie asked.

"I was hoping you'd say that," Susan replied.

That night when Dean arrived home, immediately after he stepped through the door he called out, "What is that delicious smell?"

"Why don't you get in here and find out," Sofie called back from the kitchen.

When he went into the kitchen, he found the kitchen table set, two candles lit, and the vase of roses in between.

"If I get this kind of response, I guess I should send you flowers more often. Didn't I tell you something nice would happen today?"

"And it wasn't the only thing," Sofie told him. "Guess what else happened."

"I don't know. What happened?"

"One of the neighbors came over to welcome me."

"Really? Who?"

"You don't need to sound so shocked," Sofie said.

"No . . . that's not . . . I mean I think it's great. Tell me about her."

"Why are you assuming it was a her? I just said neighbor. You know, you wouldn't be very good at solving mysteries. You can't make those kinds of assumptions."

"I don't care about solving mysteries." Dean was impatient. "I want to hear about this visit."

"All right. Well . . . she brought over a pie."

"A pie?" Dean repeated.

"Yes. By the way, that's what we're having for dessert."

"You still haven't told me who it was."

"I don't think it will mean anything to you, but her name is Susan Altman."

"Oh, I've heard about her. I believe she was originally Susan Wellingbrook. She's old money, but her husband is a self-made man. He came from nothing."

"How do you find out these things about people?" Sofie asked. "Anyway, I don't care if she grew up in a shack."

"You'd probably like her better if she did," Dean observed.

"No. I liked her just the way she is. But I haven't told you the other part."

"What's the other part?"

"She invited me to come to a meeting of their book club—their *mystery* book club."

13. The Mystery Readers

Priscilla and Ashley and Julia were all sitting in Priscilla's white living room when Susan and Sofie arrived. Susan had forgotten to tell Sofie about the shoe rule so Sofie had to leave her shoes at the door and go in her stocking feet to meet everyone.

Susan performed the introductions.

"Sofie, this is Ashley—she lives in the colonial up the street. And that's Julia. She also just moved here—a few months before you came. And this is Priscilla, our host." Susan turned to the others, "I think you all know that Sofie just moved into the Tudor, and she's a big mystery fan so I thought I'd bring her along. I told her we were reading *Nemesis*, and it turns out she's already read it, so it worked out perfectly."

Sofie smiled and tried to seem comfortable, even if she didn't feel it.

"So how do you like Greenwich so far?" Priscilla asked her. Then, slyly, "Have you made it down to the Avenue yet?"

"Yes, I went just the other day," Sofie said.

"I bet the traffic cop yelled at you," Priscilla went on. "Didn't he?"

"How did you know?"

Susan hurried to reassure her, "Oh, it happens to everyone when they first get here."

Priscilla added, with malicious glee, "It's a spectator sport in the summertime with some of the locals. They'll sit on the benches nearby and watch the out-of-towners get yelled at when they try to cross."

"It's ridiculous," Ashley said. "I mean, even if there aren't any cars coming, you have to just stand there and wait until the cop tells you that you can cross."

"I guess he got you too, then," Priscilla said.

"He gets everyone," Susan said.

"Actually, he doesn't," Julia said. "I didn't wait to cross, and he didn't say anything to me."

"You're lying," Priscilla declared.

Julia shrugged as if to say, Think whatever you want—but you're wrong.

"Why don't we talk about the book?" Susan said brightly. "Sofie, did you need a little recap? I don't know how long it's been since you read it. It's one of the Miss Marple mysteries—"

"It's the last Miss Marple mystery that Agatha Christie wrote," Priscilla inserted, "though it's not actually the final novel of the series. Christie wrote what she intended to be the final book in the series years earlier."

"Is that right?" Susan said. "I didn't know that. Well, anyway, it's the one that starts out with Miss Marple getting a kind of assignment. A very wealthy businessman—who was actually a character from an earlier novel—dies and leaves a legacy in his will for her, but she only gets the legacy if she solves a mystery. This businessman's nickname for her is "Nemesis," which apparently means "bringer of justice." He's hoping that she's going to do the same for him with this mystery and make everything right. Only he doesn't tell her *what* she's supposed to make right. He doesn't even tell her what mystery she's supposed to solve."

Ashley broke in. "I didn't understand why he kept it this big secret," she complained. "It seemed silly that he'd go to all that trouble to leave the legacy and then not tell her what he wanted her to do."

Priscilla turned to Sofie. "What do you think?"

Sofie hesitated, sensing a bit of a test. Then she said, "Maybe this is just me, but I thought it was because he wanted Miss Marple to be introduced into the mystery in a natural way—and that's why he has his lawyers sign her up for that tour of the great houses of Britain and sends the letter of introduction to his old friends. It gives her the best chance to get a sense of things without raising suspicion. I suppose he could have let her in on it, but my guess is that he was offering her up a challenge and not wanting to make it too easy."

"You remember the book pretty well," Susan said.

"I reread it for today," Sofie admitted.

Priscilla raised her eyebrows and gave a nod of approval. Then she looked over to where Julia sat staring out the window looking bored. "Julia? What did you think of it?"

Julia wrinkled her nose. "You don't get enough clues to figure it out. What's so clever about a mystery that you can't figure out? And Miss Marple is so dull. Like she says herself, in the end she solves it because the murderer reminds her of some other person she knew in that little village of hers. What's so interesting about that?"

"What's so interesting about that?" Priscilla repeated, her voice climbing. "Where do I start?"

"We're reading the mystery classics," Susan whispered to Sofie. "We started with Poe, of course. Then we did Sherlock Holmes and Wilkie Collins and, oh, who was that other person?"

"Ambrose Bierce," Priscilla said. She turned back to Julia to continue the argument. "Don't you see why that idea is so important? When Miss Marple says that someone reminds her of someone else, it's saying something really profound about human nature. It draws the parallel between Tommy, the butcher boy Miss Marple knows in St. Mary Mead who skimped on the cuts of meat, and the murderer in the mystery she's solving. Christie shows us how really ordinary what we call 'evil' actually is."

"Or just how ordinary her novels are," Julia said.

"Do you know how many copies of her books have been sold around the world?" Priscilla demanded. "Something like a billion."

"So? That doesn't mean anything. *Valley of the Dolls* sold millions of copies too. Do you want to claim that's a masterpiece?" Julia shot back.

"But this is Agatha Christie," Priscilla said.

"For God's sake, you'd think I was telling you that your child was ugly or something." Julia laughed.

It was the laughter that got to Priscilla. "It's worse," she said. "When you say that someone, who is so obviously brilliant, is *ordinary* . . ." Priscilla turned to Susan. "Help me out here."

"I liked it," Susan said rather tepidly, since the truth was she agreed with Julia and she'd been trying to figure out a way to say that without hurting Priscilla's feelings. In fact she didn't love any of the classics. Everyone knew that she preferred the modern serial killer mysteries—anything that had a string of gruesome deaths and outrageously psychopathic murderers. She didn't like an ordinary face on evil. She didn't want to think that anyone she knew could do something that awful, so she couldn't help saying, "The thing is, you're talking about the human face on evil, but I know what Julia means when she says it seems sort of ordinary. And to be honest I don't think murder is ordinary at all."

"But that's exactly what it is. Don't you read the papers?" Priscilla argued. "Besides, Christie addresses that exact idea. In one of her books she says, 'I hope you young people will never realize how very wicked the world is.' Or something like that. And that's what makes Miss Marple special—she sees it. She sees the truth of things, and not only that, she tries to do something about it. That's why she's called Nemesis. She's the avenging angel who makes sure that justice is served in the end."

"But it's not really," Susan said. "Served, I mean. Agatha Christie always seems to kill off the nicest people. She writes them so I get attached to them. And then they're suddenly dead. It's . . . unpleasant."

"I don't see how your serial killers are more pleasant," Priscilla said. "What do you think, Sofie?"

Sofie had been listening quietly. Without fuss she said simply, "I think Agatha Christie is a genius."

Priscilla sighed. "*Finally.* Someone is talking sense."

"Why do you think she's a genius?" Julia asked.

"How could you not?" Sofie said matter-of-factly, and her calm, unruffled response conveyed more authority than Priscilla had managed with all her arguing. "It's not just a mystery. Her books are about people. They're about the psychology of people."

"Yes!" Priscilla practically pounced on Sofie's words. "Like everyone talks about Jane Austen and the psychology of her characters? I think Agatha Christie is just as good at it."

"You're comparing Jane Austen and Agatha Christie?" Julia asked, her disbelief obvious in her tone.

"Yes. Why? You disagree?"

"I think most people would disagree."

"How much Jane Austen have you read?" Priscilla challenged.

Julia avoided the question by turning it around. "How much have *you* read?" she shot back.

"There are only six. And since I have a master's in nineteenth-century British literature, I've read all of them," Priscilla replied.

"Oh, so am I supposed to be impressed?" Julia said. "How long have you been waiting to slip that into the conversation?"

Susan broke in to steer the conversation to safer ground. "Why do you think Agatha Christie is better at psychology than Jane Austen?"

Priscilla reluctantly stopped glaring at Julia and turned to Susan to explain. "Well, it's true that Austen does the little foibles well. I mean, even though she was writing more than a century ago, you feel like she could be describing people you know. But the thing is, Christie does something that I don't think Austen does. Austen is describing a very mannered world. It's all very restrained. Christie's psychology tackles the big, messy emotions."

Sofie was nodding during Priscilla's explanation, and when Priscilla finished she put in, "Like what Christie said in this book about love being the most frightening word. And how sometimes love's a terrible thing."

"Why is love terrible?" Susan interrupted. "I don't think love is terrible."

"You don't want to think *anything* is terrible," Priscilla said.

Ashley jumped in. "But Susan not wanting to think anything is terrible kind of shows the whole point behind Agatha Christie's mysteries."

"And what is the 'whole point'?" Priscilla asked, and she couldn't keep a hint of sarcasm from her voice.

"Well, Christie is really writing about a kind of . . . um . . . psychic blindness," Ashley replied.

There was a moment of surprised silence following Ashley's remark.

"What do you mean by psychic blindness?" Priscilla finally asked.

"Well," Ashley said slowly, as if considering her words. "It's that underneath every mystery, Christie is really asking the question, Why don't we see? Maybe it's that we don't *want* to see. But she's asking it of both the characters and the readers."

Everyone stared at her.

"Did you read that somewhere?" Priscilla asked.

Ashley hesitated, and then confessed, "It was in this book."

"What book?"

"It's an analysis of Agatha Christie's mysteries."

"Oh yes, I've heard about that," Priscilla said. "I think the author specifically deconstructs one of her mysteries. Am I right?"

"Yes, that's the one."

"We should read it," Priscilla announced. "But we'll have to read the book that he analyzes first. Do you remember what it was?" she asked Ashley.

Ashley bit her lip. "I don't know why, but all I can think of is the actor Dan Aykroyd."

"That's it," Priscilla said. "It's *The Murder of Roger Ackroyd*. It's one of her most famous. Come to think of it, I don't know why I didn't pick it for us to read already." She thought for a moment. "I suppose we could read that next . . . or maybe . . . what do you think about taking a little break from Christie and coming back to it?"

"Yes, good idea," both Julia and Susan agreed—a little too eagerly. Priscilla frowned at them but let it pass. Instead she said, "I want to talk more about the idea that Sofie brought up. You think that people only murder out of hate and revenge. You don't ever think it could be from love."

The conversation veered off into a discussion of the characters in the book and their different motivations. Finally Priscilla said, "OK, well, we should take a minute to talk about our next selection." She turned to Sofie to explain. "I pick out the books, but I do take suggestions from everyone before choosing. Susan, do you have any ideas?"

"There's a new Jonathan Kellerman out," Susan said hopefully.

"But you'll read that anyway even if we don't do it for the group," Priscilla pointed out. "And it might be a little less interesting to discuss for anyone who hasn't read other books in the series." She turned to Ashley. "Did you have any suggestions?"

"I read about this mystery that had little recipes at the end of every chapter. I thought it might be cute if we read that and each cooked something to bring to the meeting. . . . What?" Ashley asked, looking around, sensing she'd said something wrong.

"I guess I never went over all the rules after you joined, did I?" Priscilla said.

"Did I suggest something that's against the rules?" Ashley asked, bewildered.

Priscilla ticked off on her fingers as she went over the rules that

Ashley had broken: "No themed mysteries. No themed food tied into the mystery. No themed drinks to go with the mystery. No themes period," Priscilla finished decisively. "Any group that does themes never lasts for more than a year. Actually, I should probably go over the rules again, shouldn't I? I mean since we're going to have a new member."

Susan beamed at Sofie. It was unusual for Priscilla to decide on a new member that quickly.

Priscilla went on. "The first and most basic rule is—you have to read the book. Well, you can listen to the audio book if you prefer. We're not like some groups that are so strict they'll kick someone out if they find out they've been listening to the CDs instead. I could understand it if they kicked someone out for listening to the abridged version, but the unabridged is fine. Some groups you'll get banned for any audio."

"Really? Some groups do that?" Sofie said.

"Absolutely. You haven't heard about it? They're like the Fundamentalists of book groups—strict and literal. They believe the only way to read is from the page. Believe me, I love books, but I think it's a little silly to ignore the fact that for thousands of years stories were told, not read. I have to admit that I prefer to read the book first, but if it's really good, after I read it sometimes I like to listen to it on CD. I find that I hear things I didn't notice when I just read it. So audio books are fine. But we *are* pretty strict about making sure you finish one way or another. I mean, I do understand every once in a while there might be something unavoidable—though you do have a whole month," Priscilla said, making it obvious that she didn't really believe in any excuses. "But it's even worse to try to pretend. It's so obvious when someone hasn't finished the book and they go online and read a synopsis to try to pretend like they have. That's just embarrassing. But that's pretty much all we have for rules. Read the book and talk about it when we get together. I keep it simple, and it seems to work. So are we done? Oh wait, I didn't finish getting suggestions for next month." She turned to Julia. "Since you didn't like Agatha Christie, did you have something else you'd like to read?"

Julia shrugged. Then she said casually, "I was thinking one of the mystery collections. I heard about one called *The New Omnibus of Crime*. We could read selections out of that. They've got both classics and new stories."

"That's" Priscilla started to speak, paused, then went on, almost reluctantly—"actually quite a good idea. I had been thinking we might want to look at the original *Omnibus of Crime* that Dorothy Sayers put together. But it might be a good idea to mix it up a little with some more current selections. What does everyone else think?"

With Julia and Priscilla in agreement, no one else would have dared to disagree.

May

14. Sofie & Dean

"Sofie," Dean called. "Sofie . . . Sofie!" he finally bellowed. He was standing just inside his walk-in closet as he yelled, looking at the rack of suits and shirts and jackets.

"What is it?" Sofie asked from right behind him.

Dean jumped and wheeled around. "Jesus. You could give me a heart attack."

"You would have heard me if you weren't making such a racket," she said.

"I used it to polish the furniture. What do you think I did with it?" Sofie looked past him at the closet. "It should be hanging in the closet with all your suits."

"I know where it *should* be, but it's not there."

"Wanna bet?"

He looked at her. "Why do I suddenly feel like my odds aren't good?"

" 'Cause they're not. What do you need it for anyway?"

"I've got a business thing after work tomorrow."

"But you always wear a suit to business things in the city."

"You're too good at this detective thing. You caught me." He held his hands in mock surrender. "It's actually not in the city. It's at a country club in Westchester. I'd look pretty silly in a suit at a country club, don't you think? So I hope you can find it for me."

She found the coat exactly where it was supposed to be—hanging in his closet. It had just been hidden among the suits and sports jackets Dean didn't wear as much. They had been pushed tight together toward the back of the closet so as to take up as little room as possible. Sofie didn't wonder that Dean hadn't found it, but he was a bit sheepish when she emerged from the closet with the jacket.

She held it out to him, but he snagged her waist and pulled her into a hug instead of taking it. "You're the best."

"Be careful, you'll wrinkle it," Sofie said as the jacket was crushed between them.

"That would be tragic." He pulled her even closer and leaned into her in that way she knew so well.

"We haven't had dinner yet," Sofie said. "The chicken Kiev is almost done . . . or, at least let me turn the oven off."

"Forget about the chicken Kiev," he murmured.

And within a few minutes she did, though afterward it took two days to get the smell of burnt chicken out of the kitchen, and she had to throw away the pan.

Sofie knew that at some point in the marriage the sex would become routine, but so far it was one thing that had never suffered, even during the one year when they seemed to do nothing but fight. She remembered the first time they had made love—and how surprised he had been. "You seem so shy," he'd said. "I am shy," she replied. "Not in bed," he retorted.

Later that night after she'd disposed of the chicken and they were lying in bed and Dean was just drowsing off to sleep, she asked, "So will you be back in time for a late dinner tomorrow?"

"No, not tomorrow, hon," he said sleepily, turning over on his side and tucking his hands under the pillow. When he did that he looked just like a little boy. She had always loved watching him sleep, but the problem was it seemed like the only view she had of him these days. Dean's days at the office had always been long, and now the commute made it worse. In the few weeks right after the move he'd made a real effort to get home so they could have dinner together—even if it wasn't until nine or ten. But then he was assigned to a deal and most nights he wasn't getting home until after midnight.

Dean knew this was hard on Sofie, and he tried to make it up to her—bringing her little gifts or calling her during the day, but for

Sofie it had been a long, dreary spring. The days were overcast and gray and they seemed endless, and her efforts at writing had been dismal. She'd produced exactly five sentences, four of which she had crossed out.

The book group had been a saving grace. Sofie had to admit she didn't actually *like* Priscilla, but the woman certainly was serious about her mysteries. They'd read from *The New Omnibus of Crime*, and then they'd read a Raymond Chandler and then the Edgar Award–winner for best first novel. Priscilla did a good job of mixing up the selections, and the meetings were always lively. At first Sofie had been a bit skeptical about Julia and Ashley because they didn't seem to be readers. And she had been right about that—they weren't, but sometimes that actually made their reactions to the books more interesting. Sofie was used to talking to hardcore mystery fans at her job at the Black Orchid, and she found that, as non-mystery fans, Julia and Ashley had very different responses. They weren't comparing every book to the hundreds of other books they'd read before. They didn't make pronouncements of where a book should fall in the mystery canon. They just gave their personal responses. It was refreshing.

But still the book group couldn't really compare to her old job, and she missed her life in the city. Dean pointed out that it wasn't like they were so far away—she could still go in. He went in and out every day, and she hadn't been in once. The truth was, she was scared. Scared of what she might discover going back. As it was now, she felt as if she were in some sort of precarious limbo and the wrong move might send her tumbling over the edge. So she spent most of her time waiting. Waiting for the days to pass. Waiting for Dean to get home. Waiting for things to get better—or worse.

At first she believed Dean when he said that things at work were crazy and that when it quieted down, his schedule would be a lot more regular and he'd be home more. It could happen any day, he said. So at around seven she'd keep one eye on the door. She tried to will him into coming home on time by planning elaborate meals. She clipped recipes from the paper and scoured the stores for ingredients like tamarind and beaumonde. But they were meals that

Dean almost never got home in time to eat. He'd look at the Saran-wrapped dishes in the Sub-Zero and say with mournful reproach, "You should have called. I could have saved you all this trouble. I had to stay late so I just ordered in at the office."

But that was exactly why she didn't call. She found she preferred not to know. She needed the activity, the purpose. When she was cooking the meal, she was so sure *that* night he would get home in time. And it did happen a couple of times. He would blow through the door like a force of nature at eight or nine with an armful of flowers or the latest mystery that he picked up at Posman Books in Grand Central.

Sofie consoled herself with the fact that, even if they didn't see each other much, at least they were getting along. In the beginning of the second year of their marriage they'd hit bad times. Suddenly they didn't seem to be able to have a conversation without fighting. Even when she tried to agree with everything he said, it had somehow still devolved into an argument. That had lasted for about eight months. Then her father got sick again, and Dean had rallied to her side, proving that during the tough times he was there for her.

At least now was better than it had been. That's what she told herself. But the days still dragged, and the nights were worse. She'd always had a problem with insomnia, but it seemed like since they moved out of the city she hadn't managed more than a few hours' sleep at a stretch. She'd taken to going out at night and walking along the golf course, looking up at the backs of the houses for lighted windows, evidence that there were other people who couldn't sleep.

She thought that part of the reason she couldn't sleep was the absence of noise. She'd slept all her life with the muffled sounds of traffic—cabbies leaning on their horns, trucks bumping over the potholes and, in summer, people's conversations floating up through the open windows. Out here it was quiet. All she heard was the sound of the crickets and the wind rustling the leaves. Every night she found herself lying in bed next to Dean, tense and listening. Waiting.

FOUR MONTHS LATER:

October

15. Priscilla & Susan

The season was starting to change. All of a sudden the thin Lycra shirt that Priscilla wore wasn't quite enough to keep off the chill so, as she waited on the front step for Susan, she marched in place as much to keep warm as to keep her heart rate up.

Susan burst out of the front door, her jacket half unbuttoned, waving a section of the *New York Times*.

"What? What is it?" Priscilla demanded.

Susan closed the door behind her to keep the dogs from escaping, then turned to Priscilla and demanded excitedly, "Have you seen the paper this morning?"

"No. Why?"

"Take a look at what's on the front page of the Business section."

Priscilla took the paper and glanced at it. There was a picture of Harry shaking hands with another man in a suit, and they were both smiling.

"I didn't think you'd be so excited about Harry getting his picture in the paper," Priscilla said a bit unkindly. She was very aware of the fact that Gordon would never have his picture on the front page—or any page—of the *Times*. Gordon had been comparatively young when he was made managing director in sales, and it had looked as if he might climb high on the ladder—but he'd been in the same position for more than ten years, and at a certain point it had become obvious that he was not going further.

"No, it's not that. He's been in the paper dozens of times," Susan said, not even noticing the sharpness in Priscilla's words. "It's the headline. Didn't you read it?"

"It said he's acquiring some big company or something. So what's the big deal?"

"Don't you remember? That was Harry's excuse for staying so late at work." Susan paused expectantly, but Priscilla just looked at her so Susan rushed on. "Don't you see? This means it was true. He was telling the truth. The hours are always crazy before an acquisition. There's no way he could have been doing that and have any time to spend with a woman."

"Oh. Well, that's great." Priscilla didn't want to admit that she'd forgotten about Susan's problems with Harry. Susan hadn't mentioned it for weeks, and Priscilla had other things on her mind.

"I can't tell you. I've been so worried."

"I told you that you were making too big a deal out of it, didn't I?" Priscilla said.

"Yes, but you still thought he was cheating. You just thought it would blow over. But he wasn't. See, you shouldn't always think the worst of people."

"I don't always think the worst of people," Priscilla corrected her. "Just of men."

"Even Gordon?" Susan asked.

"Oh, Gordon doesn't count. He's so . . . well, dependable."

"You say that like it's a dirty word or something. You have a wonderful husband. And he adores you."

"Being adored is boring. Or—at least, being adored by Gordon is boring," Priscilla amended.

"So maybe your relationship isn't exactly exciting. But no one's marriage is. No one's got it all."

Susan had what Priscilla considered a rather annoying habit of always trying to find the sunny side of things.

"Are you trying to condemn us all to lives of boredom and mediocrity? Besides, I don't think it's true. I think you *can* have it all if you find the right person. Other people have. Like Julia. She has it all."

"She seems to," Susan said. "But then again, you never really know."

"You mean her life may not be perfect? Don't get my hopes up. I believe Julia has gotten absolutely everything she ever wanted."

"You never really know what's going on in someone else's life," Susan repeated.

That statement was truer than Susan even knew. She had no idea that, at that moment, Priscilla was in love.

16. Priscilla

*I*n love. For the first time in her life. At the age of forty. Hopelessly, impossibly in love.

She remembered the first time she'd seen him. She'd invited the book club members and their husbands over for drinks. Since Priscilla was strict about not gossiping during the book club meetings, every month the members of the club took turns hosting a social night. It had been Priscilla's turn. She was standing with Ashley, Susan, and Julia by the side bar, sipping from her wineglass, when he appeared in the archway to the living room.

"Who is *that?*" Ashley said immediately, clutching at Priscilla's arm. "Oh my God, he's gorgeous."

"He's a dead ringer for a young Robert Redford," Susan said.

"Oooh, that's a good one, Susan," Ashley agreed.

"So don't keep us in suspense. Who is it?" Susan asked, turning to Priscilla.

At that moment the mystery man looked up and met Priscilla's eye. He smiled at her, and Priscilla felt her breath catch.

"Priscilla?" Susan prompted.

"I have no idea," Priscilla admitted.

Then a moment later the question was answered when Sofie appeared in the entryway next to him. The man looked away and down at Sofie—smiling at *her* now. Then he draped an arm across her shoulders.

After she caught her breath, Priscilla crossed the room and was introduced to Sofie's husband.

Dean.

Priscilla asked him if he wanted a drink, and he said a martini would be great. She admitted that she didn't know how to make a martini, and he said, "I think we need to correct that immediately. Lead the way to the bar."

They'd spent most of the rest of the night behind the bar, serving drinks almost like host and hostess. At one point Ashley had tried to pull his attention away, declaring that she didn't know how to make a martini either. But to Priscilla's delight Dean had replied that he could only work with one student at a time. Then he looked at her and winked. Even better was the fact that he seemed to ignore Julia completely, and Julia was obviously not happy about it.

It turned out to be a great party. The group usually just drank wine, but with Dean behind the bar almost everyone gave into his cajoling, and they had all gotten soused. It was, Priscilla thought many times afterward, the kind of party that she and Dean would have had if they were a couple.

She should have felt guilty—guilty because she was married, guilty because he was married. But then she asked herself, why should she be guilty? It wasn't like they had done anything about it. A little friendly banter over cocktails wasn't a crime. She couldn't help it if there was a spark between them—she was certain he had felt something too. And after that night, every party that came around they were practically inseparable. Those parties became the focus of her existence, the evenings she lived for. Priscilla didn't even care when her friends started to comment.

"You seem to get along well with Sofie's husband," Susan said the day after the third—or maybe it was the fourth—party that Sofie and Dean attended.

"Dean?" Priscilla said—as if Sofie had more than one husband. "Why do you say that?"

"Because you spend practically all your time talking to him."

"I do not," Priscilla said.

"Well, more time talking to him than anyone else. And you almost never talk to Sofie."

"What do you mean? I talk to her more than anyone else at the book club meetings. Didn't we have that long discussion about how the mystery genre has been dismissed for years and how Chandler and Hammett and Cain are just now finally starting to get some recognition? In fact, I don't know what I'd do without her. She even manages to get interesting comments out of Julia and Ashley."

"I'm not talking about the book group. I'm talking about other times—and about anything outside mysteries."

"She doesn't talk to me either," Priscilla said defensively. "In fact she always seems to be talking to Julia." And these days Priscilla avoided Julia at all costs. Priscilla wasn't sure when it had happened, but lately everything that Julia said to her seemed to have an undercurrent of nastiness. Priscilla had even started thinking about how to get Julia out of the book club, but the truth was, she was a bit intimidated by Julia.

Susan said, "Sofie talks to Julia because Julia actually makes an effort to talk to *her*."

"I wonder why Julia finds Sofie so fascinating," Priscilla said.

"Maybe you'd find out if you talked to her. She's really interesting."

"Why don't you go be *her* best friend, then," Priscilla said.

"I can't believe you're jealous of her."

"I am not," Priscilla protested. But she was. Well, she was jealous of Sofie's husband.

"You should invite her out for a walk one of these days," Susan said. "Ask her some questions. Get to know her."

Priscilla was about to dismiss this suggestion, but then she stopped herself. "You know, that's not a bad idea." She was thinking that it would also be a great opportunity to find out more about Dean. "So you wouldn't mind? You've been saying for a while that going every day is a bit much for you."

"Oh," Susan was obviously surprised. "I was thinking we could all go."

"But walking three across doesn't really work so well." What Priscilla didn't add was that it wouldn't be so easy to pump Sofie for information with Susan along.

Susan hesitated, but really she had no choice but to agree. It was, after all, her idea.

So Priscilla had called and asked, but Sofie had surprised her by saying no. She said it politely enough—she claimed she wasn't feeling well. When Susan heard the excuse, her response was, "She must be pregnant. Morning sickness. Makes sense, right?"

The very idea that Sofie might be pregnant was enough to make *Priscilla* sick. She would much rather think that Sofie said no because she was upset about how much attention her husband was paying to Priscilla. But if that was the case, Sofie was very good at hiding it. She hadn't shown any sign of resentment or coldness during any of the book club meetings. True, she didn't talk much, but it didn't seem like it was because she was angry or upset. She always spoke readily enough when someone asked her opinion. And just recently Priscilla had noticed that what Sofie said tended to spark a lively discussion. When Priscilla started paying attention to it she realized it happened too regularly to be accidental, and then she wasn't sure if she was grateful or annoyed. It was almost as if, with only a sentence or two here or there, Sofie was actually steering the discussion.

But despite her close study, Priscilla hadn't been able to detect any difference in Sofie's manner toward her. Sofie didn't seem to think there was anything unusual about the amount of time Priscilla and Dean spent together (though Sofie *had* missed a couple of the parties—again because she claimed not to be feeling well). Maybe that was why she hadn't been bothered by Priscilla's and Dean's behavior. She was certainly the only one; everyone else in the book group seemed to have something to say about it.

Julia was the next after Susan to make a comment. At one of the parties she came up to where Priscilla and Dean were serving drinks. "Just white wine," she said to Dean when he tried to get her to take a Cosmo. She took her wine and then she turned to Priscilla and said with a condescending smile, "You know you're making a fool of yourself." And then she turned on her heel and walked away.

It might have been awful, but Dean had leaned over and whispered, "I guess she doesn't like to see people having fun." His mouth was so close that his lips brushed her ear, and Priscilla would have listened to a hundred snide remarks from Julia just to feel his lips on her skin again.

Ashley was the last to say something. At the most recent party, when Priscilla was separated from Dean for a moment, Ashley sidled up to her and said, "If I didn't know better, I'd say you two were having an affair."

Priscilla laughed and said boldly, "Why do you think you know better?" She was a little drunk at the time.

"Because if you were having an affair, I would think you'd at least to try to hide it."

"I have nothing to hide," Priscilla said.

Ashley smiled. "That's what I was saying."

It almost sounded like a dare. If so, it was one that Priscilla was more than willing to take her up on.

17. Priscilla

$\mathcal{I}$t was Ashley's turn to host.

The moment Dean walked into Ashley's living room he glanced around, and Priscilla knew that he was looking for her. She deliberately looked away so he wouldn't catch her standing there staring at him as if she'd just been waiting for him to arrive—which in fact she had. But this pretense ended up costing her. Before she was able to pull him off into a corner, everyone settled down in the living room in a big group. Dean was stuck over on the couch between Sofie and Ashley's husband, Stewart. Priscilla got up twice, once to go to the bathroom, another time to refill a glass that was still mostly full, both times hoping Dean would take the hint and get up and come over to see her. But he didn't.

Help came from an unanticipated source when Priscilla was least expecting it—it happened when she was in the middle of an argument with Julia. Priscilla had been talking about Halloween. It was her favorite holiday, and every year, in celebration of her favorite holiday, she decorated her yard. She'd even started a little trend, with many of the other women in the neighborhood following her lead. Priscilla was enthusiastically describing what her designer was planning for this year—little ghosts in all the trees. But just as Priscilla was getting into the details of the effect they were going for, Julia started laughing.

Priscilla stopped speaking abruptly and glared at Julia. "What is so funny?" she demanded.

"I've never heard of anything more ridiculous," Julia said, still laughing. "It sounds hideous. Why don't you just hang some corpses and be done with it?"

Priscilla was about to retaliate when Ashley broke in saying, "Oh, Priscilla, you're so good with wine. Would you go pick out something? You don't mind, do you? We have a Transtherm wine cabinet in the kitchen. Wouldn't you know, our cellar is too damp."

Priscilla was annoyed to be sent on an errand by Ashley—until she heard Ashley add, "And Dean, you were mixing such wonderful cocktails at the last party. Maybe you could see if we have anything you could work with in the fridge? Priscilla, will you show Dean where the kitchen is?"

Suddenly she didn't mind the errand at all. "Of course," she said.

Priscilla led the way down the hall to the kitchen. She crossed to the wine cabinet, which was about the size of a refrigerator, to look at the wine, but instead of looking for mixers in the fridge, Dean followed her and stood just behind her as she opened the cabinet. She felt like a teenager again as he reached over her shoulder to check a bottle and his body brushed up against hers . . . except she didn't think she'd ever felt exactly like this, not even when she was a teenager.

"So what do you think?" he asked. "A Merlot? Or a Cab?"

She turned around to face him. They were standing very close. "What do *you* think?" she asked, looking up at him. She was willing him to kiss her. He had to kiss her.

"I think . . ." Dean lowered his voice to match hers. And he was leaning in. It was going to happen. She was just closing her eyes and lifting her face to him when she heard the scrape of the kitchen door being pushed open. She thought for sure they were going to be caught, but when she opened her eyes, Dean had somehow made it across the room and was standing with his hand on the fridge door as if he had just closed it. He said, "What do you think of screwdrivers? Vodka and OJ? But maybe that's a little too breakfasty."

He looked over his shoulder, and pretended to be surprised to see Julia standing in the doorway. "Well, hello there."

"Hello yourself." Julia glanced over at Priscilla, then back to Dean.

"How're things back in the living room?" Dean asked. "Are the natives getting thirsty?"

"I think your wife needs you for something," Julia said.

"Best get back then. But I shouldn't go empty-handed." He opened the fridge. "I didn't see this before," he said, retrieving a bottle of tonic. He opened a drawer in the refrigerator and added, "And I've struck gold." He held up a lime. "Gin and vodka tonics should be just the ticket. And I think you're right about the Merlot," he said to Priscilla. He looked back at Julia. "Well, I'd better get back and start mixing." And Dean escaped out into the hallway.

"I find Merlot a bit bland," Julia said to Priscilla when they were left alone.

Priscilla pulled out a couple of bottles, checked the labels and said, "Yes, that's what we decided as well. How about a Cab? Is that better?"

"It's fine," Julia said. She crossed the kitchen to the fridge and opened the door and stood there a moment, scanning the contents.

"What are you looking for?" Priscilla asked.

"Well, it's a good thing I'm not looking for orange juice." Julia looked around at Priscilla and fixed her with a stare. "Because there doesn't seem to be any."

18. Sofie

*S*ofie sat in an armchair close enough to the others to pretend to be following their conversation without really having to join in. She was listening to Harry and Gordon discuss the details of the takeover Harry had just completed. Now that it was public, Harry was eager to talk about the work that had taken months of planning and strategy.

Sofie surveyed the room. Her eyes fell on Julia's husband, Alex. A moment earlier Julia had disappeared down the hall, and now Alex was sitting all alone. But he seemed completely unembarrassed by it. He could have been sitting in his own living room. In fact he looked as if he had forgotten there was anyone else there. He held a glass of wine and was staring down into it, seemingly lost in thought.

Over the last few months Sofie felt as though she had gotten to know everyone *except* Alex—which was ironic because she found him by far the most interesting. She noticed how, even when he was standing in a group of people, he held himself slightly aloof. It was as if he were somehow apart from the others. It was comforting to have someone else there who looked like she felt.

That was what she was thinking as she gazed at him. Then, at that moment he looked up—straight at her—and something passed between them. Their eyes were locked on each other, and she felt the little hairs on her arms rise. Then she was aware of breath on the back of her neck and a light touch, and she jumped, breaking eye contact.

"So now I can't kiss my own wife?" Dean straightened from bending to brush his lips against her neck.

"You startled me," Sofie said.

"Well, I wouldn't have been able to if you hadn't been ogling Julia's husband over there."

"I wasn't ogling. I was . . ." she trailed off. What had she been doing?

"You've got goose bumps," he said.

"Have I? I guess I'm a little chilled."

He rested his hand against her cheek. "You feel hot. And you look flushed. You're not getting sick, are you?"

"No. No, it's nothing."

"Are you sure? I wouldn't want you getting sick again."

There was real concern in his voice, and there was good reason. Sofie hadn't been doing well. The spring had been hard for her—with Dean working late hours at the office, and her trying to adjust to life outside the city. But Dean had insisted it would get better. He was wrong.

On the first really hot summer day, she'd finally made a trip into the city. First she went to visit the bookstore, and it was wonderful. It felt like coming home. She could have stayed all day, but she had promised herself that she would leave time to stop by Dean's office. When she arrived, she found that he was out at a meeting. His assistant let her wait for him in his office, and when he wasn't back in an hour, she went home.

It turned out her fears about visiting the city were justified, because everything went to hell after that. She fell into a black hole of lethargy. She stopped cooking, she stopped writing, she even stopped reading—except for the one book she still read for the book club, and even that was a struggle. When she got a chance to suggest a selection, she chose *Presumed Innocent*. She chose it because neither Julia, Ashley, or more surprisingly, Susan, had read it. But also she suggested it because she had read it so many times already she wouldn't have to read it again for the discussion.

For weeks she didn't get out of bed before noon, and even when she did she often never managed to change out of her bathrobe. If Dean didn't bring food home for dinner, they had to order in because there was nothing in the refrigerator. And for the first time ever, Sofie had, several times now, gently pushed Dean away when he started kissing her neck—his unspoken signal for sex.

During the whole period Dean had been surprisingly patient and gentle. For one, he stopped asking how the writing was going. He also made a real effort to get home early, and he brought her things he thought might raise her spirits. One night it was a three-course meal from Jean-Louis, one of the best restaurants in Greenwich. Another night he rented her favorite old movie, *Diabolique*, and rubbed her back as they watched it. He had long since discovered that she wasn't much interested in jewelry—she didn't even have her ears pierced—so he brought her home a signed first edition of *The Murder at the Vicarage*, Agatha Christie's first Miss Marple book.

The last was the only gesture that seemed to get the desired response. When she opened the package and discovered what it was, she breathed, "Oh Dean" as she turned the pages delicately, as if it might fall apart.

"You like it?"

"It's wonderful," she said softly. "I love it." But usually when he gave her presents she liked she threw her arms around him and—he always joked—practically strangled him. This time she just kept turning the book over, trailing her finger along the signature on the title page.

After that when she still didn't get better, he started suggesting she might want to see a doctor. Maybe get some antidepressants.

She shook her head.

"It's nothing to be ashamed of," he told her. "These things tend to run in families, and from what you've told me it's pretty certain your mother had some serious problems with depression."

"I'll think about it," she said.

"I have a friend who went to a great doctor for this. I can call and get the—"

"I said I'd think about it," Sofie said again, this time in a tone that ended the conversation.

Maybe it was the reference to her mother that scared her out of her deep funk, but the next day when Dean's alarm clock went off, she didn't just roll away and pull the duvet over her head. It wasn't that the idea of getting up and facing the day was any easier, but somehow she found the strength of will to force herself. The next day she managed to get dressed. And the day after that she went to the supermarket. Everything felt like a struggle—like she was trying to run through water—but she did it anyway.

Dean was delighted. It was as if he thought everything was back to normal. How, she wondered, could he not see the difference? How could he fail to notice that she wasn't the same person she used to be?

She managed to get to the point where she was doing most of the things she used to, though she went about them mechanically, as if she were a robot going about its programmed tasks. The one thing she still tried to avoid was social gatherings. She went to the book group, but she avoided the parties. She'd bowed out of the last two, which Dean had not been happy about, and she had tried to get out of going to Ashley's, but Dean had insisted.

"It doesn't matter if I go or not," she'd said to him. "It's not like anyone's going to miss me."

"Now you're feeling sorry for yourself," he accused.

"No, it's just a fact. I don't blame them."

"You don't even know them," Dean said. She could tell from his voice he was getting annoyed. "You think you can just see right through people. Well, let me be the first to tell you that you can't. You don't know everything there is to know, and you're not always right."

"I don't want to be right," she said.

"So go to the party, and for God's sake, make an effort."

She'd agreed to go, but now she wanted to be anywhere else in the world but there. Dean still hovered behind her, acting concerned. "Are you sure you're all right?" he asked again.

She looked up at him and said, "No. I don't think I am."

19. Sofie & Dean

"That wasn't so awful, was it?" Dean asked as they reentered the house, into the kitchen through the door from the garage.

"I guess not," Sofie said.

Dean immediately made a beeline for the refrigerator and starting looking through it. "I'm hungry. Are you hungry? That's one thing, I thought the food was pretty awful. Ah, perfect. There's some lasagna in here. Do you want some?"

"No, thanks."

He pulled out the refrigerator dish and transferred the lasagna onto a plate.

"You're awfully quiet," Dean said.

"I'm tired," she replied. "I think I'll go to bed."

"You can't even stay up another ten minutes to sit with me while I eat?"

"If you want." She sat down at the kitchen table.

He crossed to the microwave and popped the door. "How long do I need to cook this?"

"Two and a half minutes should do it," she said. "But you need to cover it with a paper towel, or the tomato sauce will splatter."

He pulled off a sheet, covered the lasagna, and stood by the microwave as the plate revolved inside. When it was done he carried it over to the table.

"You want a bite?" he offered her the first forkful. Sofie shook her head.

He put down the fork without eating and said, "You're not still mad that we didn't leave early, are you? I know you said you didn't feel well, but you managed fine."

"I guess," she said without much conviction.

"You didn't even go to the last two parties. If you left this one early . . . well, it just would've looked bad. We're living here now, and if we really want to become part of the community, we need to make the effort." He picked up the fork again and took a bite.

Sofie watched him for a moment, then she said, "That's the thing. I don't want to keep living here."

Dean stared at her, his mouth full of lasagna.

"I want to move back to New York."

Dean swallowed his food. "You're not serious."

"Yes, I am," she said quietly.

"You want to just pull up again, undo all the work and effort and go running back to the city?"

"Yes."

"You're crazy."

"I'm not." She took a deep breath and launched into her pitch. "If you think about it, our life isn't much different than it was living in the city. We just stay in and eat dinner, maybe watch a movie. But now the video store is farther away. If we wanted trees, the park was right across the street."

"That's not the point. The point wasn't trees or what we do every night. The point was trying something different. And I like it out here. I like feeling there's a community. I don't want to live surrounded by strangers my whole life. Listen, I know you're not happy right now, but I don't feel like you can really know whether it's working or not in just a few months. I want you to give it a chance. A real chance. And if, after that, it's still not working out, I promise you, we won't stay."

"What do you mean by a real chance?"

"A year," Dean said. "Just a year. So that means only, what? Four more months? That's not a lot to ask. And if you want, we'll move on the anniversary."

"A year to the day?" Sofie asked, a catch in her voice. "That's it?"

"That's it."

"And if it doesn't work?"

"Then that very day we can start looking at moving back into the city. I promise," he said, holding up his hand. "Now will you promise to make more of an effort?"

Sofie didn't say anything for a moment.

"Sofie?"

She looked up at him. "Yes," she said. "I promise."

And Sofie kept her word. The next day she called Priscilla and asked if she could take her up on that offer of a morning walk.

PART II

20. Sofie & Priscilla

The body hung from the branch of a maple tree in the front yard. It was clothed in a gauzy white nightgown, the breeze fluttering at the hem. The body didn't move, though—it just hung.

It was a perfect October morning, a slight chill in the air, a light frost on the grass. The leaves from the maple drifted down—a bright autumn red—leaving a carpet on the ground like a huge pool of blood.

The sky lightened slowly, and a couple of cars whizzed by, lifting and swirling the piles of leaves by the curb. A few late-season birds darted from tree to tree. Then Priscilla and Sofie came striding up the street.

"What do you think of Ashley's pumpkin theme?" Priscilla asked as they walked. The yard they were passing had literally hundreds of pumpkins—the miniature kind—threaded on wire like strings of popcorn and hung through the boughs of the trees. There were also half a dozen larger pumpkins, elaborately carved, arranged on the front steps and porch. They were obviously the work of a professional and not completed in somebody's newspaper-lined kitchen by a rowdy group of children.

Sofie thought for a moment before answering. She wasn't sure if Priscilla wanted her to praise it or to claim to hate it. "It looks nice," Sofie ventured, taking a guess but not wanting to overdo it. She liked the challenge of talking to Priscilla—it was all about trying to figure out what answers she was looking for. Priscilla reminded Sofie of an English teacher she'd had in tenth grade who asked questions under the guise of generating discussion, but in actuality always had an answer in mind and was really just looking for a student to parrot her opinion back to her.

This time it turned out that Sofie had guessed right.

"Of course, it looks *fantastic*," Priscilla said. "But do you know why? She went and hired the decorator I got for my yard last Halloween."

"It's seems a bit competitive," Sofie said as a consolation.

Sofie had guessed right again.

"A bit? Oh, please. Why is it that people are always competing with me? Am I that intimidating?"

This time Sofie hesitated. Did Priscilla want her to say that she was or that she wasn't? She decided to avoid the question by asking one of her own. "Did Julia put up Halloween decorations too?" she asked, peering through the trees.

"Julia? Not likely." But then they drew nearer, and Priscilla took another look. She stopped abruptly and said, "Oh my God."

Sofie stopped as well. "What? What is it?"

"That bitch. You're right. Julia did put something up. But she didn't do it in the spirit of the holiday. She's making fun of my ghost tree."

"She's what?"

"Look." Priscilla pointed an accusing forefinger. "You know my ghost tree? Where I hung all the ghost sheets and lit them with the Christmas lights?"

"And then the lights are still up for Christmas," Sofie said. "It's really very clever."

"Exactly. I guess it takes an intelligent person to appreciate it. Well, look. Just look what she did. She went and hung up a fake corpse."

"I thought I saw something. That's a little tacky."

"She must be making fun of me, right? Because if Julia is anything, she is not tacky."

"I don't know her very well," Sofie said. "But it certainly seems a little rude."

"It is. It *is*," Priscilla agreed. "That bitch."

"What are you going to do?"

"Well, I'm not going to stand for this. That's for sure. I'm going to take it down." And Priscilla started heading purposefully up the lawn.

"Do you think that's a good idea?" Sofie asked, following Priscilla. The frost on the grass crunched under her feet.

"I think it's a very good idea," Priscilla said, moving even faster than the pace she set on her power walks.

But then Priscilla stopped.

When Sofie caught up with her, Priscilla was standing about ten feet away from the hanging figure. Priscilla reached out and put her hand against the trunk of one of the nearby trees as if to steady herself. The other hand went up to cover her mouth.

"So you decided to—" Sofie broke off. "Are you all right?" she asked instead.

Priscilla just shook her head, still staring at the tree.

Sofie looked again—for the first time since she'd gotten close. There was a metal folding chair lying on its side on the ground. Her eyes moved to the feet, suspended in midair. Looking up she saw the long blond hair hanging in a curtain around the lolled head and glimpsed, beneath the curtain of hair, the horrific face.

Sofie took an involuntary step back. At that moment she discovered that no matter how many mysteries you read, you could never imagine what it was like to see the actual thing. The face was dark and mottled, and she could see the staring eyes and something protruding from the mouth. It took her a moment to identify it as a tongue.

It was Julia.

No one in the neighborhood had ever seen Julia looking less than perfect—and the body underneath the transparent nightgown looked as perfect as ever. But that face. Sofie had never expected death could be so humiliating. So personal.

"What should we do?" Priscilla whispered, releasing her hand from across her mouth.

"I don't know," Sofie whispered back. "Call 911?"

"We need a phone. I'll go see if Alex is home. Oh my God, Alex," Priscilla's hand flew back up to her mouth. "How am I going to tell Alex? I can't believe he doesn't know. I have to tell him. He has to know," and she rushed off with the sudden import of her responsibility.

"Wait, I'm coming with you," Sofie said.

They rounded the shrubbery and climbed the steps to the door. Priscilla bravely raised a finger to the bell and rang several times as if she could convey the seriousness of their errand through this urgent ringing.

"Hold your horses, I'm coming," a voice called from inside the hall. The door swung open, and Julia's husband stood in his bathrobe with a coffee cup in one hand and a section of the newspaper tucked beneath his arm.

"Alex," Priscilla said, breathlessly.

"Good morning, Priscilla." Alex glanced at Sofie. "Hi Sofie. So where's the fire?" he asked smiling.

Sofie somehow had been expecting him to answer the door solemnly. She thought that when something so horrific had happened, even if you didn't know it yet there should be some premonition—some extra sense that tells you something is wrong. But Alex couldn't have looked more cheerful.

"Your wife—" Priscilla began.

"I'm afraid she's not up yet," he apologized.

This just got worse, Sofie thought. The poor man thought his wife was still up in bed asleep. Then Sofie wondered for a split second how he could possibly think that—until she realized that they must not be sleeping in the same room.

"No. I mean . . . I don't know how to say this . . ." Priscilla faltered and glanced beseechingly at Sofie.

"I'm afraid there's been an accident," Sofie said, but even as she said it she rethought her choice of words. It had certainly been no accident.

But it did the trick. Alex's smile disappeared and he simply said, "Where?"

He followed them out into the yard. Sofie looked down and noticed that he wasn't wearing any shoes. His feet were long and narrow and white.

They came to a halt under the same tree where Priscilla had stopped before. Both women looked at him, and Priscilla gestured toward where Julia's body hung.

Alex looked and a hush seemed to fall—not just among the three clustered together—but all around them. It was like the deep silence that you feel standing in a field of snow.

Sofie glanced anxiously at Alex's face, but she couldn't read any expression there. It was strangely, eerily blank.

"I should call 911," he said and began to turn away.

"But Alex shouldn't we . . . um . . . get her down?" Priscilla suggested, taking a step toward the body.

"Stay away from her," he said harshly.

Priscilla stopped. "But we can't just leave her there," she protested, a high wavering note in her voice.

"I know it seems awful," Sofie said soothingly, laying a hand on Priscilla's arm. "But I think he's right. We need to leave things as they are for the police."

"Yes, that's what I meant," Alex said, giving Sofie an appraising look. "Would you mind staying here for a few minutes while I go inside and call the police and change into some clothes? I'll be as fast as I can."

"Of course."

As soon as they heard the front door open and close, Priscilla turned to Sofie. "This is awful. Why do you think she did it?"

"Well," Sofie hesitated a long moment, then said, "Actually, I don't think she did."

21. Detective Peters

"That was fucking weird," Detective Peters said as he sank into his chair at the station. The big station room was almost empty, but the rows of desks were cluttered with paper and strewn with coffee mugs and Post-it notes, making it look as if everyone had suddenly gotten up and left all at once.

It was evening and most of the staff had gone for the day. Detective Peters had just returned from the crime scene. He had been there the whole day with the crew, going through all the steps. They'd started with a videotape of the "walk-through," followed by hundreds of pictures documenting the scene. Then the crime scene technicians moved in, working methodically over every inch of ground, saving the area around the body for last. Then the medical examiner had come in to examine the body and they'd finally moved inside. The husband had been cooperative and had given them permission to go through the house as well. Finally they'd bagged and tagged all items of interest—the rope, the metal folding chair, tape-lifts of both items, castings of footprints found around the scene. And everything had to be painstakingly documented. It had taken all day.

"What was so weird about it?" Officer Hamill perched on the corner of Peters's desk. Hamill had been on night shift and had missed all the excitement. "It couldn't have been weirder than the case last month where the guy got so mad at his wife that he killed her cat and cooked it for dinner."

Peters had started sorting through his notes, but he paused for a moment. "The guy stole the idea from Shakespeare, you know. But in Shakespeare it was the woman's own kids. And I think it was some sort of famous Greek myth before Shakespeare used it."

"So you mean he was a copycat?" Hamill said.

Peters groaned. "You're killin' me, Hamill."

"Oh, come on. That was a good one," Hamill said. "Anyway, I thought it was pretty clever of him. He traumatized the poor woman—I think she had a breakdown—and all he got was a citation."

"OK, you got a point. That was the weirdest case. Today wasn't weird like weirdo. I guess I mean weird like it doesn't make sense."

"Like how?"

Peters sighed just thinking about it. "We get called out there, right? And we find what looks like a suicide. Lady hung herself. But she did it in the front yard. You know, most of the time people don't do that in public places. They go to the basement or the attic—somewhere away from other people. Not right out in the yard. And when we arrive at the scene, what do we find? She's still out there, swinging in the breeze—on display for all the neighbors who've collected on the street. In a way it was great for us. The crime scene was completely intact. No one had gone within ten feet of the body. But what kind of husband would leave his wife up there? It reminded me of the Old West when they used to string someone up and then leave them up there as an example. In my experience most husbands, if they find their wives hanging from a tree in their front yard, are gonna rush over and get her down. It's pure instinct. Most of them say that their only thought was if they got their wife down, there might be some chance of saving her. Usually she's been dead for hours, but the husband's still frantic to get her down like her life depended on it. But what does this guy do? Not only does he leave her hanging, he also has the presence of mind to keep everyone away to "preserve the scene." The only way that makes sense is if at some point he trained to be a cop. But he says he didn't."

"Father a cop, maybe?"

"Nope." Peters said. "So my question is why is his first reaction to preserve the scene?"

"It doesn't make sense," Hamill agreed. "Especially when it looks like a suicide. There's no reason to preserve the scene for a suicide. I mean, *we* do it just in case it turns out to be something else—so I guess he must have been thinking it was something else."

"*Exactly*," Peters said, slapping the desk with his palm. "That's *exactly* what I thought. But when we questioned him, he claimed that it never crossed his mind—at least not at first—that she hadn't committed suicide. But that brings us right back to the same question: Why preserve the scene?"

"Because the son of a bitch killed her, and he's trying to pass it off like a suicide," Hamill said. "That part is obvious."

"Well, that's what you'd think. But if he killed her and set it up to look like suicide, why wouldn't he try to act more normal? Why *not* rush over and get her down in front of witnesses? Then he would effectively erase or contaminate any evidence he might accidentally have left."

"Oh . . . right," Hamill said.

"It doesn't make any sense."

"So what do you figure?"

"I don't know. A suicide in the front yard is definitely strange. And there's another thing—we couldn't get any prints off the chair we found under the body. Not even from the victim. It was as if it was wiped clean. But you can't rule anything out at this point. There's still a chance she just killed herself."

"And there's always the autoerotic thing," Hamill said. "That might account for her being in the front yard. Maybe she got off doing it in public—one of those exhibitionist sex addicts."

"You sound like you're writing an episode for *Law & Order*."

"Not a bad idea. What do they say? Ripped from the headlines?"

"Gimme a break. When it looks like a suicide, it usually is. When it's murder, it's usually the spouse who did it. It's pretty simple. But people watch *Law & Order*, and they think it's always some intricate mystery. Some big cover-up."

"Sometimes it is," Hamill said.

"Sure, and somebody always wins the lottery, but it's still one chance in a fucking million. You know what? Even with all the weird stuff, I bet the medical examiner rules it a suicide and that will be the end of it."

"When's the autopsy scheduled?"

"Tomorrow or the day after. I'm not sure yet."

"You gonna go?"

"Yeah, of course. Got to preserve the chain of evidence."

"Hey, Peters." One of the other officers poked his head in from the hallway. "Chief wants to see you."

"Thanks. Be right in." He got up and grimaced at Hamill. "Time to tell the chief I don't have a clue."

When Peters entered the chief's office, the chief was behind his desk, hunched over paperwork as well. People thought the lives of police officers were action-packed, but they had no idea the amount of paperwork that had to get filled out. No matter how high you got, you never escaped it.

The chief looked up, put his pen down, and motioned Peters to a seat. "So tell me about the case," he said.

Then Peters gave him essentially the same information he'd given Hamill. The chief listened silently to Peters's story without interrupting. He was good with that—letting his men tell the whole story before he started asking questions. Only when he was sure that Peters was finished did he speak.

"So you think it might really have been a suicide?" he asked.

"I don't know, Chief. It's pretty strange all around."

"Hopefully we'll get something from the crime scene to help us out. In the meantime we've got a bit of a tricky tightrope to walk. I assume you had local media show up?"

Peters nodded.

"What did you tell them?"

"I told them that it appeared to be a suicide."

"Good. A suicide doesn't get much coverage. If they get the idea that it might be a murder case, we're going to have a media circus on our hands. Rich, beautiful wife, privileged neighborhood, bizarre circumstances. This is the tabloids' bread and butter. But when you get that kind of media frenzy, it hurts the investigation"—the chief smiled ironically—"not to mention the reputation of the Department unless we get an immediate arrest and indictment. So basically, I need you to work the case like a homicide without giving any indication we might think it's anything other than a suicide."

Peters made a face.

"I know it's a tall order. But the one thing on our side is that the people you'll be talking to are the friends and neighbors, and anyone living in Greenwich isn't likely to be selling any exclusives to the *National Enquirer*. I'm sure they'd prefer not to talk to reporters. They won't want their names in the paper in connection with something like this. That will help."

"And if it looks like it *is* a homicide?" Peters asked.

"I'd like to keep that to ourselves—at least for a while. It always looks better to announce a murder investigation when you can also announce an arrest. The last thing we want is another Martha Moxley situation on our hands. We've got to be aware of the public relations side of things, but," and the chief held up a hand, "if you find this is impacting your investigation, you come talk to me. In the end that's the most important thing."

"OK, Chief," Peters agreed. "I'll do my best."

"I'm not going to let you go out there without some help, though."

"Help?"

"I got a call from the DA's office this morning. Apparently one of their detectives requested to work with you on this one. He's handled a couple of cases like this before, and I think he may even have some information or some sort of history that will be useful. I didn't get all the details, but I think it's a good idea. It will help with manpower and with the media aspect, not to mention prepping the case for trial."

"Which detective?" Peters asked, thinking of a few of the detectives he knew who worked with the DA. They were mostly political creatures, and would be more of a hindrance than a help in an investigation.

"Detective Ackerman. Have you heard of him?"

Peters nodded. "Perfect record on closing his cases, right?"

"That's right."

"Haven't heard about him in a while though."

"He had some personal issues I believe. Took some time off. But he's coming back for this one."

22. Detective Ackerman

*A*ckerman was sitting at his desk, staring intently at the paper in front of him, pencil poised, when Tracy walked over and perched herself on the edge and said, "I'm making some fresh coffee. You want some?"

Ackerman looked up. "Sure. If it's no trouble . . ."

"Not at all," she assured him.

Tracy had a crush on Detective Ackerman. Actually, most of the women there had a little bit of a crush on him, but Tracy was new and she still had hopes the flirting might go somewhere. The other women knew better.

Ackerman was single, but it was a relatively recent thing. Just eight months earlier his wife had left him. She left because she said she was tired of getting the scraps. Tired of always coming in a distant second to his job. Before the divorce his work had been his life; the irony was that now that she'd left, suddenly he didn't seem to care. Fortunately the higher-ups were understanding about his situation. They allowed him to "assist" on other cases, and that had given him some breathing room to recover. He seemed a little better in the last couple of months; he had started joking again, started taking an interest in the cases that were coming in. And that's when the women in the office had started taking an interest in *him*. They thought that if he was interested in work again, he might be interested in other things as well, but no one had managed to get asked out on a date. One of the girls had even tried asking *him*, but he'd turned her down gently. Everyone else had given it up as a lost cause. But Tracy was sure she could get him interested. She was trying the classic route—through his stomach.

"I'll even see if I can snag you a jelly doughnut," she said.

"Oh, no. Now, that would be too much to ask for."

"Then isn't it a good thing you don't need to ask?" Tracy said as she pushed off the desk and walked toward the kitchen.

Ackerman watched a moment before going back to the task in front of him. By the time she got back, he was so absorbed that he didn't even notice her return until she set a cup of coffee and a doughnut down in front of him.

He looked up.

"I thought you went into a trance or something," Tracy said. "You didn't even hear me, did you?"

"No, sorry. I guess I was concentrating. Thanks for this." He picked up the doughnut and took a bite.

"No problem. You need some brain fuel if you're going to concentrate that hard. What are you working on? A case?" She parked herself on the edge of the desk again and leaned over to get a peek at the paper in front of him. Then she laughed at what she saw. "I see you've got some very important work there."

"It *is* work," Ackerman chided her.

"A crossword puzzle? If that's work, then I want your job."

"You think it's easy?"

"Sure. How hard can it be?"

"OK"—he picked up the paper and held it so she couldn't see the answers he'd filled in—"here's the clue for five down. It says, 'Die of cold?' It's seven letters."

"Well, that's easy. Freeze."

"That's only six letters," Ackerman pointed out.

"Oh." She paused. "Freezes, then. That will fit."

"It'll fit, but it's not right."

"So what's the real answer then, smarty pants?"

"Ice cube."

She stared down at the puzzle for a moment. "Why . . . oh." She laughed. "I see. 'Die of cold.' They mean die as in dice. That is so sneaky. That's totally not what you'd think of first. You just assume that they mean die like *die*."

"That's why it's hard," he said, tapping his pencil against the list of clues. "The real challenge is that sometimes it *is* the obvious answer. And sometimes it's not. It's hard to stay flexible and be willing to follow wherever the clues take you and make it fit with the answers surrounding that clue."

"What if you're bad at crosswords? Does that mean you're not smart or something?"

"Not at all. They say there's something called a crossword-puzzle brain. Instead of straightforward deductions, people with crossword-puzzle brains think sideways—they call it divergent thinking. It's not that you're stupid, but someone with a purely logical way of thinking can't think sideways. It's like asking an alligator to jump; they just don't move that way."

"So how can you tell if you have a crossword puzzle brain?'

Ackerman leaned back in his chair and thought a moment. "I think I can give you an example. I'll give you a problem to solve, and we'll see what you come up with. OK?"

Tracy nodded.

"OK. So there's a twenty-story building with two elevators. A lot of the building's employees have complained about how long they have to wait for the elevators to arrive. How would you fix the situation?"

Tracy thought for a minute, drumming her heel against the side of the desk. Then she said, "Well, I guess I'd change it so that one elevator only worked for the first ten floors, and the second elevator worked for eleven through twenty. That should make things faster and the people wouldn't have to wait so long for the elevator to come." She crossed her arms, looking pleased with her answer.

"An absolutely logical solution to the problem," Ackerman agreed. "But you know what people with crossword-puzzle brains come up with?"

"What?"

"Installing mirrors in the lobby so the employees won't notice the wait as much because they'll be able to look at themselves and fix their hair."

"But . . . that's a ridiculous solution. It's no solution at all."

"But it works."

"They still have to wait just as long for the elevator," Tracy protested.

"Yes, but the problem was that the employees were complaining about it. If you give them something to occupy their attention so the wait *seems* shorter, they stop complaining and that fixes the problem."

"It works?"

"Like a charm," Ackerman assured her. "And it's a lot cheaper than reprogramming the elevators."

"I don't see what this has to do with solving murders," Tracy said, a little petulantly.

"No? Well, it's just handy to be able to look at a situation from a different angle."

"So this is what you do all day?"

"No," Ackerman smiled. "This is what I do when I'm waiting for the information on a case to get faxed over. And it looks like it's here," he said, looking over her shoulder at Margie, another of the secretaries, who was headed toward them carrying a folder.

"Here's the information you've been waiting for," Margie said, handing over the file and giving Tracy a look.

Tracy quickly got up from her perch on the desk.

Ackerman took it and flipped it open. He skimmed a bit of the report, then started shuffling through the photos. He got almost all the way through, until he stopped at one. He stared down at it for a long moment. Then he looked up at Tracy and Margie and said, "It's him. I've been waiting for this for ten years."

23. Alex

*A*lex shut the door behind the last of the police officers. Then he turned around and, almost like a sleepwalker, went into the dining room and dropped into a chair—it was where he'd spent most of the morning while the police were there, and after they left he returned there without even thinking. There were still paper coffee cups scattered around, an open box of doughnuts, two pumpernickel bagels left on a plate, and a scraped-out plastic container of cream cheese. Alex reached out and snagged a dry bagel and took a bite. He hadn't eaten anything all morning, and he was starving. He knew he wasn't supposed to be hungry. He was supposed to be the grieving husband. He wasn't very good at filling that role, but he had sensed that reaching out and helping himself to a bagel earlier would not have been a good idea. So instead he'd sat all morning with just a cup of coffee, staring at the food and listening to the conversation swirling around him.

After the initial questioning, the police mostly ignored him—or at least they pretended to. But Alex felt the sidelong glances, and when he got up to walk around the house, they had sent an officer to follow him. It was so uncomfortable, he had decided to stay in the dining room and see if he could pick up any information from listening to the chatter, but they did all of their real talking somewhere else because all he heard about was a son's fourth birthday party, another officer's tough decision between buying a Toyota Corolla or a Nissan Sentra, and their rankings in the fantasy football league.

At the time Alex had wondered at their choice of using the dining room as a gathering place instead of the living room—until he realized that the dining room window looked out on the front yard. It didn't look directly out on the tree where his wife hung—that was off to the left but still in their field of vision. It seemed like hours before they lowered Julia out of the tree.

From the window he could also see the interviews the detectives were conducting. They interviewed both Priscilla and Sofie. Thank goodness Sofie had been there. Alex wasn't sure that he could have handled Priscilla's hysteria without her. He knew the police must be asking the two women about him—how did he react when they told him, what did he do when he saw his wife's body, what did he say while they were waiting for the police to arrive. He wondered what they were saying. How much had they noticed? They certainly knew that his response was not that of a normal loving husband. That alone was enough to complicate things.

Suddenly, sitting there alone at the dining room table, Alex felt a wave of hate pass over him. Fucking Julia.

Abruptly he stood up, went to the kitchen to get a couple of garbage bags, then climbed the stairs to the master bedroom and crossed to her walk-in closet. It could hardly even be called a closet—it was closer to a small room, and it was stuffed with expensive designer clothes. Prada, Alberta Ferretti, Christian Lacroix, Marc Jacobs. He couldn't begin to guess how much the things in the closet had cost, but the floor was ankle-deep in clothes. When she was looking for something to wear in the morning, Julia would pull pieces off their hangers, and if she decided not to use them, she simply tossed them on the floor. The housekeeper spent at least an hour every day putting Julia's closet in order. But it was Monday and the housekeeper didn't come on the weekends. Julia was like a tornado, and she left chaos wherever she went. The house only looked presentable because Alex spent much of the weekend picking up after her, but he didn't go near her closet. These clothes had cost thousands, and she'd thrown them about like they were trash. For someone who had come from nothing, she had more of a sense of entitlement than anyone Alex had ever known.

He took a garbage bag and started cramming clothes inside. He just grabbed—silk dresses, cashmere sweaters, leather jackets—all were stuffed inside until it was full to the bursting point. And then he took another bag. He kept going until there were trash bags lined up in the closet. The shelves were bare and there were only empty hangers left along the bars. He had just finished and was standing back to survey his handiwork when he heard the doorbell ring.

He turned and went back down the stairs, crossed through the living room to the foyer, and opened the front door. There were two men standing on the stoop. He recognized Peters as one of the detectives from that morning. Then he looked at the other man. When he saw who it was standing there, he felt the shock of a different kind of recognition. "What the hell are you doing here?" Alex demanded.

Ackerman smiled. "Hello, Mr. Stowe. I'm the lead detective on this case. And we have a few questions for you."

24. Priscilla & Gordon

"Where on earth have you been? Why are you home so late?" Priscilla demanded as her husband came through the door from the garage.

"I called and left a message—," Gordon started, but Priscilla didn't wait to listen.

you answer me? Are you OK?"
he said in a little-girl voice.
ng with my baby?" he asked, climbing on the bed to
I heard what happened on the news. Did you see it?"
rinkled her nose.
e been awful. Do you want to talk about it?"
cing a pattern on the comforter—and when she
lidn't look up. "Baby," she said, then paused.
sugar?"
ave something I need to tell you."

she stalled.
mean you're afraid because of what happened

id to tell you."
ould never be afraid to tell me anything."
e mad?"
ot."
?"
d his left hand and said, "I promise. Now, what's

rward and whispered in his ear.
sharply, frowning.
," she accused.
mad. I'm just thinking."
u thinking about?"
what we're going to do about this," he said.
ey looked frightened.
cide now," he said, seeing the look on her face.
time. But for God's sake, don't say anything to
nyone. OK?"
eed.

"Do you have any idea what I've been through? Didn't you hear what happened?"

"No. What happened?" he asked almost absently, taking off his hat and putting it on the shelf in the closet.

He was reaching for a hanger for his overcoat when Priscilla said, "I found Julia Stowe hanging from a tree in her front yard this morning."

Gordon didn't even falter; he retrieved the hanger and was arranging his coat on it as he said, "Is that right? Was she playing a game or something?"

"No, Gordon. It wasn't a game. She was dead."

Finally Priscilla had managed to get her husband's attention. Gordon stopped, still holding the hanger with the coat, and looked at her.

"Dead?"

"That's what usually happens when there's a rope around your neck," Priscilla answered.

"Priscilla," he said sharply. "If you're making a joke, it's not funny."

"I know it's not funny."

"She's really dead?"

"As a doornail," Priscilla replied.

"That's . . . that's *terrible*." He looked down and realized he was still holding the hanger. He put it in the closet, closed the door, then stood there a moment, his hand flat against the wood as if he needed the support. "How can you be so flippant about it? Poor Julia."

"Poor Julia? Why is it you always think of someone else? Why not think of your wife for a change?"

"But . . . Julia's the one who killed herself."

"And what do you think it was like for me finding her like that?" Priscilla said.

That first sight of Julia—of the remains of what had been a person—had been truly shocking, but in the intervening hours Priscilla's brain had converted the memory to something more like a scene from a movie. However there were times, flashes, when all the horror of it came washing back over her.

"The best thing would probably be for you to think about it as little as possible," Gordon said soothingly.

"Best for who? Best for you, you mean," Priscilla retorted. She *wanted* to talk to Gordon about it; she *wanted* to go over every detail, but she had forgotten what her husband was like. Gordon was the kind of person who turned his head away when he passed an accident. In her mind Priscilla accused him of being weak and oversensitive, but the reality was that it annoyed her because when she passed an accident she slowed down to get a good look, and Gordon made her ashamed of that part of herself.

For a second it looked like Gordon was about to protest, but instead he said, "I'm sorry, I wasn't thinking. Of course we should talk about it if that's going to make you feel better. I can't even imagine what that was like."

Priscilla opened her mouth to tell him what it was like, but to her surprise, she started to cry.

"Hey, hey, listen it's OK," Gordon said.

They were still standing in the entryway, and Gordon took her arm and led her into the living room. "Come on, sit down. I'll get you a drink." He sat her down on the couch, went over to the cabinet where they kept the liquor, pulled out the brandy and two snifters, poured a couple of fingers in each, and returned with the glasses. He handed her one, then sat next to her on the couch. At this point, Priscilla's crying had subsided to sniffles.

"Take a drink," he told her.

Obediently Priscilla took a sip of the brandy.

"They say there's a lot of survivor's guilt when someone you know commits suicide," Gordon went on. "It's natural to think that there might have been something you could have done—talked to her, or noticed something. But you shouldn't feel responsible."

Priscilla half choked on the brandy. At first it seemed as if she were going to start crying again, but instead she startled Gordon by starting to laugh. She was still half crying, but laughing at the same time.

"What? What did I say that was so funny?"

She replied through alm[...]
would feel responsible for Ju[...]

"That's good. That's a g[...]
one who's responsible for Ju[...]

"No, you don't understan[...]
and turned to look at him[...]
murdered."

Gordon jerked back, aln[...]

"Murdered," Priscilla re[...]

"How do you know? Di[...]

"No. The police didn't [...]
yet—at least not for sure."

"So this is just a hunch [...]
obviously ready to discount [...]

"No. It's not a hunch. It[...]

"And how exactly do yo[...]

25. As[...]

Stewart burst in the do[...]
He threw his coat [...]
for which his first wife had [...]
ley not bother him about it, [...]
with her belongings so tha[...]
create too unstable a struct[...]
his coat up.

Stewart walked through [...]
the rooms dark and emp[...]
called again. He saw the lig[...]
he found her. She was al[...]
o'clock—*and* she wasn't we[...]

"Why did[...]

"I'm OK," [...]

"What's w[...]
lie next to her [...]

"Yes." She [...]

"It must h[...]

She was t[...]
spoke, she sti[...]

"What is i[...]

"Well . . . [...]

"What is i[...]

"I'm afraid[...]

"Afraid? Y[...]
today?"

"No, I'm a[...]

"Baby, you[...]

"You won't[...]

"Of course[...]

"You prom[...]

Stewart ra[...]
bothering you[...]

She leaned[...]

He drew b[...]

"You *are* n[...]

"No. I'm n[...]

"What are [...]

"I'm think[...]

At that, A[...]

"We won'[...]

"We'll take s[...]
anyone. Not [...]

"OK," she [...]

26. Sofie & Dean

*S*ofie was also in bed when her husband got home—but that wasn't so surprising, since it was after midnight when Dean pulled into the garage. She heard the garage door and then the sounds of Dean raiding the fridge. She wondered if he would find the quiche she'd left in there for him or if she should go down and get it out for him. After a moment's thought, she got up and put on a robe and slippers. Dean could have something right in front of his face and still not find it. Just last night he'd been looking for the hot sauce to put on his chili. She told him that it was in the refrigerator door, but he insisted he'd looked and it wasn't there. She had to stop what she was doing to go to the refrigerator. She'd glanced at the door and plucked the hot sauce from where it was tucked behind a bottle of Italian dressing. When she handed it to him, he said sheepishly, "I didn't see it." She'd said, "That's because you didn't look."

Sure enough, when Sofie got downstairs, she found Dean rooting through the contents of the fridge.

"I made a quiche for you," Sofie said. "Didn't you see it? I left it right in the front."

"I saw it," Dean said. "But I was thinking I'd save it so we could have it tomorrow night for dinner. I was going to have the chili again tonight."

"Oh, I threw out the chili. I had it for lunch, and then there wasn't much left—and I didn't think it was very good in the first place."

"I love your chili," Dean said. "You know your chili is my favorite."

"You love everything I make. Anyway, I needed something to do to get my mind off things. It was sort of a crazy day here. Did you hear?"

"Yes. I heard on the radio coming home."

"Well?" Sofie said.

"It's terrible. Shocking." He took the quiche from the fridge and brought it over to the kitchen table.

"Of course it's terrible," Sofie said impatiently, getting him a plate and silverware and bringing it over to him. "But what do you *think*?"

"Do you mind if we don't talk about this now?" Dean said, cutting a piece of quiche and transferring the slab to his plate.

"Aren't you going to heat that up?" she said.

"I'm too tired."

And he did seem tired. He was half slumped in the chair, and even his voice was flat and indifferent. Sofie took his plate from him and put it in the microwave.

"But I wanted to talk to you about it," she said.

"Can we do it tomorrow?" Dean asked. "Right now I think it's just about all I can handle to have some food, maybe watch a little TV, and go to bed."

"Dean, I was the one who found the body."

"What?" He swiveled in his seat and stared at her.

"Priscilla and I found her. Remember we were going on a walk this morning? Well, we were the ones who saw her."

"You found the body?" he repeated.

The microwave beeped, and Sofie popped the door and brought the plate back over to Dean. Then she sat down and said, "It was awful. Her tongue was so swollen, it was sticking out of her mouth. It looked like someone had put a cow's tongue in there."

Dean had been about to take a bite, and he dropped the fork back on the plate with a clatter. "Sofie!"

"Sorry."

"I can't eat this now," he said, pushing his plate away abruptly.

"Sorry," Sofie said again.

There was a moment of silence. Then Dean said, "Why on earth would someone do that to themselves?"

"She didn't," Sofie told him.

"Next thing you're going to tell me is Julia didn't really kill herself, but that she was murdered."

"She was."

"That's too much," Dean said, bringing his palm down hard on the table. "She wasn't murdered. Say it. Say she wasn't murdered."

Sofie shook her head stubbornly. "I won't say it. I think she *was* murdered—and so do the other women."

"What other women?"

"The other women in the book club."

"Don't tell me you've got them thinking that someone murdered Julia as well?"

"But I'm right."

"You're right, you're right," Dean mimicked. His voice took on a nasty edge. "You're always right. Someday you're going to be wrong, and it won't be about some little thing. Believe me, when you're wrong it's gonna be a biggie."

27. Susan & Harry

*S*usan waited all evening for Harry to come home, but instead, at ten o'clock when she had just settled down in front of the television to try to take her mind off what had happened earlier that day, the phone rang.

"Suze, glad I got you," Harry said.

"Why wouldn't you get me? Where else would I be?" Susan asked.

"Listen, I'm not going to make it home tonight. I've got this thing that's going to run late. I'm just going to stay at the apartment for the night."

"Can't you come home?" Susan asked. "Even if it's late. Something happened here today. Something awful."

But Harry wasn't listening. "I can't talk right now. I have to get back. I'm sorry, but this is going to have to wait."

"You don't sound sorry."

"Susan, it's an expression. Don't do this now."

"Do what?"

"Don't be difficult. I've got to go."

"Don't hang up. Harry. Don't hang up. They found Julia today—"

But Harry didn't wait to hear the end of the sentence. He'd already hung up. Susan tried calling him back on his cell phone, but he must have turned it off because it went straight into voice mail.

Susan listened to the greeting and left a message. "It's me. Call me back. Please."

She had never minded before when Harry stayed at the apartment, because she knew how hard the commute could be and it really didn't make sense if he wasn't going to get back home until after midnight only to get back on a train at six thirty. But part of the reason she never minded is that she assumed if she ever asked him to come home, he would do it. She thought she'd been storing up goodwill—that when she did finally ask, he would know that it was important, and she would get it without question. What had happened instead was Harry had learned that thinking of her was not something that was required of him.

He didn't even call her back.

28. Priscilla & the Detectives

$\mathcal{D}$etective Ackerman pulled up to the curb in front of a sprawling Georgian-style mansion, but didn't shut off the car. "Can you see, is this number eighteen?" he asked Detective Peters, who was sitting next to him in the passenger seat.

Peters leaned forward, peering through the windshield. "I don't see a number on this one, but I'm pretty sure there's a twenty on the mailbox of the next house."

"Then this is it." Ackerman put it into park and turned off the ignition.

Ackerman had been pleasantly surprised by Peters. Normally when he came in to work on a case, the detectives were . . . not very helpful. That was the diplomatic way Ackerman usually phrased it. He understood; they didn't like it when someone from the district attorney's office started horning in on their investigation. He probably would have felt the same. But Peters—unlike many of the detectives Ackerman had worked with—hadn't been outright hostile when they met. True, he had been a bit wary, but after about an hour going over the case (during which Ackerman tried to make it clear that he wasn't into the politics or the prestige) Peters had relaxed into friendliness.

"So who's our first interview?" Peters asked.

Ackerman smiled at Peters's tact. This was actually their second interview—if you could call it an interview when on their first they hadn't even gotten past the stoop and the conversation had lasted all of two minutes. That's what had happened when they went to see Alex Stowe the day before. Ackerman knew he should have sent Peters with another detective. But he hadn't been able to resist; he'd wanted to see Alex Stowe's face when he showed up at his front door—and in that at least, he hadn't been disappointed.

"I thought we'd start with the obvious—with the woman who discovered the body," Ackerman said. "What's her name again?"

Peters flipped through his notebook. "Priscilla Brenner." He read silently for a moment, then shook his head. "I remember the interview, but for the life of me, I can't remember which one she was. All the women out here look the same to me—every one is blonder and thinner than the next. It's creepy."

"Did you just transfer here?" Ackerman guessed.

"Yeah. A couple of months ago from the seventy-eighth precinct in Brooklyn."

"You'll get used to it after a while," Ackerman told him.

As they got out of the car and started up the flagstone path to the front door, Peters asked, "So how do you want to handle this?

This isn't the easiest thing—conducting an investigation when you don't want anyone to figure out that it's an investigation."

Ackerman considered for a moment. "We'll just tell them that it's routine. We have to investigate all avenues, that kind of thing. Rich, well-educated people don't like to admit to believing in conspiracy theories. They don't usually buy the tabloids. They just read them while they're in line at the supermarket."

"Do they even go to the supermarket?" Peters asked.

"OK, so they read the copies the maid leaves around," Ackerman amended.

They had reached the front door, and Ackerman lifted a finger to ring the bell. Priscilla opened it so quickly that he was taken aback. It was almost as if she had been hovering right there, waiting for them. He hoped that she hadn't heard their conversation about the tabloids.

"I'm so glad you're here," she said, ushering them in. "Let's go sit in the living room. Can I offer you some tea or coffee?"

"We don't want to trouble you," Ackerman said.

"Oh, it's no trouble," Priscilla assured them. "I'll just have Danielle make it."

"Your daughter?" Peters guessed.

"The housekeeper," Priscilla corrected him with a frown.

"Coffee," Ackerman jumped in quickly. "Thank you."

"This is the living room," Priscilla gestured through an archway. "And if you don't mind taking off your shoes, you can put them right over there. Please make yourselves comfortable. I'll just pop into the kitchen to talk to Danielle." She headed off down the hall in the opposite direction.

"Sorry about the daughter thing," Peters whispered.

"Don't worry about it. What do you think of this?" he asked, nodding toward the living room. With the white carpet, white couches, white end tables, and the sun streaming in the windows, it had the blinding effect of sunlight on snow.

"Just don't spill the coffee," Peters said as he bent to pull off his shoes.

Ackerman groaned. "Oh, great. Thanks very much. Haven't you heard about the power of suggestion?"

"Is that like saying I jinxed you?" Peters grinned.

"I'm just glad my socks match," Ackerman said as he bent to untie his laces. "My wife took care of the laundry for sixteen years, and I haven't quite got the hang of it yet."

"You know what you need to do? It's an old bachelor's trick. Throw out all the socks you have and go out and buy twenty pairs of the same kind, all black. That way your socks will always match."

"Not a bad idea," Ackerman said. He led the way into the living room and sat down gingerly on the couch.

Peters claimed a nearby armchair and pulled out his notebook and a pen.

They didn't have to wait long before Priscilla returned from the kitchen with Danielle in tow.

"How do you take your coffee?" Priscilla asked them.

"Milk and sugar," Ackerman said.

Danielle added milk and sugar to one of the cups and handed it to Priscilla.

"I thought all detectives drank their coffee black," Priscilla said as she presented it to Ackerman.

Ackerman received the cup carefully and immediately set it down. "Sorry to disappoint you. I have a sweet tooth."

Priscilla turned to Peters. "And you?"

"I take it black," Peters told her.

"There you go. He's a real detective," Ackerman said.

"No, just lactose intolerant," Peters replied.

Ackerman laughed.

Priscilla handed Peters his coffee then took her own cup from Danielle and moved to sit on the couch next to Ackerman. He noticed that she was wearing shoes—high heels, actually, with strappy things across the top.

"I only wear these shoes inside," she explained, noticing the direction of his gaze. "I keep several pairs for inside only."

"Ah. I see," Ackerman said, intentionally avoiding looking over at Peters. Somehow he knew if he looked over, he wouldn't be able to keep a straight face.

"So, how can I help?" Priscilla asked. "I imagine you want to make an arrest as soon as possible."

"An arrest?" Ackerman repeated.

"Yes. Of course you're going to want to arrest the person who killed Julia."

Ackerman heard Peters almost choke on a sip of coffee. Studiously ignoring Peters, he said, "At this point, we're still considering it a suicide. We're just covering all the bases."

"But it wasn't a suicide," Priscilla said. "It was murder."

Ackerman listened to the conviction in her voice, and he felt a prickle of anticipation. There was information to be had here.

"There's no evidence of that," he said cautiously, hoping to elicit a reaction without giving anything away. And it worked.

"Of course there is," Priscilla corrected him importantly. "There's the branch."

"The branch?" Ackerman repeated.

"You mean you didn't notice the branch? I thought for sure you would have seen that."

"*What* about the branch?"

"Well, didn't you notice that the rope made a groove in the branch where Julia was . . . well, where Julia was."

"But you can expect a mark, even if the person didn't weigh much," Ackerman pointed out.

"Sure," Priscilla agreed. "But even if she weighed two hundred pounds, if you throw a rope over a branch and hang yourself, it wouldn't make *that* kind of a mark. You'd only get that kind of deep groove from friction. For example, you would get a groove like that if you have a dead weight on the end of a rope, you throw that rope over a tree limb, and then hoist that weight up. The friction of the rope against the branch will cut into the bark."

Both detectives stared at her.

This was what you got when you made assumptions about people, Ackerman thought. He'd learned that lesson the hard way many, many times over the years—but those automatic judgments still somehow slipped in. From that moment forward, Ackerman reminded himself to take every interview seriously.

Ackerman looked at Peters. "Was there a mark like that on the branch?" he asked.

"It should show in the photographs," Peters replied, subtly pointing out that Ackerman would have had the opportunity to see the evidence as well. "Plus, we cut off that part of the branch. So at least the evidence is preserved. We'll be able to test for that."

Ackerman turned back to Priscilla. "I can assure you, we'll be going over all the evidence very carefully. So you said you saw the mark on the tree and now you think that there was a possibility it was murder?"

"No. I don't *think* it was. I know it was. It doesn't leave much doubt, does it?" Priscilla asked.

"With evidence like that, there's always some doubt," Ackerman told her honestly. "But if you believed it was murder, why didn't you say anything to the police?"

"Well, I didn't notice straight away," Priscilla hedged. "Not consciously. I think subconsciously I knew something wasn't right all along, but it was only later that I realized what I'd seen."

"Did you talk to any reporters?"

"I did right after . . . after I found Julia."

"And did you mention anything to them about your suspicions?"

"No, of course not." Priscilla said, sounding almost offended.

Ackerman didn't try to hide his relief. "Good. I want you to bring anything else you might think of to us, right away."

"I don't know if my ideas will be any help," she said modestly.

"I want to hear your thoughts right away," Ackerman repeated. "Day or night," and with that, he took a card out of his wallet. "OK?"

Priscilla took the card. "OK."

"And if you don't mind, I have just a few more questions for you." Ackerman said. He was hopeful that there might be more information there to unearth.

"Sure," Priscilla said, still fingering the card.

"What were your impressions of Julia before the incident? Was she acting different? Upset?"

Priscilla seemed to take her new role of advisor seriously, because she took a few seconds to consider her answer. "Yes, now you mention it, she did seem upset beforehand."

"For how long before?"

"A few weeks, maybe a month," Priscilla said.

"Was she upset with any specific person? Did you notice?"

"Well, at the time I thought she was upset with *me*. But that's probably because I was taking things personally. You know how if you're upset in general, you tend to be rude to whoever you're talking to?"

"What do you think she was upset about?"

"I'm not absolutely positive, but I think living out here in Greenwich might have been getting to her. She wasn't exactly a country person. She was always talking about how dull it was out here."

"So you don't think she was upset with her husband?"

"She must have been—for moving her out here."

"But she didn't say anything about it?" he pressed.

"Oh, no. She was way too concerned with appearances." Priscilla spoke with obvious condescension.

"What 'appearances,' exactly?"

"That she was perfect and her life was perfect."

Her voice revealed a little more annoyance than she intended, and Ackerman picked up on it, saying, "That must have been irritating."

"Oh, no." Priscilla backtracked quickly. "Well, it would probably bother some people, but it didn't bother me. I could see through that a mile away."

"So, in general, would you say you liked her?"

"Julia? Of course I liked Julia. I invited her to be a member of the book club, didn't I?"

"Ah, yes. You have a book club."

"Yes. We read mysteries."

"So that explains it," Ackerman said, smiling. "You've had training in this."

"Do you read mysteries?" Priscilla asked.

"No, I get enough of them in my job." He paused, then added, "But I do crosswords to relax."

She responded exactly as he was hoping she would.

"I do too," she said eagerly.

"You do? Then maybe you can help me with a clue I'm stuck on." He pulled the paper out of his back pocket.

"I'll do my best," Pricilla said, sitting up straighter.

"The clue reads, 'remote post' and the answer is four letters."

Priscilla frowned in concentration. "Remote post," she repeated. "I bet that's a reference to the Internet. Is the answer e-mail? No, wait, you said four letters, right?"

"Four letters," he confirmed.

"That was too easy anyway." She was silent for a few seconds. Then her face brightened. "It's got to be 'blog.' You know, that refers to those journals that people post on the Internet from all over the world, and that fits, doesn't it? Or did you have any other letters filled in that conflicted?"

Ackerman took out the paper and penciled it in. "No, I've just started the puzzle, so I don't have any other letters yet. But that's a very good answer. Thank you. And now we'd better get going. We have to interview your fellow book club members."

"But Detective, you haven't even touched your coffee," Priscilla protested.

"Ah, yes." Ackerman cautiously picked up the little china cup and sipped. "It's very good," he said, but he put the cup down again almost immediately. "I'll have to trouble you for another when we come back. We'll need to speak to your husband as well."

"Gordon? Gordon won't be able to help you."

"We need to cover all the bases anyway. Besides, it will give us another chance to check in with you." And Ackerman gave her a smile intended to flatter.

"Whew," Peters said as they walked away from the house. "Who lives like that? The maid? Making us take off our shoes? And that

room? Jesus. I guess maybe all that money makes you go a little"—
Peters circled his forefinger up near his temple.

Ackerman couldn't resist pointing out, "But that woman you're
calling crazy noticed something on a crime scene that you missed.
If it turns out that she's right about that branch, it could be an important piece of evidence."

"You had to bring that up, didn't you?"

"Yes, I did. So what else did we get? Let's just review it before
we go to our next interview."

Peters flipped his notebook open. "She said she thought that
Julia might have been angry with her."

"I'm inclined to put that down to ego," Ackerman mused. "She
seems the type to think that the whole world revolves around her. I
think that's the most likely explanation."

"I'm with you on that one." Peters glanced down at the notebook
again. "She also said that Julia wasn't happy about moving out to the
'country.' Did you know we lived in the 'country'? I always thought
of the country as farms and stuff."

"Different language," Ackerman said.

"So now rich people have a different language to go along with
their different standard of living?"

"Yep. Anything else?"

"She said that Julia was image conscious, but that she liked her."

"Yeah. I don't know about that. She didn't sound very fond of
her, did she?"

"Why can't people just tell the truth?" Peters wondered aloud. "I
mean, it's not like she killed the woman. And it would make our job
so much easier."

"Yeah, well, people always lie. They have a lot more practice at it
than telling the truth. Anyway, this particular case is one of the easier ones," Ackerman said. "We don't have to figure out who did it—
just how to nail him for it. And I think that branch is going to help.
Let's see what else we can find out from"—he glanced down at his
own notebook—"from Susan Altman."

29. Susan & the Detectives

"What did I think of Julia?" Susan repeated.

Ackerman and Peters were talking to Susan, and once again they had coffee in front of them—but this time they were both actually drinking it. Susan had served it in big, thick ceramic mugs that looked like they would crack the tile floor before they even chipped. And even better, there was no way to stain tile.

The visit had been different from the moment Susan opened the door, and they'd been swarmed by two big dogs—one Newfoundland and one golden retriever. Not exactly guard dogs, Ackerman noted as their tails wagged like pistons and they enthusiastically licked any exposed piece of skin. The Newfie actually tried to rear up and give Peters (who was the shorter of the two) a face-to-face greeting.

"Bo, Hector, down," Susan pleaded. They ignored her until she managed to snag their collars and drag them back inside.

"Come in, come in," she said rather breathlessly. "They're just excited. I haven't taken them for a walk yet today. Do you want to go sit down in the living room? Or would you prefer the kitchen?"

When Ackerman and Peters said "Kitchen" almost in unison, Susan grinned. "You just came from talking to Priscilla, right? Let me guess. She took you into the living room and she served coffee. It's terrifying, isn't it? If you think that's nerve racking, try drinking red wine in there. But I'm glad you chose the kitchen. I think if we sat in the living room, you'd leave with evidence of Bo and Hector all over your suits."

Both Ackerman and Peters laughed and followed her into the kitchen. On the way, Ackerman snuck a peek into the living room as they passed. It looked comfortable and lived in, and, as she had claimed, decorated with dog hair.

In the kitchen it turned out the coffee was already made. "It might be a bit burnt," she apologized. "It's been on since this morning."

"That will just make us feel right at home," Ackerman assured her. "That's what we always drink. I've even come to like it."

"Please, sit," Susan motioned them toward a couple of stools that were pulled up to the counter. Then she went to the cabinets and pulled out three mugs and three plates as well.

"I have something to go with the coffee," Susan explained as she took a pumpkin pie out of the cupboard. "Fresh from the store. I find I can never have coffee without having something to eat with it. It always has to be coffee *and* something, and since I don't smoke, I end up eating too much. I've always said if I gave up coffee, I'd lose twenty pounds." As she talked, she cut three slices and transferred them to plates without even giving them the chance to decline.

It was only after the plates in front of them were empty that Ackerman finally managed to segue into the interview. But after Susan's hospitality, he didn't feel like he could jump right into the details of the death, so instead he started out with a general question: What had Susan thought of Julia?

Susan sat with her mug cradled between her palms, mulling over their question aloud. "What did I think of Julia? Well, to be honest—I couldn't stand her."

Ackerman couldn't hold back a bark of laughter. Yet again, he had been caught off guard.

But Susan mistook the sound for disapproval because she said anxiously, "Does that sound too awful? To speak that way about someone who's . . . well, who can't defend themselves? I just figured that I shouldn't whitewash it. There was just something. . . ." Susan trailed off, thinking about it for a moment, then shrugged.

"No, it's not awful. It's much more useful to us if you're completely honest. It helps to get a sense of the victim. What about everyone else. Did they like her?"

Susan hesitated. "Well, we didn't actually talk about it much. But I know that Priscilla didn't like her either. I know what you're going to say. Then why be friends with her at all? Right?"

"You're doing my job for me," Ackerman said, smiling. "I don't even need to ask any questions."

"Like my husband says, just wind me up and I'll keep going. The thing is, Julia was actually pretty nice at the beginning. Or at least she pretended to be. And anyway, Julia was the type of person who always gets invited. You'd be afraid not to."

"Afraid?" Ackerman repeated.

"Oh, now stop it," Susan chided. "You're just giving me a hard time. You know what I mean."

"I do know what you mean," Ackerman said. "But I have to ask because someone obviously did hate Julia, or was afraid of her, or both."

"What?" Susan said nervously.

"Priscilla told us about the branch," Ackerman said. "And she told us that she didn't believe it was suicide. Do you agree?"

"Well, yes."

"So that means that someone had to have some strong feeling about her in order to kill her, wouldn't you say?"

"Oh. Well, yes . . . I suppose I didn't think of that."

"What *did* you think when Priscilla told you what she noticed about the branch?"

"What *she* noticed about the branch?" Susan echoed. Then quickly, "Oh, right. Sorry, what was the question?"

Ackerman frowned, sensing something off about her response but not quite knowing what it was. "I wanted to know what you thought when you discovered that Julia might have been murdered."

"Yes. God, it sounds so awful when you put it that way. I only thought how it meant she didn't kill herself and how that was a relief. It would have been so disturbing to think that someone was that unhappy and you had no idea."

"It's less disturbing to think someone else killed her?" Ackerman asked.

"Yes, I think so—maybe it's the idea you'd been so wrong about someone. Has that ever happened to you? That you've really misjudged someone and they turn out to be completely different than you thought?"

"Yes," Ackerman said, without hesitation.

Susan looked at Peters.

"Sure," he agreed.

"Then you might know what I'm talking about when I say that, to me, that's much more upsetting. I never in a million years would have thought that Julia was the type to commit suicide."

"But you could see someone wanting to kill her?" Ackerman asked.

"Well . . . yes. To be honest, I could see that a lot more easily."

"What does your husband think about the situation?"

"Harry? Oh . . . Harry thinks it's awful."

Again, there was something a little strained in her response, but Ackerman couldn't quite pinpoint what was wrong.

"We'll also want to speak to your husband at some point," he said.

"He's been swamped at work, and when that happens he generally stays in the city. So I don't know when he'd be around," Susan hedged.

"Then do you have a number where we can reach him?"

Ackerman thought there was another strange hesitation before she said, "Um. Sure. I'll get a pen and write it down for you." Then she was suddenly very busy opening drawers, rummaging through papers and clips and rubber bands, looking for a pen.

"Here, use mine," Peters said, holding out the one he'd been using to take notes.

"Oh, thank you." Susan took the pen and wrote down Harry's work and cell-phone numbers.

Ackerman took it and inspected it for a moment, as if he might see what was wrong in the numbers on the scrap of paper.

"Anything else I can do to help, just let me know," Susan said.

It was a conversation closer, and Ackerman recognized it immediately. Why, he wondered, was she suddenly so anxious for them to leave?

"Thanks for taking the time to talk to us," he said. "We'll probably be back soon to talk to you and your husband."

"Of course."

"Oh, there's one more thing," Ackerman said as he and Peters got up and followed her back out into the hallway. "Mrs. Brenner mentioned that you all do crosswords. I got stuck on a clue from today's puzzle, and I was wondering if you had any ideas."

"That's funny. I just started the puzzle right before you arrived."

"You did?"

"Well, most days I start it. I can't say I always finish. Just a minute, let me get it." She ducked into the living room and retrieved a section of the newspaper off the coffee table. "Which clue?" she asked when she rejoined them in the hall.

"Three down—the clue is 'Remote post.' Four letters."

She frowned down at the paper in her hands. "I didn't tackle that one yet, but I think I might have gotten the first letter. I have it starting with an 's.' Did you have that?"

"I actually don't have any of the letters," Ackerman said apologetically.

"Anyway, I think that's right. Remote post, four letters," she repeated. "How about Siam? It's remote. Both geographically and historically." She looked down at the paper in her hands again, as if that had the answers. Then she looked back up. "I don't know if that's right—I'll have to fill in some more to see—but it's something to work with. I have to admit, I usually do a lot of erasing. I'm definitely not one of those people who can use a pen."

"I don't use a pen either," Ackerman told her.

"You don't?"

He shook his head. "Even if I was good enough, I wouldn't on principle."

"What principle?"

"I think that everyone makes mistakes."

"So Mrs. Brenner lied about liking Julia," Ackerman said as they got back in the car. "That may or may not mean anything. But the strange thing is that I feel like Mrs. Altman lied to us about something as well. She seemed a bit agitated. At least at the end. So who do we see next?"

"You have the list," Peters reminded Ackerman.

"Oh, right." Ackerman checked. "Next is Ashley Turkel."

30. Ashley & the Detectives

*A*shley greeted the detectives at the door, and Peters pursed his lips in a silent whistle. She wore a halter dress with a short skirt and plunging neckline, with high-heeled pumps that any woman in the neighborhood would have immediately identified as Jimmy Choos.

"It's about time you came to see me," she said. "I can understand you going to Priscilla first since she was the one who found Julia, but why did you go to Susan's next?"

"We wanted to talk to whoever knew Julia the best," Ackerman explained. "But I was much better friends with Julia than she was," Ashley said, sounding annoyed.

"We didnt' know that from the information we gathered," Ackerman explained diplomatically.

"Oh. Well, I guess that's true. All right. Come in. We'll go sit in the conservatory."

She led them to a room that extended past the back of the house and was all glass on three sides. The leaves were just peaking and there was a riot of color outside: red and yellow and orange, all made brighter by the contrast with the dark green of the conifers.

"So you were good friends with Julia?" Ackerman said as they sat down. The furniture here was white wicker with flower-patterned cushions: it seemed like the room functioned as a sort of indoor patio. The chair creaked ominously as Ackerman sat.

"I didn't say I was good friends with her," Ashley corrected him. "Just better friends than Susan. But I guess I was the closest woman friend she had. I mean, we were both relatively new to the neighborhood. And we were both younger than Susan and Priscilla."

She said that she was younger as if informing them of some extraordinary achievement, Ackerman thought. He suspected that he was not looking at a woman who was going to be able to grow old gracefully.

"So did she confide in you?" he asked.

"Sure," Ashley shrugged. "She told me lots of things. She probably told me more than she meant to."

"What do you mean, 'more than she meant to'?"

"I think she thought it was safe to say stuff to me."

"Safe because you wouldn't tell anyone?"

"No, safe because she thought I wasn't smart enough to use it against her. That's what they all think—just because I didn't go to Wesleyan like Stewart's first wife, and I don't need to show people how *intelligent* I am all the time. But I don't care. Stewart always says you have an advantage if people underestimate you."

"Are you looking for an advantage?" Ackerman asked.

"Isn't everyone?" Ashley countered.

Ackerman allowed himself a smile. "So what did Julia tell you?"

"Oh, lots of stuff."

"Like what?"

"I guess it doesn't matter if I say it now. She told me stuff like what she thought of Priscilla and Susan and some of the other women in the neighborhood. She wasn't very impressed. She thought Susan's taste was awful. She was right about that. Have you seen that pink Juicy tracksuit she wears? I mean, I love Juicy Couture too—I have the best cashmere hoodie—but she's not twenty. She can't pull off that color. And her house . . ." Ashley shuddered. "It's *so* New England country. I mean, I guess that's where she came from and everything, but you can overdo something. Julia said she didn't know how Susan could come from so much money and have so little class."

"So she didn't like Susan very much?"

"You know, I don't think it was Susan; I don't think she liked *anyone* out here—including me. She was always saying how this place was a backwater, and she couldn't wait to move back to the city."

"They were planning on moving back?"

"I thought so. She talked like she was. But then once I mentioned something to Alex, and he didn't seem to know anything about it. He thought she was perfectly happy out here. Men are so slow sometimes."

Ackerman perked up when he heard Alex's name. "So what else did she say?" Ackerman asked, hoping for more about Alex.

When Ashley shared the next piece of information, she leaned forward and dropped her voice. "She talked about Priscilla, too," she told them, as if revealing a shocking secret. But neither detective must have looked sufficiently impressed because she added, almost impatiently, "I don't think you get it. *Nobody* around here dares to talk about Priscilla. They're always afraid she'll hear about it. But Julia didn't seem to care. She said that Priscilla was like a dictator from a tiny island in the South Pacific who acted like she ruled the entire world instead of just a tiny island."

Peters laughed.

Ackerman shot him a look.

"What?" Peters said.

Ackerman shook his head and turned back to Ashley. He wasn't interested in Priscilla. He was interested in Alex. He gave up hinting and asked directly, "So what did Julia say about her husband?"

Ashley smiled. "Now, that's the strange thing," she said. But then she stopped, obviously milking the drama.

"What's the strange thing?" Ackerman asked, trying to keep the impatience from his voice.

"Well, Julia had something bad to say about just about everyone—everyone except her husband. She *never* talked to me about him."

"Oh," Ackerman said, disappointed.

"But don't you see how weird that is? I mean, I love Stewart, but I complain about him all the time—to my girlfriends, not to him," she clarified quickly. "Like, he's a total slob, but I'm smart enough not to say anything to him. It's unnatural not to complain about your husband sometimes. So, for all that Julia told me, I don't think any of it is really useful to you guys—at least, not in getting Alex for the murder."

"Why do you think we're interested in *Alex* for murder?" Ackerman asked sharply.

"Well, if you're not, you should be."

"First of all, what makes you think it was a homicide? Secondly, do you know anything that makes you think that he did it?"

"Didn't Susan or Priscilla tell you about the branch?" Ashley asked.

"Yes, they both mentioned it," Ackerman said.

"That takes care of the murder part. And isn't it always the husband? I've read enough mysteries to know that the husband is always the number-one suspect."

Ackerman only barely held back a sigh. He thought he was on the verge of a real piece of information.

But then Ashley went on. "Besides, there was that thing that Alex said at their dinner party. It was a little strange at the time, but thinking of it now, it positively gives me the chills. It's like he wanted us—maybe wanted Julia—to know what he was going to do."

Both detectives sat up straighter at that.

"What did he say?" Ackerman demanded.

"Don't tell me that no one told you this yet? We were talking about our book club. Somebody, I think it was Susan's husband, Harry, said that we should be reading biographies because that would be useful. We'd learn something from it. But then Alex said that mysteries can be useful too . . . if you have a murder to solve. And *then* he said, 'You never know when that might happen.' "

"He said that? Are you sure?"

"Well, it was something like that," Ashley said breezily. "I remembered it almost right away when Sofie told us about the branch."

"You mean when Priscilla told you about the branch," Ackerman corrected her.

"Priscilla? Did she tell you that she noticed the branch?" Ashley laughed. "*Priscilla* didn't notice anything. It was Sofie."

"Sofie claimed she was the one who saw it?"

Ashley must have heard the skepticism in Ackerman's voice. "No. She told everyone—me, Susan, and Priscilla at the same time."

"It definitely wasn't Priscilla who noticed and maybe Sofie just repeated it?"

"No way," Ashley said firmly. "In fact, at first Priscilla was saying how ridiculous it was—the idea that Julia was murdered. She thought it was silly. I can't believe she tried to take credit for it."

"But we talked to Mrs. Altman about this too, and she didn't say anything about Sofie being the one who noticed the branch," Peters put in.

"That doesn't surprise me. Susan's totally under Priscilla's thumb. Besides, Susan hates any kind of conflict. She just wants to smooth everything over—so it doesn't shock me that she'd cover for Priscilla if only just to escape the unpleasantness of having to say that Priscilla lied. Sofie is the one you should be talking to. She's smarter than three of Priscilla Brenner."

"Well, she's next on the list," Ackerman said. "We'll see what she has to say."

Peters shook his head. "With the way things are going so far, we'll get yet another version of events."

Ashley turned to look at him. "You're a detective and you expect people to agree on how things happened?"

"She's got a point," Ackerman said.

"Of course I do." Ashley tossed her hair. "I told you I'm not stupid."

"Then maybe you can help me with something else," Ackerman said. "I'm doing today's crossword puzzle, and I'm stuck on this one clue. The clue is 'remote post.' Four letters. Any ideas?"

"He's a detective and expects everyone to tell the same story"— she jerked her head toward Peters—"and now you're asking me for help with your crossword? I'm going to let you figure that one out on your own, but since you guys seem to need a lot of help, I'll give you this advice: Keep your eye on that husband of Julia's. It's unnatural for a woman not to complain about her husband—there must have been something really wrong."

"She's a piece of work," Peters said on their way back out to the car. "She's almost as good as the first one. Can you imagine being married to a woman like that? In fact, they're all bonkers."

"I thought the second one, what was her name? Susan—I thought she was all right," Ackerman said.

"All right in comparison, maybe. But I don't trust people who have that much money and are that friendly. It's got to be fake."

"Anyone who loves dogs can't be so bad," Ackerman said.

"You think so? What would you say if I told you that Hitler loved dogs?"

"Did he?"

"Yes. Or at least he loved *his* dog. And anyway, it's not like that Susan woman was so honest with us either. She lied to cover for that friend of hers—Priscilla, the South Pacific dictator." Peters chuckled again at that. "Julia Stowe hit the nail on the head with that description. She seems like she was a smart lady. Smart and nasty."

"Susan Altman did say she could see someone killing Julia before she could see Julia killing herself. That was a rather vivid description of character," Ackerman agreed.

"True, but this last one, Betty Boop, gave us that that thing the husband said at dinner."

"That could be important in court," Ackerman agreed. "That's something that could influence a jury. It's just a little too much of a coincidence. I think he got cocky. I think he basically told everyone what he was going to do before he did it."

"*If* he said it," Peters pointed out. "You know about witness testimony. Notoriously unreliable. And don't you find it a little strange that neither of the other women remembered it?"

"We'll have to check with them. See if they remember it too."

"Do you want to do that now?"

"No, we'll go see Sofie Wright first and find out if she's as smart as Betty Boop seems to think she is."

31. Sofie & the Detectives

ofie met them at the door and ushered them into a room at the front of the house. At one glance Ackerman could tell it was the room for "company." It was filled with dark, formal, antique furniture, which was certainly very expensive—and very uncomfortable. While Priscilla's white living room made sense for her, and Susan's comfortable, dog-hair covered furniture was an obvious match, these stiff antiques somehow didn't jibe with the woman in front of him. She wasn't haughty like Priscilla, or welcoming like Susan, or provocative like Ashley. He couldn't quite get a sense of her yet.

She seated both detectives on a small couch—more like a love seat—and asked them if they would like some coffee. Ackerman opted for decaf this time to avoid caffeine overload.

Sofie disappeared to get the coffee—and she was gone quite a while. They saw the reason why when she returned with a tray. She'd brought the coffee, but there was also a plate of sandwiches—tomato and mozzarella, prosciutto and provolone, ham with melted Gruyere, and turkey with melted Brie. She put the tray on the low table in front of them, saying, "I thought you might be hungry by now—because I'm sure Priscilla and Ashley didn't give you anything to eat. And Susan probably gave you pie. Apple, maybe?"

"Pumpkin," Ackerman said. "Though apple is my favorite."

"She brought me key lime over the summer. The thing is, when I'm hungry, I can't really eat something sweet. I thought you might want something a little more filling. So I . . . well, I made these." She talked nervously, filling the silence as she poured them coffee.

"Thank you. These look great."

Peters picked up a prosciutto and provolone and took a bite. He chewed for a moment, then asked Sofie, "Is there sage in this?"

"Is there too much?" Sofie asked.

"No, not at all. It's just I never thought of adding sage."

"I probably wouldn't have either. There's a place I used to go in the city that added sage to their prosciutto sandwiches, and that's where I got the idea. I'm not like some people who can experiment and throw in random spices or ingredients they have lying around."

"I do that," Peters admitted. "But only because I can't be bothered to follow the directions. I just throw stuff in and cross my fingers. The thing is when I cook, half the time it's great, but the other half it's practically inedible unless I'm using ingredients I've already tried together. There's a book you should get—it tells about which spices go together and which don't and basically how people put recipes together. I'm trying to think of the name . . ."

Ackerman ate two sandwiches while Sofie and Peters were talking. Finally he had to interrupt. "Enough with the cooking talk," Ackerman said. "I feel like I'm trapped in one of those shows on the Food Network."

"Sorry," both Peters and Sofie apologized.

"If you don't mind, we have some questions for you," Ackerman said to Sofie. "But first I'd like to clear up a discrepancy that concerns you."

"Discrepancy?" Sofie echoed. "With *me*?"

"It's over who actually noticed the groove on the branch where Julia Stowe was hung."

"Oh, that," Sofie said.

"Priscilla Brenner said that she noticed it, and Susan Altman seemed to back that up. But Ashley Turkel says it was you. Which was it?"

"We both found the body . . . so I suppose we could have seen it at the same time. . . ."

Ackerman shook his head, letting her know that answer wasn't going to cut it. "According to Mrs. Turkel, Mrs. Brenner actually ridiculed you for suggesting it was a homicide instead of a suicide. That doesn't sound like you both noticed it at the same time."

Sofie hesitated, then admitted, "I was the one who noticed the branch. But I'd prefer if you didn't make a big deal about it—if that's all right."

Ackerman raised his eyebrows.

"I know," Sofie smiled apologetically. "I know it seems silly. But it will make my life a lot easier."

"What do you mean, easier?" he pressed.

"I mean with Priscilla."

"No insurgents allowed on this island," Peters commented.

"What?" Sofie looked at him.

"Nothing," Ackerman answered for Peters. "Don't pay attention to him."

"Thanks a lot," Peters said.

"We won't make a big deal about it," Ackerman told Sofie. "But that's on the condition that from now on, you come to us with anything you notice regarding this case. I noticed you didn't mention anything about your suspicions of it being a homicide when you talked to the police."

"But you figured it out," Sofie said. "You didn't need me to tell you that. By the way, how did you know?"

The other women hadn't thought to question what the detectives had discovered from the investigation—they had been too caught up in their own discoveries. But it looked like Sofie was different. Ackerman thought that he was going to have to be a bit more careful with her. He wanted to make sure that he was the one asking the questions. "As far as I'm concerned, we still don't know for sure if it's a homicide," Ackerman said evasively. "Now, I'd like to start out by asking you a bit more about the branch," he said. "Did you notice it right away?"

"No, not right away," Sofie said slowly.

"When?"

"It was after we told Alex, and he went back into the house to call 911."

"Was there something that triggered you? Do you remember what you were thinking when it occurred to you?"

Sofie's eyes seemed to fix themselves on an indistinct point in front of her as if she were looking back in time at the scene itself. Then she started to describe it.

"Priscilla was talking. She said to me, 'I wonder why she did it.'

I was looking at Julia, and all of a sudden I saw the groove in the bark and I said to Priscilla, 'I don't think she did.' "

"So you noticed it even before the police arrived. Why didn't you mention anything about it when you were interviewed?"

"I mentioned something to Priscilla, but she laughed at me. So I thought maybe I was blowing a little detail way out of proportion. My husband always accuses me of being a conspiracy theorist and seeing hidden motives everywhere," she admitted.

Ackerman had met a lot of conspiracy theorists in his time, but this woman didn't seem like the type.

"Was there anything else that made you think it might not be a suicide?" Ackerman asked her.

"Yes, I suppose the way her husband reacted made me think something was strange about the whole situation."

"What was strange about it?"

Sofie took a few seconds to answer. When she finally spoke she said, "A better question is what *wasn't* strange about it. I can't seem to figure it out. . . ." She was silent for a moment, then she shrugged. "Anyway, Julia's husband's reaction wasn't the only thing that was strange. I thought it was even stranger that Julia chose to hang herself in the front yard. That just didn't seem to be like her. But of course it made sense if she was murdered."

"How do you figure that?" Ackerman asked.

"I know that sounds crazy, but I can explain," Sofie said. "About a week ago I was at a dinner at Ashley's house, and at a certain point while we were sitting around having drinks, Priscilla and Julia got into a discussion. Priscilla was talking about Halloween and what her decorator had planned for her yard. She was describing these little ghosts that she was going to put in the trees around her house. They're up now, did you see them?"

"Yes, I saw them," Ackerman said. Then he added, "Very nice," since Sofie seemed to be waiting for some other response.

"Well, Priscilla was excited about it, and she was telling everyone about the design, and Julia started laughing—and not in a nice way. So Priscilla asked Julia what she was laughing about. That's when

Julia told her that she thought it sounded hideous, and that Priscilla might as well hang corpses in the yard."

"I remember Mrs. Brenner mentioned something about her Halloween decorations when I was interviewing her, but I didn't understand the relevance," Peters interjected.

Sofie nodded. "When Priscilla saw something that looked like a corpse hanging in Julia's yard, she thought that Julia had put it there to make fun of her decorations. So she went charging up to take it down."

"So you think there's a connection there?" Ackerman asked. "Between that conversation at the party and the fact that Julia was hung in her front yard?"

"*And* that Priscilla would probably see the body," Sofie added. "She goes out on a walk every morning, and everyone knows it."

"I see," Ackerman said. "You think it's all connected."

"I think it could be."

"So do you remember who was at this party and overheard that conversation?"

"Priscilla and Julia were there. And their husbands. Plus Ashley and her husband. And Susan and Harry, and me and Dean. And I'm pretty sure that everyone was in the room."

"So Alex Stowe was definitely there and overheard that conversation?"

"Yes, he was there too."

"You seem to have thought a lot about this."

"I . . . well, it's sort of a hobby of mine. I read a lot of mysteries. And I was thinking of trying to write one, but I haven't gotten very far."

"When's the last time your husband accused you of coming up with a conspiracy theory?" Ackerman asked on impulse.

"Other than this murder? A few months ago. When we were buying this house. I told him I thought the real estate agent had put a bug in the kitchen and was listening to our conversation."

"And?"

"My husband asked her to walk him through the upstairs again, and I found it under the counter."

Ackerman nodded thoughtfully. "By the way," he said, remembering something else, "were you at the other party where they were talking about the usefulness of reading mysteries?"

"I'm not sure. Can you be more specific?"

"Apparently Harry Altman was talking about how your book club should be reading biographies because they would have a much more practical application." Ackerman paused, waiting for recognition from Sofie.

Sofie shook her head.

"And Ashley Turkel told us that Alex said that mysteries can be useful too when there's a murder to solve—and you never know when that's going to happen."

Sofie looked up sharply.

"Interesting, isn't it?"

"Strange," Sofie murmured.

"It's a word that seems to be getting a lot of use in this investigation," Peters observed.

"You see a lot of strange things in this profession," Ackerman said. "The fact is, a lot of the time people simply aren't logical. As a detective, you think, why did they do this or that or say this or that—but really you can't know. Sometimes because you don't have all the information, but sometimes simply because they don't know themselves. Thanks goodness we don't have to figure everything out. All we have to do is find out who did it."

"And that part's not too hard," Peters said.

"You already know who did it?" Sofie asked.

Ackerman shot a look at Peters then tried to cover. "What Peters means is that if you look at the percentages, it's usually the person closest to the victim who turns out to be the perp. Serial killers, though they get a lot of press, are statistically very rare. When you're a detective, you see that ninety percent of the time, it's the obvious suspect, and in this case, the obvious suspect is the husband."

"But you can't just go by the percentages," Sofie protested. "Because even though I'm sure you're right, and it is the most obvious suspect ninety percent of the time, it's still someone else ten percent of the time. And ten percent is a lot if you think about it. If you go on that assumption, ten innocent people out of a hundred would be wrongly convicted."

"Hold your horses, no one's getting convicted yet," Ackerman said. "I promise we won't just go on percentages. In the meantime, you could help by giving us your husband's phone number, as we'll want to speak with him as well. And here's my card. Call me if you notice anything—even if Priscilla tells you it's ridiculous. All right?"

"OK," Sofie agreed.

Ackerman glanced down and saw that between them, he and Peters had polished off all the sandwiches. "Thank you for the food. It was delicious."

Sofie looked pleased. "You're welcome."

"I guess that's it for today, unless . . . do you happen to do crossword puzzles?"

"A little," Sofie said—and smiled. It was a smile Ackerman would come to recognize as the sign of a gross understatement.

"I'm having trouble with one of the clues from today's puzzle."

"Let me see," Sofie said, holding her hand out for the paper.

He fished it out of his pocket and handed it over.

"Which one?" Sofie asked.

"Number three down. The clue is 'remote post.' Four letters."

Sofie stared down at the puzzle, frowned, and shook her head slightly.

"No?" Ackerman said. He'd thought Sofie would certainly pass the test. "No ideas?"

"What?" Sofie looked up. "Oh, no. Or rather I mean yes. Three down is sofa. I remember that one because it made me laugh. That's certainly my husband's 'remote post'."

"If you know the answer, what was it you were frowning about?"

Sofie hesitated. "I don't want to be rude."

"Not at all," Ackerman said.

"Well, I did the puzzle earlier today. And I just noticed what you put in for two down."

"What's the clue?"

" 'Were up to date,' " Sofie read.

Ackerman leaned over. "That's right. I remember. I put in 'apt.' "

"Right," Sofie said. "It seems to fit."

"Did you have something different?" Ackerman asked rather skeptically.

"Umm, yes. I thought of apt at first too, but did you notice that the wording of the clue is a little awkward?"

"So what did you come up with?"

"The word 'are.' Because it's present tense of the verb 'were.' See? Were up to date? And you'll see that fits when you fill in thirteen across."

Ackerman stared down at the puzzle.

"It's a tricky one," she said apologetically.

"She got you on that one," Peters said as they left Sofie's house and walked down the walk to the car. "You should have seen your face when she told you you'd got an answer wrong. She beat you at your own game."

"She did, didn't she?" Ackerman smiled.

"What did you think of her idea about the location of the body?"

"I thought it was pretty interesting," Ackerman admitted. "Something to keep in mind."

"Did you notice she didn't claim she knew something when she didn't. Like the whole thing with Julia's husband and how strange he was acting. She didn't pretend to be able to make any sense of it. If he did it, why wouldn't he at least pretend he thought it was a suicide? It would cover his tracks and explain away any physical evidence he might have left."

"What do you mean, *if* he did it? He did it."

"I know. But it *would* be more exciting it there were something more to it. I'm as bad as all these mystery-reading housewives. They're probably dying for a little excitement."

"One of them did die," Ackerman pointed out. "But I don't think a little excitement was the reason."

32. Priscilla

$\mathcal{E}$veryone ended up gathering at Priscilla's house that night—at least, almost everyone. Of course Julia wasn't there, and they didn't invite Alex, and Susan made an excuse for Harry (though the truth was she still hadn't heard from him). But everyone else was there: Ashley and Stewart, Priscilla and Gordon, Sofie and Dean, and Susan.

For once Priscilla was more interested in talking to the other women than to Dean. He tried to get her to mix drinks with him again, but she put him off. She didn't even notice his look of annoyance because she was already hurrying over to the corner where Susan, Ashley, and Sofie were waiting.

When she drew a chair up to join the little circle, there was a little break in the conversation, and Priscilla jumped right in. "So Detective Ackerman really thinks I can help," she announced. She looked around, but she didn't get the response she was looking for. "He does," she insisted. "When he was leaving, he even asked me to help him solve his crossword puzzle."

That got a response. Everyone looked up at her.

"What?" Priscilla asked, sensing something. "What did I say?"

"He asked me to help him with a clue too," Ashley said, enjoying the disappointment that showed on Priscilla's face.

"Me too," Susan admitted.

They looked to Sofie, and she nodded.

"*What* clue did he ask you?" Priscilla said suspiciously.

"The clue was 'remote post,' " Susan replied.

"That's the same one he asked me!" Priscilla exclaimed. "And he went to see you *after* I gave him the answer, so I don't see why he asked you the same question."

"He's testing us," Sofie said. "He wants to see how we think. Why else would he ask everyone the answer to the same clue?"

"That's pretty clever," Susan said, smiling.

"I'd say it's pretty sneaky," Priscilla countered. She turned to Susan. "What did you come up with?"

"I wasn't very clever. I said Siam. I found out later it didn't fit."

"What did *you* tell him the answer was?" Priscilla asked, turning to Ashley.

"I told him that he was the detective, and if he couldn't figure it out, he was in trouble," Ashley said.

"You mean you didn't know the answer," Priscilla said.

"Not a clue," Ashley admitted.

"It was a tough one," Priscilla said, attempting to be generous.

"So you didn't get it right either," Ashley concluded.

"No, I did."

"What was it then?"

"Blog. Someone posts a blog on the Internet remotely. From their computer."

"I don't think so," Susan said. "I'm pretty sure the answer started with an 's'. Did you fill in the rest of the puzzle?"

Priscilla didn't want to admit that she hadn't bothered.

"What did you say, Sofie?" Ashley asked.

"Um. I thought the answer was 'sofa.' "

"What does that have to do with—," Priscilla started to say, then she got the pun. "Oh."

"I don't think it was a big deal," Sofie said. "It's just the answer to a clue in a crossword puzzle. It's not the answer to who killed Julia."

"Well *that* one's not hard," Ashley said. "It's Alex. He basically told us that he was going to do it."

Now all the attention was on Ashley.

"What? What do you mean he told us he was going to do it?" Priscilla demanded.

"Oh, that's right—the detectives were surprised you didn't tell them about this."

"About what?"

"Don't you remember when we went to Julia's house for dinner and we were talking about reading mysteries? Harry said we should read biographies because they were much more practical than mysteries, and then Alex said that you never know when you might have a murder to solve."

Priscilla's mouth opened in a silent O.

"I'm not sure I remember it exactly like that," Susan said. "I think it might have been Harry who mentioned murder, and then Alex just said that you never know."

"What difference does that make?" Ashley said. "It's pretty much the same thing."

"Not really," Susan said. "It means that Alex didn't bring up murder at all."

"But he said you never knew when it might happen."

"I took that to mean you never know what's going to happen in general—not that you never know when someone is going to be murdered. Besides, it can't be Alex who did it. It's too obvious."

"This isn't like a crossword puzzle, Susan," Priscilla said. "There's no one orchestrating this, trying to get us to guess the obvious answer."

"Well . . . that's not necessarily true," Sofie said.

"What, you think that someone is orchestrating this? Don't be ridiculous," Priscilla scoffed.

Ashley pointed out, "You thought the thing with the branch was ridiculous too. So I want to hear what Sofie has to say."

Priscilla glared at Ashley.

"I'm sure what Priscilla meant was that it *seems* ridiculous—which it does," Sofie said, trying to smooth things over.

"That's exactly what I meant," Priscilla said.

Ashley snorted, earning herself another glare.

"OK," Sofie said. "So Alex is the most likely person. I think we all agree on that. But what's his motive? Why did he kill his wife?"

"He couldn't stand her?" Ashley suggested.

"All right," Sofie said. "That's possible. But why kill her? Why not just get a divorce? Or was she the one with the money?"

"Oh, no," Ashley said. "She came from some tiny town in the Midwest. I think her father was a butcher or something awful like that. The money all came from Alex."

"So why not get a divorce, then?"

"Maybe they had a fight, and he killed her and then tried to make it look like suicide," Susan suggested. "I think Alex could do it. I can see him strangling someone."

They all looked to Sofie to see what she would say to that. She shook her head. "That doesn't necessarily mean anything. The thing is, I think a lot of people are capable of killing someone—probably a lot more than you think. So just because he *could* doesn't necessarily mean he *did*. And the idea that they got in a fight and he accidentally killed her doesn't fit. When you strangle someone you have to press pretty hard. It would have left bruises that would have been visible. The rope wouldn't cover those bruises because that was right up under her chin—not actually around her neck."

"What about smothering her with a pillow?" Susan said.

Sofie looked at Susan appraisingly. "I hadn't thought of that. Yes, you're right, that wouldn't leave any bruises around the neck. And Julia wasn't exactly a big person, so it wouldn't have been too difficult to hold her down. The only problem with that theory is that it's not how you would kill someone in the heat of passion. Can you see them fighting and then, in the middle of the argument, he suddenly throws her down and grabs a pillow? Doesn't seem likely, does it? No, he'd grab her by the neck or bash her head against the wall—something dramatic and violent. He wouldn't be thinking about the fact that he shouldn't leave any marks. If you think about it that way, smothering her with a pillow is something he would have done at night, while she was sleeping. Which leads us to the same conclusion."

"Which is?" Ashley prompted.

Sofie looked around at the group. "Whoever did this planned it out beforehand."

They were all silent for a moment, thinking about that.

Sofie went on. "Where did the rope come from? Where did the chair come from? Why did whoever killed her hang her outside? And why did they kill her in the first place? If this ever goes to court, this is going to be a case that's tried on circumstantial evidence. Detective Ackerman knows it. That's why he's talking to us—and why he's going to *keep* talking to us."

"What about the forensics?" Priscilla said. "Like hair and fibers and all that CSI stuff?"

"You still need supporting evidence. There have been plenty of trials where the physical evidence was there, but they still couldn't convince a jury. But you're right. It should get interesting when they get the results from the autopsy and the crime lab."

At that moment, Stewart called out, "Are you girls going to sit over there gossiping all night?"

The men had obviously run out of conversation.

They reluctantly got up and went over to join their husbands.

About ten minutes later, when they were all standing together still discussing Julia's death, Priscilla felt a touch on her elbow. She turned and saw that Dean was passing behind her. At first she thought he'd brushed her by accident, but then he glanced back at her and she knew that it hadn't been an accident. She turned back to the group and for the next few minutes she pretended to listen, but really she didn't hear a word. She was just waiting long enough to be able to follow Dean. She was sure that's what he'd meant by that little touch.

When she couldn't stand it anymore, she murmured, "I'm going to go check on Danielle, see where she is with those appetizers," even though Priscilla had specifically instructed her to wait to bring out the food. It was always a better party when people got drunk, and they got drunk quicker if they didn't have food to eat right away.

She did go first into the kitchen, and she told Danielle that she could start bringing out the appetizers. But then instead of returning to the living room Priscilla slipped into the hallway. It was dark, but she didn't want to turn on the lights. She started to make her way down the hall, and just as she was passing the door to Gordon's study, a hand reached out and Dean pulled her inside. He swung her around against the wall and pressed up against her, his lips finding her mouth.

When he finally drew back, he looked down at her intently. "I've been waiting a long time to do that," he said.

"So why did you wait so long?" she asked.

"That's a good question," he said as he leaned in to brush his lips softly against her neck.

"I wasn't even sure you liked me," she told him.

"I think it's a little more serious than that," he murmured, moving lower to kiss the base of her throat. Then he pulled the collar of her shirt aside to kiss her collarbone. "You drive me crazy."

"In a good way?"

"What do you think?" he asked, trailing his fingers along her neck and down over her breast then along her side. When he reached her waist, he hooked them just inside the top of her pants, his fingertips brushing her skin. Her breath caught as his fingers tickled her stomach.

It was too fast. Priscilla felt out of control, and the feeling scared her. She had to say something. Anything. So she said the first thing that came into her mind.

"What about Sofie?"

"What about her?" he said, his hand sliding lower.

"What if she finds out?"

"Don't worry about Sofie," Dean said, his voice low, persuasive as he took his hand out to unbutton her pants. "She's clueless. Even if she walked in on us now, she'd probably just apologize and back out. I can do whatever I want. She wouldn't say a thing." He eased open her zipper.

"So you don't love her?"

"What do you think?" Dean whispered as he slid his hand back inside.

And at that point, Priscilla couldn't answer.

33. The Detectives

Ackerman and Peters reported to the morgue early the next morning for the autopsy. They were there at eight thirty, dressed in scrubs and masks, when the body, still enclosed in the white plastic body bag, was taken from the refrigerated storage.

Whenever Ackerman attended an autopsy he always thought that the autopsy room had the feel of a men's shower room because of the tile floor interspersed with drains. But no men's shower room had anything like the massive stainless-steel autopsy table. It, like the floor, had perforations as well as a second level catch-basin.

Ackerman dreaded the autopsies, but he always went because it was part of the job. Some people wouldn't understand how he could be fine with a crime scene but be bothered by the morgue. But in a crime scene it was all right there to see—the violence, the horror, the tragedy. In the morgue it was all cleaned up and sanitized, but it was still there, underneath. Sort of like buying ground chuck all packed up in Styrofoam and plastic wrap and pretending it didn't come from a cow.

But what bothered him even more than the clinical nature of the violence was the manner of the people observing. Sometimes there were upward of ten people in the room during an autopsy: other police officers who worked the crime scene, an assistant DA, the police photographer, and sometimes a medical student in to observe. More often than not the group watching was made up of men, and there was a macho atmosphere as if everyone were trying to show how little they were affected by the gruesome scene in front of them. They made jokes and laughed and they made a point of going out to eat afterward—usually to an Italian restaurant where they would order big plates of spaghetti and meatballs. If a rookie by chance didn't eat, he'd be sure to hear about it at the station for weeks. Ackerman knew that it was just their way of dealing with the brutal reality that a person had been killed and was now being dissected on a table in front of them, but it still made him uncomfortable. Whenever he had the opportunity, he tried to limit the number of people present for the autopsy. This time he had been successful, and there were only four of them in the room: Ackerman, Peters, the medical examiner, and the diener (the medical examiner's assistant). The early hour might also have had something to do with the limited attendance.

The diener unzipped the bag and released the smell, and both Ackerman and Peters put on their masks. Then the medical examiner searched the bag for trace evidence. That was the reason the bag was white—so evidence would be easier to detect. For extra protection of potential evidence, the body was wrapped in a white sheet as well. When that was unwound, the first thing the medical examiner did was to listen for a heartbeat. Everyone had heard the stories of the body that woke up on the autopsy table. It wasn't myth. It had happened. Even though one look at Julia's face showed quite clearly that there was no possibility that she was still alive, procedure ruled—both at the crime scene and during the autopsy. It was how they ensured against careless mistakes. The tags had to be checked to make sure it was the right body, the height measured, weight estimated, and photographs taken. Finally the paper bags that had been tied around the hands and feet were removed and the investigative work began.

The medical examiner was meticulous. He made note of everything—jewelry; the color, size, and make of clothing; whether buttons were undone; the purplish color of the skin on the face; any bruises or scrapes—everything went on record. Then came time to pick trace evidence off the body. It was an excruciatingly slow process, with every hair and fiber going into a separate envelope, but it was ultimately productive. The medical examiner showed the detectives several hairs that obviously did not belong to the victim before depositing them carefully into their own envelopes.

The nightgown was removed and the body examined. X-rays were taken and finally the first cut: the Y incision. Samples of blood and urine were collected and sent off to toxicology, then each organ was removed and weighed on the scale and more samples were taken. Lastly the medical examiner used the circular saw to cut through the skull to examine the brain. At the end of the autopsy the deiner returned the organs to the body cavity and sewed up the incisions.

They had to wait for the results from the lab on the hair and fiber and blood work, but in his preliminary findings the medical examiner ruled that the cause of death was asphyxia by hanging. However, the ME had noted some possible bruising around the mouth. And that's why Ackerman and Peters were back at the precinct, anxiously awaiting the toxicology report. It could be the answer to the still-open question: suicide or homicide.

The detectives had returned to the office to do paperwork, but they were both listening for the phone. When it finally rang, Peters managed to grab it first. While Peters was listening and saying, "Uh-huh. Yes. I understand," Ackerman was trying to figure out how to pick up on the same line. But before he managed it, Peters had hung up and announced, "It's official."

"What's official?" Ackerman demanded.

"Homicide. No doubt about it."

"I knew it," Ackerman said. "What did they find?"

"Chloroform in her blood in amounts high enough that they were able to determine that when Julia would have been hanging herself from that tree . . . how do I say this? She would have been out cold. Stringing a rope up and hanging yourself while unconscious? Now, that's a suicide I'd like to see."

34. Priscilla & Susan

*P*riscilla was in high spirits, and the weather mirrored her mood. Overnight a balmy southern wind had blown in, bringing with it a perfect Indian summer day. She was sitting outside on the terrace, waiting impatiently for Susan to arrive. The breeze was just strong enough to ruffle her hair, and it brought the leaves swirling down around her like huge, colorful snowflakes.

Finally Susan appeared around the corner of the house.

"Priscilla?" she called.

"Up here."

Susan climbed the steps leading up from the lawn.

"I'm glad you called," Priscilla said

"Well, I needed to talk to you."

"I need to talk to you, *too*," Priscilla exclaimed.

Susan took the chair next to Priscilla's and she opened her mouth to speak, but Priscilla beat her to it.

"By the way, what was up with Ashley last night?" Priscilla said.

"What about Ashley?"

"Don't tell me you didn't notice how she was acting? She was positively rude."

Susan didn't know what to say, because she hadn't actually noticed. The night before she had worked hard at trying to participate in the conversation, but her mind kept slipping back to Harry. Where was he? When would he call? Or would he just show up? He couldn't be leaving her. He wouldn't do that. Not Harry. She told herself that over and over—but more to stave off panic than because she really believed it was true. So she had been too preoccupied to notice any difference in Ashley's manner.

"I suppose she was a little outspoken," Susan said, thinking back to the conversation.

"Rude," Priscilla corrected. "I think I know why she's acting like this. She's upset because she's losing her looks. Haven't you noticed that she's gained weight? I'm as sympathetic as the next person. Lord knows when I gained a bit a few years ago, I felt awful until I lost it again, but I certainly didn't take it out on other people. She has to know she can't behave this way, and if she thinks that I won't kick her out of the group just because there's only four of us, she's wrong."

"You shouldn't let her get to you," Susan said.

"Oh, I won't. And anyway, that's not what's really bothering me. I'm glad you came over. I needed to talk to somebody."

"Is it the Julia thing? I mean, finding her like that and everything?" Susan asked sympathetically.

"What? Oh—no. It's not that. I mean that was awful. But I'm talking about something worse."

"What's worse than finding your friend hanging from a tree?"

"I think I'm in love."

Susan was silent for a moment. Then she said quietly, "You're right. That is worse."

Priscilla waited, but Susan didn't continue.

"That's it? That's all you have to say?" Priscilla demanded.

"Is it . . . Dean?" Susan ventured.

"Of course it's Dean."

"Does Sofie know?"

"What, you think I discussed this with her or something?"

"No, I didn't mean that. I meant . . . it's just that Sofie seems to notice things. Like the branch. So I just thought she might have, I don't know, sensed something?"

"Last night did it look like she 'sensed' something?" Priscilla asked sarcastically.

"No," Susan admitted.

"She's not a real detective, you know. She noticed a few things. That's it. You make it seem like she's got extrasensory perception. Sometimes people can be smart about one thing and incredibly stupid about something else. But what are we doing talking about Sofie, anyway? That's what Gordon always does to me. When I try to talk to him about a problem I'm having, he's all worried about someone else. How do you think that makes me feel?"

And, just like Gordon, Susan apologized immediately. "I'm sorry."

"So do you want to hear this or not?"

"Of course," she said automatically. Really the last thing Susan wanted to do right then was to listen to Priscilla talk about her affair. It struck right at the heart of Susan's own tortured imaginings— she pictured Harry in some romantic restaurant in New York, in a dark, secluded booth with some young, beautiful woman, and they were laughing and holding hands and obviously very much in love.

"It's so crazy, but it feels like I've known him forever. And the chemistry . . ."

"So you slept with him?"

"Of course not. We only had a few minutes alone. But it was more intimate and personal than any sex could ever be."

Susan thought that Priscilla must never have had really good sex, but she kept that thought to herself.

Priscilla went on, "I can't stop thinking about him. Before I was telling myself that it was just a fun thing. You know, just a break from regular life. A break from Gordon. A little excitement, a little romance. But now . . . Susan," she paused and took a deep breath. "I would leave Gordon to be with him. I mean, I want to."

Susan started to say something, but Priscilla rushed on. "I know, believe me, I know what you're going to say, Susan. But just listen. Gordon's a wonderful person. I know that. They don't come better than Gordon. But we're just not right for each other anymore. We probably never were. He's more like a best friend than a husband. I want something more."

When Priscilla finally stopped for a breath, Susan got a chance to speak. "But you barely know Dean. You and Gordon have been together for fifteen years, and you've seen Dean . . . how many times? How can you even compare them?"

Priscilla shook her head, annoyed. "That's exactly my point. I've been with Gordon forever, and I just met Dean, and I feel so much closer to him. I feel like he knows me so much better than Gordon does."

Listening to Priscilla go on about the bond she felt with Dean—and especially hearing her compare and dismiss her husband of more than a decade—Susan felt something rising within her. At first she could barely identify the sensation—she hadn't felt it in so long. It was anger. And when Priscilla finally paused, Susan couldn't stop it from coming out. "Sometimes you're so stupid, Priscilla," she burst out. "I can't believe you're thinking of leaving Gordon. After everything you and Gordon have been through together. And the idea that you're closer to Dean—that he knows more about you than Gordon does—well, you know how you always tell other people they're being ridiculous. That's beyond ridiculous."

Priscilla stood up, the legs of the chair screeching across the wood. "I don't let anyone speak to me that way."

"Oh, sure. You don't let anyone else speak to you that way, but you do it to other people all the time."

"Why are you attacking me like this?" Priscilla gripped the back of the chair as if she needed the support to remain standing.

"Everything isn't always about you, you know," Susan said.

"But that's what we were talking about—me."

"That's *always* what we're talking about. You. Your life. Your problems."

"If that's the way you feel, why are you even my friend at all?"

"That's a good question," Susan shot back.

"Then what are you still doing here?" Priscilla asked.

"I have no idea."

Then Susan carefully pushed back her chair, gathered up her purse, and without another word, walked down the terrace onto the lawn and around the corner of the house. She was shaking as she left, and she burst into tears almost as soon as she was out of sight, but she didn't even consider going back.

35. Alex

"So, what have you heard?" Alex asked as he settled himself in the chair across from Ruth's desk.

Ruth Zimmerman was an old friend, not to mention one of the most respected—and feared—criminal attorneys in the state of Connecticut. Alex had called Ruth the moment he found Ackerman on his doorstep. She'd advised him not to talk. Then she said would get on the phone and find out what she could, and he should come into her office first thing the next morning.

As he sat across from her, he tilted the chair onto two legs and put his feet up on her desk.

"Hey, get your feet off of there," she said, swatting at the soles of his shoes with her newspaper.

"I don't pay you enough that I can put my feet up?"

"No, not on this desk. It's an antique," she told him.

"Ah," he took his feet off. "I thought it was an imitation. I didn't know you could afford a seventeenth-century Queen Anne desk."

"Oh, you're so smart. You *would* know something like that. Fine, you win—it's an imitation. Put your feet up."

Alex grinned and put his feet back up on the desk and asked again, "So what have you got for me?" Then, seeing the look on her face, he said, "Is your news the real reason why you're letting me put my feet up."

"Did you expect me to have good news?"

"No, of course not. I'm talking to a lawyer, aren't I?"

"Not just a lawyer, a criminal lawyer. Being a criminal lawyer is kind of like being an oncologist. If we're talking, it's probably bad news.

"OK, enough with the metaphors. What's going on?"

"It doesn't look good. Officially they're still calling it a suicide, but that's just for the press. The truth is they think it's homicide, and they're coming after you."

"That fucking Ackerman's got it in for me."

"With good reason. You have to admit, with your history you can't blame him for suspecting you."

"Whose side are you on?"

"The wrong side—as usual," she said with an exaggerated sigh, making Alex laugh.

Ruth Zimmerman was about sixty. She had been doing criminal law for more than thirty years and had been at the top of her profession for almost as long. She had managed to make it to the top through a combination of fierce intelligence, relentlessness, and humor. It was the last that made her so popular with the juries, but also made her somewhat unpopular with her clients. People facing criminal charges didn't usually like to laugh about it. Alex was an exception.

"Just as long as it's not the losing side," Alex said.

"We can cross our fingers."

"Hopefully you have a bit more strategy in mind than that," he said wryly.

"First we have to see what we're up against. They're going to go after a search warrant for your house and grounds and maybe even your office."

"But they already went through the house."

"I guess they want another look."

She read something in Alex's face. "What? Did you do something?" she demanded.

He shrugged. "I took all Julia's clothes and put them in garbage bags."

"Why on earth did you do that?"

"I was angry."

"Did you throw them out?"

"Not yet."

Ruth heaved a sigh of relief. "Thank God. Take them out and hang up every single item. I even want you to fold every goddamn piece of underwear—and I want you to do it yourself. Don't have your maid to do it because then she'd be able to testify that you had all the clothes packed up in garbage bags. You're a smart man. You have to start using your head. We're not just managing evidence. We're managing opinion. Because that's essentially what it comes down to. The opinions of twelve people."

"Then I'm doomed."

"That's not true. You can be very charming when you want to be. And people often choose to believe what they want to believe, regardless of the evidence. So we'll just have to get some women on that jury. Now for the other news."

"There's more?"

"They're not just going for the search warrant. They want samples of skin and hair. If they find samples on the body, they want to be able to match it." She looked at him. "It might be better to fight them on this than have them be able to match hairs and blood to you."

There was a long pause. Then, in exasperation, Ruth said, "I'm asking you if we should fight them on this, Alex."

"Oh, come on, Ruth. The only way I could guarantee that they wouldn't find anything is if I vacuumed her off after I killed her. *Of course* there's a chance they'll be able to match some hairs. She was my wife. We lived in the same house. Can you say for sure that sitting here right now, you don't have some of your husband's hairs on your jacket? Or a piece of fiber from his coat that rubbed off when you gave him a kiss this morning before coming to work?"

"Actually, yes, I can. I know because he moved out of the house about two months ago," Ruth said.

"Oh. I'm sorry . . ."

Ruth waved a hand. "Don't be. But I see your point. So we'll fight them."

"That won't look good either," Alex pointed out. "And think about how great it would be if the hairs *didn't* belong to me."

"Who would they belong to?"

Alex shot her a disgusted look. "They'd belong to the guy who killed her. You have to at least consider the fact that I didn't do it. Don't you remember? I told you she had a lover."

"Right. I remember you telling me that. But honestly, Alex, you have no proof. You even hired a private investigator who couldn't come up with anything. I mean, what are the chances that your wife is having an affair, and an investigator can't find any evidence of it?"

"The only thing that proves is that my wife was smarter than the gumshoe. Doesn't it look like it was serious if I actually hired someone?"

"No. It looks like you were jealous and paranoid. At least that's how the prosecution is going to paint it, and without any evidence that's probably how the jury is going to see it too. It's actually ammunition against us because it gives you motive. So you'd better find out who this mystery man is."

"How am I supposed to do that?"

"*You* look this time. Go through her things."

"I've gone through her things before."

"Go through everything again. Maybe you overlooked something. Maybe she got careless."

"I was thinking I might try talking to her friends. I thought they might know something."

"That will be a bit awkward, won't it?"

"They don't know the police think it's a homicide. As far as they're concerned, I'm the grieving widower."

"But the detectives have been to see them, right?"

"They wouldn't say anything if they're trying to keep the investigation under wraps."

"They might have said enough to create some suspicion. Let me

ask you this. Do you have a fridge full of food from neighbors bringing dishes over? A ton of messages on your answering machine?"

"Actually, no," Alex said.

"Then they know something."

"Damn. You're probably right."

"So don't you think it would be a little awkward to go to them
asking about your wife?"

"It would be more awkward to get twenty-five to life for murder,
wouldn't you say?"

"Good point. You do what you think best. But back to the issue
of giving samples—what do you want to do? Should I try to stall
them? It could be a big piece of the case, so I can't decide for you."

Alex considered for a moment. "Well, if we fight it and lose *and*
the samples match, that would be pretty bad. But if I volunteer and
the samples match, we can always use the husband-wife excuse.
Plus, if the samples don't match, then that's big. Right?"

"Right."

"OK. I'm a gambling man. Let's do it."

"You sure?"

"Your confidence is underwhelming," Alex said.

"Experience has taught me to be a pessimist."

"So your experience tells you I did it?"

She looked at him. "Let me give you another piece of advice that
I've learned as a lawyer: Don't ask a question when you don't really
want the answer."

36. Alex

$\mathcal{I}$t took Alex all afternoon to rehang and refold Julia's clothes.
Ruth instructed him that he should make everything look as
natural as possible. At the time Alex remarked that if Ruth really
wanted things to appear natural, then he could just dump the trash

bags onto the floor of the closet, as that was its natural state before the maid got to it.

"Ah, but I said it needed to *appear* natural," Ruth shot back. "Not *be* natural. It's not at all the same thing."

So Alex obediently hung and folded neatly, but not too neatly. In the process of restoring Julia's closet, he came across at least a dozen pieces with the tags still on them, obviously never worn. Others, however, hadn't been cleaned, and he could smell her scent on them. Smell was a powerful trigger, and Julia's scent brought a rush of emotion: He felt an overwhelming surge of frustration and rage.

As he put the clothes back he also took the opportunity to do something he should have thought of when he dumped them in the garbage bags: he checked all the pockets. He found odds and ends: the card of a restaurant in the city, a receipt from Barneys, another one from La Perla, a few twenties, two lipsticks (both a bright, aggressive red), and a single diamond stud. Then he checked her coat pockets, her jewelry chest, he flipped through the pages of the three books on the bedside table—all mysteries from that book group. He flipped through, but nothing fell out from the pages.

Julia didn't have any files because she hadn't had to do any paperwork. Alex handled the bills and the taxes and the important documents like passports and birth certificates. All she had were stacks of *Vogue* and *Harper's* and *W*. There was no diary. There was only one computer in the house, and the police had confiscated it. But he knew there was nothing on it. He'd hired a computer expert to try to retrieve the Web history and discover Julia's mail account. But she must have gotten some expert advice as well, because the computer hadn't stored any history of browsing except for the Web sites that he regularly visited. The technician told him that she might have purchased a device called a memory stick. With a memory stick, he explained, you could plug it into the USB port on a computer and set it so the sites visited and files downloaded would be recorded on it instead of the computer's hard drive. The memory stick itself was tiny—about the size of your pinky finger—and Alex had searched for it but hadn't found it.

Alex knew it was time to implement the next plan of attack. It was too late to do it that day, but he decided that early the next morning he would visit his wife's friends. And he knew where he had to start.

37. Sofie & Priscilla

*T*he next morning Sofie found herself sitting in Priscilla's living room, which she had started calling (though only to herself) the sanitarium. The stark white made her think of the padded white rooms they always showed in old movies when someone went crazy and they put them in a straightjacket.

Priscilla had called her the night before and asked her to come over for coffee. Sofie had been there a quarter of an hour, though it felt more like an hour, and Priscilla was well into her rant.

"I just don't understand it. I swear, I think everyone's going crazy. Didn't you think Ashley was rude the other night?" Priscilla asked, and not for the first time.

"It did seem like she was trying to provoke you," Sofie agreed automatically.

"It did, didn't it? That's exactly what I thought. Can you believe that Susan said she didn't really notice anything?"

"Susan seemed a bit distracted," Sofie offered in Susan's defense.

"I haven't even told you yet what happened with Susan," Priscilla replied.

"Something happened with Susan?" Sofie tried to sound surprised, but really she had been expecting something like this. When Priscilla called, Sofie knew there must be a reason she had been summoned instead of Susan. She felt tired at the very thought of having to fill Susan's role. She knew she wouldn't be good at it, and she was afraid she might lose her patience and just come out and tell Priscilla she was an idiot.

"God, yes. Something happed with Susan. She came over yesterday, and we were talking—just about things. Relationships and all that nonsense. Then all of a sudden she just started attacking me. Out of nowhere."

"Attacking you?"

"Saying things like I was stupid and selfish and ridiculous."

"She did? That doesn't sound like Susan."

"I know. I could barely believe it. You think you know someone . . ."

"I know," Sofie agreed.

"Then they go and do something like that, and you realize you never knew anything about them at all."

"That's true."

At that moment, Priscilla's doorbell rang.

"I bet that's her," Priscilla said. "I knew she'd come and apologize."

The entryway was visible from where they sat in the living room. The doorbell rang again, and Danielle appeared in the hallway. "Would you like me to get it?" Danielle asked.

"No, I'll get it. Thank you, Danielle."

Priscilla rose, went to the front door, and pulled it open. But it wasn't Susan standing there on the stoop. It was Alex Stowe.

38. Alex at Priscilla's House

"What are *you* doing here?" Priscilla demanded.

It was the exact phrasing Alex himself had used when he found Ackerman standing on his doorstep, and he was quite aware that it did not imply pleasant surprise. Then again, he hadn't expected to be welcomed. In fact, when he thought about it beforehand, he had debated whether to call first or just go over. In the end he'd calculated he would have a better chance by just showing up at the door. He thought it might be harder to send him away if he was actually standing in front of her than it would be to give some excuse over the phone. In general it was a good strategy. But this was Priscilla.

"I was wondering if I could come in and talk to you for a few minutes," Alex said.

"You must be insane if you think I'm going to let you in this house," Priscilla retorted.

Alex tried to answer as mildly as possible. "You've let me in before," he pointed out.

"Yes, but that was before you killed your wife."

There it was. This was what Ruth had predicted. But he still had to try, so he said, "Is that what Ackerman told you? Because you can't trust anything he says about me. He made up his mind about this case before he knew a single detail."

Priscilla wasn't buying it. But even if it hadn't been plain from the expression on her face, he would have known when she opened her mouth.

"I didn't need anyone to tell me. I saw you. Remember? I was the one who came and knocked on your door. And your reaction was probably the most cold-blooded thing I've ever seen in my life."

"But I didn't do it. That's the truth. And I came to you because I'm going to need your help proving that."

"If you need *my* help, then you can bet you'll be spending the rest of your life in a room smaller than my closet."

Priscilla swung the door shut, right in his face. Then she turned on her heel and marched back into the living room.

"I'm so glad you were here because if I told you about how he tried to force his way in here, you probably wouldn't have believed me," she said to Sofie. "*I* almost don't believe it. The nerve of that man."

"I suppose someone who might have killed his wife wouldn't think twice about doing something like that," Sofie said.

"I guess you're right, but still . . ." Priscilla was so agitated she couldn't sit down. Instead she paced the room as she talked. "He must be insane to think I would talk to him—much less try to help him."

"Actually, I wish you had let him in," Sofie said.

"What?" Priscilla rounded on her. "And what would I have done when I invited him in? Should I have served him coffee and encouraged him to tell me all about how he killed his wife?"

"Well, yes. I mean yes to the coffee part. He wasn't going to tell you how he killed his wife. He was going to tell you how he didn't do it."

"He was going to spin a bunch of lies."

"Probably," Sofie agreed.

"And you think I should have let him in here and served him coffee and smiled and nodded and agreed to help him?"

"Well, yes."

Priscilla threw up her hands. "Now it's official—everybody's gone completely crazy."

"It might seem crazy. But really it makes sense."

"You're going to tell me how that makes sense?"

"If you'll listen."

"Go ahead." Priscilla said, crossing her arms.

"So you think he did it, and you want to help the detectives prove it, right?"

"I plan to do whatever I can."

"Then you should have invited him in," Sofie said. "You should have told him you believed him and that you wanted to help him. Then get him talking. The more he talks, the better it is. Who knows, you might have been able to get him to slip up, or even catch him in an outright lie—especially if you got him to trust you, and he let his guard down. He would have talked to you about things he wouldn't say to the detectives. I doubt if he's talked to them at all."

Priscilla blinked. Then she said something she didn't often say. "You're right," she told Sofie. "You're absolutely right."

"It would have been interesting to hear his story, wouldn't it? He didn't try to claim it was a suicide, so I wonder if he has an idea of who did it since he's claiming it wasn't him," Sofie mused.

"Oh God, I'm such an idiot. I could have gotten him talking and then just fed all the information to the police."

Sofie nodded.

"And it's too late now. I don't see how I could go and tell him I changed my mind. Not after what I said to him."

"It would be a little tough," Sofie agreed.

Priscilla shook her head. "Damn."

"Um . . . I guess . . . Well, maybe I could."

"You?" Priscilla said dubiously. Then she thought about it for a moment. "Yes, why not? All you have to do is go see him and tell him that you were here when he came by and you heard what he said and you want to help him."

"You think that would work?"

"Of course it would," Priscilla assured her.

"I don't know . . ."

"I do. And you shouldn't wait too long, or it might look strange. You'll go this afternoon," Priscilla declared.

Sofie didn't try to argue with Priscilla. Instead she simply asked, "Do you want me to come over here after and tell you what happened?"

Priscilla was about to agree, and then she remembered that she hoped to have another visitor that evening. She and Dean had talked about him coming by—so she certainly didn't want Sofie popping over. "How about this? I'll come pick you up first thing in the morning. We can go walking, and you can tell me all about it then."

"But it's a Wednesday. Don't you walk with Susan on Wednesdays?"

"Not anymore," Priscilla said.

39. Alex at Susan's House

After he was turned away from Priscilla's house, Alex decided to try Susan next. He thought he might catch her before Priscilla had a chance to call and tell her friends not to speak to him. He didn't know that Priscilla and Susan weren't talking anymore—and he couldn't have known about the plan that Priscilla and Sofie were hatching at that very moment.

Alex walked up the flagstone path and took a deep breath. At least it couldn't be worse than Priscilla's, he told himself as he rang the bell. A moment later he heard the howling barks of Susan's dogs scrambling to sniff at the door.

Susan was listlessly surfing eBay when Alex rang the doorbell. Surfing was just a way for her to pass the time between checking her e-mail every three minutes. She had tried sending an e-mail to Harry that morning, saying how she had been trying to get in touch with him for the last two days and that she was really worried so if he could just let her know that he was all right, she'd feel so much better. In the hours since she had sent it, she must have checked for a reply several hundred times.

For the last two days, she had been expecting to hear from Harry at any moment. Every time the phone rang, she was certain it was him. She told herself that when she actually spoke to him, he would have a reasonable explanation. Then everything would be fine.

When she heard the doorbell, Susan was sure that, instead of sending an e-mail, Harry had come himself. She didn't even stop to think that if Harry came home he wouldn't be ringing the front door. He would have simply let himself in with his keys. But in her imagination, Harry was standing on the stoop with a huge bouquet of red roses in the crook of his arm.

Susan ran to the door, her dogs swarming around her legs, and put her eye to the peephole. Even though she hoped for Harry, in the back of her mind she admitted to herself that more likely it was the UPS deliveryman or maybe even Priscilla stopping by to apologize. The last person she expected to see standing in front of her door was Alex Stowe. When she saw him standing there, she'd never felt further from being able to deal with a situation. Susan, who always had a moment to listen to someone else's problems, now felt like it was taking every ounce of her strength just to keep from falling apart.

Even so, she reached out to open the door. He'd probably heard her footsteps. It wasn't like she could just pretend not to be home. It would be incredibly rude not to let him in after that. She actually had the knob in her hand and was about to turn it when she stopped. For maybe the first time in her life Susan decided that even though it might be rude and selfish, she was not going to open that door.

On the other side Alex stood and waited. He thought he heard footsteps, but with the noise from the dogs he couldn't be sure. He waited another minute, and then he knew that this time he wouldn't get the door slammed in his face—because it wouldn't get opened at all.

40. Alex at Ashley's House

*A*shley opened the door almost immediately after Alex rang the bell. She opened so quickly he found he wasn't ready, and he didn't know quite what to say. So he simply said, "Hello, Ashley."

"Hello, Alex," she replied.

"I was wondering if I could talk to you for a minute."

"Sure." She swung the door open wider and stepped back to allow him to enter. Then she led the way into the house to the conservatory at the back where she had taken the detectives as well. Just in the last two days the leaves had fallen and now the ground was carpeted with red and gold but the trees themselves showed branches against the sky. It was starting to look like winter.

"Thanks for letting me in and talking to me," Alex said.

"You thought I wouldn't?"

"Well, Priscilla slammed the door in my face, and I don't know if Susan wasn't home or if she just didn't answer."

"Why is it everyone always comes to see me last?" Ashley demanded. "And don't tell me you were doing it alphabetically."

"What?"

"That's what the detectives said. They went to Priscilla and Susan first too."

"Then we all obviously made the same mistake."

"Yes, you did."

There was a pause and Alex was trying to figure out how to bring the subject around to his wife when Ashley did it for him.

"I guess you wanted to talk to me about Julia, right? You probably wanted to tell me you're innocent."

"You're right," Alex admitted.

"Well I should give you fair warning. You're wasting your breath. I know you killed her."

"So . . . why did you let me in?"

"I wanted you to know that I knew," Ashley said. "And I wanted to tell you that you're not going to get away with it. Detective Ackerman is going to make sure of that, and we're going to help him."

"We?"

"The book club. We've been training for this. Remember? You yourself said that you never know when you're going to have a murder to solve."

"I never said that," Alex protested.

"At the dinner party you had with your . . . wife. Susan's husband said we should read something useful like biographies. And you said—"

"I remember now," Alex said abruptly. He shook his head and laughed.

"You think that's funny?"

"Yes, that's about what passes for funny these days," Alex said. "So you and Susan and Priscilla are going to solve the mystery, is that it?"

"With some help."

"From Ackerman," Alex said bitterly.

"I wasn't thinking of him, actually."

"Who then?"

"Sofie. She was the first one to realize that it wasn't a suicide. She knew even before the police."

Alex raised his eyebrows and said, "Then I guess I'd better go see Sofie."

41. Alex at Sofie's House

*S*ofie had just gotten home from Priscilla's house and was in the kitchen unloading the dishwasher while trying to think of what on earth she would say when she went to talk to Alex Stowe—when her own doorbell rang.

Unlike Priscilla, Susan, and Ashley, Sofie knew who was at her door.

She froze for a moment. Then she closed the dishwasher, turned, and walked down the hallway to the front door. And opened it.

They had seen each other at the dinner parties, but they'd never actually had a real conversation, so it felt like they were supposed to know each other—but they didn't. There was a moment of awkward silence.

"I hope I'm not intruding," Alex said.

"Not at all," she replied. "Um, would you like to come in?"

"That would be great."

Sofie instinctively knew she couldn't bring him into the front room filled with stiff antique furniture, and the kitchen seemed too informal, so she led him into the room that she thought of as her "not writing" room. It was the room where she kept her computer—and where she had intended to write her book. But over the summer, as the days slipped by and she hadn't managed to put a single sentence into that blank document, she had started calling it her "not writing" room instead. In addition to the desk by the window it also had a couch and a chair with an ottoman—and the chair was where she'd actually spent most of her time, with her feet up, a cup of coffee on the side table, and a book spread open in her lap.

Sofie took the armchair while Alex sat on the couch.

Sofie glanced down. She saw her hands were twisted together in her lap. She loosened them.

When she glanced up again, she found Alex studying her. Then suddenly he smiled. He looked completely different when he smiled.

She smiled back, but she couldn't think of anything to say. He spoke first.

"I wanted to thank you for your help the other morning. You were very . . . calm."

"I didn't feel calm," she admitted. There had been times when she felt calm in nerve-racking situations, but that had not been one of them.

"No, I suppose you didn't. But you kept your head. You knew exactly what I meant when I told Priscilla not to touch the body, and I have to say, without you there, I don't think she would have listened to me. You know, it could turn out to be crucial that the scene wasn't . . . compromised. What made you think of it?"

She tried to deflect the praise by saying, "My husband would say it was the result of too many mysteries and an overactive imagination."

He smiled again. "Well, I guess I should thank your mysteries and your overactive imagination, then. Besides, I don't think you can have too much imagination. Even in your wildest dreams, you can never predict the crazy things that happen in your life."

"That's true," Sofie agreed, wholeheartedly.

"Is that why you like mysteries? Because you get to use your imagination?"

"Not exactly." No one had actually ever asked her *why* she liked mysteries before. She tried to think about how to express it. "I think it's because of the sense of justice in the end. Because a lot of the time you don't actually get that in life. But in most mysteries everyone gets what they deserve."

"You don't believe that justice wins out in real life?"

"No, not usually. How about you?"

"You mean do I believe that justice wins out?"

She laughed. "No, I meant do you read mysteries?"

"Oh." He grinned. "I used to devour them. When I was a kid, I couldn't get enough of Sherlock Holmes."

"I have a friend who loves those books," Sofie said. "He's always saying how they're the best mysteries ever written."

"I don't know about that. These days I think I prefer Agatha Christie."

"You do?" Sofie said. "I do too."

Alex leaned forward and lowered his voice. "Can you keep a secret?"

Sofie nodded.

"My absolute favorite sleuth is Miss Marple. Most guys wouldn't admit that, would they? I suppose you prefer Poirot?"

"No. I love Miss Marple. Dean just got me a first-edition copy of *The Murder at the Vicarage*. Would you like to see it?"

"I'd love to."

Sofie got up and took it down off the bookshelf and handed it over.

With great care, he opened the cover and turned the pages. "This is wonderful. What a fantastic gift. Your husband is a fan too?"

"No, he's not much of a reader. I mean except for newspapers."

"My wife isn't . . . I mean, she wasn't much of a reader either."

There was a short silence.

Then Alex said, "I wanted to say thanks for inviting me in. I tried to talk to all the other women in the book club, but Priscilla wouldn't let me in, and Susan didn't even answer the door. I guess I can't blame them. Still, I'd hoped they would give me the benefit of the doubt. Ashley let me in, but only so she could tell me that she knew I was guilty and that everyone was going to be working their hardest to help Detective Ackerman prove it."

"That's not what I'm doing," Sofie said.

"No?"

"No. I'm going to try to help find out *who's* guilty. Not prove that *you're* guilty. The evidence will prove it one way or another."

"Right now the evidence is against me," Alex pointed out.

Sofie smiled. "Well, that's true."

"So you think I did it?"

"Let me put it this way—I don't think that I've got the entire crossword puzzle correct until I've filled in all the clues."

"You know what's funny? Ashley said that you were the person to talk to. I have to tell you, the last thing I expected was to get good advice from Ashley, but that just goes to show, you can always be wrong."

Sofie found the color rising in her cheeks. Pretending to be very interested in pushing back her cuticles with her thumbnail, she said, "I wouldn't read too much into what Ashley says. She just likes me because I don't make her feel stupid, and maybe because she felt a little left out with Priscilla and Susan being so close."

"You're not giving her much credit," Alex said. "It seems to me she might have a little more to her opinions than just ego and jealousy."

"You think so? What about her opinion about the murder? Do you think there's more to that one?"

Alex surprised her by laughing. "Actually, yes, I think there's something to that one as well. As I said, the evidence against me at the moment doesn't look good. But that's what I'm here for. To try to find some more of your 'clues' to fill in the puzzle."

His good-natured response disarmed her. And then, at that moment, Agatha stalked into the room.

"You have a cat," Alex exclaimed.

"Her name's Agatha."

"After our favorite author I assume. She's beautiful. May I?" he asked, as he leaned over to pick Agatha up just as she was sliding by him.

Sofie was about to warn him not to—Agatha never allowed anyone but Sofie to pick her up—but before she could say anything, Alex had scooped Agatha up and was cradling her in the crook of his arm and scratching her behind the ears.

Agatha didn't even struggle. She just narrowed her eyes in pleasure.

"She doesn't let anyone do that," Sofie told him.

"No?"

Agatha started purring.

"Tell me how I can help," Sofie said.

"Do you really want to know?" Alex asked, hopefully.

Sofie nodded.

"OK. I'll tell you."

42. Sofie & Dean

"*J*ulia Stowe was having an affair," Sofie announced at dinner that night.

Dean stopped chewing and stared at her.

"How do you know that?" he asked, his mouth still full of food.

"I talked to Alex Stowe today and he told me."

Dean swallowed. "You *what?*"

She asked carefully, "Are you angry?"

Watching him, Sofie felt like it could go either way. He was teetering on the edge. This happened sometimes. Either Dean would start yelling, or he'd catch himself and make a joke instead. She could see the struggle.

Dean didn't answer right away. He took a sip of his wine. Then he set down the glass and said slowly, "Well, I can't say I'm happy. I mean, I know you like mysteries, but this is a little crazy, don't you think? I didn't think you'd actually go over there and grill him about his wife's death."

Sofie relaxed. Now she knew it wasn't going to be a bad fight.

"I didn't. He came here," she told him.

That made Dean pause.

"I'm not sure that's not worse," he said after a long pause.

"He went to see everyone. He tried Priscilla and Susan and Ashley before he came here."

"And?"

"None of them would talk to him."

"That sounds like they were smart. I don't suppose you followed their lead, though."

"How am I supposed to get information about the murder if I don't talk to him?"

"I'm not real happy about you talking to a murderer."

"So you admit that I'm right about Julia being killed?"

"The police called me today," Dean said grudgingly. "And when

I asked them, they didn't confirm it—but they didn't deny it either. So it looks like there's a possibility that you're right. And I don't want you talking to a murderer."

"What if he didn't do it?"

"Oh, come on, Sofie. You can't possibly be so naïve. Of course he did it. Who else? Some crazy person came along and just decided to murder his wife and make it look like a suicide? Give me a break."

"But he's not saying that. He's not saying it was some random person. He's saying that his wife was having an affair."

"He . . . oh, you have to be kidding me," Dean said.

"People do have affairs," Sofie pointed out. "How many of your friends at the office have cheated on their wives?"

"I don't know. You think they come into my office and say, 'Hey, I just slept with a stripper last night,' or, 'I just banged my secretary in the bathroom'?"

"Yes."

"You make it sound like all the guys at work are barbarians and go around bragging about their sexual conquests."

"Don't they?"

"No, they don't. People don't go around spilling their guts."

"Now *you're* being naïve," Sofie said.

"All I know is they're not spilling their guts to me. But what else did Alex say, other than the fact that his wife was having an affair? Did he tell you who she was having an affair with?"

"No. Because he doesn't know," Sofie said. "That's the problem. He said he's sure this other person was the one who killed his wife, and he's trying to find out who it is."

"How's he going to do that? Is he hoping you're so smart you can figure out who his wife was sleeping with?"

Sofie looked down and smiled. But Dean knew his wife's expressions, and he said, "What?"

She tried to look innocent. "Nothing."

"I know you. What were you just thinking?" he demanded. "And don't tell me 'nothing.' "

"If you must know, I was just thinking that you wouldn't make a very good detective," she told him.

"Oh, really? Why's that?"

"Because you're already making assumptions."

"What assumption did I make? I said I didn't think you could figure it out."

"No, you said I couldn't figure out what guy his wife was sleeping with."

"And?"

"Well, you automatically assumed it was a guy. What if she was sleeping with a woman?"

Even Dean couldn't hold back a snort of laughter. "You take the cake," he said like he always did when she surprised him.

She grinned.

"So did he think you could find his wife's lover? Is that better? It's gender neutral."

"Much better," she said. "And no. Not exactly. Actually, he was hoping that Julia might have confided in one of her friends."

"But you weren't really friends with her," Dean said.

"No. Not really. That's why he went to see Priscilla and Susan and Ashley first. Though I didn't get the sense that they were her friends either. But I'm going to ask them if Julia told them anything."

"Or if they were sleeping with her," Dean joked.

"I don't know that they'd volunteer that," Sofie said seriously.

Dean looked at her more closely. "You mean you're actually thinking of helping him?"

"I just want to find out what happened. If Julia was having an affair, I want to find out who she was having it with."

"So the great detective Sofie Wright is on the trail of the unknown lover who she's going to help prove was the real killer," Dean said sarcastically.

"Not necessarily. I'm just looking for evidence. The evidence isn't biased."

"People control evidence," Dean said. "And people are biased."

"And your point is?"

"My point is that he's trying to use you."

"And I'm using him right back."

"When have you ever used anybody?" Dean scoffed.

"I've used people," Sofie protested.

"When? Give me one example."

Sofie paused, then said, "Well, it's never too late to learn."

"See what I mean? You're a novice. He's an expert. You're way out of your league here."

43. Susan & Harry

*H*arry hadn't come home, and Susan hadn't been able to get in touch with him. He didn't answer his cell phone, and his secretary claimed that all she knew was that he said he would be away for a few days.

Susan started to think, What if something had happened to him? What if he'd been kidnapped? Or worse? She had to do something. And that's when she decided that she would call the police and report him missing. But then she asked herself, what number did you call for this kind of thing? It wasn't exactly a 911 call. Did she just look up the number for the local precinct? Then she remembered the card that Detective Ackerman had left with her. She went and got the card and was about to dial when she started to imagine the questions Detective Ackerman would ask her. When had Harry disappeared? When was the last time she talked to him?

When she realized what her answer would be, she put down the phone, and covered her mouth with her hand. She would have to tell Detective Ackerman that her husband had disappeared the day that Julia was killed. What if the two events were connected? She couldn't possibly bring the police into this.

So she waited.

She had been waiting for days now, but of course he finally turned up the moment she stopped expecting him. It was nine thirty at night, and Susan was already in bed. She didn't usually go to sleep that early, but she didn't know what else to do. She wanted the day to be over, so she took two Tylenol PM and got into bed, hoping to escape into oblivion. She was exhausted—she hadn't slept properly in days—but it was the kind of exhaustion where her body felt like it had been run over by a truck, and yet she couldn't stop her mind from racing.

She had turned on the TV and was flipping through the channels—she couldn't even concentrate enough to watch a sitcom—and the TV was the reason she didn't hear the car, didn't hear the garage door, didn't hear the footsteps on the stairs. She just happened to look up and see her husband standing in the doorway of their bedroom staring at her with a look she had never seen before—and never wanted to see again.

She was in her oldest pair of pajamas. Her hair was still wet from the shower she had taken in the hopes that the warm water would relax her and help her go to sleep. She had just applied the moisturizer that cost a hundred dollars an ounce and which promised to keep the skin looking full and dewy well past the age of forty, but also, when applied, looked greasy and made her face shine as if she were slicked with oil. Of course Harry had seen her this way hundreds of times, but that was before he started looking at her with pity instead of with love.

To make matters worse, she hadn't seen Harry looking so good in years. He was in her favorite suit, the one that made him look stocky instead of heavy, and he was wearing a white shirt and the dark blue tie that matched his eyes. His salt-and-pepper hair looked like he'd just had it trimmed. And he was *tan*, she realized with a shock.

The first day Harry had been missing she'd thought obsessively about what she would say to him when she finally saw him. She wanted to tell him how he, who had always prided himself on his fair dealing in business, had exhibited zero integrity in his marriage. She wanted to remind him of his vows and ask him if his word meant anything. She wanted to demand how he could do this. It was like expertly engineered torture or, at the very least, it showed complete and utter disregard of how she might be feeling. She wanted to tell him that she never thought he was capable of acting this way. She wanted to tell him that never in a million years would she have treated him the way he had treated her.

That was in the first day. In the second day she had gotten scared and started thinking about how she might have misread the situation. Maybe he was hurt. Maybe he was in trouble. Maybe he had been kidnapped. Then she realized the timing of his disappearance, and she became convinced that it was linked to Julia's death. Since then Susan had been constructing elaborate scenarios to explain the coincidence. She thought—maybe he was having an affair with Julia. Maybe Julia had threatened to tell Susan all about it, and Harry, in order to protect his marriage, had killed her to keep that from happening. Or maybe he had promised to run away with Julia but hadn't actually been able to go through with it, and when he told her Julia flew into a rage and tried to attack him, and he'd killed her while defending himself. Susan envisioned a dozen different scenarios, but all of them had been a version of the same thing: Harry doing whatever he had to do to try to protect Susan and keep his marriage intact.

She'd thought of her imaginings as nightmares—she hadn't thought she might actually prefer them to the ordinary, utterly mundane, devastating truth: that Harry had been away with another woman. That he had been away at some luxurious beach resort somewhere, dancing, drinking cocktails, sitting in the sun, making love. But she knew that was the truth the moment she saw him.

"You have a *tan*?" she practically spit the words at him.

"I had to get away for a few days. I had to have time to think," Harry told her.

"Did you happen to do this thinking alone? Or did you bring someone along to help you . . . think?"

"I'm not going to lie to you. I wasn't alone."

"You're not going to lie to me? What have you been doing for the last six months?" she demanded.

"Well, that's one of the things I decided over these last few days. I'm not going to lie to you anymore. It's not fair to either of us."

"*Now* you've decided. Did the other person help you with that?"

"Being sarcastic isn't going to make this any easier, Suze," Harry said.

"And why would I want this to be easy? Do you think it's been easy for me these last few days, not knowing where you were, what happened to you, or what was going on?"

"Didn't my secretary give you the message that I'd be in touch in a few days?"

"No. No, she didn't. All your secretary said to me was that you weren't available. That's the only message I got from her."

"Then I'm sorry. There was a misunderstanding."

"But why would you leave that message with your secretary? Why didn't you tell me that yourself? Don't you think you owed me that much?"

"I'm here now," Harry said. "I could have just had my lawyer send the papers."

"The papers?" Susan repeated. "What papers?"

"Come on, Suze. You know what papers."

"Divorce papers?" she almost whispered.

Harry nodded.

Then, right when she needed it most, her anger deserted her.

"This isn't the way it should happen," she said. "Harry, we've been together for almost twenty years. Isn't that worth something? Don't you think there's something there worth saving?"

"Believe me, Suze, this is tearing me apart. It's been tearing me apart for months. But it just wasn't working. It hasn't been working for a while."

"Why didn't you say anything?"

"Because I didn't even know. I mean I knew in my gut, but I didn't *know*."

"It's not too late," she pleaded. "We can talk about things. You can tell me why you've been unhappy. Tell me what I need to do. All I ever tried to do was to make you happy."

"I know that. But . . . I'm not happy."

"So tell me what to do. What can I do?" Then, desperately, "I can change."

"You can't become a whole different person," Harry said. "You're wonderful just as you are. But I'm just not happy in this marriage. I'm sorry."

"So I assume you've found the person who's going to make you happy?"

"Yes," Harry said simply.

"Who is she?"

"Do we have to do this now?"

"What, did you think you'd just come home and say 'I want a divorce' and I'd say 'OK' and that would be it? Is that how you thought this would work?"

"It's just that I don't want to hurt you."

"If you really didn't want to hurt me, you wouldn't have had an affair. If you didn't want to hurt me, you wouldn't have disappeared for days off to . . . where did you go?"

"Suze, don't."

But Susan just went on. "If you didn't want to hurt me, you wouldn't have come here telling me that you want a divorce and that you've made up your mind. You've already hurt me. I think I deserve to know the rest."

Harry sighed. "You're right." He crossed to the armchair in the corner that faced the bed and sat down. Suddenly he looked very tired. All the energy and vitality he'd had when he first appeared seemed drained from him. "You're right. Ask me whatever you want, and I'll tell you."

Susan took a deep breath. "Is there any hope for us, Harry? Is there anything I can do? Any way you'll change your mind."

"No, Suze. I'm sorry."

She sat in bed, stunned. She'd asked the question blindly hoping for another answer. Alex's lawyer would have said the same thing to Susan that she did to Alex: Don't ask any questions you don't want the answer to.

"But why?" It was a last appeal.

Harry shook his head. "I don't know why. These things just happen. We grew apart."

"I didn't grow apart from you. I love you," Susan told him.

"I know. I know you do. But maybe I need something more than love."

"What else is there?"

"You need love on both sides, right? It isn't just enough for one person to love."

"You don't love me?" She almost couldn't get enough breath to get the words out.

"See? I told you we shouldn't do this. It's just hurting you." Harry started to stand up.

"No. No, I need to hear it. I need to hear the truth," Susan said. "Please."

Harry looked at her, then slowly sat back down again.

"You love . . . her?"

"Yes."

"Who is she?"

"She's . . . she's a colleague."

"She *works* for you?"

"No. She works for the company we just took over. Or, rather, she used to. She was the one we brought in to help us with our strategy."

"She sold out her own company? What kind of person can she be?"

"See, Suze, this is part of the problem. You just don't understand the business world."

"So you're saying I need to understand the business world for our marriage to work?"

"It's my world. It's the world I live in from seven in the morning to seven at night. Twelve hours a day. It's part of who I am. So yes, I guess that is what I'm trying to say."

"You said you liked it that I didn't work. You said the thing that was really important was that someone created a home."

"That's what I thought. What can I say? I was wrong."

"You were wrong." Susan laughed, and there was an edge of hysteria to it. "You say it like it's no big deal. Like, oops, sorry. I was wrong. But do you realize what you did? Do you realize what I gave up for you?"

"Do we have to go there?" Harry asked wearily.

"Yes, we have to go there. Of course we have to go there. All my life I've wanted a family. I wanted children. More than anything in the whole world. But you said you didn't want kids, and I gave that up for you. I gave up my dream for you. That's how much I loved you."

"I think that was part of the problem. You shouldn't have given that up for me—or for anyone. And it put too much pressure on me to be worth it for you, to be worth that sacrifice. And I'm not worth it. I can't live up to that."

"But you did. You were enough for me."

"No. I wasn't. If you really look in your heart, you'll see that you never forgave me for that. You never forgave me for making you give up the family that you wanted. You should have followed your dream."

"You tell me that now? Now when I'm forty, and it's too late?"

"People make mistakes, Susan. I made some, and even if you won't admit it, you made some too." Harry stood. "I know you're hurt and angry now, but I think at some point you'll look back and see that I was right. We'll both be happier."

"That's just what you're telling yourself to make you feel better. And you know what? It's a crock of shit."

"All I know is that this is something I have to do. You only get one go around at this. And I can't stay here and give up the rest of my life because I'm scared to hurt you. Then we'd both be miserable. I was hoping I would have your blessing."

"Really? You thought I might give you my blessing? You thought I would do something like that?"

"It shows how highly I think of you," Harry said.

"Actually, I don't think anyone has ever said anything so insulting to me in my entire life. You must think I'm a total schmuck. You come in to tell me that you're leaving me for another woman. You tell me that I never made you happy. You tell me that I made a mistake when I gave up the one thing that was more important to me than anything in the world—for you. And now you expect me to give you my *blessing*?" Susan had found her anger again, just in time.

"I thought you were a caring, rational person who just wanted the best for the people you love," Harry tried to explain.

"No, you thought I was a schmuck who you could walk all over, and I would just say, 'I want you to be happy, if that means divorce then I understand.' Well, I might be a schmuck, but I'm not going to say that."

"I don't think that's so unreasonable."

"I don't care what you think anymore. You can get the hell out of this house, and out of my life too."

"This isn't like you," Harry said. "This isn't you. This is just your hurt talking. I understand you're angry. But . . . you're not going to be unreasonable about this divorce, are you? You're not going to make this hard for everyone just to get revenge. That's not you. That's not the kind of person you are."

"Didn't I tell you before?" Susan said. "I can change."

44. Priscilla & Sofie

The days Priscilla went walking with Susan, she usually did two loops first before stopping to pick up Susan. But that morning she went straight to Sofie's house, and the moment Sofie opened the door, Priscilla started peppering her with questions.

"So what happened? What did he say? Did you find out anything?"

Sofie stepped out and pulled the door closed behind her. "It was . . . interesting."

"What is that supposed to mean?" Priscilla demanded as they started down the walk to the street.

"I don't know where to start," Sofie said.

"Start at the beginning. How was it going over there? Did he think it was strange that you wanted to talk to him?"

"Actually, I didn't need to go over there. He came to see me."

"He did?"

"Well, he also went to see Susan and Ashley."

"Did they talk to him?" Priscilla demanded.

"Susan didn't even answer the door. Apparently Ashley let him in to her house, but not to listen to what he had to say. She let him in so *she* could talk. She told him that we were trying to prove he murdered his wife."

"Oh, that's just great. So he knows what we're planning. He's not going to tell us anything now."

"I think I was able to fix it," Sofie said.

"You were able to convince him that you were going to help him?"

"I think so—or, at least that I wasn't out to get him. Anyway, he's pretty desperate. Things aren't looking too good for him right now, and he says the detective has some sort of vendetta against him."

"Detective Ackerman? I can't see him going after anyone."

"I know," Sofie agreed. "He doesn't seem to be the type."

"Did you ask Alex why Detective Ackerman supposedly has it in for him?"

"He wouldn't tell me."

"It sounds like he's making it all up," Priscilla declared.

"I didn't tell you all of it yet. What he really came over to say was that Julia was having an affair, and he was hoping that maybe she'd confided in you or Susan or Ashley."

"Julia was having an *affair?*"

"That's what he says. So she didn't mention anything to you about it?"

"To me? God no."

"Do you think it's possible?"

"Possible? I suppose it's *possible*." Priscilla thought for a moment. "So he's claiming that Julia's lover is the one who killed her?"

Sofie nodded.

"And he has no idea who that person is?"

"No. That's why he needs help. He needs any insights you might have. Anything you might have noticed. Any little thing you might have picked up on."

"Sounds like a wild goose chase to me. It's probably something he cooked up with his lawyer to throw at the jury to create—what is it they call it? Reasonable doubt, right? And making up this theory that Julia had a lover is his only option. He can't really suggest that some random stranger murdered her and made it look like a suicide."

"That's true. But he didn't just start thinking she had a lover since she was killed. He thought so beforehand," Sofie said.

"Because he said so?"

"Because he hired a private detective to try to find out."

"He did? And the PI didn't find anything?"

"Nothing. But if her lover lived around here, the PI wouldn't have been able to really do anything. All he'd be able to do would be to sit in the car out front. And when it got dark, with all the trees around the houses, he wouldn't have been able to see anything. Julia would have been able to avoid getting caught by simply slipping out the back door. Or even one of the windows. And *that's* why she was killed outside. Because it's where she and her lover met."

"Oooh," Priscilla said. "That's good. But hold on—wouldn't Alex have noticed all those times she just 'slipped out the back'?"

"They had separate bedrooms," Sofie told her.

"No, *really?*"

"Don't you remember the day we found Julia and went to tell Alex, he told us she was still sleeping? But Julia had been hanging in that tree for hours. So the only way he could think she was still sleeping was if they had separate bedrooms. Alex confided as much to me yesterday.

"Riiight," Priscilla said. "I can't believe I didn't notice something so obvious. Did he say why?"

"No."

"Did you ask?"

"*No.* I can't ask him something like that. I barely know him."

"Why not? He brought it up in the first place. He volunteered the fact that he and Julia had separate bedrooms. Why can't you ask how that happened? I mean, you don't have to grill him like you're an investigative reporter. You pretend to be sympathetic, you get him talking about his relationship with his wife and how bad it was, and you get some real information that's going to be useful to Detective Ackerman."

"But I'm really not trying to prove him guilty. I think there's a chance he didn't do it," Sofie said.

"Oh, so the mystery lover did it?"

"Like you said, anything's possible. Julia being killed outside fits the facts—even you admitted as much."

"What facts? I don't see any facts. Does he have any evidence that there was an affair at all? I mean, I know the PI couldn't figure out who it was, but did he even find any evidence of it at all?"

"I don't think so," Sofie admitted.

"Nothing?"

Sofie shook her head.

"And you say you think maybe he didn't do it? *You're* the one's who's innocent—innocent like a baby. You'd better watch out. He's doing a snow job on you."

"Dean said practically the same thing. But I know what I'm doing," Sofie assured her.

"What is it you're doing?"

"Helping with the case."

"But who are you helping?"

Sofie didn't answer that.

"I don't believe Julia was having an affair at all. It's just a paranoid fantasy he had, which, as a matter of fact, gives him a motive. In fact it's one of the oldest in the book. It's Othello all over again."

"I don't know," Sofie said. "I don't think it's a paranoid fantasy. Something tells me he's right, and Julia did have a lover."

They walked in silence for a moment, and when Priscilla spoke next, she switched topics completely. She said, very casually, "Oh, before I forget, I wanted to tell you I'm thinking of having a little get-together. I was going to do it during the week, and I wanted to see if that would be possible. I know the crazy hours Gordon sometimes works, but he says he thinks he can get out early. Would it be impossible to get your husband home by eight? Because I seem to remember he works late a lot too, doesn't he?"

"Dean? Yes, Dean generally works long hours. But it's actually been a lot better recently. I think he's been making a real effort to get home earlier so we can spend more time together."

"He has?"

"We've had dinner together every night this week. I don't even remember the last time that happened. Last night he was home before seven."

"That's so sweet," Priscilla said.

But she wasn't thinking that was sweet. She was thinking that Dean had no excuse—he could easily have stopped by to see her the night before. She'd called his work number and left a message that Gordon wouldn't be around until late. When Dean didn't show, she had given him the benefit of the doubt, telling herself that he hadn't gotten back in time and that was why he didn't come over.

Sofie interrupted Priscilla's thoughts, saying, "I think we could make it any day."

"Make what?" Priscilla asked, forgetting for a moment the pretense she had used to find out about Dean's hours. But she recovered quickly, "Oh right. The get-together. Yes, I'm going to plan it for sometime in the next week. The only thing is that since we've lost Julia and Alex and Susan and Harry, it would be absolute disaster if someone couldn't make it. So tell your husband that his presence is required—or there will be dire consequences," Priscilla said playfully. Since she couldn't get through to him on the phone, she would send a message to him through his wife.

"Of course, I'll let him know."

"You won't forget?"

"I'll tell him," Sofie promised.

45. Dean & the Detectives

" $\mathcal{S}$ o this isn't just a delusion of my wife's?" Dean asked the two detectives as he led them into his office.

Ackerman had arranged to meet with Dean, Gordon, and Stewart at their offices in the city. He'd hoped to manage all the men in one visit, but he had not yet been able to get in touch with Susan's husband, Harry.

Ackerman had decided to meet with the men at their offices because he wanted their true opinions, and he'd interviewed enough husbands to know that they wouldn't always speak their minds in front of their wives—or even when their wives were in the next room.

Dean was their first interview, and his opening seemed to justify Ackerman's strategy.

"What's not just your wife's delusion?" Ackerman asked in response to Dean's question.

"That Julia Stowe was murdered. My wife doesn't seem to believe in Occam's Razor—" He paused, looking at Ackerman. When the detective didn't respond, he explained, "It's the idea that the simplest theory is the one that should be selected. There are thousands of examples. Like the crop circles that were reported in the seventies—there were two different theories about that. One was that the grass was matted down by flying saucers. The other was that someone had used some kind of instrument to push the grass down. People like to say that anything is possible, and that may be true, but if you apply Occam's Razor to the problem, you see that there's a lot of improbabilities in the flying saucer theory—what with the difficulty in traveling across galaxies and the problem of light speed and the lack of evidence of the existence of flying saucers—and since there's not a lot of evidence for flying saucers, you'd probably have to go with the second theory, that the crop circles were man-made. And, you know, years later two people actually admitted to making the original crop circles. The rest were probably copycats. And yet, contrary to all logic, some people still believe that they were made by flying saucers. Because otherwise it's just too boring. Too mundane. They prefer the fantastic to the truth."

"You raise a good point," Ackerman said diplomatically.

Peters looked up. He'd only been with Ackerman a few days, but it was long enough for him to know that that kind of statement was a precursor to Ackerman destroying the other person's "good point."

And sure enough, Ackerman continued after only a slight hesitation, as if he were thinking out loud. "In theory, at least. But as a detective who often has to put theory to practice, I think you've left out an important part. Occam's Razor doesn't actually say that the simplest theory is always the best one. It's the simplest theory *that fits the facts*. That's an important distinction. But you're not the first person to make that mistake. Occam's Razor is prone to oversimplification. I actually prefer something that Einstein said. He said that everything should be made as simple as possible, *but not simpler*. Of course, when you see a person hanging, the simplest theory would be to conclude that it's a suicide. All the more so because hanging is the most common form of suicide and not really what you think of when you think of a murder. But there's a reason that, in police procedure, we're instructed to treat all suicides as homicides until proven differently. It's because we don't yet know the facts. And the facts in this case indicate that it wasn't suicide. The facts tell us that it was actually a homicide that someone was trying very hard to make *look* like suicide."

"How can you know that for sure?"

"We don't know for sure," Ackerman lied. "But there are indications."

"Sofie was going on about some silly mark on some branch . . ."

"That was an important piece of evidence your wife discovered."

"You're just being kind."

"No. Not really. Am I being kind?" Ackerman asked Peters.

"He's not the type," Peters said.

Ackerman turned back to Dean. "Do you have any ideas about who you think might have killed her?" Ackerman asked.

"If it was anyone, it was that husband of hers."

"Why do you say that?"

"I don't know. Just a feeling. There's something . . . wrong about him. If I were you, I'd have a look at his history."

Ackerman glanced at Peters and raised his eyebrows.

Dean went on, "And I can tell you, I'm not too happy about my wife spending time with him."

"What?" Ackerman said, sitting up straighter.

"Yes, just yesterday my wife apparently sat around all afternoon, having coffee with him. She claims she's 'investigating,' but it looks to me more like she's getting snowed. I think she actually might be buying some story he's come up with about his wife having a lover and that it was this other person who killed her. Maybe you can talk some sense into her. Tell her that the detective work is your job, and she should stay out of it."

"I'll talk to her," Ackerman said.

"Would you? I'd really appreciate it. It's just that I worry about her. I mean, what if she did inadvertently discover something—something that would help convict him? She could be in real danger."

"I think you might be getting carried away, Mr. Wright," Ackerman said soothingly.

"People always say that—until something happens. I just have a very bad feeling about this," Dean said. "I have the feeling that something's going to go wrong."

"Nothing's going to go wrong," Ackerman said. "Not if I can help it."

46. Stewart & the Detectives

"Who's next?" Peters asked as they left Dean's office building and emerged onto the street. "And how far do we have to go?"

"Stewart Turkel. And it's not far. Just a few blocks."

"Which one is Stewart Turkel married to?"

"Betty Boop," Ackerman said.

"What kind of man do you think he is? I mean, who marries that kind of woman?"

"What kind? Probably the type of guy who that type of girl wouldn't have looked twice at in high school."

"You think it's that simple?" Peters said.

"I don't think it's simple at all," Ackerman replied.

They walked five blocks north to a building on Central Park South, took the elevator up to the forty-seventh floor, and were shown into an office with a view that you might find on a postcard of Manhattan.

Stewart stood to greet them, and Ackerman threw one look at Peters to say 'I told you so." Stewart was short, stocky, and bald. But there was an unmistakable air of power around him. It wasn't just the expensive suit and the overwhelming view behind him. Ackerman immediately sensed a keenness to Stewart's inspection. Ackerman had the feeling that his suit was being assessed for how much it had cost, how old it was, and the last time he'd gotten it cleaned. His wife had bought it for him on sale at Century 21 two years ago. He knew he needed new suits, but he hadn't yet managed to find the time to buy them. His wife had always done that for him. She'd also taken care of the dry-cleaning, which was why he didn't even remember the last time he'd taken it in.

"Please, gentlemen, have a seat," Stewart said, gesturing to the two chairs facing his desk. "So, where do we start? Crossword puzzle clues?" He smiled, showing too many teeth. "I hear you like to play little games."

Stewart was trying to show Ackerman that he was on to him, but Ackerman was actually pleased. He had hoped the women would talk and discover what he had been up to with the clues. It had been calculated to create a little bit of competition. He wanted them to try to impress him—in trying to do that, they would give him all the information they had.

"Do you like crosswords?" Ackerman asked politely.

"They're a waste of time in my opinion," Stewart replied.

Ackerman took that to mean that Stewart wasn't very good at them. He had never known someone who was really good at them who could resist the feeling of satisfaction when you filled in the last letter on the grid.

"I mean, you don't really learn anything from them," Stewart continued. "It's mostly useless trivia or ridiculous puns. What do you actually get from finishing one? Nothing."

"Do you work out?" Ackerman asked.

"What?"

"Do you work out?" Ackerman repeated.

"Yes, I try. As often as I can. I try to get it in in the morning, but if I can't, there's a gym in the building, and I go at lunchtime when I can get away."

"What do you get from working out?"

"That's a stupid question. You get into shape. You build up your muscles. You improve your cardiovascular system. There are all sorts of health benefits."

"Did you know that a lot of doctors are recommending that as people get older, they do a crossword puzzle a day to keep their brain in shape? They think it may help stave off the effects of Alzheimer's."

"You're joking."

"Not at all."

"Huh." Stewart sat back in his chair.

Ackerman didn't say anything. He knew he'd accomplished what he needed to do. Stewart had been testing him—seeing if he could intimidate Ackerman with his big office and his impressive view and an aggressive attitude. It was crucial not to back down. Now the test was over, and Ackerman could get on with his job.

"We have some questions for you about Julia Stowe," Ackerman said, and Peters opened up his notebook and clicked his pen to the ready.

"I assumed you didn't come for stock advice," Stewart said.

"Personally, I'd welcome some stock advice," Peters said.

"Do you have any extra cash lying around that you don't need and could afford to lose?" Stewart asked.

Peters snorted. "Extra cash lying around?"

"Then my advice would be to stay out of the market right now."

"Julia Stowe," Ackerman interjected. "What can you tell me about her?"

"Probably more than anyone else" Stewart said.

"Why's that?"

"Because I knew her before she moved out to Greenwich. I met her a bunch of times at society parties in the city."

"And?"

"Well, out in Greenwich, she tried to play nice, but underneath she was a real bitch—though I say that with the utmost respect. She knew what she wanted, and by God, she was going to get it."

"What did she want? Money?" Ackerman asked.

"I'm sure she started off wanting money. But she probably found out pretty quickly that money is easy to get. So she set her sights higher. You can't buy what Julia wanted. I mean, you need money to even be in the running, but money alone doesn't do it."

"What is this thing Julia wanted?"

"Status," Stewart said succinctly.

"What exactly does that mean?"

"What is status? Well, it changes depending on where you are and who you ask. In the Hamptons it would mean being able to get into any club or get an invitation to every party—at least every party that mattered. I think of status as the triumvarate: money, power, and the ability to inspire envy."

Ackerman thought it was well put—and it showed that the subject was obviously something Stewart had put some thought into.

"Did she manage it?" Ackerman asked. "Status, I mean."

"There's always someone higher on the totem pole, isn't there? I think she thought she was at the top, and then she realized she was only halfway, but by then it was too late. Maybe that's why she agreed to move out to Greenwich. Usually the reason women want to move out of the city is to get a big house and have kids. But Julia was not the mothering type. She knew that mothers don't have status. Kids mean mundane things like car-pooling and dentist appointments—even when you have a nanny and a housekeeper. Kids are not glamorous."

"You make her sound almost inhuman," Peters said.

"In a way I suppose she was. Being human means having messy emotions and making mistakes and feeling insecure. And Julia never showed anything like that. I mean, I suppose there was a person under there somewhere, but I never saw it."

"What about her husband?"

"Alex? What about him?"

"Do you think she felt anything for him?"

"They never seemed less than the perfect couple."

"But?" Ackerman prompted.

"There were times I thought I sensed something underneath," Stewart admitted.

"What?"

"It was just a feeling," Steward cautioned. "But . . . I think she might have hated him."

47. Gordon & the Detectives

*T*hey were in the middle of the interview with Gordon, and it wasn't going well.

"Julia and Alex?" Gordon repeated. "I don't know. They seemed fine."

"Fine?" Ackerman prodded. They'd had to go all the way downtown to Gordon's office, and Ackerman was starting to think that it might have been a waste of time. They had been there for ten minutes, and Ackerman hadn't managed to get anything substantive from him.

"What about looking at it in hindsight?" Ackerman asked.

"It's terrible. I don't like to think about it," Gordon admitted.

At that moment Gordon's secretary arrived with coffee she'd run down to Starbucks to get. Apparently the coffee in the cafeteria was undrinkable.

"Thank you, Elizabeth," Gordon said.

The detectives echoed the thanks. When she'd left, Ackerman returned to the questioning.

"So were you close with them?"

"No. I suppose not. I see what you're saying. It's not that it's a personal loss exactly. But it's always shocking when something like this happens to someone you know. And I don't like to think about the fact that these things happen."

Sheltered upbringing, Ackerman guessed, resulting in the proto-typical sensitive soul. Ackerman himself couldn't even fathom what it was like to be like that. When your job is murder, and you look at tragedy every day, it tends to dull what feeling you have. Ackerman supposed it was part of the reason his marriage fell apart. That was something *he* didn't like to think about. He tried to use that to work up some sympathy for Gordon, but it had been a long week, and he found himself getting annoyed.

"Surely you noticed something? Had some opinion? Some sense of something wrong?"

"I tend to put rose colored glasses on things."

"But you're not blind. You do notice some things, right? If it's extreme enough."

"Yes, if it's extreme enough, I do eventually notice it," Gordon said sadly.

"So did you notice anything?" Ackerman repeated.

"I don't think I'm the best person to be asking about this. What did everyone else say?"

"Well, for one thing, pretty much everyone we talked to knew that Julia was unhappy living out in Greenwich. They thought she might have been angry at her husband."

"Why would she be angry at her husband?" Gordon asked.

Ackerman had to control his impatience. "For making her move out there."

"But—he didn't make her move out there."

Ackerman and Peters looked at each other. "What?"

"Alex didn't make Julia move out of the city. That was Julia's idea."

"I think you must be mistaken," Ackerman said.

"No, I'm pretty sure about that," Gordon said. "I ran into Julia's Realtor over the summer and we got to talking. But if you want to double-check, you can call her."

Ackerman and Peters called the Realtor on their way back to the train station. She confirmed what Gordon had told them: It had been Julia, not Alex, who wanted to move out of the city.

48. Sofie & The Detectives

*T*hey had taken an early morning commuter train, but it was almost three o'clock when Ackerman and Peters returned to the Greenwich train station and walked back to their car.

"How do they do it every day?" Peters wondered. "I'm exhausted from commuting just one day."

"And it wasn't even a full day," Ackerman said.

"So how do they do it?"

"Habit," Ackerman replied. "You can get used to just about anything."

"I don't know, I don't think I could get used to that."

"So you can get used to dead bodies and autopsies but you couldn't get used to commuting into the city? Is that what you're saying?"

"Pretty much," Peters said. "All I want to do is go home and crawl into bed. And instead we've got mountains of paperwork to fill out."

"We've got something to do before we even get to the paperwork," Ackerman said.

Sofie had been anxious and jittery all day. She tried to read, but she just couldn't concentrate on the words. She knew better than to try to bake anything in this mood. In the midst of measuring out four cups of flour, she'd lose track of how many she'd put in. Was that four? Or only three? Or she'd forget if she'd already added the vanilla or not. Something always ended up going wrong. So she decided to attempt to go through her files and clean out the junk that she had been accumulating for years. She was in the middle of that when the doorbell rang. Alex had said he was coming after four, but maybe he was early. She jumped up and hurried to the door. But when she opened it, it wasn't Alex on the stoop. It was Detective Ackerman and Detective Peters.

"Sorry to just drop by without warning," Ackerman said. "Could we come in for a few minutes?"

"Sure, sure. Come on in." As she led them back into the kitchen, in her head Sofie was calculating how much time she had before Alex did show up. It would be a disaster if he arrived and the detectives were still there.

It was as if Ackerman was reading her mind. As soon as they sat down he said, "I heard that you spent the afternoon with Alex Stowe the other day."

"Who told you?"

"Your husband—he's concerned about you."

"That's silly," Sofie said. "Even if Alex did kill his wife, he's not going to do anything to me. It's not like he's a serial killer or anything."

"It's not silly. You should be careful," Ackerman said. "People are unpredictable."

"Is that why you came by? To tell me to be careful?"

"No, I came by to ask you why you were talking to him. Your husband seems to think you're getting conned."

"My husband doesn't seem to have a lot of confidence in my ability to judge for myself," Sofie observed wryly.

"I wouldn't put it that way. He thinks you might be vulnerable to being . . . manipulated."

"And you agree?"

"I don't know. That's why I came to talk to you."

"I'm not being manipulated," Sofie assured him. "I know what I'm doing."

"So will you tell me what it is you're doing?"

"I'm filling in the grid. The more he talks, the more information I have. And if he gets comfortable with me, if he starts thinking I'm on his side, then maybe he'll say more than he intended."

Ackerman looked skeptical.

"He'll certainly say more to me than he will to you." Sofie dangled the carrot in front of the detective, wondering if he would bite.

"And you'll pass along any information you get from him?" Ackerman asked.

"Of course. That's the whole point."

Ackerman hesitated.

"Well?" Sofie prodded.

"All right," Ackerman agreed reluctantly. "See what you can get from him. But I want regular updates, and I want you to be careful."

"I will," Sofie promised.

Peters and Ackerman were silent as they walked back down the driveway and climbed into the car, but it was one of those loud silences.

Instead of turning on the car, Ackerman turned to Peters and said, "OK, what is it?"

"Nothing."

"Bullshit. You might as well say it."

"I was only wondering . . . do you think that was the best idea?"

"What?"

"Letting her loose with her own little amateur detective work with this guy?"

"She may get some good information—something we can use in court."

"You're using her," Peters said.

"She volunteered."

"It doesn't matter. She doesn't have all the facts. Here you are warning her that Alex Stowe might be manipulating her, but you're just as guilty. You're withholding information as well. Admit it—when you went in there, you didn't have the slightest intention of trying to get her to stop. You just wanted to make sure she wasn't switching sides."

Ackerman shrugged, but that in itself was an admission.

Peters looked at him. "I'm worried that you're getting a little too involved in this case."

"I get involved in every case," Ackerman said.

"But I don't think it's every case you would let a woman get this close to a killer just on the possibility she might get some information we could use in court."

Ackerman didn't say anything to that—because he didn't know how to answer.

49. Alex

"It worked," Alex said, sitting in his lawyer's office in his favorite pose—feet up, hands behind his head.

"What worked?"

"Going to Julia's friends. Well, actually it didn't work for most of them. But one of them agreed to help me. She's going to help me find out what I need to know."

"You mean like a kind of spy?" Ruth asked, amused.

"Sort of. She's a member of that mystery book club Julia belonged to. But apparently their latest project isn't a book—it's solving the mystery of my wife's murder. Except they've decided that it's one of those mysteries where you pretty much know all along who did it, it's just a question of whether the murderer is going to get away with it. And guess who they've decided the murderer is?"

"I can't imagine."

"Can you tell me whatever happened to innocent until proven guilty?" Alex asked.

"Nothing happened to it. It never existed. It's one of those unrealistic ideals that people like to pretend are real, like fidelity and loyalty and justice."

"Has anyone ever told you you're not the most comforting person?" Alex said.

"I'm not in the mood to be comforting. I met with my divorce lawyer this morning. It appears my soon-to-be ex is trying to take me for all I'm worth."

"How did I end up with a depressed lawyer in the middle of a nasty divorce?"

"Oh, we've gone way beyond nasty," Ruth assured him. "I've found that the void love leaves behind can only be filled satisfactorily with another, equally powerful emotion."

"Dreaming of killing your husband? Want some tips on how to get away with it?"

"No, I don't want to kill him. That's too easy. I want to make him suffer. That's what nasty divorces are all about."

"If you saw my wife's body, you wouldn't think it was too easy," Alex said.

"Yes, well, enough chitchat."

"Chitchat?" Alex echoed. "I wouldn't want to know what you considered a serious conversation."

"You were telling me about your new ally. So you say she's going to help you even though all her friends are out to prove you guilty?"

"Yes, she is. I think in her quiet way, she's had quite a bit of sway over what the others think. And are you ready for the best part? Apparently she's won over Detective Ackerman as well. She may even have some influence with him."

"And can you tell me why she's going to do all this for a murder suspect she doesn't even know?"

"Well, she claims that she'll believe whatever the evidence shows. But that's not the way it works, is it? You see what you want to see. So I have to make her *want* to believe I'm innocent."

"Make her want to believe?" Ruth repeated. "Let me guess. You think you can make her fall in love with you just like that."

"Yes," Alex said.

"Isn't she married?"

"Yes," Alex said again. "But her husband is a jerk."

"So? You think women fall in love with the nice guys?"

"All right, you've got a point. And I'll admit he is charming, but he's a little too aware of it. You can tell he thinks he's the greatest thing since sliced bread. I figure all I have to do is build *her* up a little. Make her feel like I'm the lucky one in getting to spend time with her."

"You're going to break the poor girl's heart," Ruth remarked.

"You disapprove?"

"Not if it helps us win the case. When are you going to see her again?"

"I'm going straight from here. How do I !ook?"

"Handsome as the devil," Ruth said.

50. Alex & Sofie

*A*lex and Sofie were laughing—throw your head back, can't catch your breath laughing.

"Oh, my stomach hurts," Sofie managed to get out.

"Mine too," Alex said.

He had shown up at Sofie's door with a bottle of wine. It was only three o'clock, but Sofie thought it was only polite to offer to open it up. They'd polished that one off, gone through a second, and were now on their third. Plus they'd eaten almost all of the stuffed cabbages Sofie had made for Dean's dinner that night.

Actually, it was the stuffed cabbages that had started it. They were halfway through the second bottle when they went to raid the fridge, and when Alex heard she'd just made stuffed cabbages, he couldn't believe it. "Stuffed cabbages? With raisins?"

"Of course with raisins," Sofie said. "You can't have them without raisins."

"Meat with raisins. It sounds so disgusting, and it tastes so good," Alex said.

"A lot of people think it *is* disgusting. But one of my nannies was from Eastern Europe, and the only thing she cooked was Ukrainian food. So for three years, it's pretty much all I ate."

"It's practically the only thing I ate for my entire childhood," Alex told her.

"You had an Eastern European nanny too?"

"No, an Eastern European mother."

"Oh, I'm so . . . sorry," Sofie said, but she had already started to giggle—she wasn't used to having more than a glass or two of wine, and she'd had almost an entire bottle.

"So you think that's funny?" Alex said. "For years I thought that any food except for Hungarian food was disgusting because my mother didn't know how to make it. One time she tried to make spaghetti, but instead of putting spaghetti sauce on top, she put ketchup on it."

That had set Sofie off in another fit of laughter, and it had also gotten them started swapping horror stories about their parents and their childhood. The more awful the story, the harder they laughed.

Alex had grown up in Coney Island the oldest of four. Until he'd left home at the age of sixteen, he shared a bedroom with his brother and two sisters. His father was an alcoholic and his mother had to take in laundry to keep them afloat. Sofie had the run of an entire brownstone on the Upper East Side. She was an only child with a whole staff at her disposal. Both her stepmothers (neither of whom lasted long) only owned clothes that could be dry-cleaned, but the more stories they told, the more they found they had in common.

Alex told her about how he used to run track in high school. His father went to only one meet during his freshman year. At the meet, Alex came in second in the 100m, and his father said, "Why am I going to bother coming if you're not going to win?" Over the next year, Alex became a track star and eventually went on to win the all-city competition, but his father never went to another race.

"You think your family was tough?" Sofie demanded. "Listen to this." And she told him about how, when she was first sent to kindergarten, they thought she was slow. When she spoke, they couldn't understand what she said. They were going to suggest that she be switched into a special school when a teacher finally figured it out. Usually a driver dropped her off and picked her up. But there was one day the driver had off and the nanny came to get her in a cab. The teacher overheard Sofie jabbering away to the nanny—in Slavic. "I wasn't mentally handicapped, I just didn't speak English very well. I must have forgotten what I learned from my mother. But do you know what that means? It means not only did I not speak to my father or stepmother enough to learn much English, I didn't even speak to them enough for them to *realize* I didn't."

"I don't believe you," Alex said, laughing. "Admit it. You made that up."

"I wish."

Alex and Sofie went toe-to-toe with their stories, but in the end they couldn't decide who'd had a worse time of it. From the funny stories, they segued into the tougher parts. Alex told her about his father's drinking bouts. She told him about her father's rages. Alex told her how his mother had gotten lung cancer when he was eight, and how it dragged on over two years with her getting sicker and sicker. She died when he was ten. Sofie told him about her mother's suicide and how she had been the one to find the body.

As they talked, the light outside slowly faded. There was only one lamp on, and it threw a small pool of light between them. Maybe it was the darkness, or the wine, or the revelation of past tragedy, but Alex started talking about the more recent past—his marriage to Julia.

"I don't know," he said shaking his head. "Maybe I was still trying to impress my father. Julia was probably the only person who could have done it. She wasn't intimidated by him. In fact, I think my father might have been a little scared of her. You see, she had a way of walking into a room, something about her always made everyone look up. But I guess you know—you saw the way she carried herself, how it set her apart. Everyone noticed it. When she first arrived in the city, everyone knew who she was after a week.

After a month, she became known as the ungettable woman. But I got her. I won this prize that everyone else had tried for and failed. So when she said she wanted to get married right away, I was thrilled. I didn't invite any of my family to the wedding. I was barely in touch with my brother and sisters. My father—he wouldn't have wanted to come anyway, but I took Julia out to meet him after we were married. I have to admit, I wanted to show her off. I thought he would be impressed. I thought he would look at her and say, gosh, if my son can get this woman to marry him, he must really be something. Why not? It's what everyone else was saying." Alex smiled bitterly. "My father took one look at her and laughed in my face. He told me, in Hungarian, that he thought this was the stupidest thing I'd ever done. This woman, he said, was going to make my life a misery. Hadn't I learned anything? This type of woman was not for marrying. You married someone like my mother, and you screwed around with someone like this. And then you left the money by the bed." Alex laughed. "My old, immigrant father, who didn't even have a high school education, saw what all the big-shots in Manhattan couldn't see. I would have seen it eventually, but at least I might have had a couple of happy months. Thanks to him, I didn't even have that. Once someone takes the blinders off, they're off."

"That's true," she said.

"I realized that Julia's real talent was her ability to arouse emotions in people. But I don't mean emotions like love—I'm talking about emotions like envy, inadequacy, inferiority. She was like a siphon, empty at the core. When I bought her—because that's what I did—I bought other people's envy and admiration. But you find that's not worth much when you know the thing they envy you for is a big fraud. It's like they're admiring a piece of beautiful jewelry, and they're telling you how lucky you are to have it, but you know it's a fake."

They were silent for a bit. Then, trying to lighten the mood, Alex said, "Did your father say that your husband was going to make you miserable when you brought him home for the first time?"

"No. My father loved Dean. After they spent one evening together, my father told me that Dean might have been the first thing I actually got right."

"That was the response I was looking for from my dad," Alex said.

"Yeah, but you know what? It didn't feel as good as I thought it was going to. It was almost like he was saying, how did you get a great guy like this to fall for someone like you?"

"But it all worked out okay in the end. You're happy with your husband, right?" Alex asked.

"I was head over heels crazy in love with him," Sofie said.

"I don't think I've ever been head over heels crazy in love with anyone," Alex admitted.

"Maybe you just haven't met the right person."

"Maybe. And maybe I made sure that I wouldn't meet the right person."

"Why would you do that?"

"The more you care about someone, the more they can hurt you," he said. "It's a lot safer not to risk it."

Sofie smiled and went to pick up her wineglass. When Alex saw it was empty, he picked up the bottle to pour some more, but the bottle was empty too.

"I guess we drank some wine," he said, looking at the two other empty bottles.

"You drank most of it," she said.

"I think you're right. But even two to one, you still drank a whole bottle."

"But over how many hours?"

Alex glanced at his watch. "My God, I had no idea it was so late. I should probably get going."

"I guess you'd better," Sofie said reluctantly. "You've probably got stuff to do."

"No. I just figured your husband would be home soon, and I didn't want to still be hanging around." He grinned. "Especially since I helped polish off two bottles of his favorite wine."

"Hmm. You've got a point."

"Actually I'm probably just going to go home and watch TV to anesthetize myself—and maybe get to sleep before three a.m. for a change. The only good thing about not being able to get to sleep at night is that sometimes I sleep late the next morning, and then there's less of the day to get through."

"You're not working?"

"I can't. Not with all this going on."

"That must be awful," Sofie said. "If you need someone to talk to—"

"Are you sure?" Alex asked before she should even finish her sentence.

Sofie nodded. "It's the least I can do."

"I'll call you tomorrow."

51. Dean & Priscilla

*D*ean parked in the country club lot, walked across the golf course, and let himself into Priscilla's kitchen by the back patio.

She was waiting for him. She started over toward him as he pulled open the sliding glass door, saying, "I'm so glad you're here," but as she advanced, Dean took a step back.

"What is it?" she said, stopping abruptly. "What's wrong?"

"I got the message that you wanted to see me," he said, leaning against the counter and folding his arms across his chest. "So now I'm here. But I want you to know, I don't respond well to threats."

"Threats?" Priscilla laughed nervously. "What on earth are you talking about?"

"I'm talking about sending me threats through my own wife if I didn't come to see you right away."

"That wasn't a threat, silly. It was supposed to be a secret message."

Dean's frown only deepened.

Priscilla took a tentative step forward and laid one hand on his folded arms. "You can't pay too much attention to what I say. Really. I didn't mean anything by it. I just really wanted to see you. That's not bad, is it? I wouldn't in a million years try to force you to do anything you didn't want to do."

Of course she *had* meant for him to hear the veiled threat in her words. Priscilla was used to getting what she wanted, and she was used to doing whatever it took to get it. But she was also sensitive to when her tactics didn't work, and tonight she discovered that Dean wasn't someone she could push around.

"I'm sorry," she whispered, sidling up closer. "Really."

Dean stared down at her a moment, and she thought she saw something—some emotion flicker in his eyes. Then he relented. "All right," he said, unfolding his arms. "So where's your husband?"

"Gordon? Oh he's staying late at the office. He got stuck with some ridiculous work, as usual. If there's something unpleasant to be done, Gordon's always the sucker who ends up doing it. God knows when he's getting home tonight. You'd think he'd make an effort to get back earlier considering it's so soon after . . . after the most horrific experience of my life. I've been having such awful nightmares. I can barely sleep. I tried to take a nap this afternoon, and it happened again. I'm afraid to close my eyes."

"Come on, let's go sit down." Dean took her hand and pulled her into the living room. "Tell me about it," he commanded as he crossed to the bar and started making them drinks.

"In the dream, I start out in a house, and it's my house, but it's not my house. You know how that is in dreams? How you can know it's your house without it looking anything like your real house?"

"Sure," Dean said from across the room.

"So, I'm in my house, and it's dark. I can barely see anything. I'm going through all the rooms, searching for someone. I don't know why I don't just turn on the lights, but I don't. And suddenly I start getting the feeling that something awful has happened in this house. I walk into the bedroom, and even though it's dark, I can see stains on the sheets. Like someone died there. And then someone comes out of the shadows at me. Then I see their face, and suddenly I can't breathe."

"And?"

"And that's when I wake up," Priscilla said.

"No, I meant, and . . . whose face is it? I bet it's mine, right?"

"No, it's not yours. That would be understandable if it was yours. I mean the meaning would be obvious, right? You represent emotional danger."

"Alex?" Dean guessed.

"Well, that would make sense too. But this is the strange thing. The face"—she paused, then said—"it's Gordon's."

52. Susan & Detective Ackerman

"Mrs. Altman, it's Detective Ackerman calling," Ackerman said when Susan picked up the phone.

"Oh, hello."

Susan sounded distracted, as if she were in the middle of something, so Ackerman asked, "Did I catch you at a bad time?"

Susan thought of saying, yes, a very bad time, but she knew he wasn't referring to that kind of bad time.

"No, not at all," she said.

"Well, this won't take long. I'm just calling because I haven't been able to get in touch with your husband. I've left a couple of messages, but he's never called me back, and his secretary won't put me through."

"Oh." Susan said with a strange choked kind of laugh. "Now I understand."

"Understand what?" Ackerman asked, bewildered.

"You didn't leave a message regarding what you were calling about, did you?"

"No. I figured he'd know what it was about."

"And here I was thinking Harry was going off the deep end when all along it was just you."

"I'm not following," Ackerman said.

"Of course you're not. I'm sorry. It's just that my husband and I are getting a divorce, and in the last few days he's been calling me and leaving messages saying things like I'm insane, and this detective stuff isn't going to work, I'm not going to find anything, and there's nothing I can do about the divorce because Connecticut allows no-fault divorce. I thought he might be going crazy. I thought that was maybe why . . ." She started to laugh again. But then Ackerman realized it wasn't a laugh. Susan was crying.

Twenty minutes later Ackerman was at Susan's door. As usual, getting the door open was a challenge while trying to hold on to the dogs. She wasn't successful and when Ackerman stepped in, they rushed forward, pressing up against his legs, tails pumping. Bo jumped up, and Susan grabbed at him saying, "Bo, down. I'm so sorry."

"That's OK. I love dogs. We always had at least two in my house growing up."

"No dogs now?" Susan asked, shooing hers away from the door so Ackerman could get in.

"No. I'd love to have a dog, but it would be cruel. I'm not home enough to take care of one."

"Should we, um, go sit down?" Susan asked awkwardly. Now that he was here, she wasn't quite sure what to do with him. When they had settled into chairs in the living room, Susan started to say, "I'm sorry to impose on you like this. I just—"

"I'm happy to come," Ackerman said. "Really. I know what you're going through. And it's not your fault,"

It was the one thing that Susan needed to hear the most, and when he said it, she promptly burst into tears again.

Ackerman just leaned over and patted her knee. Then he sat there calmly while she cried. He didn't show any signs of discomfort or impatience. Susan imagined that in his line of work, he must be used to people crying in front of him.

When she finally calmed down a bit, she asked him, voice still wavering, "How do you know it's not my fault?"

"First of all, I happen to know that in general the people who sit around thinking that it must have been their fault and going over endlessly what they could have done differently . . ."

Susan looked up sharply. It was as if he had read her mind.

Ackerman saw her look and smiled. "Those people are not usually the ones at fault. If you want to find the one at fault, all you need to do is look for the person who is most energetically pointing the finger at other people."

"It's not usually just *one* person's fault though," Susan said. "And anyway, even if it was, what good does it do sitting around thinking about what someone else did wrong?"

"What good does it do sitting around blaming yourself if you're actually not responsible?" Ackerman countered. "Because in the end, that's really what it's about. It's not about blame—it's about responsibility."

"What's the difference?"

"How do I explain it? OK, let's say managing a relationship is like baking a cake. You have a husband and a wife adding the ingredients together. And let's just say that it comes out tasting terrible, and the wife says, 'Oh, it must be my fault. I probably stirred it too much. Or maybe I didn't measure carefully enough.' OK, maybe that's true. Maybe she did stir it a little too much, and she added a half a teaspoon instead of a quarter of a teaspoon of vanilla. But that's not what made it taste so horrible. The reality is that the husband, instead of adding sugar, added salt. What good does it do for the wife to pick on all the little things she did wrong? They have to figure out what the real mistake was and who was responsible. Until that happens, all their cakes are going to taste terrible."

"But what if he goes to bake a cake with someone else and adds sugar in that one?" Susan asked. "What if it's something about me that made him want to add the salt?"

"You're still trying to make it so that it's your fault."

"But what if it is? Maybe I've just gotten old. Maybe it's that he's not attracted to me anymore."

"That's not it."

"How do you know?"

He smiled. "Because I'm a man, and I have eyes."

"Now you're just being kind."

"No, I'm not."

Susan glanced at him and something in his expression made her flush slightly. But she went on. "Well, it was something. I must have done something."

Ackerman smiled sadly. "Do you want me to prove it wasn't your fault?"

"Can you?"

"Yes. But you'll need to answer a few questions first."

"Of course."

"Do you want this divorce?"

"No. I'd do anything to save this marriage."

"So you'd do anything he asked? I mean anything reasonable."

"Of course I would. I love him."

"Did he ever ask?"

Susan frowned. "What do you mean?"

"I mean did he ever really ask you to change something or do something different and you said no? Did he ever even tell you he was unhappy with the relationship and was thinking of leaving?"

"No," Susan said. "No, he just stopped coming home."

"So how is this your fault? Are you supposed to be a mind reader too?"

"I should have seen that he wasn't happy."

"And then what?"

"And then I should have been able to make him happy."

"How do you 'make' someone else happy? I would say that your one mistake was concentrating too much on making your husband happy. Were *you* happy?"

"You mean was I happy in my marriage—before all this?"

"Not in your marriage," Ackerman corrected. "Just in general."

Susan was about to say yes automatically, without even thinking. But then she stopped herself. Had she actually been happy? She thought of the big empty house and her long empty days. She thought about how she felt every time she saw children out playing in their yard.

"No," Susan admitted. "I wasn't happy. But that wasn't Harry's fault."

"I didn't say it was. But if your not being happy wasn't his fault, then why should Harry being unhappy be your fault?"

"I don't know."

"That might be something you want to think about. How long have you been applying one standard to yourself and another to your husband?"

"How do you know all these things? Do you moonlight as a therapist or something?"

"No. I wish that's how I knew."

"Oh." Susan said after a pause. "You've been through it."

Ackerman nodded.

"And not too long ago," she guessed.

"No. Not too long ago. And in my case, it *was* my fault. I spent all my time and energy on the job—and it's a job that takes a lot out of you, so I didn't have anything left for my wife when I got home. I'd always been a bit of a workaholic. I don't think you become a detective otherwise. But I guess it got worse over the years. You know how it is. You slip into routines. You stop making the effort. And my wife tried. She asked, she pleaded, she threatened. I guess I just didn't believe she would really leave me—until she did. And then it was too late."

"Why was it too late?"

Ackerman shrugged. "It had to get pretty bad for her to leave. And then at that point, it was easier for her to start over than it was for her to try to repair the damage. In general, we don't like to think that there's a too late. But there is."

"What did you do that was so awful?"

"I neglected her. I know it doesn't sound awful, but it adds up over the years. All the little betrayals. All the nights I said I'd be home for dinner and I didn't show. The times when we had plans on the weekend and I had to cancel. The family gatherings, weddings, even funerals that I begged off attending because of work. I forgot what was really important. I mean, my job is important, but my wife should have been more important. When it came to priorities and what got my time and attention, somehow she always came last on the list. I figured she understood. And she did. She knew how important my work was to me. She didn't want me to give it up. She just wanted to feel important too. But I didn't listen. I didn't— It would have been so easy to give her what she wanted. And it would have made my life better too. But I didn't realize that until after she left."

Susan jumped in, saying, "I don't know if you should take all the blame there. My husband was almost never home. You couldn't have been worse than him with that stuff, and I never thought of leaving him."

"Maybe you should have," Ackerman suggested gently.

53. The Mystery Readers

"So what have you found out?" Priscilla asked Sofie. They had gathered for a book club meeting, but now it was just Priscilla, Ashley, and Sofie gathered in Priscilla's white living room.

"Well . . . I told you about the lover, right?" Sofie asked.

"Yes, you found that out the first day," Priscilla said impatiently. "You've seen him again since then, haven't you?"

"Yes, I saw him yesterday."

"Did he say anything about what he told the police? Or his lawyer?"

"No, we didn't talk about that."

"Then did he at least say anything about Julia?"

"No," Sofie lied. "Not yet."

"I don't know why you're bothering with him," Ashley put in.

"Isn't that obvious?" Priscilla said—though she hadn't seen the obvious when Alex had shown up at her door. "She's getting information." Priscilla turned back to Sofie. "So what did you find out when you spoke to him last?"

"I found out he grew up out in Coney Island."

"That's it?" Priscilla was obviously disappointed.

"We talked about growing up and our families. I'm building a relationship with him so that when we start talking about the case, he'll confide in me."

"And why would he do that?" Ashley said.

"Maybe because he likes her," Priscilla countered.

"You mean *likes* her likes her?" Ashley's disbelief was obvious.

"Just because he wasn't interested in flirting with *you*, you assumed he was gay," Priscilla goaded Ashley. "Maybe you just weren't his type. Maybe Sofie is."

"If you want to know his type, look at who he married," Ashley said. "You couldn't get much different than Sofie and Julia."

"Yeah, well maybe he found out that he wanted something different," Priscilla shot back.

"Stop it," Sofie said. "There's nothing like that going on."

"Maybe there should be," Priscilla suggested. "A little something on the side can be fun. Add a little spice to life."

"Yeah, you should know," Ashley said under her breath.

At that moment, Priscilla was saved by Danielle's appearance with the coffee.

"Oh, good," Priscilla said. "I've been dying for some coffee. Everyone wants some, right?"

"There are only three cups," Ashley said, looking at the tray.

"There are only three of us here," Priscilla pointed out.

"What about Susan?"

"What about her? Does it look like she's here?"

"She might just be a little late," Ashley said.

"No, she's not late."

"But Susan *never* misses a meeting," Ashley said.

Priscilla turned to Danielle and said, "Thanks, I think we can pour for ourselves." When Danielle had left the room, Priscilla turned back to Ashley and said, rather stiffly, "Susan's not coming." In fact, she had been waiting for days for Susan to call and apologize, and she was only just now starting to suspect that the call wasn't coming.

Ashley glanced over at Sofie, and Sofie just shook her head

slightly. Ashley looked back to Priscilla and asked, "Why? What happened?"

"Why do you think that something happened?"

"Because I know Susan."

"I don't know what happened," Priscilla said. "The other day she was over here, and she just turned on me."

"That doesn't sound like Susan. Did you ask her what was wrong?"

"No. She didn't exactly give me a chance. She was too busy insulting me."

"Have you gone over to see her since?"

"I don't think it's up to *me* to go over and see *her*."

"This is starting to feel like the club I was in when I was in fifth grade. There's obviously something wrong. I'm going over to see Susan," Ashley said, standing up.

"You're leaving?" Priscilla asked, half angry, half scared. She couldn't afford to lose Ashley too. She stood up, knocking over her coffee. It spread out over the table and dripped onto the white rug.

Ashley said, "You might want to get some stain remover on that carpet." And then she turned and walked out.

"Danielle," Priscilla called. "Danielle!"

Danielle appeared a moment later.

"We've had a spill. Would you get the spot cleaner and get it up? If that doesn't work you'll have to call the carpet people."

Danielle glanced at the stain that was still spreading on the white carpet, and she turned and hurried back into the kitchen.

Sofie stood up then as well.

"You're not going too," Priscilla said.

"I should. You know, in case Alex calls. We're supposed be going down to Coney Island today. I've never been, so he suggested . . . anyway, it's something to do to take his mind off things."

"You're going to Coney Island with him?"

"It's not a big deal. It's just a last-minute thing."

Priscilla struggled with herself. On the one hand, the more involved Sofie got with Alex, the better it would be for her and Dean. But on the other hand, Priscilla knew that Alex wasn't someone to trust, and in the end, her better impulses won out.

"Just don't get too close to him, OK?" Priscilla said. "It might not be safe."

"Funny, that's what Detective Ackerman said."

"Well, then you might want to listen."

54. Sofie & Alex

$\mathscr{S}$ ofie had lied when she told Priscilla that she hadn't found out anything about Alex's relationship with Julia, but she'd been telling the truth when she said that the Coney Island trip was a last-minute thing.

Alex had called her early that morning. In fact, he called so soon after Dean had left for work Sofie wondered if he had been standing at his front window watching for Dean's car to pass by.

"Hey," he said when she picked up the phone. "It's me."

The mood of the day before had been intimate, but she knew it had been brought about by circumstances: the rainy afternoon, the bottles of wine, the shared confidences. She didn't expect it to hold. She thought the next time they talked the intimacy would have been replaced by the awkwardness of strangers who had gotten drunk and revealed too much. But she was wrong; it was still there.

"Hi," she said.

"My lawyer called me last night. I'm going to give DNA samples to the police this morning. And I'm a little nervous about it."

"I'm sure it will be OK," she said, but she knew her words were just empty platitudes.

"They're going to let me know by the end of the day if it's a match or not, but I don't think I can stand sitting around, waiting for that call. I was wondering if you'd consider going on a little trip with me."

"What kind of trip?"

"Yesterday you said you'd never been to Coney Island. For someone who's grown up in New York, that's practically a crime. The rides and stuff are closed—so I can't take you on the Cyclone, which happens to be the best roller coaster in the country. But you can still get a feel for the place. I'd love to take you there and show you around."

"I don't know . . ."

"It's going to be a beautiful day. And it would be an act of charity. What do you say?"

"I've got the book club meeting and I don't know how long that's going to go—"

"And I'm not sure how long giving the DNA samples is going to take. Why don't we just leave when we're both ready?"

"But how long is a trip to Coney Island going to take? If we don't leave until midday, when do you think we'll get back?"

"Maybe not late. We don't want to have to hurry. Manhattan's got one pace, Coney Island's got another."

"But my husband . . ."

"Call him. Tell him you might not be home until later."

"What reason will I give him?"

"Tell him the truth—or make up a lie. Whatever you have to do. Just as long as you say you'll go."

She hesitated, but only because she was trying to think what she would tell Dean; she had never really considered saying no.

55. Alex

"How did it go?" Ruth asked as Alex came into her office.

"It went fine," Alex said, taking the seat across from her. "Anyway, it's done."

"How do you feel? You nervous?"

"Nah. It's just my life on the line. No big deal."

Ruth smiled. "Well, at this point, we're just going to be waiting for the results. We'll know more about where we are with the case when we find out."

"If it's a match, I know exactly where I'll be."

Ruth didn't bother to contradict him. If it was a match, his arrest would be a matter of course. If it wasn't a match, he still wasn't off the hook, but it would weaken the case against him considerably. "We'll deal with that when we get there. In the mean time, are you going to be OK? I mean today, while we're waiting to hear?"

"I've actually planned a trip."

"Oh yeah? Not to South America, I hope?" She tried to pass it off as a joke, but Alex heard the worry in her voice.

"I'm taking Sofie to see the neighborhood where I grew up. Can you believe she's a native New Yorker and she's never been to Coney Island?"

"Sofie . . . ?"

"You know, Sofie—the one who's friends with Julia's friends."

"Oh, right. That's the person who was going to convince all her friends as well as the two detectives on the case that you're innocent."

"Sarcasm is always so helpful," Alex commented. "Remember, I have to convince *her* first."

"Right. I almost forgot. That's the part where you romance her into believing you. How's that going?"

"Actually, pretty darn well."

56. Sofie & Alex

"*I* didn't know there was any part of New York that was like this," Sofie said.

They were sitting at the end of the pier at Coney Island looking back at the beach and the boardwalk and the brightly colored Ferris wheel.

"I told you, you had to see it. Was I right, or was I right?"

"At least there was one thing you were right about."

"Oh, ho," Alex said, laughing. "I hear an accusation in there. What was I wrong about?"

"You said it was going to be a beautiful day."

"Isn't there a beautiful sunset right behind you?" he demanded.

"Yes, and there's also gale force winds to go along with it," Sofie said.

"Are you cold?"

"I can't feel my nose anymore. We should maybe head in soon."

"We can't go in before the sun sets," he protested. "How about this? Is this better?" he asked, draping his arm around her shoulders.

"It's not better, it's predictable," Sofie scolded shrugging his arm off. "Did that even work when you were sixteen?"

"Like a charm. So you won't even let me put my arm around you?"

"No, I won't," Sofie said simply.

"I suppose this is completely out of the question then," he said as he leaned over and brushed his lips against hers.

She sat perfectly still, not pushing him away, but not responding either.

"That must have been really awful, right?" he asked.

"Well, it was awfully stupid. Your wife died a week ago. How do you think that looks?"

"I wasn't thinking," he admitted.

"I suggest you start. What if they called me to the stand and they asked if anything happened between us?"

"Who said there's even going to be a trial?"

"Oh, there's going to be a trial. But I didn't say I know *who's* going to be on trial."

"You're the only one who doesn't know, then. Even my lawyer thinks I did it."

"You just have to wait until there's some concrete evidence in your favor."

"And what if the concrete evidence points to me as well?"

"You're starting to sound like someone who's guilty," Sofie said.

"We're all guilty of something."

"Don't talk like that," she said, annoyed. "Are you trying to make me think you did it?"

"Don't you?"

"Now you're fishing."

"I want to know. I want to know what you think—before the test results come back."

"Why does it matter what I think?"

"It just does. So do you believe me that I didn't kill my wife?"

Sofie just looked at him. She didn't give him an answer.

57. Priscilla & Dean

"No," Priscilla said, trying to push Dean off of her and sit up on the couch.

"No?" he said, running his hand along her thigh. "You don't like that?"

"You know I do," Priscilla said. She was flushed and short of breath. The truth was she liked it too much. Gordon had never made her feel this way.

"So why stop?" Dean said, showing that he didn't intend to.

"No. Dean, please. Stop."

And this time he did stop. And she felt like the proverbial woman who says no but means yes. She'd meant it—but now she found that she was disappointed that he'd listened to her.

He sat up and passed a hand over his hair to smooth it down.

"Are you mad?" she asked anxiously.

"No. I'm not mad."

"It's just that I want it to be special," she explained. "I don't want it to happen here on the couch half an hour before Gordon gets home.

"You want to save yourself? Have an old-fashioned wedding night?" Dean joked.

He had hit, inadvertently, on her exact fantasy. On one level, she knew it was crazy. She knew that everyone would say that it was way too soon. But on another level, she thought it wasn't too soon at all. In fact, it was almost too late. She'd had to wait forty years to feel this.

"Yes," she said. "I do."

He looked at her more closely.

"Are you serious?" He sounded alarmed.

She backtracked quickly. "Of course not, silly."

He still looked a bit uncertain, so she said, "Relax, I was *kidding*."

"OK. Good. I just wanted to make sure we're on the same page here. We're just having some fun, right?"

"Absolutely," she told him, but as she said it, she felt a wave of something close to nausea. Was it possible that she could feel something so powerful, and he didn't feel the same? She immediately dismissed the thought. He felt it too, but he was scared. He wasn't ready to face up to how big this thing was between them was. It would come. She'd just have to be a little patient with him. But in her mind, she had already started planning. She had imagined the scene with Gordon. She knew how she would tell him—calmly, rationally. She had envisioned his response. Incredulous, pleading, but finally reasonable—because Gordon was always reasonable. She even knew the lawyer she wanted to get, and she knew, from all the divorces her friends had been through, that the divorce laws in Connecticut were better than almost any state except for California . . . Well, good if you were the one wanting a divorce and your spouse was the one with the money.

It was almost as if he heard her thoughts and wanted to argue.

"We don't want to cause a whole lot of problems. Sofie would be devastated if she found out."

"I thought you didn't care about Sofie."

"It's not about caring about her. It's about having to deal with her. She'd freak out. I don't even know what she'd do. But whatever it was, I'd have to deal with it."

"You might be surprised. Sofie might not be quite as devastated as you think," Priscilla blurted out before she realized what she was saying.

"What do you mean?" Dean asked sharply.

She knew she shouldn't say anything else, but she couldn't help herself. "It's just that she seems to be really enjoying the 'detective' work she's doing with Alex."

"What do you know? Is there something going on?"

"Well, would you say that there's something going on with us?" Priscilla asked coyly. "She was going to spend the day with him today. He was taking her down to Coney Island. Apparently he grew up around there. Very romantic."

"She told me she was going to the movies," Dean said. "I can't believe she lied to me."

"That's a little hypocritical of you, seeing as you're here," Priscilla pointed out.

Dean barely seemed to hear her. When he spoke, it wasn't like he was trying to convince her—but more like he was trying to convince himself. "Anyway, there's no way she'd ever be interested in Alex," he said. "She's not the kind who cheats."

"Are you sure?" Priscilla asked.

58. Sofie & Alex

"Another glass of wine?"

Sofie covered her wine glass with her hand. "I'd better not. Dean will be able to smell it on my breath, and I don't think they serve wine in most movie theaters. Besides, I should probably get going. I want to get home before Dean if I can."

"Stay," Alex urged. "Stay here with me until I get the call. If he gets home before you do, just tell him you went to a later movie. It can't be too much longer now. Please?"

She hesitated, then said, "OK. I'll stay."

She didn't have to wait long; the call came about five minutes later. When the phone rang, they both froze.

It rang again, and still Alex didn't move. Sofie wanted to yell at him to pick it up, but she forced herself to keep quiet. She was here to help, not make things harder. When he finally moved the two steps over to the phone and reached out, she could see his hand was shaking. He picked it up and said, "Yes?"

She watched his face, but not a muscle moved. He seemed to listen for an eternity. Finally he said, "Yes, I understand. Thanks for calling. I'll see you tomorrow." He put the phone back down, sank into the nearest chair, and dropped his face into his hands.

Sofie felt her own knees go weak. She wanted to ask him what had happened, but she found that when she opened her mouth, she couldn't make any sound come out. She was suddenly light-headed. Her cheeks felt hot, but her lips were strangely cold.

At that moment Alex looked up. He was going to speak—until he saw her face. Then he leapt up and, putting an arm around her to steady her, he guided her to the chair he had just been sitting in.

"It's OK," he said, once she was sitting down. "It's OK. That was my lawyer. She called to tell me it wasn't a match. The hairs and skin—they're from someone else. I'm not off the hook, but at least I've got some breathing room. Are you all right? You're white as a sheet."

Sofie gave a shaky laugh. "I know. I feel really . . . I thought . . . When you got the call and then you sat down like that . . ."

"I'm so sorry. I didn't think how it would look. It was just such a relief. And you seemed so calm beforehand. Like you weren't worried at all. Was that all just an act to make me feel better?"

"Yes," she admitted. "And then it looked like it was bad news. . . ."

Alex stared at her, a peculiar look on his face. "If it had been bad news, you would have cared that much?"

Sofie avoided his gaze. "Apparently so," she said.

59. The Detectives

*P*eters and Ackerman were in the empty precinct. Ackerman sat with his head in his hands—the same pose Alex had taken when he'd gotten the call. Peters had tipped his chair back, his feet propped on the desk, and was staring at the ceiling.

"Well," Peters said. "That was a surprise."

Ackerman lifted his head. "So you thought he did it too?"

"Yeah."

"I don't understand. I was so sure. . . . I thought by this time today we'd be on our way to arrest that bastard."

Peters sighed. "I guess it's back to the drawing board."

"What do you mean?"

"We'd better start looking for the match to that evidence. Because it's not the only thing that points away from him. We've got those footprints that are a good size and a half smaller than his."

"Those could be from a gardener," Ackerman said.

"And there are carpet and clothing fibers on the body that don't match anything in his house."

"He would have gotten rid of whatever he was wearing. And maybe the carpet fibers are from his office."

"It's just that the evidence is piling up, and it seems to be pointing away from Alex Stowe."

"You're not ruling him out as a suspect, are you?"

"No, I'm not ruling him out. But he's not my favorite anymore. And after this, you can't be so sure it's him either."

"But I am sure," Ackerman said. "The fact that the DNA didn't match could be explained in a lot of different ways. For one, he could have planted those hairs to get himself off. Maybe that's why he didn't want the crime scene disturbed. Did you ever think of that?"

"It's a little far-fetched," Peters said.

"But you know it happens. You've heard about cases—"

"I know it happens. It's just . . . you're the one who told me that before your divorce you sometimes let a case get to you. Tell me that's not happening here."

"It's not happening here," Ackerman said, but Peters didn't look convinced.

60. Sofie & Dean

"Where have you been?" Dean demanded.

Sofie had just come in the front door, and she was in the hallway taking off her coat.

"Don't you remember?" she said, opening up the closet and hanging up her jacket. "I told you I was going to be late."

"Yes, but where were you?"

"You know where I was—I went to a movie."

Dean stared at her.

She looked at him. "What? Why are you acting so weird?"

"I'm just a little surprised."

"That I went to a movie? You're easily shocked, aren't you?" She walked past him down toward the kitchen.

"No, not that you went to a movie. That you're so good at lying about it."

Sofie stopped in her tracks.

"I had no idea you could do it so well," Dean said.

She turned around, crossing her arms over her chest. "Why do you think I'm lying?"

"I don't think you're lying. I *know* you're lying."

"Then how do you *know* I'm lying?"

"It doesn't matter how I know. That's beside the point."

"Is it?"

"Don't try to turn this around, Sofie. This is about you. It's about you flat-out lying to me."

"You make it sound like I did something horrific," Sofie said. "Fine, if you want to know, I was with Alex today. I didn't tell you because I knew you'd give me a hard time about it. That's all. Now, if you'll excuse me, I'm starving." And she turned back around and continued toward the kitchen.

"Don't you walk away from me," Dean said, but Sofie didn't even pause.

"What? Why is this such a big deal? Are you going to tell me that you never lied to *me*?" Sofie said as he followed her into the kitchen.

"You said you were going to the movies, but you were spending time with another man. That's a big deal."

"Come on, Dean. Don't be ridiculous. I lied to you because I knew you didn't want me talking to Alex. You know this is just about the case."

"There you go again. You're lying, but to look at you, butter wouldn't melt in your mouth. Who are you? You're not the person I married. I don't even know you."

"Oh, don't be so melodramatic," she said, pulling a plate of stuffed peppers from the refrigerator. "Why do you care so much if I talk to Alex?"

"I care that you lied about it."

"Oh, so if I told you the truth, you wouldn't have a problem with it?"

"No, I'd still have a problem with it."

"What? You think I like him? You think I'm having an affair?"

"I don't know," Dean said. "How would I know? I only just discovered how good you are at lying."

"I told you I'm only interested in the case. And I'm telling you the truth."

"Well, Priscilla seems to think differently." The retort was out of his mouth before he had time to think better of it.

"Oh?" Sofie's eyebrows rose. "When did you talk to Priscilla?"

"I ran into her on my way home," Dean said.

"So I guess she's the one who told you I was with Alex today?"

"Yes, she told me. But don't tell her I told you."

"Why not?"

"She felt really bad that she'd gotten you in trouble."

"I bet she did."

"What?" Dean said innocently. Too innocently.

"So you ran into her on the way home? When was that?"

"A little while ago."

"How long?"

"I don't know. I didn't check my watch."

"Because when I was at Alex's house, I saw you drive by. And I left about two minutes later. That's not a whole lot of time to *talk* to Priscilla."

"What are you implying?"

Sofie looked at him. Then she said, "Only that if I wanted to be paranoid, I could just as easily start accusing you of having an affair."

Dean decided to back off the issue. "OK, you've got a point. You have to have trust in a marriage."

"That's what I'm saying," Sofie agreed.

"I didn't really think you were having an affair."

"Then why did you imply it?"

"I guess I was just . . . scared."

"Scared? Of what?"

"I just don't want you to see him anymore," Dean finally said.

"Listen, there's nothing to worry about."

"What if I forbid you to see him?"

"*Forbid* me?" Sofie echoed.

"Ask you," Dean amended. "I'm asking you not to see him anymore, OK?"

"Dean, I've been reading mysteries my whole life. Now you're asking me to give up my chance at solving a real one?"

"You really think you're going to solve this?"

"At least I'm damn well going to try," Sofie said.

61. Sofie & the Detectives

"*T*hat was delicious," Ackerman said, taking the last bite of apple pie and putting his fork down. "But if I'd known you were going to go to all this trouble—"

"It's no trouble," Sofie assured him. "I remembered you said that apple was your favorite, and I haven't made one yet this fall. It's a crime to go through apple season and not make an apple pie."

Sofie and Detective Ackerman were sitting in Sofie's kitchen with their empty plates in front of them and a copy of the *New York Times* Sunday crossword puzzle folded next to Ackerman's plate.

"So what did you think of the puzzle this week?" he asked.

"It was a tough one," Sofie admitted.

"I thought so too. We've got another tough one on our hands, don't we?"

"You mean the case?" Sofie asked.

"Yes. We had a little setback."

"I heard they couldn't match the DNA evidence found on the body to Alex, but I don't see how that's a setback," she said. "I would assume that's valuable information to redirect your efforts. What about Julia's lover?"

Ackerman gave a short laugh. "I know that Alex claims she had a lover, but I also know there's absolutely no evidence of it."

"Have you *looked* for evidence?"

At that, it was Ackerman's turn to look uncomfortable. When he spoke, his voice was defensive. "No. But we didn't have to—did he happen tell you that he hired a private detective and couldn't come up with anything? Not a scrap of proof that his wife was having an affair."

"Yes, but I never thought that you'd be the kind of detective who would leave someone else to do your work for you. If I were you, I'd want to make that determination myself. You have a lot more resources than some private eye."

"It's a waste of time," Ackerman said.

"You *want* him to be guilty," Sofie said accusingly.

"I don't *want* him to be guilty. He *is* guilty."

"I just don't see how you can be so certain, especially now."

"Listen, I came by today because I got a call from your husband this morning."

"Dean called you?"

Ackerman nodded. "He's worried that you're getting too caught up with this case. And I think I agree."

"But I talked to you about this. You knew I was going to be spending time with Alex, trying to get information about the case."

"I know. And in retrospect, I don't think I should have sanctioned that. I have to agree with your husband—it's not safe for you. Plus I think you're getting too . . . well, emotionally involved."

"What do you mean?"

"I mean that it seems you've come to like Alex Stowe a little too much."

Sofie opened her mouth to answer indignantly, but Ackerman held up a hand. "Don't get angry. Just tell me the truth, you're starting to like him, aren't you?"

"It's not that I like him," Sofie insisted. "It's that you don't. What do you have against him?"

Ackerman looked at her for a moment. Then he said, "You're not going to let this alone, are you?"

"No."

"And to think when I first met you, I thought you were this shy, nervous person."

"See, you can be wrong about people sometimes," Sofie said.

"I'm not wrong about Alex Stowe."

"*How do you know?*"

"I know," Ackerman said slowly, "because this isn't the first time. You see, he's done it before."

Sofie stared at him, frowning in confusion. "Done what before?"

"Killed his wife," Ackerman said succinctly.

"He tried to kill Julia before?"

"No, not Julia. His first wife. And he didn't just try. He succeeded."

"He . . . I don't understand," Sofie said, shaking her head. "You're saying that he was married before Julia, and he killed his first wife?"

"Yes. That's exactly what I'm saying."

"But—did he go to jail for it?"

Ackerman smiled, but it was a smile without humor. "No. He didn't."

"Was anyone convicted for the murder?"

"No. They um"—Ackerman cleared his throat—"they ruled it a suicide."

"A suicide?" Sofie echoed. "You're kidding, right?"

"No."

"His first wife committed suicide?"

"No. He made it *look* like his first wife committed suicide."

"But"—Sofie paused, still trying to take in the new information— "but how can you know that? I mean, if it was ruled a suicide . . ."

"Come on, now. You're asking me that after what just happened with his second wife? And you haven't even heard the details. She died of carbon monoxide poisoning. She left her car running in the garage."

"That's quite common, isn't it?" Sofie said.

"They also found that she had taken a large dose of Klonopin. It's an antianxiety drug that she had a prescription for. She took about five times the normal dose."

"Well, I imagine that committing suicide would be anxiety-producing," Sofie said.

Ackerman gave her a look. "There was no suicide note. At the time of her death Alex Stowe was at a friend's party, and there were twenty witnesses to confirm that. *But*, even though he was at the party during the time of death, the ingestion of the Klonopin probably occurred before his departure. Also, he was the one who discovered the body, and he brought his wife into the house from the car, so the scene was impossibly compromised. *And* some of the wife's friends said she was thinking of divorcing him. So"—Ackerman ticked off the points on his fingers—"we have the fact that she was heavily drugged and certainly disoriented when she got in the car. He had a good alibi—but it was almost too good. I think that in itself is suspicious. Plus there was no suicide note, and he compromised the scene by removing her from the car."

"So what happened? Did it go to trial?"

Ackerman shook his head. "We didn't even have enough to indict. A lot of people don't know this, but it's easier to get away with murder than you think. Make sure it's unwitnessed, that you don't tell anyone, and you work alone, and it's going to be very tough to prosecute successfully. Not impossible, but tough."

"But all that seems like enough at least to get an indictment," Sofie said.

"There were some extenuating circumstances."

"Like what?"

"The wife had a history of depression and a couple of incidents."

"Incidents?"

"A couple of attempts at suicide, but in both cases she called friends right after she took the pills, and of course they called 911 and got an ambulance rushed over, and they pumped her stomach."

"Those are some pretty important extenuating circumstances," Sofie pointed out.

"Sofie, he killed her. How can you doubt it after what's happened with his second wife?"

"If he really did it once, do you really think he'd be stupid enough to try the same trick again?"

"Yes. It worked the first time. Why not the second?"

"Well, you could look at it another way," Sofie said. "If someone else knew about his history, they might have staged it."

"You mean the O.J. defense? He was framed?"

"It's possible."

Ackerman made a noise in the back of his throat.

Sofie ignored the derisive sound and plunged on. "You have to at least admit it's possible. It could explain some things, like why this time he didn't want anyone to disturb the scene and that comment he made at dinner. Remember you told me about it? Apparently he said that you never know when you might have a murder on your hands. Of course he was referring to his first wife and that whole situation."

"It explains a whole lot more than just a casual comment at dinner," Ackerman said, annoyed.

"Can you tell me why he killed his first wife?"

"The oldest reason in the book. Money. When he married her he was twenty-five, broke, and ambitious, and she was forty, loaded, and lonely. She'd just gone through a messy divorce, and her ex had taken her for half of everything. Her ex told her it was all she was good for. That no one would ever be interested in her if it wasn't for her money."

"And she married Alex? I'm surprised she ever got married again," Sofie said.

"I've got one word for you: prenup. He signed away any rights to a single penny. She was desperate to believe that someone cared about her completely separate from her money. Apparently her lawyers assured her that it was airtight; they promised her that there was no way Alex would ever be able to get any money from her from a divorce. But they didn't think that he might find another way to get her money."

"I don't know," Sofie said uncertainly. "I just don't think you can be sure."

"Yes, you can. At least I can. According to the Police Department, I have a perfect record—that means I've closed every case I've ever worked on. It looks good on paper, but it's not true. This case was considered closed because they ruled it a suicide. But I know he got away with murder. Now I've got a chance to set the record straight. Are you going to help me, or not?"

Sofie looked down at the floor, biting her lip nervously.

"Well?" he demanded.

62. Sofie & Alex

"Hey I'm glad you—"

Sofie silently brushed past Alex and went into the house.

"Called," he finished. She headed through the living room and down the hall without saying a word.

He followed her into the kitchen, where she had already pulled out a bottle of wine—that they'd been drinking the night before—and was getting down a wineglass.

"Would you pour me a glass?" he asked, but she didn't reach up for another glass. She just uncorked the bottle and poured into the glass she had gotten for herself.

"All right, I'll get my own. It looks like I might need it."

She swung around to face him. "Why didn't you tell me about your first wife?" she demanded.

"Oh," he said. "That."

"Yes, *that*."

"Who told you?"

"It certainly wasn't you," she retorted. "Detective Ackerman told me."

He curled his lip. "That asshole."

"No, actually he's not. I thought he was persecuting you. I couldn't figure out why he was so convinced that you were guilty without hard evidence to back it up. Now it makes sense. A lot of things make sense."

"Oh, so now you think I did it?"

She looked at him for a long moment. "It doesn't look good," she told him. "How am I supposed to trust you if you lie to me?"

"I thought there wasn't any way you'd help me if I *didn't* lie to you."

"You've got it backwards. Being honest about the bad stuff is the way you really earn trust. But when I find out you lied about it, it makes me wonder why."

"I'm sorry," he said, helplessly. "You're right. What can I do?"

"You can start by telling me about it."

"Didn't you get all the gory details from the detective?"

"Yes, but I thought you might want to tell your side of the story."

"Detective Ackerman probably tried to make it sound as bad as possible. I bet he didn't mention that my first wife had a history of depression, and she'd actually had several suicide attempts before that."

"No, he told me that."

"And he still thinks I did it?"

"He doesn't just think; he's sure."

"Don't you think that's a little crazy?"

"No. He had some valid concerns."

"Like?"

"Like he said there was no suicide note."

"But there was paper and a pen in the car—in the seat next to her. I think she meant to write one, but the Klonopin hit harder and sooner than she expected. She had the phone out there with her too. Maybe she was planning on calling for help again . . . I don't know."

"Detective Ackerman also told me that she was thinking of divorce?"

"Lies," Alex said. "It was her friends. They never liked me. They were jealous old hags who didn't like the fact that Beth had found someone who made her happy. It was true at the time she was going through a bit of a rough patch. But that had absolutely nothing to do with me. She always said she didn't know what she'd have done if I hadn't come into her life."

"And you going to that party? Detective Ackerman said that was suspicious."

"Since when is going to a party on a Saturday night suspicious? Beth said she wanted some time alone. And it was going to the party or going to the movies, and I didn't feel like sitting alone in the dark on a Saturday night. So now you know everything."

"Are you sure?"

"I'm sure."

Sofie looked down into her wine, rolling the stem of the glass between her fingers. "Sofie?" His voice was soft, hesitant.

She looked up and said almost ferociously, "From now on, no more lies. If you lie to me again— I can handle just about anything, as long as you're honest with me."

"No more lying," Alex promised.

She shook her head. "Jesus, you're lucky this stuff isn't admissible in court. And you're *really* lucky there weren't any hairs on the body that matched yours. But you know, even though evidence on the body doesn't match up, you're still a suspect."

"Oh, they made sure to tell that to my lawyer."

"So we've got to do something."

"You mean you're still going to help me?"

"Well, I'm not giving up completely."

"That's not exactly a vote of confidence."

"Take it or leave it," she retorted.

"I'll take it. So what do we do now?" he asked. "Have any ideas?"

"Actually, I do."

63. Sofie & Alex

"So what is your brilliant idea that's going to save my skin?" Alex asked.

"Actually, it was your brilliant idea," Sofie said.

"Oh, great. Then we're in trouble."

"Remember why you originally came to see me? You wanted help finding the person your wife was having an affair with. Now, I bet if we find that person, we'll find the match to those unidentified hairs."

"Why didn't I think of that?" Alex said, with exaggerated sarcasm. "Oh wait a second, I did. And you know what? I already tried looking."

"You didn't try looking with me," she pointed out. "Sometimes a new set of eyes can make all the difference in the world."

Alex still looked doubtful, but he shrugged and said, "OK. Where do you want to start?"

"Let's start with her things."

"I went through it all. There's nothing there."

"You can't be sure of that."

"No, I really mean nothing. No diary, no letters."

"Computer?"

"The police took it. But I looked before that. I hired a technician, and apparently she used one of those little memory sticks so she wouldn't leave any trace on the computer."

"And I guess you didn't happen to find the memory stick?"

Alex shook his head.

"What have we got then?"

"Clothes, jewelry, a few receipts."

"OK. Let's take a look."

Alex led the way upstairs. "I slept at one end of the hall," he said, gesturing. "And Julia slept at the other. I wanted to be as far away as I could get."

"You hated her that much?"

"Yes, but that's not why. The truth is, she snored something awful."

"She *didn't*."

Alex grinned. "You bet she did. It was why she would never stay over at my place before we got married—not even just to sleep. I found out about it on the wedding night. Very romantic—she sounded like a moose. She claimed it was a genetic disorder—obstructive sleep apnea. But I think it was just that she snored really loud."

"How loud?"

"*Really* loud. You can't imagine how loud."

Sofie laughed.

"That's why I took the room furthest away, and I still had to put in earplugs."

"So you've got a reason to explain away the separate bedrooms and why you didn't hear Julia go out," Sofie said.

"Very true."

They reached the master bedroom and Alex pushed open the door. "Where do you want to start?"

"How about the jewelry?" Sofie suggested.

"I should probably put this stuff in a security deposit box now or something until I can sell it. God only knows how much all this is worth."

Sofie expected him to lead her to a jewelry box, but instead he gestured toward a small dresser.

"Which drawer?" Sofie asked.

"The whole thing. She was a total slob with everything except her jewelry. She had a healthy respect for jewels. So she had that cabinet made."

Sofie opened the top drawer. It was lined with felt and divided into tiny partitions, with a pair of earrings nestled in each. She ran her fingers down the rows. She opened the next drawer and that held bracelets and brooches. The bottom drawer held the necklaces.

"Discover anything?" Alex asked.

"Yeah. That stuff is worth a fortune—if it's all real."

"It was when she bought it, if you go by the price tag."

"You should check if it still is," Sofie said. "Wasn't there that Agatha Christie mystery where they stole the jewels and replaced them with fakes?"

"Isn't that a bit far-fetched?"

Sofie shot him a look.

"OK, OK. I'll do it. What next? The clothes?"

Sofie nodded.

He pointed her to the walk-in closet.

Sofie opened the door. "Wow."

Alex came to stand beside her. "She had a lot of clothes."

"It's the kind of stuff I wish I could wear," Sofie said.

"Go ahead. Take anything you want."

"I couldn't do that."

"A lot of the stuff still has the tags on it."

"No, that's not what I mean. I wish I could wear it—but I can't. I can't pull it off."

Alex looked at her. "You wouldn't want to. It's not your style."

"I know," she said.

"That's a good thing." When Sofie looked doubtful, he said, "Trust me."

"Let's start going through the pockets," Sofie said, stepping into the closet and checking the pockets of the first pair of pants.

"I already did that."

"You did?"

Alex answered the unspoken question. "Nothing there. Just some odds and ends."

"Let me look at it anyway."

"I think I put the stuff over here."

He went over to one of the bedside tables, opened the top drawer, and took out some items and put them on the bedspread.

Sofie picked them up one by one. First she picked up the lipsticks and opened them one after the other. They were both a bright, scarlet red—and they were both almost gone. "Huh. Guess she liked that color." She moved her hand over to the receipts. "She went to Jean-Georges for dinner. With you?"

Alex shook his head. "But that doesn't mean anything. We didn't do much together."

She picked up the next receipt and laughed.

"What's so funny?" Alex demanded.

"She bought something—looks like a lot of things from the amount—from La Perla."

"So?"

"La Perla is a lingerie store."

"Ah."

"If it wasn't for you . . ."

"It wasn't for me," Alex confirmed.

"Then it was for someone else."

"But we still don't know who."

Sofie brushed the covers straight and caught sight of the diamond earring. She reached out and picked it up with her thumb and forefinger and held it up.

"What?" Alex asked, seeing the look on her face. "What is it?"

64. Priscilla & Gordon

*P*riscilla heard a small noise—and when she turned around and saw Gordon standing in the doorway of the kitchen, she jumped.

"You scared me. What are you doing home at this hour?" Priscilla demanded. "I thought you had that big project at work."

"I thought I'd come home a little early for a change and surprise you."

"Well, I'm surprised all right," Priscilla said. She was surprised—but she was definitely not pleased.

"Are you *cooking*?" Gordon asked, looking around the kitchen.

"Yes, I'm cooking. What's the big deal?"

"It's just I don't think I've seen you cook anything in years."

"That doesn't mean I can't."

"Sure," Gordon said, not very convincingly. "What are you making?"

"Beef Wellington."

"Wow. I had no idea you knew how to make beef Wellington. I was going to suggest we go out to dinner. But I guess we should stay in." He saw the look on her face and said, "Or we can go out if you were making this for a party or something. Whatever you want."

What Priscilla wanted was for Gordon to be back at work, slaving away at his big project. Dean was coming over for dinner—at least, that had been the plan. If Gordon had been just half an hour later, he would have found her with Dean. Part of her wished it had happened like that. It would have been awful, but then it would have been over. It would have forced . . . well, everybody's hand in that case.

"Excuse me a second," Priscilla said, wiping her hands on a dishrag and leaving the room. She went into Gordon's study, closed the door, and made the phone call. She got Dean on his cell. He was in his car already, on his way from the station. She told him that Gordon had unexpectedly shown up.

"That was close," Dean said. "I'll take a rain check, then. I hope Gordon enjoys my beef Wellington."

"Yeah, thanks a lot. I'm sure you'll get some sort of gourmet something from your wife."

"You're not getting jealous of my wife now, are you?"

"Of course not."

Gordon knocked softly, then opened the door.

Priscilla covered the mouthpiece with one hand. "What?" she said annoyed. "You can't leave me alone for five seconds?"

"It's just that . . . it smells like something's burning."

"Oh, shit. I've got to go," she said into the phone, and she could hear Dean laughing on the other end of the line.

The pastry crust of the beef Wellington was charcoal.

Gordon tried to comfort her. He rubbed her back saying, "Don't worry about it. It's OK. We'll just go out."

"It's not OK." Priscilla slammed down the pan. "I've been work-ing on that for"—she gestured helplessly—"I don't know . . . hours."

"Hey, let's just have a glass of something. Sit down. And talk. OK?"

"You think that's going to solve anything?"

"I thought we might try."

"Well, you know what? I don't think I'm in the mood for this tonight," Priscilla said, turning away.

"I think it's important that we talk."

She couldn't contain her annoyance. She had been looking for-ward all day to this dinner with Dean. She had wanted to talk to Dean—and now she had *Gordon* there.

"You know what? I don't care what you think."

Gordon stared at her. "You really don't, do you?"

"No, I really don't. I don't care what you think. I don't care what you do. I just don't care."

"I guess that's our talk, then," he said.

"I guess it is."

Gordon nodded, as if confirming something in his own head. "OK." Then he turned around, but instead of going upstairs or into the TV room, he went out the front door. A moment later she heard his car start up.

She ran to the front window—just in time to see Gordon pulling out. She had a moment of panic . . . until she realized that if she called Dean right away, she might catch him before he got home.

65. Sofie

*T*he house was dark and quiet when Sofie returned. Dean hadn't gotten back from work yet, and there was no message on the machine, so she didn't know if he was going to be around for dinner. She usually had some leftovers she could serve as a backup, but when she checked the fridge, it was completely bare. She decided that she didn't feel like cooking. Instead she pulled out the stack of take-out menus and started sorting through them, but she was too restless even for that. She wandered into the other room and turned on the TV and flicked through some channels—then turned it off again almost immediately. She picked up the book she had started several days ago but had put down because it didn't hold her interest. When she read a couple of paragraphs, she found it wasn't any better now.

She finally realized that she wasn't going to be able to do anything that required her to sit still. So even though it was pitch black already and there was a wind that made it feel like deep winter, she decided to go out for a walk. It had been ages since she'd gone on one of her solitary rambles. She put on her heavy jacket, got out a scarf, gloves, and a hat, and called to Agatha. Then she slipped out the sliding glass doors and walked down the hill to the golf course.

Agatha trotted along beside her, slipping into the woods then darting back out again. The moon was just rising over the tree line. It was almost full and it lit up the open golf course in an eerie half-light. There was even a moon shadow cast by the trees. Sofie walked along the edge of moonlight and shade, peering in among the trees, trying to pick out Agatha's form, but it was like a solid line of impenetrable darkness.

Then Sofie heard a noise, like something big moving in the underbrush. Sofie called to Agatha, but when she looked down, Agatha was beside her. She scooped her cat up, saying, "I don't want you off hunting that thing. With our luck, it would turn out to be a skunk or something." But as Sofie continued walking, she realized that the noise was still there. She stopped and the noise stopped as well. Her pulse spiked.

She took a few tentative steps forward, and once again, she heard the ominous rustling. She stopped and the noise stopped. She could hear her own breathing in the silence. Now she knew what the noise was; it was the sound of footsteps in the brittle leaves.

She started walking again—and again she heard the rustling behind her. She broke into a run. Her heart was pounding, her breath coming fast, and she was clutching Agatha so hard that she started squirming.

Sofie sprinted along the grass, heading for a break in the trees where she could run up the hill and through to the street. She thought she heard the noise getting louder—and closer—and she put on a burst of speed up the hill. She reached the road and kept going, glancing back over her shoulder. In her imagination, the other person was right behind her, actually reaching out to grab her. Then someone did grab her; someone in front of her.

Sofie screamed, Agatha clawed her way free, and a familiar voice said, "Hey, it's OK. It's OK. It's me."

Sofie blinked, gasping. Detective Ackerman was standing in front of her on the street, holding both arms firmly.

"Just take deep breaths. Can you tell me what's wrong?"

Sofie gulped air, trying to speak.

"It's OK. Take a minute if you need."

"Someone following me . . ." Sofie gasped.

Ackerman glanced over Sofie's shoulder. "Where?"

Sofie gestured down toward the golf course.

"I'll go check it out."

Ackerman disappeared down the hill.

Sofie moved to stand right under a street lamp. Even in the center of a pool of light, she didn't feel quite safe. It was funny, the neighborhood where she lived, where she'd gone out to walk at night dozens of times without even thinking about it, and now she was scared just to stand there.

Ackerman returned a minute later, shaking his head. "No one's there."

"But there was," Sofie insisted. By this time she had managed to catch her breath and she was able to speak almost normally. "I heard something. I thought it was just a skunk or a raccoon or something, but every time I stopped walking the sound stopped—and then it started up again when I started walking."

"Oh, I believe you heard something," Ackerman assured her. "You were scared. Anyone could have seen that."

"But do you think I was imagining things?"

Ackerman hesitated, then said, "I don't think so. I think someone was *trying* to scare you."

"But why?"

"Maybe you're getting too close to finding out something they don't want discovered," Ackerman suggested. "I'm going to get the team down here first thing tomorrow. See if we can find anything."

"Do you think someone was really trying to hurt me? Do you think I should be . . . worried?" Sofie asked.

"I think whoever it was probably could have caught you if they wanted to. But, just to be on the safe side, I think you should be careful. Very careful."

66. Sofie & Dean

"See?" Dean said. "See, I told you to stay away from that man. I knew he was dangerous."

Dean had just returned home and Sofie had finished telling him what had happened to her on the golf course.

"There's no reason to think it was Alex," Sofie protested.

"What did Detective Ackerman think?"

"He said it looked like I might be getting close to discovering something important and that might be making somebody nervous. He said he's going to get the crime scene people down at first light to see if they can find anything."

"Well, I'm glad to hear he's taking this seriously," Dean said. "Now, I want you to promise me you'll stay away from Alex. At least for a little while until things calm down."

"But—"

"I want you to promise me," Dean repeated.

"All right," Sofie said reluctantly.

"By the way, what was Detective Ackerman doing around here at that hour? It must have been almost nine o'clock."

"I don't know. That's a good question."

"Come to think of it, I think I saw his car here the other night when I was driving back as well. It's a blue Corolla, isn't it?"

"Blue sedan type thing, you mean?"

Dean nodded.

"That's his car," she agreed. "Are you sure you saw it here at *night*?"

"I'm positive," Dean said.

67. Sofie & Dean

*T*he next morning Sofie took the men out to the golf course and showed them where she had been walking and where she had heard the noise. When checking the woods, they said they found what looked like a trail. Then, in a bare patch of earth, they found a footprint.

"So what did you do today?" Dean asked as they sat down to dinner that night.

"Well, I spent the morning with the police down at the golf course," Sofie said.

"Did they find anything?"

Sofie nodded, but she had just taken a bite so she had to chew and swallow before she could answer him. "A footprint. They're going to compare it to the footprints they found near Julia's body. They said it looks like the same size. And, you know, the prints they found near Julia's body were at least a size smaller than Alex's. So if the footprints they found this morning were the same size as the ones near the body—"

"OK, I see where you're going with this," Dean broke in. "But first of all, the footprint they found might not have been the person following you. It could be a groundskeeper or something. And second of all, he could have hired someone. Did you go over to see him today?"

"No."

"Are you telling me the truth?"

"I said I didn't go see him."

"What did you do this afternoon?" Dean asked suspiciously.

"I don't quiz *you* about where you've been when you come home late," Sofie retorted.

"I'm asking because I'm *worried* about you."

Sofie sighed and said, "I've been making bread all afternoon. It's not exactly something you throw together in half an hour. After the detectives left, I went to the store, then I came home and started the bread. I let the dough rise. I read a little bit of my book. I kneaded the dough. I read some more, I kneaded the dough again. The bread's over there." She gestured. "I thought you could have it for breakfast."

"I'm sorry." Dean reached across the table for her hand. "Will you forgive me?"

Sofie ignored his question, and said instead, "I was thinking of coming into the city sometime this week. I was going to visit the bookstore, and I thought I might drop by to see you at your office."

"Do you think you should?" Dean asked.

"Why on earth not?"

"It's just that you seemed to get so upset the last time you came in."

He was referring to when she'd spiraled into her depression.

"Upset? Is that how you'd describe it?"

"OK, more than upset. Then isn't that all the more reason to be careful not to trigger it again?"

"I think I can handle it."

"I don't want you to—"

"Dean. You can't control my every move. I'm coming into the city. If you don't want me to come by to see you—"

"No, of course I want you to come by."

"Are you going to be around? Last time you weren't even there."

"That wasn't my fault," Dean protested. "I told you I was going to be out."

"No, you didn't."

"Well, anyway, let's not argue about it. I have a meeting the day after tomorrow, and I'll be out most of the day, but other than that, I should be around."

68. Sofie

Sofie rode the elevator up to the twenty-sixth floor and went through the double glass doors and into the posh lobby of Dean's company. It actually had a two-story ceiling with a large curving wooden staircase. Sofie climbed the stairs and took the hallway to the left down to Dean's office. Right outside his office was a smaller room with his assistant's desk.

"Hi, Jenny," Sofie said to her husband's secretary. "I dropped by to see Dean."

"Oh, Mrs. Wright. I'm so sorry. He's out. He's at meeting with a big corporate client over at their offices."

"Today? Did it change? He told me it was tomorrow."

"No, it's always been scheduled for today," Jenny said

"I can't believe this. This is the second time he's done this to me."

"It's men," Jenny said, leaning forward conspiratorially. "They can't remember anything. I don't know, I think it's something with their brains. I tell myself it's why my husband forgets my birthday every year."

Sofie checked her watch. "When do you think he might be back?"

"I'm not sure. I can page him, and he'll call as soon as he gets a break."

"Could you?"

"Of course. But it might be a little while."

"That's OK," Sofie said. "I can wait. I've been walking around the city all morning, it will be good to sit down for a while. Do you think I could go wait in his office again? I didn't bring a book, so I thought I could maybe use the Internet."

"Sure," Jenny said. "Go right in."

Sofie opened the door to Dean's office. She circled around his desk and sat down.

Dean's work area was very neat. There was an in-box and an out-box, and aside from those two neat piles, there wasn't another scrap of paper on the desk. There was only the keyboard and the flat-screen monitor. The screen was black, but when she moved the mouse it came to life.

Sofie clicked on the icon to open to the Internet. Then she glanced up. Through the open doorway she could see Jenny at her desk just outside, but Jenny was focused on her own work.

Sofie minimized the Internet window so she would be able to click on it if Jenny were to decide to come into the office and come all the way around the desk to where she could see the screen. Then Sofie clicked instead on Dean's e-mail program.

The prompt for a password popped up, and she entered the password she knew he used for all his accounts.

It worked. The mail program opened. With another quick glance out at Jenny, Sofie went straight to the archives and started searching.

69. Sofie & Dean

Sofie was sitting at the kitchen table with a book open in front of her and a glass of red wine when she heard the garage door. A moment later Dean appeared in the kitchen. Sofie didn't even look up from her book.

He stood in the doorway a moment. Then he said, "Aren't you even going to say hello?"

Sofie glanced up. "Hi," she said briefly, and then went back to her book.

He frowned. Putting down his briefcase, he went to get a glass and crossed the room to join her at the table. He reached for the bottle to pour himself some wine, but there was only a swallow left.

"Did you drink this all yourself?" he asked.

She shrugged.

"You're angry about today, aren't you? But I *told* you I was going to be out."

"I thought you said it was tomorrow," Sofie said, turning the page.

"No, I didn't. This is the same conversation we had before. You got the days mixed up. And why didn't you wait for me? Jenny paged me, but when I called she said you'd gone."

"I wanted to get back."

"What was so important you had to get back for?"

"Nothing," she said. "I was tired."

"So . . . how was your day in the city?"

"Fine."

"And everyone at the bookstore? I bet they were happy to see you."

Sofie shrugged. "I guess."

He tried once more, "Something smells good. What's in the pot?"

"See for yourself."

He got up and crossed to the stove and lifted the lid off the big pot. "Hey, you made my favorite."

"Chili was the fastest thing I could think of to make," Sofie said. "I didn't have a lot of time."

"But you left the city by two. That's when I called Jenny."

"It takes time to make dinner," she said. "I had to go to the store. And then I had to come back and chop everything up. And put in the rice. And grate the cheese. I don't just snap my fingers and food appears, even though that's what it looks like to you."

"We could have just ordered in if you were too tired."

"OK, next time I won't bother."

Dean tried to pacify her. "That's not what I meant. I love your chili. You know what? Let's have another bottle. Why don't I open a bottle of the Montrachet."

"What's the occasion?"

"Do we need an occasion?"

Dean disappeared into the cellar and returned with a bottle in hand. "Should we go sit down in the living room?"

"No, I want to stay here to keep an eye on the chili," Sofie said.

He set the bottle on the table. Then he took the empty bottle and her old glass over to the counter and returned with the bottle opener and two clean glasses.

"Is there something bothering you?" Dean asked as he peeled off the foil and started to twist in the corkscrew.

"Actually, yes," she said.

Dean had screwed in the opener as far as it would go. Now he eased out the cork and poured a generous amount in the two glasses. He slid one over to her and took his and sat down across from her. He had been waiting for her to continue, but Sofie stayed silent. Finally he said, "If there's something wrong, you're going to have to tell me what it is. I can't read your mind."

Sofie looked straight at him and asked, "Are you having an affair?"

Dean had just been raising his glass to take a sip, and he almost spilled the wine all over himself. Instead it spattered on the table. "What?! No. I'm not. Of course I'm not. Why are you asking me that?"

"Because I think you are."

He set down his glass and blotted at the spill with a napkin. "What made you think that all of a sudden?"

"Actually, I've thought so for a while," she told him.

"Honey, if you were worried about it, why didn't you say something to me?"

"Because I knew you'd either lie to me and say you weren't having an affair, or you'd admit that you were and tell me you loved this other person and you wanted to be with her. And neither of those options seemed terribly appealing."

"What about me telling you that you're imagining things? It's just all the craziness around here that's got you imagining things. Everything's fine, hon. I promise." He reached out across the table, hand open, waiting for her to reach out and take his.

She ignored the gesture.

"Dean," Sofie said. "I know."

He slowly drew back his hand. The struggle was evident on his face, whether or not he should try to keep up the front. But another look at Sofie was enough to give him the answer to that question.

He said quietly, "What if I told you it was all a big mistake? You're right, there is something—but it's hardly an affair. We barely did more than kiss. And the fact is, I don't care about her."

Sofie was gazing down into her wine, turning the stem between her fingers. "Then why did you do it?"

"I don't know. It just . . . happened. I admit I was flirting with her. And then she took it seriously, and I didn't quite know how to get out of it at that point. So I just kind of went along with it."

Sofie looked up in a flash of anger. "That's bullshit. You could have stopped it at any point. You didn't because she might have made a fuss, and you were afraid it would affect this perfect little life that you wanted out here."

"My wanting to be here in Greenwich was about us. Starting a new life. Having a family."

"And when was that going to happen?"

"I don't know. It's kind of hard to start a family when you won't have sex with me," Dean pointed out.

"You expect me to sleep with you when you're having an affair?"

"I told you that nothing happened. Besides, now that I think of it, you stopped sleeping with me before all of this. So you can't claim that you weren't sleeping with me because I was having an affair with Priscilla."

Sofie finally raised the wineglass and took a sip. Then she placed it carefully back down on the table and said, "I didn't say I stopped sleeping with you because you were having an affair with *Priscilla*."

"What?"

Sofie sighed. "Are you going to pretend that you don't know what I'm talking about?"

He leaned forward and put his palms flat on the table for emphasis—or to steady himself. "But I *don't* know what you're talking about," he said.

"I'm talking about the affair you were having *before* Priscilla."

"I swear, there wasn't any affair before Priscilla."

She stared at him until he looked away.

"Dean, I thought you were going to be honest with me. I thought you were going to finally tell the truth."

"I *am* telling the truth. You're just paranoid and insecure," Dean said, changing tactics and going on the offensive. "You've always been like that."

"Maybe so," she allowed. "But maybe I've had good reason."

"So everybody's always taking advantage of poor Sofie—your father, your stepmothers, now me. Is that it? It seems to me that you're awfully good at playing the victim."

"You're right. I have been a victim," Sofie said.

"Whose fault is that?"

"It's my fault that I'm a victim. But you can't tell me that it's my fault that you've been cheating on me."

He sat back in his chair and rolled his eyes heavenward as if asking for patience. Then he tried again, speaking slowly as if to a child. "Sofie, I haven't been cheating on you—this thing with Priscilla, it's a joke. And it's over. As of right now. And that's it. There hasn't been anyone else."

Sofie reached into her pocket and held out her hand. There was a diamond earring resting in her palm.

Dean frowned. "What's that?"

"I found it when we were moving out of our apartment in the city," Sofie said. "I don't even have pierced ears."

"So? That's evidence that I've been cheating? Look at the size of it—it's got to be cubic zirconium. It's probably the maid's or something."

"Mmm. Then can you explain to me why Julia Stowe owned a single diamond stud that exactly matched this one?"

His reply was too quick. "There could be any number of explanations. Everyone has diamond studs. It's not so crazy to think that Julia had a pair and lost one, and that someone else lost one in our apartment."

"They're from the same pair; both earrings have diamonds that are point three-four carat in a platinum setting, and they're sold at Tiffany's."

"That doesn't mean they're the same set," Dean said. "How many pairs of those earrings do they sell a year? Thousands, probably."

"You're such a big one on Occam's Razor. You're always applying it to my theories. It seems to me, in this situation, the most obvious explanation is that Julia lost her earring in our apartment. In our *bedroom*."

"But that was before we even moved out here," Dean pointed out. "How is that obvious?"

"You were having an affair. She moved out here, you followed. Very simple."

"It's not obvious. It's paranoid. It's this great big conspiracy that you've cooked up."

"I'm sure the police could send the earrings to the lab. They could compare traces of skin on the post and determine if they were worn by the same person."

She let the earring tumble onto the table and nudged it with her forefinger.

Dean's eyes were fixed on the diamond as he said, "You can't seriously be thinking of wasting the time of the Police Department on this?"

"No," she said, plucking the earring off the table and depositing it back into her pocket. "I'm not going to waste their time with that."

With the earring gone, it was almost as if a spell had been broken. Dean relaxed back into his chair. "Thank God. I was beginning to think that you were really losing it."

"Anyway," Sofie went on as if she hadn't even heard him. "It wouldn't hold much sway in court because there's no real way to prove that I found the earring in our apartment. Your lawyer could just claim that I got the earring from Alex and simply pretended that I found it in the apartment since I didn't show it to anyone or mention it."

"This is madness," Dean said. "I'm not going to need a lawyer."

Sofie continued, not even breaking stride. "No, I don't really need to prove the earrings match to prove that you were having an affair. Because I've got these." Sofie pushed her chair back and got up, went over to a drawer by the phone, and pulled out a manila folder. She brought it back over and put it on the table in front of Dean.

"What . . . ?" Dean looked down at the folder and up at Sofie, but she had turned away to pour herself some more wine. She heard the sharp intake of breath when Dean opened it. When she turned back around, he was flipping frantically through small pile of papers.

"Did you go into my work e-mail when you were in my office today?" he demanded. "How did you access it?"

She rounded the table and sat back down across from him. "You use the same password for everything," she said. "It's what we use to log into our bank page, our cell phone account, even the security system."

"I can't believe you did that." His voice was outraged.

"Are you sure this is the tack you want to take, Dean?" Sofie asked. "You want to get all indignant about my going into your e-mail account?"

He took a deep breath, and said, "You're right. I'm sorry. I'm so sorry."

"So now you admit you were having an affair with her?"

"Yes," he said. "Yes, we were . . . involved."

"Were you still involved with her when you started up with Priscilla?"

He glanced down at the stack of paper. He hadn't been able to look at everything—and he obviously didn't remember what he'd said in the e-mails and what he hadn't.

"You're going to have to be honest now," Sofie said.

"Neither of them meant anything to me. They were just flings. It was a terrible thing to do, I know. But at the time it seemed harmless. Maybe because I knew how much you meant to me. I knew that no one else could interfere with that."

"So you were lying to Julia when you wrote to her that you were going to leave me?"

"Yes. I was. I'd never leave you. You know that. I'd do anything to keep you."

"Anything?"

"Anything," Dean vowed.

"Even kill Julia?"

"God, no," Dean flinched if she had raised her hand to hit him.

"So you didn't kill her because when she got upset about your flirting with Priscilla, she threatened to tell me everything?"

"No, it wasn't like that. Sofie, listen to me. I didn't kill Julia. I swear."

"You mean like you swore you weren't having an affair with her? And like you swore you'd be faithful to me forever. Like that?"

"No, not like that," Dean said helplessly.

"I didn't think so. Is this why you didn't want me talking to Alex? Because you thought I'd find out? By the way, how did you manage to fool the private eye he hired?"

Dean didn't answer.

"Dean," she prompted. "The truth."

"We paid him off," Dean said.

"You must still be paying him?"

Dean nodded.

"What, were you prepared to pay him for the rest of your life? Because from what I can tell, as long as he had a hold over you, you'd have to keep on paying him."

"I knew it wasn't going to be forever—just until I broke it off with Julia."

"And then?"

"And then I was going to tell you everything."

"And you thought I'd forgive you?"

He hesitated, then admitted, "I did. I thought you'd forgive me. What we have is so strong. I was sure that a stupid affair couldn't really change that. I thought you loved me more than that."

"You were right," Sofie said. "I did love you more than that. And I probably would have forgiven you. But that's not what happened, is it? Look at how I had to find out."

"That's because I knew how bad it would seem. I was afraid you wouldn't believe me . . . wouldn't believe me when I told you how much I love you," he said, reaching out across the table. This time he didn't wait for her to put her hand in his. Instead he captured it and gripped it tightly. But she didn't squeeze back.

"I loved you so much," she whispered.

"I know you did. But it's not too late. Couples work through these things. I know it takes time to heal, but people do manage to stay together after an affair."

Sofie gently pulled her hand out of his.

"What about after murder?" she asked.

"Sofie, I swear—"

Sofie held up a hand—the hand she had just reclaimed. "Please, no more swearing. So why did you follow me the other night when I was out on the golf course?"

"I—"

"The truth," Sofie reminded him.

"OK."

"OK?"

"You're right. It was me."

"But why?"

"It was a spur-of-the-moment thing. I saw you out walking, and I thought maybe I could scare you a little."

"What were you doing out on the golf course?"

Dean didn't answer right away.

"Oh, I see. You were going to see Priscilla, weren't you?"

He nodded.

"But why did you want to scare me?"

"I thought you might stop looking into the case. I was afraid you might find something."

"Something . . . ?"

"The affair. Just the affair. Because I know how it looks, and I knew it might muddy things enough that Alex might not get convicted."

"So you were just worried about justice being served, is that it? You weren't worried about what else might turn up?"

"No, I wasn't."

"That's a relief," Sofie said. "So you won't mind if I go to the police with this then." She motioned to the folder that was still open on the table in front of him.

He looked down, flipped the folder closed, and rested his hand on top of it, as if he could keep the contents safe that way. "Sofie, our lives will be ruined if you go to the police with this. There's no reason for it. Baby, please, think about this. I swear—" He stopped when he saw the look she shot him. "I'll make it up to you. Just promise me you won't go to the police."

"I can't," Sofie said.

"Please. For me. For us."

"I told you I can't promise you that."

"You mean you won't."

"No, I mean I can't," Sofie repeated.

"Why not?"

She looked at him and said, "Because I already did."

70. Sofie & Dean

$\mathcal{R}$ ight there, before Sofie's eyes, the cajoling, affectionate, reasonable Dean disappeared. His face twisted with anger. "You—you—" Dean couldn't even manage a sentence. "You stupid bitch," he finally managed to spit out.

Sofie started to get up, but Dean leaned forward over the table and grabbed her hand again—this time he grabbed her by the wrist and it hurt.

"Ow, Dean, let me go," she said, trying to free herself.

"You're. So. Fucking. Stupid." Dean practically spit the words at her, as if they were little bullets.

Sofie twisted her hand, trying to free herself. "You're hurting me," she told him.

"Good," he spat.

She yanked herself loose from his grip and rubbed her wrist, suddenly angry as well. "If I'm so stupid, how did I find out about you?"

Dean laughed. "Oh, boy."

"What?"

"You don't have a clue."

"I don't have a clue? Well, I know that it's strange that you're so angry about my telling the police. Why are you so angry if you don't have anything to hide?"

"I told you before. You could be giving Alex Stowe a get-out-of-jail-free card with this. It's like a gift. But maybe you knew that. Maybe that's what you wanted."

"Why do you care so much anyway?"

"Because I loved her," Dean said. "She's the only person who ever really understood me. We both came from nothing. We wanted the same things. It felt like we were the same person. Do you know what it feels like to meet someone who knows you like that? No. Of course not. How would you? What she and I had—it was a once-in-a-lifetime thing. I fucking loved her. And I want that asshole to rot in jail for the rest of his life for what he did to her."

Watching him, Sofie realized that he looked different as he spoke. A layer had been stripped away. The layer of artifice. It had been invisible to her before because she had never seen him without it.

"The truth. Finally," she said softly.

"Yes. The truth. Finally."

"So you did love her."

"More than anything in the world. . . . She meant more to me than anything in the world." He didn't say it forcefully, he just . . . said it. And it was as if Sofie had disappeared and all he could see was the image of Julia.

"And me?" Sofie asked.

Dean eyes refocused on her. "You? What about you?"

"What was I?"

When he looked at her, his eyes were flat. Expressionless.

"Nothing," he said.

"Nothing? Nothing at all?"

He shrugged.

"So why did you marry me? I didn't have any money. Not even a trust fund. My father was a big deal, but I wasn't going to get anything until . . . oh. I see. That's right. I remember now—we met right after my father was diagnosed."

"And then he had his miraculous recovery," Dean said bitterly.

"And that's when we started having problems and getting in all those fights," Sofie remembered aloud. "Because you started to realize you didn't know how long you were going to have to wait. So the entire time you were planning to—to . . ." She found she couldn't say it. "Nothing was true, then. You were lying to me all along."

"And you had no idea. So who's the detective now?"

Sofie looked down at the floor. "And moving out here?"

"For the Connecticut divorce laws. Julia and I planned it. I thought there was a chance you might refuse to give me a divorce. This is a no-fault state, so you can't stop it. And the division of property is much more generous with respect to the division of an inheritance." The matter-of-fact way he said it seemed to make it worse.

"And that's why you wanted me to agree to stay?"

"That's why. You get residency after a year."

"I guess you'd rather hurt me than get the money," she said. "Since you're telling me all this."

Dean smiled. It was the kind of smile that appears on the face of someone who is about to win—but the kind of win where most of the satisfaction is coming from the fact that the other person is about to lose.

"Why do you think that?" he said.

"Because . . . I mean now you won't get it."

"Oh, really? How do you figure that?"

"After what you've said . . ."

"You can't prove I said anything."

"We won't be under Connecticut divorce law, so the inheritance . . ."

"True. But anything we bought with the inheritance is marital property," he pointed out. "So the house and the antiques and the wine and the art—"

"*That's* why you weren't more keen about keeping my father's things. And all that stuff you said about loving English antiques, that was all baloney, wasn't it?"

"You're finally starting to get it."

"Finally," Sofie echoed.

"Are we done here?" Dean asked.

"I think so," Sofie said quietly.

"Then I'm going upstairs."

He pushed back his chair, picked up his glass of wine, and then after a second's thought, picked up the bottle as well, and turned and left the room.

As soon as she heard his footsteps climbing the stairs, Sofie went to the closet to retrieve her coat. Then she slipped out the back through the patio, circled around the house to the front, and walked a few paces down the street to where a dark blue sedan was parked. She opened the door and slid into the back seat.

Detective Ackerman and Detective Peters were sitting in the front.

"Hey," she said. "Everything OK here?"

"You did a good job," Peters told her.

"So you heard everything?"

"Yes, we got it," Ackerman told her.

"Then you know that I didn't get him to confess," Sofie said.

"I didn't expect you to," Ackerman replied.

"Hey, you did great," Peters put in. "No one expected a confession. You got him to admit to the affair, and you got him to admit to following you on the golf course. Both those things are big."

"But the e-mails would have proved the affair," Sofie said. "And you'll probably be able to match the footprint you found out on the course to the one near the body, right?"

"You'd be surprised what lawyers can do with reasonable doubt. They somehow manage to stretch that concept so the jury thinks if they're not one-hundred-percent sure, they can't convict. So we need every scrap we can get because this case is going to be circumstantial, and circumstantial cases always leave that little bit of wiggle room. All the evidence can be right there, but which way a jury goes is pretty much decided in the end by what they think of the defendant. And in that respect, I think this is gonna make a huge difference. After a jury hears this tape, they're not going to believe a word your husband says. I mean, how many times did he change his story?"

"Would a jury actually hear the tape?" Sofie asked.

"If he gets indicted, almost surely. I don't see on what grounds a lawyer could get it excluded. We made double sure that all the paperwork was in order."

"That's good" Sofie said.

"Are you feeling OK?" Peters asked.

"Yes. I'm OK," Sofie said quietly

"That's a tough thing you did," Ackerman told her. "Not an easy choice to call us, and then agreeing to the tap."

"Well, it's not the first one in that kitchen," Sofie said, smiling a little.

"Right, that Realtor of yours."

"Now I know why he wanted the house so much. And what *friend* recommended that Realtor. You probably don't think a lot of me after hearing all that stuff that he said."

"No, I don't think a lot of your husband after hearing that," Ackerman corrected her.

"I think you should look on the bright side," Peters said.

Both Sofie and Ackerman looked at Peters like he was crazy.

"The bright side?" Sofie echoed.

"After that conversation, even if it turns out he's not guilty, you don't have to wonder if you did the right thing."

71. Sofie & Alex

$\mathcal{S}$ ofie left the detectives' car, but she didn't go back to her house. Instead she walked down the street and rang another doorbell. A moment later she heard footsteps, and then Alex was opening the door and pulling her inside, asking, "Are you all right? Did anything go wrong?"

"That depends on your definition of wrong," Sofie said. "I can't stay long. I didn't tell Dean where I was going. Not that he cares at this point."

"So you really did it?"

Sofie nodded.

"Let me get you a drink . . ."

That afternoon after coming back from the city Sofie hadn't gone straight to the police station with what she found—instead she'd gone to see Alex.

Now she sat down with her drink, and she told him everything that had happened after she'd left his house. She told him about going down to the station, talking to the detectives, coming up with the idea of taping her conversation with Dean, setting up the bug, and then, finally, the conversation itself.

Alex listened, though not silently. He couldn't help certain exclamations at parts of her story.

"So, what now?" Alex asked when she finished.

"The detectives say they're going to come by in the morning before Dean goes to work and ask him to go down to the station with them. They'll know first thing in the morning if they matched the footprints, and if they did, they're going to get a search warrant to compare the fibers and hair samples."

"The same routine that I went through."

"Mmm."

They were silent for a minute.

"Listen," Alex said, "I want to thank you."

Sofie tried to wave him off, but he wouldn't listen.

"No, I'm serious. What you've done . . . I don't really know what to say."

"You don't have to say anything. I didn't do it for you."

"No? You want me to believe the bullshit you told the detectives? That you did it because you thought it was the right thing?"

"No. I didn't even expect *them* to believe that. But I wasn't about to admit straight out that I was pissed off and wanted to get back at my husband for being a cheating bastard."

"So you did it because you were angry?"

"Of course I was angry."

"And I had nothing to do with it?"

Sofie didn't answer.

"Nothing at all?"

Sofie looked away from him as she spoke. "Listen, we probably shouldn't be seen together for the next little while."

"Why not?"

"Because my husband is about to be under investigation in connection with your wife's murder. I think *that's* bad enough without anyone starting to talk nonsense about us—speculating about how I turned him in for you. Do you want that in the papers? You think that's going to help anything?"

"You've got a point," Alex conceded. "Maybe we shouldn't see each other for a bit."

"I should get back," she said, and she started to get up, but Alex caught her by the wrist. Dean had also grabbed her by the wrist, but this was a completely different type of touch.

"Don't go yet."

"No?"

He shook his head. "Not just yet."

"Did we have other stuff we needed to talk about?"

"No."

"What then?"

"Nothing," he said. He leaned in and kissed her on the side of her mouth. Then he kissed her bottom lip. She just sat there, frozen. He pulled back to look at her, as if to gauge her reaction.

"It's been a really long time since I kissed anyone but my husband," Sofie whispered.

"It's been a really long time since I kissed anyone at all," Alex replied.

"I should go," Sofie said, but she didn't move.

"I want you to stay," he said.

She stayed.

72. Alex

*A*lex sauntered into his lawyer's office the next afternoon. He dropped into the chair across from her desk, and as usual, started to put his feet up when she said, "Hey, get 'em off of there."

"I'm sure we've been through this before," Alex said. "I've already gotten permission."

"Revoked."

"Revoked?" Alex repeated, pretending to be outraged.

"That's right. If you want to be able to put your feet up on my imitation Queen Anne desk again, you'll have to go get implicated in another murder."

"What, being a suspect in one isn't good enough?"

"No, that would be enough."

At that, Alex leaned forward. "What do you know?" he demanded.

Ruth smiled. "I don't know an awful lot, but here's one thing I do know, and that's unless you get caught up in another murder case, you won't be needing my services anymore."

Alex stared at her a moment. Then he whooped. He practically leapt over the desk to pull her out of her chair and give her a big, smacking kiss on the cheek.

"Hey, be careful there. You don't want to be giving me ideas. I'll be a single woman soon."

"In that case," Alex playfully bent her back in a dip and leaned over her.

"Let me go," Ruth said, swatting at him. "I'm getting dizzy."

"You're at *my* mercy now, instead of the other way around."

"I have a feeling that you were never at anyone's mercy. But if you don't let me go, I won't tell you the news."

Alex quickly helped her back into her chair then retreated back around the desk. "What's the news?"

"They brought Dean Wright in for questioning this morning. She paused, studying him shrewdly. "You don't seem very surprised."

"I'm not. He was my wife's lover."

"But when did you find out? And how? And why didn't you tell me? I can't believe you let me find out from the police."

"It looks better that way," Alex said. "Besides, it wasn't my place to tell you."

"But how did you find out?"

"Do you remember Sofie?" Alex asked.

"Sofie? You mean your little helper?"

"Yes, well she's married to Dean Wright."

Ruth pursed her mouth in a silent O.

"She was the one who figured it out," Alex said.

"Do you know about these e-mails then?"

"Yes. She showed them to me."

"Ah," Ruth appraised him for a moment. "I also heard something about a conversation and matching a footprint on the golf course to one at the scene?"

"They matched it?" Alex asked eagerly.

"Apparently, but I don't know what a footprint on the golf course has to do with anything. Would you care to explain it to me?"

"Later," Alex said impatiently. "What else?"

"Well, they used that to get a search warrant for the house and to compel him to provide hair for DNA comparison. Apparently he wasn't prepared to be as accommodating as you were. They brought him down to the station, but he wouldn't talk. He asked to retain a lawyer. Guess who he called."

"No! He called you?" Alex laughed.

"Of course I had to tell him that I couldn't."

"So he had to settle for the second-best criminal lawyer in the county," Alex said.

"You don't have to flatter me anymore, remember?"

"I thought I might get my privileges reinstated," Alex suggested, patting the desk.

"Not a chance. Do you want to hear this story or not?"

"There's more?"

"There sure is," Ruth assured him. "They put the investigation on full speed because they found out that it was about to come out in the press. It will probably be in the papers tomorrow. I guess they wanted to have something to feed to the reporters."

"Did they?"

"You bet they did. Match on the suit. Match on the shoes. Match on the hair. They charged him this afternoon."

73. Detective Ackerman

*D*etective Ackerman sat across from the DA in her office. "I want you to know I'm against this," he said. "I think it's a mistake."

The DA was sitting on the other side of her desk, eating a chicken Caesar salad. She pierced a piece of chicken with her fork, then loaded the rest with pieces of lettuce. "I think you've made that clear," she replied. She put the forkful in her mouth, chewed, swallowed, and added, "But this is out of your hands now."

"I just want to reiterate—," Ackerman started to say.

"I know how you feel about the case, Mike," she said, interrupting him. "I just don't agree. You've done a great job. We've got a strong case."

"It's *too* strong," Ackerman said. "There's *too* much evidence. He planted it on the body after she was dead. I'm sure of it."

She looked down at her salad, carefully constructing another perfect bite. But this time after she had loaded up the fork, she set it down and looked at him.

"Listen, Mike, how many years have we been working together? I know you're a great detective. But I think you're not exactly objective about this case anymore. . . . You're not objective about this man."

Ackerman closed his eyes for a moment, as if summoning up the last reserves of calm. When he spoke, his words were carefully chosen. "I don't know about great, but I am a detective. A detective, not a reporter—I'm not supposed to be objective. I'm supposed to solve crimes. I'm supposed to have opinions. And now I'm giving you my opinion. The whole thing feels wrong."

"I heard you. And I've taken everything you've said into consideration. But it's my decision now . . ."

"And you're going ahead with the case," Ackerman finished for her.

"I'm just trying to do my job the best I can."

"I know. But you're making a terrible mistake."

74. Sofie & Detective Ackerman

"Detective Ackerman!" Sofie exclaimed when she answered the door.

"I hope I'm not catching you at a bad time?"

"Please," she stood back and held the door open.

"How are you?" he asked, following her back to the kitchen.

"Oh . . . I've been better," Sofie said, retrieving the coffee from the freezer and the coffee filters from the cupboard. "Dean came back after spending the morning at the station, and he was only home about an hour and a half before they came back to arrest him."

"I know."

"I was surprised you weren't there," Sofie said. "Detective Peters came."

"I'm sorry. I was down at the District Attorney's office."

"Oh. Right. I imagine you had to talk to them about the case. They told me it's going to hit the papers tomorrow." She turned away to fill the coffee pot. She ran the water slowly, then turned back and came over and poured the water into the coffee machine. "I don't think I'm ready to face it. I still can't—" She shook her head, at a loss to even finish the sentence. "It's just all too much. I wanted to ask you—how do other people deal with it? When they find out . . . well, you know."

"That's what I came to talk to you about," Ackerman said.

"I'm not sure if I can take any more revelations."

"I know. And I'm not sure how you'll take this."

Sofie closed her eyes and seemed to brace herself.

"I don't think your husband killed Julia Stowe."

Sofie's eyes snapped open. "But all the evidence they told me about . . . was it a mistake?"

"No, they definitely matched the trace evidence to your husband. But there's too *much* evidence."

"I don't understand."

"First of all, don't you think it's a little coincidental that Alex came to you for help, and it just so happens that it was your husband having an affair with his wife?"

"But he didn't know it was my husband," Sofie protested.

"Sure. That's what he *said*. But I think he knew. I think he knew and he decided to use that information to get away with murder."

"How?"

"I think he planted that evidence. He knew he was going to be the prime suspect. But he also didn't want to point the finger too quickly at your husband. That might look suspicious as well. So he pretended not to know who his wife's lover was, and instead, he used you to 'discover' the secret."

"No," Sofie said shaking her head. "No, he wouldn't have."

"Are you sure?"

"Why are you telling me this?"

Ackerman answered her question with a question. "Why are you so upset?"

"I'm not upset," she insisted. "At least not about what you think. I'm upset because I think you've got it all wrong."

"Think about it," Ackerman urged. "He arranged everything. Every little detail. And he played it out perfectly. He set up the scene. Then, when you found the body, he made sure it was preserved so no one would disturb the evidence he'd planted—"

Sofie broke in. "Did you ever think he might have done that because he knew he wasn't guilty and he wanted to preserve the scene so he could prove it? And as for framing, I was just thinking—it might have been the other way around. It could have been Dean trying to frame Alex. What if Julia told him about Alex's first wife? And when he heard that, he decided to fake a suicide because he knew that Alex would be implicated."

"You seem to really want Alex to be innocent. Even if it means your husband is guilty."

"It's not a matter of wanting someone to be innocent," Sofie protested. "It's just about the evidence."

"Is it? Are you sure?"

"How about you, Detective? Is it really about the evidence for you? Maybe you're as blinded as I am."

Ackerman sighed. "Listen, you've had a tough time of it. Your husband turned out to be a bastard. I just don't want to see you fall for someone even worse. Stay away from Alex Stowe. That's all I wanted to tell you."

75. Priscilla

*P*riscilla saw the vans from her window—they were lined up all along the street. The satellite dishes that sprouted from the roofs told her what type of vans they were.

She didn't even stop to put on a coat. She just rushed out the door and headed down the street. As she drew closer, she could see the lettering on the sides of the vans were from all the major news channels. The reporters themselves were all out of their vehicles— gathered on the street in front of Sofie and Dean's house.

Priscilla raced up to the closest person—a cameraman who was still setting up.

"What's going on? Is someone hurt?" she demanded.

"Woman killed a few weeks ago," the reporter said.

"I know about *that*. What's *this* all about?"

"They arrested someone for it."

"But he lives down the street," Priscilla said.

"Who lives down the street?"

"The man who did it. The husband."

"It wasn't the husband. It was the lover."

"What lover?"

"This guy," the cameraman gestured toward the house. "His name is Wright or something like that."

Priscilla just shook her head. "No."

"He got arrested yesterday." The cameraman looked more closely at her. "Hey, are you a friend? Would you be willing to say a few words on camera? Mandy"—he called over to the group of reporters—"Hey, Mandy, get over here."

Priscilla turned and fled back to her house, ignoring the calls of the cameraman. When she closed the front door behind her, she had to sit down because her legs were shaking so much, she didn't feel like they could hold her.

It couldn't be true. She told herself that it couldn't possibly be true. Snatching up the phone, she dialed Dean's home number. It rang and rang. There wasn't even an answering machine that picked up. She hung up and tried Dean's cell phone number, but that went straight to voice mail—and the mailbox was full.

She sat back down at the kitchen table and put her head in her hands. She didn't know what to do with herself. She had to talk to someone. Normally at this point she would have gone straight to Susan's house. But she couldn't do that now. She'd replaced Susan with Sofie, but she couldn't call Sofie. The only person left was Ashley.

Five minutes later she was ringing Ashley's doorbell, and a moment after that, Ashley opened the door.

"Priscilla," Ashley said, surprised but not pleased. "You should have called."

"I really need to talk to you. Have you seen what's going on over at Sofie and Dean's house? Do you have any idea what they're saying?"

"I saw it on the news early this morning," Ashley said. "Stewart always insists on turning on the TV first thing in the morning. It's so annoying."

"Why didn't you call me?"

"I figured you would have seen it too. And the truth is, I'm not feeling so well right now," Ashley said, putting a hand on her stomach.

"Oh, no, did you eat something that disagreed with you?" Priscilla said, her voice full of pretend concern.

"Not exactly. I guess I might as well tell you now. I'm pregnant."

Priscilla's face looked so blank that Ashley added, "Stewart and I are having a baby."

Priscilla felt a mounting sense of being caught in a nightmare. "So this is why you've been such a bitch."

"Excuse me?" Ashley said.

"You knew you were going to be switching over to the other book group. You knew you wouldn't need me anymore. So you feel like you can say whatever you want to me. Is that right? You just throw people aside when you don't need them anymore?"

"No, actually, that sounds more like you," Ashley said.

"What did your husband think about your news?" Priscilla sneered. "I bet that's just what he wanted—a second load of brats. To tell you the truth, I'm surprised he didn't insist that you get rid of it."

Ashley drew herself up and looked at Priscilla with narrowed eyes. Stewart, when they got married, had told Ashley very clearly and firmly that he didn't want any more children. Priscilla, in her anger, had inadvertently hit a little too close to home. So Ashley struck back with the rumor that had been circulating the neighborhood for years. The rumor explained a lot: why Priscilla had banned women with children from the book club, her ridicule of the lives of new mothers, her insistence that she would never, ever make the "mistake" of having kids of her own.

Ashley said, her voice icy, "I'm sorry *you* can't have children, Priscilla. But I never said anything to you because that was your personal business. But you don't seem to have any boundaries. You've crossed the line—and I'm not just talking about what you said to me just now. You crossed the line when you went after Sofie's husband, and when you turned on Susan after what happened with her husband, and I've had enough. Everyone's had enough." Ashley said it with great import, as if she were making some sort of big announcement.

"Now tell me why I'm supposed to care?" Priscilla said, but she couldn't quite pull it off because her voice was shaking.

"You'll see," Ashley said. "And when you do, I think you'll care."

76. Priscilla & Dean

*P*riscilla was upset when she left Ashley's—but then something happened that made her forget about Ashley completely.

She was almost back at her house when she noticed a commotion over by the TV vans. When she looked over, she saw a car pulling into the driveway, and she thought she recognized Dean's profile in the passenger seat. She knew for sure when she caught a glimpse of him as he got out of the car—and before he was surrounded by a swarm of reporters. He escaped from them when he ducked into the house with the person who had been driving.

Priscilla made a split-second decision—she had to see him. Now.

Instead of going back to her house, she headed toward Dean's. If she had taken a moment to consider, she might have realized that now was not the best time to go barging in. But Priscilla didn't often think—at least, not about other people. So she marched up to the lawn and braved the onslaught of reporters.

At the front door she rang the bell several times, hoping that Dean would at least come look to see who it was. She had to keep her finger on the bell for almost a minute before the door finally opened and she was able to escape from the shouted questions of the reporters as she slipped inside.

"Oh my God, they're like jackals," she said, smiling weakly up at Dean.

He didn't smile back.

She tried again. "How are you? I've been frantic with worry."

"Who was it?" a woman's voice called from the kitchen.

"Nobody," Dean yelled back. "Just a neighbor. I'll be there in a second."

"Who's *that*?" Priscilla demanded, staring toward the kitchen.

"That's my lawyer. Not that it's any of your business."

"A woman?" Priscilla said skeptically.

"What do you want, Priscilla?" Dean asked impatiently.

"What do I want? I wanted— I needed to see you," she told him. "To find out what this nonsense is all about."

"This 'nonsense,' as you call it, is that I've been charged with murder."

"But that's ridiculous."

Dean leaned back against the wall and crossed his arms. "Great, I'll tell the judge you said it was ridiculous. I'm sure he'll drop the charges right away."

"But what about your alibi?"

He shrugged. "What alibi?"

"Didn't Sofie tell the detectives that you were together all night?"

"No, she told them that she went to bed and I stayed downstairs to watch some TV, and that she didn't know when I came to bed."

"But . . ." Priscilla shook her head, trying to think. "But even if it was true, why wouldn't she lie?"

"Isn't it obvious? Because she *wants* me to go to jail."

"But why?" Priscilla cried.

"Because I was cheating on her. Because I was planning to leave her."

"Oh, Dean. That's awful."

He snorted. "I don't think I needed you to tell me that."

"But *no wonder* you're angry at me. Sofie's trying to punish you, and it's all because of me—"

"Because of you?" Dean echoed. "This has nothing to do with you."

"What do you mean? You just said that Sofie didn't give you an alibi because she found out about us."

"No, that's not what I said. I said it was because she found out I was cheating—but not with *you*." Dean's voice was filled with such disgust, Priscilla actually recoiled as if he'd hit her.

"But you weren't . . . I mean, you couldn't . . ."

Dean just stared at her.

"Who?" Priscilla finally managed to ask.

"Who? Julia, of course."

"Of course," Priscilla repeated, dazed. "And us?"

"I think you should go home."

"I'm not going anywhere," she declared. "Not until we work this thing out."

"*We're* not working anything out. There is no 'we.' Don't you get it?"

"Of course there's a 'we.' If you think this is going to scare me off, you're wrong. I know you loved me. I know it."

"You're so stupid, Priscilla. I was using you."

"Using me?"

"As cover. If I was flirting with you, no one would think I was actually in love with Julia. Then when she died and the investigation started, I figured it would be even more convincing if we actually had something. That way if Sofie suspected anything, I could say the affair was with you."

"No. You're lying. I don't know why, but you're lying. I know what we had was real."

"Real? You obviously don't have the slightest idea what real is."

"And you do?"

"Yes," Dean said. "I do."

"Oh, right. You mean the woman you murdered?"

Priscilla knew she'd gone too far when she saw the expression on Dean's face.

"Get out," he said softly. "Now."

Priscilla turned and fled.

77. Priscilla & Gordon

The rest of the day was the worst time Priscilla could remember. After leaving Dean's house, she had managed to make it through the pack of reporters, back into her house, and upstairs to her bedroom. But as soon as she shut the door behind her, she slid to the floor. And she lay there, curled in a ball, crying.

At a certain point she crept to the bed and burrowed under the covers. She only came out to use the bathroom. She had calmed down a little then, but she made the mistake of looking at herself in the bathroom mirror. She looked haggard and drawn and—old. How, she asked herself, had she ever thought that she could still attract a man like Dean? She had to face facts. She was stuck with Gordon—steady, dependable, boring Gordon. The thought of it depressed her, but that's how it was. By the end of the day, she managed to pull herself together and go downstairs to wait for him, but she found that she was actually glad when he got back.

"Oh, Gordon, thank God you're home," she said as soon as he stepped through the door that night. "I've had the most awful day imaginable. I tried you at the office, but your secretary said you'd left for the day. And that was ages ago. Where have you been?"

Gordon opened his mouth to answer, but Priscilla didn't even give him a chance.

"I don't even know where to start. First of all, I went over there to see Ashley this morning and she . . . she—"

"I know," Gordon said.

Priscilla assumed Gordon's words were simply emotional support, and she went on. "You know how strange she's been acting the last few weeks? Well, I found out the reason today. She's pregnant, and she's probably already started cozying up to the women in the other book club. Anyway, that's why she was so rude to me. She thought she didn't need me anymore. And then she said the most hurtful things."

"I know," Gordon said again.

This time Priscilla noticed Gordon's words—or maybe it was something in his tone.

"You know? What do you mean you know?"

"I know all about it," Gordon said.

"How do you know all about it?"

"Because Ashley called me."

"She . . . called you?" Priscilla's heart started beating faster as she remembered asking Ashley why she should care, and Ashley's parting words: *you'll see.* Priscilla had taken them for an empty threat. Now she was starting to think she had underestimated Ashley.

"Yes, she did," Gordon said.

"Why did she call you?"

"Why do you think?"

"I don't know. At this point, I don't feel like I know her anymore. I get the sense that she'd say anything—absolutely anything—just to hurt me," Priscilla said, scrambling to cover for herself. "And I never did anything to her. I don't know what she has against me."

Gordon didn't say anything. He just looked at her.

"What? Why are you looking at me like that? What did she say to you?"

"She said she was sure you were having an affair with Dean Wright."

Priscilla didn't even have to pretend much shock—she couldn't believe that Ashley had actually said that to him. "See? I suspected that she'd make up some sort of craziness like that. You didn't believe her, did you?"

"Yes," Gordon said quietly. "I did."

"So you're going to take her word over mine?"

"No. Of course not."

Priscilla was about to breathe a sigh of relief—until she heard Gordon's next words.

"So I called Susan."

"You what? But you can't take Susan's word for anything. She's not exactly a friend anymore. I'm sure there's nothing she'd like better than to break us up. She'd say anything to make that happen."

Gordon smiled.

"What's so funny? I don't see anything funny."

"*I* do. When I spoke to her, Susan denied that there was anything between you and Dean."

Priscilla tried to recover by saying, "Well, I guess Susan's honest at least."

But Gordon had seen the surprise and had understood it all. "No, actually I don't believe she is. In fact, she's a terrible liar. But she tried to cover for you."

"No, it's true. I told you, there wasn't anything between us,"

Priscilla insisted. And in that statement at least, she was telling the truth.

"Nothing?"

"Absolutely nothing."

"When's the last time you saw him?"

"Ages ago," Priscilla lied. "I don't even remember when it was."

Gordon shook his head sadly. "I saw you," he said. "I saw you today on the news. They showed you going into his house."

Priscilla had the mounting sense of being trapped. But maybe she could still talk her way out of things. "I—," she began, but Gordon cut her off.

"Don't lie to me anymore, Priscilla. The thing is, I knew before Ashley even called me. I've known for a while."

"But it was nothing. Really, Gordon, we didn't do anything. We kissed. That's it. I swear. You can ask anyone. And it's over now."

"Yes, it's over," Gordon said, in a tone she'd never heard before.

"What . . . what do you mean?"

"Priscilla, I want a divorce."

"Gordon, please. It was a huge mistake. I'm so sorry. It will never happen again."

"It's not just the affair. It's also the fact that you weren't going to tell me the truth unless you absolutely had to. And I believe it's over between you two, but only because Dean was arrested. Then you probably couldn't get out of it fast enough."

"That's not true—" Priscilla started to protest, until she realized what she was going to reveal. It was already too late.

Gordon gave a bitter little laugh. "I see. You weren't even going to break it off; he was the one who did it. Funny. I didn't think you could hurt me any more."

"Oh, Gordon, that means you still care about me."

"No. I think it just means that I still have some pride left. Which is kind of amazing, after being married to you all these years."

She decided not to respond to that comment. Instead she tried reasoning with him. "But we can't just give up on our marriage without at least trying to save it."

"I've *been* trying. I'm tired of trying."

"Listen," Priscilla said persuasively, putting a hand on his arm. "We'll start counseling. The sooner the better. I have a friend who went through counseling, and they're still together. I'll call first thing tomorrow and get the name of the—"

"No, Priscilla," Gordon said.

"You have to try counseling. Everybody tries counseling."

"No."

She'd never seen Gordon like this before.

"Please Gordon, just take a month. Just a month. I think you owe me—you owe us—that much at least. If it doesn't work out, it doesn't work out." Though even as Priscilla said it, she didn't mean it. She was determined it would work out. It had to. "If you leave now, you might always regret it."

"You know what I regret? I regret that I didn't do this a long time ago."

"So you're not even going to try?"

"No. I told you Priscilla. I'm done."

This wasn't like him. Gordon would never do this on his own.

"There's someone else, isn't there?" she demanded. "You hypocrite. You're accusing me, when you've been having an affair too. I can't believe I didn't see it. All those late nights. And then there was that dream I had. I must have known, subconsciously."

"There's no one else," Gordon said.

"I don't believe it. There's no way you would leave me unless there was someone else pushing you to do it."

"There's no one," Gordon said again.

"I don't believe you."

Gordon shrugged. "You know what? I don't care. If you want to think the only way I could leave you is for someone else, if that somehow makes you feel better, fine. You can think that."

"See? I knew it," Priscilla seized on his words. "You're admitting it now."

Gordon just shook his head. "Good-bye, Priscilla."

"Wait. Gordon. You can't just walk away from me."

But she found out that he could.

78. Priscilla & Susan

*P*riscilla was crying when she walked up to Susan's door and rang the bell. Just a few minutes before, Gordon had packed his bags and left, and nothing she did or said seemed to have the slightest effect on him. When she realized that he was really leaving, she'd broken down and started to cry, and now she couldn't seem to stop.

When Susan answered the door, she didn't seem surprised to find a sobbing Priscilla on her porch.

"He's divorcing me," Priscilla hiccupped.

"I'm so sorry," Susan said. "He called me, and I tried to tell him—"

"I know you did," Priscilla said.

"He didn't believe me, did he?"

Priscilla shook her head.

"I'm so sorry," Susan said again.

"But I don't think that's the real reason. I think there's someone else."

"Really? That doesn't seem like Gordon."

"There *is* someone else," Priscilla insisted, almost hysterically. "You of all people should know the signs. All those late nights when I thought he was working on a project . . . I was such an idiot. Even though I think on some level I knew. I was having these dreams—"

"It's really hard," Susan said. "And I know it seems impossible to believe now, but you will get over it."

"Get over it? How?"

"Well, it's an old cliché, but the easiest way is to meet someone else."

Priscilla stared at Susan a moment, her mouth open. "Have you met someone else?" she said, when she'd recovered enough to speak.

Susan looked both shy and proud. She nodded.

"Who? Who is it? How did you meet him?"

Susan glanced over her shoulder. "Now's not the best time. . . . I'm in the middle of cooking something."

"But you don't cook," Priscilla started to say. Then she heard a familiar voice call out from the kitchen, "What's keeping you, Sue? I swear, I'm going to burn this thing."

Priscilla looked at Susan. "Is that . . . ?"

Priscilla didn't even have time to finish her question, because at that moment Detective Ackerman appeared in the hallway, wearing jeans and a T-shirt, a dishtowel thrown over one shoulder.

"Detective Ackerman," Priscilla said. "I didn't expect to see *you* here."

"I didn't expect to see you here either," Ackerman said, rather pointedly.

Priscilla heard the accusation and her natural response kicked in: retaliation. "Well, I guess you've got a lot of time on your hands now that the case is solved. You sure were wrong about that one, weren't you?"

She had expected to score a real hit with that one, so she was shocked when Ackerman just shrugged.

"Yeah, well, it's not the most important thing in the world," he said, and his eyes slid over to rest on Susan for a second.

"That's proof that an old dog can learn new tricks," Susan said.

"If you really want to prove that, you'd better come back and finish cooking dinner," Ackerman replied.

"Are you calling me an old dog?" Susan demanded. She turned back to Priscilla. "We're making dinner," she said apologetically.

"We're burning dinner," Ackerman said, flashing a grin at Susan.

"I told you I can't cook," Susan shot back.

"I thought you were just being modest. Boy, was I wrong. I seem to be making a habit of that."

Susan turned back to face Priscilla, still smiling. She tried to look more serious, but she couldn't quite quench the look of happiness. "I'm so sorry, Priscilla. Really I am. I wouldn't have wished this on anyone. But you'll make it through. You'll see."

And she closed the door, albeit gently, in Priscilla's face.

PART III

NEW YORK

July

79. Sofie

*N*ine months.

It had been nine months without a word.

And then—on the day the trial ended and the jury went into deliberation—he called.

Sofie was in her apartment—her new apartment. She'd never lived anywhere but the Upper East Side, so when she moved back into the city she bought an apartment downtown. The place she'd shared with Dean was a classic six, so the new apartment was a loft. And, when she furnished it, she made sure there wasn't a single antique in sight. She'd chosen all modern furniture from designers like Salotti, Cavali, and Montis. It felt like a new beginning.

But the even bigger step was Sofie's other purchase. She had spent the last few months looking for the perfect retail space. She'd finally found it and had put in a bid, and contractors were working on the renovation. She was going to open up her very own mystery bookstore.

When she first decided to do it, Sofie realized it wasn't a particularly good business venture. Her father would have been appalled, but she decided to throw caution—and money—to the wind. She'd had too much of both, anyway.

After she found the space, she sat down with an architect. He was a mystery reader himself, and what they came up with was a completely impractical and, they thought, completely wonderful design. They decided to make it like a house—only, a house lined with bookshelves. One room would be a kind of large living room where people could talk. There would be a few quiet rooms for reading, as well as a kitchen with a couple of big oval tables where she was planning on serving free coffee. The back opened up onto a courtyard that was shaded by trees, and the front had big casement windows, like a house, opening up onto the street.

In addition to the standard readings, Sofie was planning on hosting book-release parties, organizing a crossword puzzle group on Sundays, and last, but not least, organizing her very own mystery book club.

Everyone told her it wouldn't work. But Sofie didn't care. She could afford to lose money on it—though it was looking like she might do better than she had expected. In fact, she'd already gotten quite a bit of press. It made for a nice little story—the wife of an accused murderer opening up a mystery bookstore.

Sofie supposed she should have anticipated the media attention she would get as Dean's wife. She had expect to get hounded a bit by the press in the beginning, but when she let it be known that she wasn't planning on having any contact with her soon-to-be-ex-husband, she expected it to die down after a few weeks. It didn't.

She also hadn't anticipated the results her actions would have on Dean. His lawyer had made it clear just how crucial it was for Dean to have his wife there at the trial. Sofie's silent support would send a strong message to the jury; it would say, I knew this man, I married him, and I still believe in him. If she wasn't there in court, her absence would speak volumes. The message Sofie sent back to Dean through the lawyers was simple: No. Then he sent a request that she at least put out a statement saying that she believed he was innocent of the crime. Her answer was the same.

Then Dean, against the advice from his lawyer, called her directly.

He called from a blocked number, so she was completely unprepared when she answered the phone and she heard his voice say, "Hello, Sofie."

She didn't answer. It felt like her throat had closed up and she was having trouble just getting air.

"Sofie?" he said again. "Are you there?"

She said "Yes." It was all she could manage.

"How can you do this to me when you know I'm innocent?" he said.

She drew a deep breath then. Anger had freed up her lungs. "You're hardly innocent," she said.

"But I didn't do it. You have to believe me."

"You think so? Because I believed you when you said you loved me. I don't *have* to do anything."

His voice took on a plaintive, defensive tone. "It's not like I'm the only man who ever cheated."

"If that's an apology, it stinks."

"Is that what you want from me? An apology?"

"No. Actually, I want you to leave me alone. I'm not going to help you, Dean. Don't call me again."

"Don't do this, Sofie. You're not like this. I know you. You're not this person."

"It seems like neither of us knew each other as well as we thought," Sofie said, and hung up the phone.

She hadn't talked to him since—though she'd thought about him every day. But she'd expected that. What she hadn't expected was the fact that she thought about Alex just as often, even though they hadn't spoken since the night before Dean's arrest. That is, until the day the jury went into deliberations.

She was just finishing her coffee when the phone rang. She was expecting a call from the construction foreman about the progress of the store. But instead when she picked up she heard a voice say, in a low, familiar tone, "Sofie. It's me."

"Who is this?" she asked, though she knew exactly who it was.

He didn't fall for it. "You didn't use to play games," Alex chided.

"Well, what can you expect when you don't call me for nine months?"

"But I've thought about you."

"Thought about how you didn't want to call?"

"You told me that we shouldn't see each other for a while," he reminded her.

"Oh, give me a break. Who's playing games now?" Sofie said.

"OK, you're right. But I can explain."

"I'm listening."

"Not over the phone."

"OK, well then . . . should we get together?" She tried to sound casual about it, but she didn't think she quite pulled it off.

"I hope to be on a plane later today," he said.

"Where are you going?"

"St. Barts."

"You mean you waited to call me until right before you were planning on leaving the country?"

"I haven't been planning it very long. I just bought the tickets this morning," he told her.

"Just a whim?"

"Well, sort of. I was thinking that it might be best for you to get away for the next little while. At least until the verdict comes back."

"So . . . you mean you . . ."

"I was hoping you'd come with me," he said.

Sofie laughed. "You call me out of the blue after I haven't heard from you in nine months, and you expect me to get on a plane with you to St. Barts with only a few hours' notice? Are you crazy?"

"Yes," he admitted. "But I'm betting that you're crazy too."

80. Susan & Detective Ackerman

Susan hung up the phone and called out, "You're not going to believe it."

Ackerman popped his head out of the kitchen. He was holding a spoon and was wearing the apron Susan had given him for Christmas. It read CAUSE MY WIFE CAN'T COOK. But before she gave it to him, she had crossed out the word "wife" and wrote "girlfriend" above it. When he opened the box and took out the apron he looked at it a moment and said, "I love it. But there's a problem," and he pointed to the crossed-out word.

"But I fixed it," Susan said.

He'd shaken his head no and pulled a small box out of his back pocket.

Now the apron had the word "girlfriend" crossed out as well, and "wife" written in again above it.

"Come into the kitchen and tell me," Ackerman commanded.

So Susan followed him back into the kitchen. "Mmm, that smells good. What are you making?"

"Tacos."

"Oh, remember don't put in too much Tabasco."

"I never put too much in."

"You only say that because it's never too hot for you. I swear I couldn't taste anything for hours after I ate your tacos last time."

"You want to make them?"

"Do you want to hear the news or not?" Susan responded.

"I bet it was just your ex calling again to tell you what a mistake you're making in not dumping me and taking him back."

"That would hardly be news," Susan said.

Just before Christmas Harry called to say he was planning on getting married again and could they expedite the divorce and leave the settlement of property until afterward. Susan agreed. Harry admitted later that he had only asked because his girlfriend insisted, and he had only agreed to it because he was so sure Susan would say no. He was already starting to feel a little pressured, but he went ahead with the wedding plans—until they came to the matter of the prenup. Harry's girlfriend had tried every way she knew how to try to persuade him to forgo the prenup, but in the end, when he'd given her an ultimatum and said that she had to sign or the wedding was off, she'd left him.

It didn't take long before Harry turned to Susan for comforting—and got a nasty shock when he found out the reason why Susan had been so ready to give him the divorce was that she was engaged herself. There was nothing more attractive than unavailability, and after that Harry had launched an all-out campaign to get her back. The fact that Susan and Ackerman had gotten married didn't seem to discourage him. Even when Susan told him the news that she was pregnant, it still didn't deter him. In fact, it seemed to spur him on. He called so often, Susan had to screen their calls.

"So it wasn't Harry on the phone?" Ackerman asked.

"No. It was Sofie."

"Oh. Of course she'd be calling. The jury went into deliberations today, didn't they?"

"She was actually calling me back. I tried her earlier to see how she was doing."

After Dean's arrest—and before Sofie sold the house and moved back into the city—she and Susan had become good friends. One of the first things Sofie told Ackerman when she found out that he and Susan were together was, "So *that's* why you were here that night I was being followed—and why Dean said he'd seen your car parked out here other nights as well." Ackerman had grinned and said, "You've turned into quite the detective."

"So what did Sofie say?" Ackerman asked Susan. "Is she doing OK?"

"I'm not sure. She was calling me back from a plane. She's on her way to St. Barts."

"Actually, I think it's a great idea for her to get out of the country for the verdict."

"It's not that," Susan said. "I think that's a good idea too—since she wouldn't come stay here with us."

"So, if you think it's a good idea, then what's bothering you?"

"It's who she's going *with*."

Ackerman looked up sharply. "Not . . ."

"Yes." Susan said. "Him. I don't understand why Sofie is doing this. She's making the same mistake all over again."

"Maybe she can't help it."

"Of course she can help it. The whole experience with Dean should have taught her something. When you go through something like that, you've got to take a lesson from it. Look at me. At least I've learned from my mistakes."

Ackerman moved over to stand in front of her and, cupping her face with his hands, leaned over to kiss her. "You think so?" he murmured.

"Yeah," Susan said. "I think this time I picked a good one."

81. Sofie & Alex

*T*he week in St. Barts was magical.

It was the only word Sofie could think of that could capture it. She was feeling something she thought she would never feel again. It was that crazy glow she'd had when she first started seeing Dean. It should have concerned her—considering how that relationship had ended—but she tried to convince herself that this time she knew better. This time she would sense if something was wrong. The problem was, she already did.

She'd been sensing it all week. She saw it in his face when he didn't know that she was looking at him—though whenever he noticed her gaze, he would immediately rearrange his expression into a smile. She wasn't afraid of him. It wasn't that. It was almost as if . . . it was almost as if he was afraid of her. But she told herself that was ridiculous.

The truth was, she knew that whatever was wrong was also part of the reason for their happiness. It heightened every moment, sharpened every sensation, the way hunger makes everything taste better.

On the fifth day things came to a head. It was the day they got the news. Sofie and Alex were on the balcony. They had just finished eating breakfast and were sitting, looking out at the view. The sun glittered off the surface of the ocean, and the only sound was the soft rush of the waves against the beach. Then the phone rang, and the sound shattered the quiet morning like glass breaking.

They looked at each other. Only one person had the phone number where they were staying, and that was Alex's lawyer, Ruth. He had told Ruth not to call under any circumstances—except when the jury came back with the verdict.

This was it.

"I'll get it," Alex said. He got up and went back into the room.

Sofie stared out over the ocean. She found herself breathing in time with the gentle swells.

In the room behind her she heard Alex pick up the phone. There were a few seconds of silence, and then he said, "Thanks for letting us know. Bye."

A moment later he came back out onto the balcony and sat back down in the chair next to her.

Sofie kept her eyes fixed straight ahead.

Alex cleared his throat awkwardly. "The jury came back with a verdict." He paused, seemingly waiting for some reaction from her.

She didn't move.

So he told her.

"They found him guilty."

She remained very still as she asked, "And his sentence?"

"Twenty-five to life."

She closed her eyes.

"Sofie?"

"Can I be alone for a little while?" Sofie said.

"Sure. Of course."

She heard Alex get up, and when she heard the door close behind him, she opened her eyes again. Everything looked exactly the same. She waited for emotion to come back. She wasn't sure what she was going to feel. It took a few quiet minutes before she was sure. She felt . . . relief.

82. Sofie & Alex

Alex returned to the room an hour later. He entered cautiously, ready to leave again if he got any signal that she needed more time.

She was still sitting on the balcony in the same spot as if she hadn't moved the entire hour.

Alex went out and sat down next to her. He glanced over, but she was still staring out at the ocean. So he turned and looked out as well, as if there were some answer out there on the horizon where the blue of the ocean bled into the blue of the sky. Neither spoke for a while. Then Alex turned to her and said, "Do you want to go snorkeling?"

She smiled, and the solemn mood was broken.

"Yes," she said. "I'd love to."

So they put on their bathing suits, went down to the beach, and hired a speed boat to take them snorkeling at a secluded spot a ways south, down the coast. The boat flew, bouncing over the surface of the waves, the motor so loud they couldn't hear themselves speak over the roar. When the man finally cut the engine, it felt like being dipped into liquid silence. They put on their flippers and masks and slipped into the water and into another world. The fish that flitted past them were outrageous, unbelievable colors: brilliant yellow stripes against velvet black, orange so bright and luminous it looked as if the fish was lit from the inside, azure paired with deep purple. Alex reached out and took Sofie's hand, and they swam like that— holding hands, gliding through the impossibly clear water.

Back in the hotel room, Alex let her shower first. Then he washed off and joined her on the balcony. The sun was just setting.

"Dinner?" he asked.

She nodded.

At dinner Sofie surprised herself with her appetite. She'd felt absolutely no hunger—until the food was set down in front of her. Then, suddenly, she was ravenous. She ate absolutely everything on her plate—but she noticed that Alex barely touched his food.

After dinner she suggested they take a walk. She led the way down the beach, away from all the cabins and all the people and in ten minutes they couldn't even see the bungalows. Behind them was the dark line of trees. In front of them, the dark undulating water.

Sofie sat down on the sand. It still held some of the heat from the sun.

Alex lowered himself beside her.

They sat in silence. Most of the day had been spent in silence, but it was a silence of understanding. A silence of unspoken accord. Now it was subtly different. This was a silence of anticipation.

She burrowed her toes into the sand until she felt the cold layer of sand that hadn't been warmed by the sun. Then, finally, she asked him. "Is something the matter, Alex?"

She sensed him stiffen beside her. But his voice was casual when he said, "What do you mean? Nothing's the matter."

She nodded and let the silence stretch out for a while longer. Then she tried again. "There's something I've been wanting to ask you."

He turned to look at her, but she couldn't make out his expression in the dark. "What is it?"

"I wanted to ask you why you waited nine months to call me. Over the phone you said you wanted to tell me in person. But you haven't said anything about it."

He didn't answer immediately. Instead he scooped up a handful of sand, then spread his fingers and let the sand dribble back out. Only when all of it had leaked through his fingers did he answer her. "I know I owe you an explanation for that. I've been meaning to tell you . . . but I've kept putting it off."

"I think it's time," Sofie said.

He sighed. "I should have done it before this, but I've been selfish. I wanted this week with you—so much. And it's been wonderful."

"You're talking like it's all over."

Alex looked up at her.

"Is that it? Is it over?" she asked.

"That's going to be up to you to decide . . . when you hear what I have to say."

"OK," Sofie said. "I'm listening."

Alex looked back down, this time absently drawing his finger through the sand. Then he wiped the mark clean with the side of his hand. "I have to go back a bit—back when I first came to you for help after Julia was killed. Do you remember how close we seemed to get so quickly?"

Sofie nodded.

"Well, on my part that was . . . how do I put it?"

"Calculated?" Sofie suggested.

"Yes. It sounds so cold. But yes. It was calculated. I set out to make you fall in love with me."

"I understand." Sofie spoke, staring down into her lap, noticing how tightly her fingers were laced together. "You needed my help. When it was over, we were over. You didn't call me because you weren't in love with me."

Alex spoke quickly. "No that's *not* why I didn't call you. It's the opposite."

"The opposite?" Sofie looked up at that.

"I realized I loved you, silly. I mean, I love you."

"And that's why you didn't call?"

"Yes. It's why I made a vow that I would *never* call."

"Why? Were you scared to risk it?"

"No. At least, not for myself."

"You were scared for *me*?"

"Yes. Because I knew what you'd just been through. I'd set out to use you just as coldly and deliberately as your husband had used you. I knew that I lied to you just like he had lied to you. And I knew that you deserved more. You deserved a partner who was completely honest and open with you. You deserved someone you could trust. And . . . I knew I couldn't be that person."

Sofie felt her throat tighten, signaling the onset of tears. "Then why did you bring me here? Why did you do this to me? I wish you had never called. I wish you had just left me alone." She started to push herself up off the sand. Her eyes had filled with the tears she'd felt coming, and she couldn't see very well.

Alex leaned over and caught her wrist, not letting her get up. She struggled to free herself.

"No, wait. You haven't let me finish. I was wrong."

With those words she stopped struggling to pull away. "What do you mean?"

"I was sure I couldn't be that person. But as the months went by, and I couldn't get you out of my head—I thought I saw a way that I *could* be that person for you. But it took me nine months to work up the courage."

"Courage to do what?" she demanded.

"The courage to be honest with you. The courage to tell you the truth."

"Courage? Why? Was that so hard? Saying that to me?"

"No, that wasn't hard."

"Then why did you wait all this time?"

"That's not what I meant," Alex said. "I haven't yet."

"Haven't what?"

"I haven't told you the truth. Not the whole truth. You see, there's something else."

"I don't understand," she said. "What else could you possibly have to tell me?"

He didn't really answer her question. Instead he gripped her hand so tight it hurt as he said, "Listen, I know you're going to have to do whatever you think is right. I want you to know I understand that. It was something I knew when I made the decision."

"You're scaring me," Sofie said.

"You would never, ever have any reason to be afraid of me, Sofie. I want you to know that. OK?"

She wanted to yell at him, *What is it?* But he spoke so urgently that she just said, "OK."

"You remember when Detective Ackerman said he knew for certain that I was guilty?"

Sofie nodded.

Alex took a deep breath. "He was right. I *am* guilty."

Sofie shook her head. "No. I don't believe it. You're lying."

"I'm not lying. He was right about me. I killed my first wife."

"You . . . you . . ."

"I killed her," Alex repeated softly.

"But the history of suicide attempts . . ."

"That part was true. When we met, she had just gotten out of the hospital. That was her second try. She was in bad shape. But after we started dating, she was like a different person. She said I made her feel alive again. She told me that I had saved her life. It felt wonderful to be needed like that—to feel like I made such a difference. And she had all that money, and all she wanted to do was spend it on me. One night, we were drunk, and I said, "Why don't we get married." Of course I knew her history—she'd been taken to the cleaners before—so I signed the harshest prenup her lawyers could draft. And then we did it. We got married. And everything was really good . . . for a while. We had been married a little over a year when she started getting bad again. Maybe her medication stopped working, maybe she stopped taking it, I don't know. But I tried everything I could think of. I encouraged her to see different doctors. Try different medication. But she wouldn't even get out of bed. She didn't shower for days. Then one day she got up and got dressed and told me that she wanted a divorce. She had decided that instead of being her savior I was actually the cause of her problems. When I asked her about what she'd said about us—about how she felt about me—about how she needed me, she said that I had been a nice toy . . . a nice toy. And she laughed about how stupid I'd been to sign that prenup because I wasn't going to get a penny.

"I didn't even really plan it. I mean, I suppose I did. But I just went over the details in my mind of what I *could* do, even though I told myself I would never go through with it. It was like a little day-dream. Just a fantasy. Harmless. Except that one night I ended up doing it. It was like I was a robot. I told her I wanted to talk about separating. That I wanted to make it as easy as possible and couldn't we talk about it over a drink. I dissolved a handful of her Klonopin in a gin and tonic because it's bittersweet anyway. We sat down and both had a drink. And I couldn't believe how fast she passed out. I carried her to the car. Put a pen and paper and the phone in the seat next to her, then turned on the ignition. Then I went out to a party. I felt fine. I chatted with people. I stayed a long time. When I went home . . . well, I took her out of the car and laid her on the floor of the kitchen. I called 911 and even tried CPR a couple of times be-cause I thought that's what anyone would have done, even if it was obvious there was no hope. The initial police response was wonder-ful, very sympathetic. Everything seemed like it was going fine until Detective Ackerman arrived. I only talked to him for about a minute before I realized that he knew. He knew I had killed her. I don't know how, but he did.

"But Sofie, I swear, I didn't kill Julia. I couldn't do that again—I don't think I really knew what I was doing the first time, but I just had so much hate in me. And it wasn't really from what my first wife did. It's just that she released a sort of avalanche from things that went way back. That's the only way I can think to explain it. It's true, I hated Julia, but I didn't kill her and frame your husband like Ackerman thinks. Though, you know, I don't really blame Ackerman for believing it. It makes sense. He knew I was guilty of killing my first wife. It was natural to think I was guilty of the second as well. But I'm not. I don't know if you'll believe me, but it's the truth."

Sofie had sat quietly throughout Alex's story, staring out across the water, watching the slow progress of the lights of a big cruise ship moving slowly across the horizon.

When she answered him, she kept her eyes fixed on the distant blaze of light, and her voice gave away nothing of what she might be feeling. "Why are you telling me all this?" she asked.

"I want to be with you, Sofie. I know it sounds crazy, but I want to marry you. You'd think I'd have had enough of marriage by now. But it's just I want a different kind of marriage. I want to be with someone who really knows me. I'm not a good person. But I want to be good to you. You said to me once that you could forgive almost anything as long as I told you the truth. I'm not holding you to that. I know you didn't imagine the truth would be something like this. I've done the worst thing you can do. And I told you why, but I know there's really no excuse for something like this. I figured you'd probably feel it was your duty to turn me in, but I decided to risk it anyway. What I wanted to say was . . . well, whatever you decide to do, I understand."

He waited for a response, but she didn't speak. She was still gazing out over the water.

"It's OK," he said softly. "You can say whatever you're thinking. In the last few months, I've gone over this conversation in my head a thousand times. I've imagined every possible response. Nothing you can say or do will surprise me."

She finally turned to look at him, and though he desperately tried to read her response in her face, her expression was unreadable.

After a few seconds, he nodded as if confirming something. "You don't have to say it. I knew it was impossible."

"That what was impossible?" Sofie asked, still with that strange, impenetrable look.

"Well, it's ridiculous to think that someone like you would even consider being with me after what I've done."

"Someone like me?" Sofie echoed. "What do you mean someone like me?"

"Someone who's—" Alex searched for a word, but all he came up with was—"good. Someone who's truly good."

"And what makes you think that I'm good?"

"You make all the hard decisions. Like when you found out that your husband was having an affair with Julia. Even though you loved him, you made the hard decision to go to the police with the information. That's why part of me knows you'll feel like you have to do the same with this information. And maybe that's even what I want. I don't know."

There was another long silence. And then she said abruptly, "Did I ever tell you my favorite quote?"

"No. Is it one from Agatha Christie?"

"No, but it could have been one of hers. The quote is, 'Nobody knows anybody—not that well.' "

Alex frowned. "So you're saying I don't really know you?"

"The thing is, until recently I don't think I even knew myself."

"I don't understand. What do you mean?"

"I always thought that I was as different from my father as a person could be. It was kind of a shock to realize I'm just like him. All the things you said that make me a good person—making what you called the 'hard' decisions. Well, it's not what you think."

"You mean you really turned the evidence over to the police because you were angry at your husband and you wanted to punish him? Is that it? Because that's just human. And you did so many other things that were good. Like helping me when you didn't have to—when you weren't even sure if I was guilty or not."

"But I had a reason to help you," Sofie said.

"You mean because you fell in love with me?"

"No. That's not why."

"Then what was it?"

"I helped you because I knew you didn't do it."

"But how could you? Did you see your husband go out that night? Did you follow him and see it all? Is that what happened?"

"No. He didn't go out. He was exactly where he said—sleeping on the couch."

Alex shook his head in confusion. "I don't understand. Then there's no way you could have known unless . . ."

Sofie finished his sentence for him. "Unless I killed her."

83. Sofie & Alex

"No," Alex said. "No, you didn't. You couldn't." He paused and was silent for a few seconds. Then, in wonder, "How?"

"With chloroform and a rope."

"That's not what I meant."

"But you know how," Sofie said. "With so much hate you feel like you don't have room for it all. With so much hurt, you want to make the people who did this to you hurt just as much as you do."

"So why didn't you kill your husband?"

She laughed. "Believe me, I thought of it. I didn't do it partly because I knew there was less of a chance I could get away with it—but mostly because I wanted him to suffer more than that. I wanted him to feel what it was like to have your whole life torn apart by someone you thought loved you."

"So you decided to frame him for Julia's murder?"

Sofie nodded.

"Then, you must have known all along that they were lovers."

Sofie nodded again.

"Since when?"

"I suspected he was having an affair for ages," she admitted.

"Since way back before my father died. But I knew for sure the day we were moving and I found that earring. But I thought maybe he had ended it. I thought maybe he was telling the truth when he said we were moving because he wanted a new start for us." She smiled. "That illusion didn't last for long. When the late nights got even worse, I knew it was still going on."

"When did you find out it was Julia?"

"That was a bit of luck. Did you know they used to meet on the golf course behind your house? Dean would park his car at the country club and walk across to the grove of trees right down the hill. He didn't know that I'd started taking walks along the golf course at night, and one night when I was on my walk I heard his voice. And then I heard a woman's voice. And then . . ." Sofie shrugged. "Then I knew it was bad. That's when I knew he hadn't moved out here for a new start. He'd moved out for her."

"Is that when you decided to do it?"

She shot him a look. "Of course not. People have affairs. It happens, and then a lot of the time the affair ends and they go back to their spouses. And I loved Dean. God knows, but I might even have let him go on with his affair if that's what it was going to take to stay married. There was even a part of me that thought, Well, of course I wouldn't be enough for him. It sounds awful, doesn't it?" She made a face.

"So what changed your mind?" Alex asked.

Sofie didn't answer right away. Instead she piled some more sand on top of her feet, scooping it up in handfuls. She patted it down, then continued.

"I found out that it was all a lie. From the very beginning. My father had been diagnosed with cancer right before we met. He wasn't supposed to live more than six months or so, and then I was going to inherit. At least, that's what Dean thought. That's why he married me."

"No prenup?"

"Of course not. I was in love."

"When do you think that Julia came into the picture?"

"I'm not sure. I don't think it was before we were married,

though I can't be sure. Anyway, I know the move to Connecticut was deliberate. Dean was worried I might not give him a divorce. But Connecticut is a no-fault state, and it's a lot more lenient than New York in division of property from an inheritance. Plus the house and the furniture and everything gave Dean a chance to convert some of the inheritance into actual marital property."

"That's cold," Alex said.

"Ice," Sofie agreed. "I think his heart was made of ice."

They fell silent for a moment. There was only the quiet of the night and the smooth movement of the water. Then Alex picked up the thread again.

"So . . . how did you find all that out?"

"Do you remember how I got the e-mails for the police?"

"You went to visit him at work when you knew he wouldn't be there. You asked to wait in his office, and you knew the password to get into his e-mail."

"Well, I'd actually already done that once before."

"When?"

"Months earlier. Back in the summer. After I'd seen them together. And that's when I found out."

"You mean you knew everything?"

"Yes. It was . . . it was like my world came crashing down on top of me." She glanced up, as if she could see the world hovering above her. The sky was strewn with clouds, but there were patches where it was clear, and those patches were thick with stars. "I felt like I lost myself."

"What did you do?"

"Nothing. Absolutely nothing. I could barely get out of bed. I spent most of my days crying. I thought about how I had never accomplished anything. I was a pathetic excuse for a human being. I had all the advantages in the world—"

"Except a family who cared about you. . . ."

"But so many people have done so much more with so much less. What had I accomplished? My big achievement was marrying a man who didn't love me and who was only interested in my money. And when I read those e-mails . . . you should have seen some of the things Dean wrote about me in those e-mails. He said I was the most boring, unimaginative person he'd ever met. I had so much money I could have done anything, but reading mysteries and doing crosswords were all I could come up with. He said I was always so apologetic that the sound of my voice made him want to scream. He said he thought he'd go out of his mind if he had to go through another year."

"It sounds to me like he was an even bigger asshole than I thought," Alex said.

"But the thing is, there was a nugget of truth in everything he said. That's what made it so awful. It was like I was seeing myself through his eyes. And I hated what I saw. I thought a lot about killing myself. I came pretty close one day. You know what stopped me?"

"What?"

"Dean said that I was getting like my mother. And I realized he was right. More right than he even knew."

"You told me that your mother committed suicide," Alex said.

"Yes, but I didn't tell you why." Sofie drew her knees up to her chest.

Alex, who'd kept his hand resting on her leg now let it fall on the sand between them.

"She was younger than I am now when she did it. Did I tell you that?"

Alex made as if to reach out to her again, but Sofie wasn't even looking at him so he just said, "No. I didn't know that."

"My mother killed herself when my father asked her for a divorce. I found her suicide note when I was ten and I was going through my father's things, trying to find a picture of her. I found a few pictures—and the letter. In it, she said she was doing it to punish him. She said she was doing it so that her death would be on his conscience for the rest of his life. But it didn't work. I know. I lived with him. And I wanted revenge that was going to work. If I killed myself, he'd get all the money and he and Julia would live happily ever after."

"Well, I don't know about the second part. I wouldn't have given them more than a couple of years. But it's true. He would have gotten—"

"Everything," Sofie said. "Absolutely everything. And it would have been just as if I had taken all his insults and just let him walk all over me. Both Dean and my father always said I was a pushover. They thought I let people get away with anything. I always told them that I could take care of myself. They didn't believe me."

"Big mistake," Alex said.

She looked at him then and smiled. "They didn't think I could get angry. But I can. I did. I was so angry I thought, *I could kill someone.* And that's when I got the idea. Did I ever tell you that I've always wanted to write a mystery?"

"No. You never told me that."

"It was what I'd planned to do after I quit my job. But I never got very far. So I decided to create one instead. A real one."

"I still can't figure out how you managed it." Alex said.

"It wasn't that hard. It just sort of fell into place. I knew I wanted to frame Dean for the murder. I knew I was going to do it outside because I could get Julia out of the house at night if she thought she was meeting Dean. And I knew in order to frame Dean I had to make sure that the scene was intact, so I had to be the one to find the body. Then I overheard that conversation between Priscilla and Julia about the Halloween decorations, and I got the idea of hanging her in the front yard. On the walk with Priscilla I could make sure that we would find the body together."

"But how did you get Julia out there? And what did you do with Dean?"

"I put a note in the mailbox. I know it was a little risky, but I can copy Dean's handwriting pretty well. And I knew the way he wrote to her from all those e-mails, so I didn't think she would doubt it was from him. As for Dean, that day I made him his favorite meal— chili. I had it all ready when he got home, complete with some heavy-duty tranquilizers crushed and blended into his serving. Half an hour later he was passed out on the couch in front of the TV. I put on one of his suits, some extra pairs of socks, his shoes, and I filled a backpack with about fifty pounds of dumbbells so the depth of the imprint would be closer to someone of his weight. I also tucked my hair under a bathing cap and put on Dean's hat and his gloves. Then I got some hairs—right from his head so as to make sure to get the roots. He didn't feel a thing. He was completely passed out. Finally I went out to meet Julia."

"And?"

"It felt like a waking dream. That's what it was like. After she passed out, it was so quiet. And then I . . . I did it. At the time, it seemed very peaceful. It was the next morning, when I saw her hanging there . . . there was nothing peaceful about that." Sofie's face twisted at the memory, as if she had inadvertently touched a spot and found it to be more painful than expected.

"And then you came to get me," Alex said.

"Yes, and that's where the surprises started. I thought I was going to have to keep you away from the scene, but you did it for me. I couldn't figure it out. I knew you would be the first suspect, but I thought I could turn the detectives toward Dean pretty easily. But I guess there's always something that goes wrong. There was Detective Ackerman set on you, and you were acting pretty strange, which wasn't helping things. So I realized I'd have to get involved and help clear you."

"But *I* came over to see *you*," Alex pointed out.

"If you'd waited ten minutes, I would have been on your stoop, knocking at your door," Sofie said.

"So the whole time I thought I was using you—you were actually using me?"

"Well, pretending to fall in love with you gave me a good excuse to stick by you, even when it seemed crazy."

Alex laughed. "You were like the chess master, and we were all the little pieces you were moving around the board."

"No. I was scared to death half the time. You should have seen me when the detectives first came to my house. I thought for certain they'd take one look at me and know that I'd done it."

"So it was you all along," Alex murmured, shaking his head.

"I told you, I'm not a good person. And I know I have to live with what I've done. But at least now I've *done* something."

"I'll say. You certainly don't start small."

"I know. I guess that makes me a villain. But I'd rather play the villain than the victim," Sofie said, half defiantly.

"The villain always has the best role anyway."

She smiled, but it was half-hearted, and when she spoke next, the defiance was gone from her voice. "The thing is, I thought it would get easier."

"What would?"

"Living with it," she said.

"Oh. That."

"Does it get better? I mean, after more time?"

He looked at her steadily. "No."

"I didn't think so." There was a moment of silence between them. She dug her fingers into the sand. Then she asked, "Do you still worry about getting caught?"

"On the bad days I used to almost want it."

"It's that bad?"

"It was. But I have a feeling it won't be anymore."

She looked up and he was smiling at her.

"So you haven't changed your mind about . . ."

He reached out again, captured her hand, and gently pulled open her fingers. He brushed the sand from her palm and twined his fingers through hers. "About you? Not a chance. You were right. I didn't know you. But I think, underneath, I recognized something."

His words won him a little smile. "You're such a romantic," she said.

"You've found me out." He lifted her hand and tried to kiss it, but she pulled it back, laughing.

"Oh, that's right," he said. "I forgot, you're not the traditional heroine. Anyway, we might be the villains, but do you think we might have a shot at happily ever after?"

She shook her head. "I don't think it works that way."

"I think it does. Or it could."

Sofie only raised her eyebrows.

He went on. "The way I see it, we've been through a lot, the two of us. We know what it takes to make a marriage work. And we've learned the hard way that you need trust more than anything."

"You forgot the most important thing," Sofie said.

"What's that?"

She smiled.

"We both know better than to ask for a divorce."